SEA CHANGE

SEA CHANGE

Robert Goddard

The Mysterious Press
New York

First published in Great Britain in 2000 by Bantam Press, an imprint of Transworld Publishers. Reissued in Great Britain by Corgi in 2011.

Printed in the United States of America

ISBN 978-0-8021-2477-7
eISBN 978-0-8021-9026-0

The Mysterious Press
an imprint of Grove Atlantic
154 West 14th Street
New York, NY 10011

Distributed by Publishers Group West

groveatlantic.com

16 17 18 19   10 9 8 7 6 5 4 3 2 1

It has been very judiciously observed that a commercial country has more to dread from the golden baits of avarice, the airy hopes of projectors and the wild enthusiastic dreams of speculators than from any external dangers.

John Millar, *An Authentic Account of the South Sea Scheme* (1845)

'I have made a profit of a thousand per cent – and I am satisfied.'

Robert Walpole (1720)

Contents

Book One

January–March 1721

Chapter One

Stags at Bay

It was dismal weather for a dismal time. The night was damp and clammy, clinging to London like a cold sweat. A fire burned in the grate, but Sir Theodore Janssen stood on the far side of the drawing-room from it, one arm propped on the sill of the open window, the other raised to his chest, his hand splayed across his brocaded waistcoat. He glanced out into Hanover Square and seemed to see in the drizzle-smeared gloom the deepening shadow of his future.

Until so very recently, he had been a man of high repute as well as substance. A baronet at the 'special request' of the Prince of Wales, a Member of Parliament, a director of the Bank of England, a landed gentleman, a financier of almost legendary acumen, he had been able to look forward to an old age of comfort and esteem. He had transformed himself from a friendless young Flemish émigré into a pioneer of a new era of commercial freedom. Yet now, here he stood, on the brink of ruin, a self-unmade man too close to the biblical term of life to delude himself with hopes of recouping what he was surely about to lose.

The South Sea Company was his mistake, of course, as it had been many men's. If he had resigned his directorship twelve months ago, or better still never accepted it in the first place, he would be free of this. Not of all financial loss, naturally. No doubt he would have gambled on the stock continuing to rise, like everyone else. But he could have borne that. His wealth was such that he would scarcely have noticed. This was different, however. This was a shameful and unavoidable acknowledgement of his own greed and stupidity. And it would come with a price, one even he might be unable to pay.

To make matters bleaker still, on the other side of the room, warming himself before the well-stacked fire, stood the man who had lured him onto the board two years before: Robert Knight, chief cashier of the company, keeper of its accounts and guardian of its secrets. Knight too faced ruin, but did so with a blithe smile and an unfurrowed brow. He still looked ten years younger than he had any right to and retained a twinkle in his eye that owed nothing to the candlelight.

'Why are you here, Mr Knight?' Sir Theodore asked, turning from the window and coughing to clear the gruffness from his throat.

'Because I am to appear before the committee the day after tomorrow, Sir Theodore.' The committee to which Knight referred was the House of Commons Secret Committee of Inquiry into the South Sea scandal. It had been sitting like an army of occupation in South Sea House all week, interrogating whomever it pleased, appropriating whatever documents it deemed likely to lead it to the truth. But the truth was in essence already known. The South Sea scheme had always been an impossible dream, sustained only by a universal determination to believe in it. Now was the winter of cruel disillusionment, of frozen credit and frost-shattered fortunes. The search was on, not so much for truth as for culprits. Everyone was a victim. But not everyone could be a villain. 'I will be hard pressed, I think,' Knight continued. 'Do you not agree?'

4

'Very hard,' said Sir Theodore with a nod. 'I have no doubt of it.'

'What should I tell them?'

'You have come here for my advice?'

'Your advice – and your assistance.'

Sir Theodore frowned. 'Assistance with what?'

'The disposal – if I may so phrase it – of the contents of my valise.' Knight stooped to pick up the bag he had brought with him and advanced to a table halfway across the room. 'May I?'

With the faintest inclination of his head, Sir Theodore consented. Knight opened the valise and slid a thick leather-spined book out onto the table. The edges of its pages were marbled and well turned. Its cover was green.

'You look surprised, Sir Theodore.'

'I am.'

'You know what it is?'

'How should I?'

'How should you not? Unless—' Knight moved round the table and leaned back against it, trailing one hand behind him that came to rest on the cover of the book. 'Perhaps it is your intention to plead ignorance. And perhaps this is a rehearsal for such a plea. If so, let me spare you the effort. You know what this is. And I know that you know. You may fool others. I wish you luck in the endeavour. But you cannot fool me.'

'No.' Sir Theodore scowled. 'Of course not. It is quite the other way about, when all's said and done.'

'You were aware of the risks attendant upon our enterprise, Sir Theodore. Do not pretend otherwise.'

'Was I? I wonder now that I thought it could ever have succeeded.'

Sir Theodore was unlikely to be alone in that. All over England, the great and the good, the newly poor and the no longer rich, were asking the same question, if not of others then of themselves. How could they have supposed it would work? To snap one's fingers and convert thirty million pounds of the National Debt into the booming stock of a company whose hard commercial assets amounted to vastly less, but whose *potential* profits from the South Sea trade were surely limitless, had seemed magically appealing. And the smooth-tongued Mr Knight had swayed every doubter, if not with words then with . . . more tangible methods of persuasion. Now, however, the magician was exposed as a trickster. And those associated with him were left with the stark choice of proclaiming themselves either his dupes or his accomplices.

'I had hopes of more than my personal enrichment, Mr Knight,' Sir Theodore continued. 'I saw this as the beginning of a glorious new world for all. I believed we were engaged in the practice of philanthropy.'

'I should not recommend you to present that argument to the committee.'

'It is not an argument. It is the truth.'

'But will it keep you from prison? I think not.'

'Will anything?'

'Perhaps.' Knight's fingers drummed on the cover of the book. 'A harder kind of truth may save us.'

'*Us?*'

'You and me, Sir Theodore. You and me and your fellow directors and all their friends in high places. So many friends. So very high. Too high to be allowed to fall, I think. But the fear of falling will work wonders. And it is wonders we need.'

'I thought what you needed was assistance.'

'Precisely. A small thing to a great end.' His fingers stopped drumming. 'This book represents our salvation. But only so long as it remains safe, both from our friends, who would destroy it, and from our enemies, who would shout its secrets from the rooftops.'

'Then I suggest you keep it safe, Mr Knight.'

'How can I? There is no safe place left at South Sea House. Mr Brodrick has sent his ferrets down every hole.' Thomas Brodrick was chairman of the Committee of Inquiry, a sworn opponent of the South Sea Company and all its works. Sir Theodore did not need to be told that he had set about his task with relish as well as dedication. It went without saying. 'If I stay, they will find it.'

'*If* you stay?'

'Or if I flee, like as not.'

'Do you propose to flee?'

'I did not say so.' Knight smiled. 'Now did I?'

Sir Theodore's eyes narrowed. He pulled the window shut behind him with sudden and excessive force. Then he said, as if tiring of their mutual prevarication, 'What do you want of me?'

'I want you to take charge of the book.'

'Why me?'

'Because you are the most eminent member of the board. Also the most reliable. And, I would judge, the least inclined to panic. Caswall and Master fell to blows in the street today outside South Sea House. It was not an edifying spectacle.'

'You flatter me, Mr Knight.'

'Not at all. I present you with the simple facts. You are the things I have said you are.'

'Supposing that to be so, why should my hands be safer than yours?'

'Because they are not the hands into which I might be expected to surrender such a document. And because you have acquaintances of long standing in your native land to whom it could be entrusted. In that event, I would not know where it was. The information could not be wrung out of me. And no-one would think to try to wring it out of you. While the book remains abroad, so to speak, there would be limits to the action that could be taken against us. It would be an insurance policy for both of us. And for our colleagues.'

'You are thinking of them?'

'No.' Knight grinned. 'I mention them in case you are.'

'If it became known that you had handed it to me, it might be supposed that I was familiar with its contents.'

'Which you are not, of course.' Knight's grin broadened, then abruptly vanished. 'But it would not become known. Why should it? I have confidence in your choice both of recipient and of courier. I have confidence in you altogether.'

'I think you have as little of that in me as I have in you, Mr Knight.'

Knight looked genuinely hurt. 'How can you say so?'

'But confidence is no longer the issue, is it? If it were, we would all still be riding high.'

'What then is the issue?'

'Desperation.' Sir Theodore gave a heavy sigh and walked slowly to the table, where he halted and stared down at the green-covered book. 'Sheer desperation.'

'Perhaps so. I'll not argue the point. The question is a simple one. Will you do it?'

'I would be mad to.'

'And madder still not to. There is a great deal at stake. More than just our personal circumstances. Far more. But it so happens' – Knight's voice took on the syrupy tone he had used to persuade so many in days gone by that the South Sea project could not, would not, fail – 'that our interests and those of the nation coincide. Our salvation is the salvation of all.'

'How gratifying.'

'Will you do it?' Knight repeated.

Sir Theodore looked at him long and hard, then said, 'Let me not detain you, Mr Knight.'

8

'May I leave what I brought?'

'You brought nothing.' Sir Theodore cocked one eyebrow. 'I trust that is understood.'

Knight nodded. 'Very clearly.'

'Then there is no more to be said.' Sir Theodore picked up the book and carried it to a bureau in a corner of the room. He slid it into one of the drawers, turned a key in the lock and dropped the key into his waistcoat pocket. 'Is there?'

An hour later, with Knight long gone, Sir Theodore rose from his seat at the bureau in which the green-covered book was still locked. He drained his glass of port and looked down at the letter it had taken him the better part of that hour to write. Yes, on balance, it seemed to him, he had disclosed as much and as little as he needed to. And the precaution he had urged on his oldest and most trusted friend, though extreme, was undoubtedly necessary. He sealed the letter, crossed to the bell-pull and tugged at it.

A few minutes passed, during which Sir Theodore gazed into the dying fire. With the thumb and index finger of his right hand, he slowly revolved the gold and diamond ring that sat fatly on the little finger of his other hand. It had been a gift from the Prince of Wales, presented at the King's birthday party at St James's eight months before, when riches seemed to rain from the clear spring sky and no-one doubted, for no-one dared to, that a pound of South Sea stock would be worth ten tomorrow and a hundred the day after. His own holding must have amounted to a million then. A million pounds and a billion delusions. They were nothing now, nothing but ashes in his mouth.

There was a tap at the door. Nicodemus Jupe, Sir Theodore's valet and loyal factotum, entered the room. A lean, grave-faced, hawk-nosed fellow of forty or so, Jupe had about him the air of one who never over-estimated his

9

importance in the world and yet never underestimated it either. He was humble without being obsequious, perceptive without being presumptuous. He had always been utterly reliable, yet the cold edge of efficiency in his soul that was the essence of his reliability was also the key to the understanding that subsisted between him and his master. He expected Sir Theodore to extricate himself from the difficulties that had overtaken them both. Indeed, he required it of him. And he himself would do anything he could to bring that about. That was the measure of his loyalty. It ran far. But it did not run to the ends of the Earth.

'There is a letter on the bureau,' said Sir Theodore. 'It must be on its way tonight.'

Jupe fetched it and glanced at the address. His face betrayed no reaction.

'I am sorry to ask you to turn out at such an hour. But it is a matter of the utmost urgency.'

'I understand, sir. I'll leave at once.'

'Before you do, there is one other thing.'

'Yes, sir?'

'The indigent mapmaker. Spandrel. We still have our eye on him?'

'Indeed, sir. I don't doubt he'll stray eventually. Then we'll have him. But for the present—'

'He adheres to the rules.'

'He does.'

'I wish to see him.'

Jupe's eyes widened faintly in surprise. 'And is that also . . . a matter of the utmost urgency?'

'It is, Jupe. Yes.'

Chapter Two

The Idle Waywiser

Dawn came slowly and grudgingly to the ill-lit room William Spandrel shared with his mother beneath the eaves of a lodging-house in Cat and Dog Yard. Spandrel did not welcome its arrival. The grey, soot-filtered light only made the cracks in the plaster and the crumbling condition of the brickwork beneath more obvious. As he shaved himself with a blunt razor through a thumb's-smear worth of soap, he studied his fractured reflection in a shard of mirror, noting the ever hollower cheekbones, the charcoal-shadowed eyes and the cringing look of defeat that tried to hide itself behind them. Who could welcome dawn when darkness was at least a kind of refuge?

He had nailed the mirror to the south-facing wall within the dormer-window, reckoning that would at least ensure enough light to cut his throat by, should he ever need to do so. It seemed likely enough that the need would one day arise, considering the intractability of his plight. If he glanced out of the window, he could see, looming beyond the sagging roof-tree of the Punch Bowl Tavern, the palisaded wall of the Fleet Prison, where he had been confined for ten purgatorial days last autumn, an unconsidered victim of the sudden tightening of credit following the bursting of the South Sea Bubble and several thousand fond dreams of wealth along with it. His own dream,

11

strictly speaking, had not been among them, but commercial catastrophe on the scale of the South Sea runs deep and hard, afflicting even those who believe themselves immune from it.

His immunity, Spandrel now realized, had been imaginary, based as it was on the slender truth that he had not himself dabbled in South Sea stock. He had been far too busy assisting his father in the painstaking survey work for what was to have been their proudest achievement – An Exact and Definitive Map of the City and Environs of London in the Reign of His Britannic Majesty King George the First – to engage in stock market speculation, even supposing he had possessed any capital with which to speculate. But the world and his wife *had* speculated, at first successfully, at length disastrously. Those fine gentlemen who had assured William Spandrel senior that they would buy a copy of his map with which to adorn their soon-to-be-gold-leafed drawing-room walls had eagerly lent him the funds for his enterprise. But they had become equally eager to retrieve those funds when a financial chasm opened beneath their feet. The map was tantalizingly close to completion, but what use was that? Suddenly, there had been no customers, only creditors. William senior had fallen ill with the worry of it. William junior assumed responsibility for his debts to spare him a spell in prison he was not well enough to survive. And the bailiffs duly came for the younger man. But the older man had died anyway. Spandrel's sacrifice had been in vain.

So sombre had his situation then been that his mother was able to persuade her normally tight-fisted brother to donate the five guineas that bought him the freedom to live in lodgings within the rules of the Prison, but outside its walls. It was freedom of a limited kind. And it was certainly preferable to the horrors of the Fleet. But as those horrors faded slowly from his mind, so new ones took their place. Would he ever be truly free again? Was he to pass the prime of his life as a fly in a jar? Was there no way out?

On this dank January morning there certainly did not appear to be one. In the corner, half-hidden by the washing Mrs Spandrel had hung in front of the fireplace, stood one of the waywisers he and his father had pushed round the streets of London, calculating distances to an obsessive nicety. Now, its wheel was limned with rust. Everything was corroding, even hope. The sheets that made up as much of the map as they had drawn were with the engraver and seemed likely to remain there, since the fellow had not so far been paid for the work he had done. And while Spandrel stayed cooped up in Cat and Dog Yard, as the rules of the Fleet demanded, there would be no more sheets. That much was certain.

Surveying was all he knew. He had been his father's loyal apprentice. But no-one had need of a surveyor at such a time. And the only thing he could survey from this rotting garret was the wasteland of his future. To think of what he had lost was too much to bear. Last summer, he had entertained hopes of marriage, to the beautiful Maria Chesney. And the map had seemed like the best idea his father had ever had. Now, there was nothing. Maria was lost to him. His father was dead. His mother had become a washerwoman. And he had become a washerwoman's assistant.

At a sound from the door, he turned, expecting to see his mother, though surprised she should be back so soon. But, strangely, it was not his mother.

A thin man in dark clothes and a grey-black wig stood in the doorway, stooping slightly to clear the lintel. His eyes, deep-set and darting, combined with his sharp-boned nose, gave him the look of some strange bird of prey, searching for carrion. And perhaps, it occurred to Spandrel, he thought he had found some.

'William Spandrel,' the man said. It was not a question. It had more the sound of an announcement intended to forestall any denial.

'Yes,' Spandrel cautiously admitted.

'My name is Jupe. I represent Sir Theodore Janssen.'

'You do? Well . . .' Spandrel put down the razor and wiped the remaining soap from his jaw. 'As you can see, there's nothing I can do for Sir Theodore.'

'You owe him a great deal of money.'

That much was undeniable. Sir Theodore was, in fact, his principal creditor by some way. Spandrel's father had surveyed an estate at Wimbledon Sir Theodore had bought a few years previously and had turned to him for backing when the idea for the map came to him. Sir Theodore, awash with cash at the time, had happily obliged. As a director of the South Sea Company, he was now likely to be a desperate man. Spandrel had gleaned that much from borrowed newspapers and overheard conversations in the yard. But he was surely not so desperate as to apply to the most hapless of his many debtors for help.

'Sir Theodore would like the debt settled,' said Jupe, advancing into the room and gazing round at the sparse and shabby furnishings.

'So would I. But I've better things to do than torment myself with thoughts of what I'd *like*.'

'So has Sir Theodore.'

'Then why are you here?'

'To present you with an opportunity to settle the debt – and your other debts along with it – by rendering Sir Theodore a small but significant service.'

'Is this some sort of joke?'

'Do I look like a man who makes jokes, Mr Spandrel?'

That he assuredly did not. 'What you should be considering is whether you can afford to ignore the chance

I am offering of extricating yourself – and your mother – from the life you are leading here.' Jupe peered curiously at a sagging flap of plaster. 'If it can be called a life, that is.'

'Your pardon, sir.' Spandrel forced himself to smile. Perhaps, he told himself, Sir Theodore had decided to be generous to those his own malpractices had helped to bankrupt. Stranger things had been known, though he could not for the moment think of any. If it was true, maybe there really was a way out of his troubles. 'There's naturally no service I'd not be willing to render Sir Theodore in exchange for a remittal of the debt.'

'Naturally.' Jupe smiled back at him with thinly veiled superciliousness. 'As you say.'

'What would he require of me?'

'He will explain that to you himself, Mr Spandrel. When you meet.'

'He's coming here?'

'Certainly not.' Jupe beetled his brow to let Spandrel know how absurd the suggestion was. 'You are going to him.'

'But I can't.'

'You must.'

'Do you take me for a fool, Mr Jupe?' The outline of a crude but effective trap was forming in Spandrel's mind. 'If I set foot outside the rules, I'll be arrested.' And that, perhaps, was the sole object of the exercise.

'Not on Sunday.'

It was a valid point. No debtor could be arrested on the sabbath. It was Spandrel's weekly breath of liberty, when he walked the streets of London a free if penniless man. Occasionally, he would stray further, into the countryside, though never so far that he could not return within the day. There was an invisible leash around his neck and always it tugged him back.

'Sir Theodore will see you then.'

'Very well.'

'Nine o'clock, Sunday morning. At his house in Hanover Square.'

'I'll be there.'

'Be sure you are, Mr Spandrel. And be on time. Sir Theodore values promptness.'

'Is there anything . . . I should bring with me?'

'Bring yourself. That is all Sir Theodore requires.'

'But . . . why? What can I—'

'No more questions.' Jupe's raised voice had suddenly filled the room. Now it dropped once more to its normal pitch. 'You will have your answers on Sunday. And I wish you well of them.'

Spandrel did not know whether to feel elated or perturbed by his summons to the presence of Sir Theodore Janssen. Just when he had least expected it, an escape route from all his difficulties had opened before him. But it might lead him into yet worse difficulties. There was the rub. The likes of Sir Theodore Janssen did not shower benefactions on the likes of him. It was not in the nature of things; not, at any rate, in the nature of merchant princes.

Folly and overconfidence had plunged Spandrel's father into debt. He had insisted on the most expensive equipment available for their project: brand-new theodolites, waywisers and measuring chains, of which none remained, the waywiser beside the fireplace being so old even the bailiffs had turned their noses up at it. He had lavished entertainment on potential customers, stinting them little in the way of food and drink while he explained the glory and precision of their map. He had thrown money around like a farmer sowing seed. But all he had reaped was broken promises and unpaid bills. And all Spandrel had inherited from him was a mapmaker's turn of mind and debts ratcheted up by interest to several hundred pounds.

Spandrel might as well have dreamed of flying through the window and mapping the city from the sky as of earning such a sum. Yet a way of earning it was what Sir Theodore had apparently decided to offer him. Why? And what did he have to do for it? What service could he render that was worth so much? It made no sense.

Yet he would go to Hanover Square on Sunday morning, of course. He would go and, like as not, he would agree to do whatever Sir Theodore asked of him. He had no choice. But that did not mean he had no doubt. Hope had been reborn. But doubt kept it company.

When Margaret Spandrel returned to Cat and Dog Yard later that morning, laden with dirty washing, she found her son staring out of the window of their room at a view so familiar to both of them that contemplation of it was surely futile. Already weary, she was at once irritated by his apparent listlessness.

'No tea brewed to welcome me back?' she snapped. 'Have you done nothing but sit there like a moon-calf while I've been gone?'

'I've been thinking,' William replied.

'Thinking?' Mrs Spandrel was a warm-hearted woman, who had married for love and been rewarded with five children, only one of whom had lived beyond the cradle, early widowhood and greater poverty than she had ever imagined descending into. Thinking was, on the whole, something she preferred not to do. 'I despair of you, boy, I really do.'

'No you don't, Ma.'

'I come close, believe me. Now, do let's have some tea before we set to scrubbing this load.' She dropped the vast bundle of washing on the floor and lowered herself into the fireside chair with a sigh. 'Then you can tell me who our mysterious visitor was.'

'We've had no visitor,' said William, as he threw some fragments of sea-coal onto the all but dead fire to warm the kettle by.

'I met Annie Welsh downstairs. She said a stranger called here earlier. Neat and clean-looking, she reckoned.'

'You know what a busybody that woman is.'

'But not often wrong.'

'Well, she is this time.'

'Are you saying she made it up?'

'No. He must have called on someone else, that's all.' William smiled at her, which was rare these days, and always cheered her. 'What would a neat and clean-looking stranger want with me?'

Chapter Three

Knights Errant

It is doubtful if William Spandrel would have been able to guess the service Sir Theodore Janssen required of him, even had he been a fly on the wall of the board-room at South Sea House that Saturday, when, with candles lit against the gloom and rain drumming on the windows, the Secret Committee of Inquiry began its examination of Robert Knight. With his fluent tongue and agile mind, Knight was more than a match for his interrogators, but even he could be worn down eventually. That must have been Chairman Brodrick's calculation, at any rate. As the questions grew more specific and the answers more evasive, the crux of the scandal would inevitably emerge. Time was on the committee's side, after all. When they adjourned that evening, they had still not hacked a path through Knight's artfully cultivated thicket of obfuscations. But, on Monday, they surely would.

Sunday dawned grey and chill, the rain spent, the city silent. Spandrel had left his mother sleeping, but knew she would not worry when she woke to find him absent. His sabbath wanderings were familiar to her. But he was not wandering this sabbath morning. He had both a purpose and a destination. He strode along High Holborn with the vigour of a man refreshed by the knowledge that he had business to attend to, even though he did not know what that business was.

The map he and his father had expended so much time and effort on might no longer be in his possession, but it was still in his mind, the great rats' maze of London printed indelibly on his memory. Few could know it as well as he did: the yards, the courts, the squares, the alleys. He could have chosen half a dozen circuitous routes to Hanover Square and negotiated them unerringly. It was not caution but urgency that prompted him to press on along the most direct route, following the southward curve of Broad Street past St Giles. He literally could not afford to be late.

Soon, he was on the Tyburn Road, with elegant modern houses to his left and open fields, alternating with building sites, to his right. This was the very edge of the city, where new money had pushed out its tendrils into old land. But the South Sea disaster had cut those tendrils. Building had stopped. The half-built houses he saw to the north might never be finished now. His father had been assured by several potential customers that there would soon be a labyrinth of streets for them to map as far west as Hyde Park. But horses and cattle still grazed the pastures beyond Bond Street and surely would for many years yet.

Hanover Square was both the limit and the apogee of this abruptly halted surge of building. Here many of the favoured servants of the new monarchy had chosen to reside in Germanically ornate splendour, Sir Theodore Janssen among them. Whether the dukes and generals still wanted him as a neighbour was a moot point. The distinct possibility that he had become an embarrassment to them gave Spandrel some comfort as he approached the great man's door and rapped the knocker.

It was Jupe who answered, so swiftly that he must have been waiting close at hand. He said nothing at first, merely looking Spandrel up and down as if wondering whether his clothes were the best he could find for a visit to such a distinguished person. (They were, in truth, the best he could find for a visit to anyone.) Then a clock began striking nine in the hall behind him and a flicker of something like surprised approval crossed Jupe's face.

He stood back, gesturing for Spandrel to enter, and closed the door behind him, then said simply, 'This way,' and led him along the hall and up the stairs. Spandrel's immediate impression was of great wealth, evident in gilded friezework and oil paintings as big as banqueting tables, weighed down by a pervading silence that magnified the striking of the clock into an ominous toll.

A door on the first floor opened and they were in a drawing-room, whose high windows looked out onto the square. There were paintings here too, along with busts and urns aplenty. A fire was burning, almost raging, it seemed to Spandrel, so unaccustomed was he to anything beyond the bare minimum of fuel. A man was standing in front of it, dressed in a purple shag gown and turban, sipping from a cup of chocolate. He was short and broad-shouldered, clearly old, but with none of the weakness of age. If he was desperate, he did not show it. Sir Theodore Janssen had not perfected a demeanour of calm authority for nothing.

'Mr Spandrel,' he said simply, handing his cup to Jupe, who left the room at once and without another word. 'I knew your father.'

'He spoke often of you, Sir Theodore.'

'Did he? As what, pray? A fine patron – or a merciless tormentor?'

'He did not enjoy being in debt.'

'No man does, Mr Spandrel. Yet you took on that state, to spare your father imprisonment.'

'There was nothing else I could do.'

21

'Some sons would not have taken that view of the matter.'

'Perhaps not.'

'Jupe tells me your present accommodation is . . . lacking in most comforts.'

'It's not Hanover Square.'

'No. Nor the Fleet Prison. There's that to console you.'

'So there is.'

'But I've not brought you here for consolation.'

'What have you brought me here for, Sir Theodore?'

'To business, yes? A sound principle. Well, our business is the money you owe me, Mr Spandrel.'

'I can't pay you.'

'Not in cash, no. Of course not. But in kind. Yes, yes. I rather think you *can* pay me in kind.'

'How?'

'By acting as my courier in a confidential transaction.'

'Your . . . *courier*?'

'I require an article to be delivered to a gentleman in Amsterdam who is known to me. And I require a trustworthy person to deliver it.'

'Me?'

'Exactly so.'

'But . . . why?' Spandrel could not have disguised his puzzlement even had he tried. The simplicity of what he was being asked to do was somehow more disturbing than had Sir Theodore wanted him to murder a business rival. 'Surely you have servants to run this kind of errand. Why not send Mr Jupe?'

'I have my reasons. And you have no need to know what they are. Indeed, the less you know the better. I will cancel your debt to me upon written confirmation that the article has been safely delivered. That is as much as you need to understand. Do you accept my terms?'

'Mr Jupe mentioned my debts to other parties than yourself.'

'There are no other parties. I have bought in all your debts. I am your sole creditor, Mr Spandrel. In passing, let me tell you that your debts came exceptionally cheap. No-one believes they will ever be paid. But no-one is likely to be as flexible as me in devising a means of payment.'

'And all I have to do to pay them off is to act as your postman?'

'Yes. That is all.'

'On this one occasion?'

'This occasion only.'

'That's very generous of you.' It was, indeed, suspiciously generous. How could Spandrel be sure further, more onerous, demands would not be made of him if he proved himself useful by accomplishing this straightforward task? The inescapable answer was that he could not.

'No doubt you are wondering what guaranty you would have that these terms would be honoured.' Sir Theodore seemed to find it easy to read Spandrel's thoughts. 'Well, you would have my word.'

'In my situation, Sir Theodore, would you find that . . . sufficient?'

'Your situation, Mr Spandrel, is that of someone who has nothing to lose and nothing to bargain with. In *your* situation, I would find any guaranty sufficient.' Sir Theodore raised his hand to forestall objections, though in plain truth Spandrel could conceive of none. 'I have to trust you with an article of some value and the money you will need to travel to Amsterdam. You have to trust me that your reward for undertaking the journey will be a release from indebtedness. You could abscond. But the consideration you showed your father suggests that you would not lightly abandon your mother. I could break my word to you. But to what purpose? I cannot profit from your imprisonment. I *may* profit from your feeling obliged to me. I still regard your father's map as a worthwhile

23

commercial project. Only you can complete it. I have no wish to prevent you. Who knows but that if you do, we may not be in a position to contract more . . . orthodox business together.' Sir Theodore smiled. 'We all take a risk, Mr Spandrel, every day that we live. The one I am inviting you to take is not so very great, now is it?'

'I suppose not.'

'You agree, then?'

'Yes. I agree.' Spandrel refrained from adding that he really had no choice *but* to agree.

'Good.' Sir Theodore walked past him to a table in the centre of the room. Turning, Spandrel saw that an old leather satchel lay on the table. Sir Theodore pulled it upright and opened the flap. 'This is the article I require you to carry.'

Spandrel moved closer. Inside the satchel was a maroon leather despatch-box, with brass reinforcements, catches and lock.

'You are to deliver the box personally to Mijnheer Ysbrand de Vries at his home in Amsterdam. He lives on the Herengracht, near the centre of the city. You will have no difficulty finding the house. Mijnheer de Vries is well known. He will be expecting you. You will obtain a receipt and return here with it.'

'Is that all?'

'It is. The box is locked, Mr Spandrel, and I will retain the key. You understand?'

'Yes.'

'Mijnheer de Vries is a man of about my own age. We are old friends. There must be no mistake as to the identity of the person to whom you deliver the box. You will say that you are instructed to ask him to recall to mind the third member of the party on the occasion when he and I first met. The person he will name is Jacob van Dillen. You have it?'

'Jacob van Dillen,' Spandrel repeated.

'Van Dillen is long dead. I should doubt if there is anyone now living who remembers him, other than Ysbrand de Vries and myself. And now you, of course.'

'I won't give him the box unless he can name van Dillen.'

'Good.'

'When do you want me to leave?'

'Immediately.'

'I must see my mother first.'

'There is no need for that. Write her a note. Say you will be away for a week or so, but do not say why. Jupe will deliver it to her and assure her that there is no need for her to worry.'

'Surely—'

'That is how it will be, Mr Spandrel. Sit down and write the note. I have pen and paper to hand.'

Almost, it seemed to Spandrel, before he knew what he was doing, he was seated at the table, scrawling a few words that read as vaguely to him as he knew they would be baffling to his mother. Sir Theodore stood over him as he wrote, waiting for him to finish.

'Good enough.' Sir Theodore plucked the barely signed letter from Spandrel's fingers. 'You may leave that with me. Now, to your travel arrangements. You will be driven in my coach to Hungerford Stairs, where my skiff is waiting to take you to Deptford. The sloop *Vixen* is due to sail from Deptford for Helvoetsluys on the afternoon tide. Your passage is paid for. For your expenses beyond that . . .' Sir Theodore crossed to a bureau in a corner of the room and returned with a well-filled purse. 'This will be ample.'

'Thank you,' said Spandrel, pocketing the purse without examining the contents but judging by the weight of coin that it was, as Sir Theodore had said, ample. 'I'd, er, always understood the quickest passage to Holland was from Harwich.'

'I did not know you were an experienced traveller, Mr Spandrel.'

'I'm . . . not.'

'Have you ever been to Holland?'

'No.'

'Have you, in truth, ever left this country?'

'No.'

'Then accept the arrangements made for you by one who was born far from these shores. You will land at Helvoetsluys some time tomorrow. From there it should take you no more than two days to reach Amsterdam. Mijnheer de Vries will be expecting you on Wednesday. In the event of unforeseen difficulties, apply to my banker in the city – the firm of Pels. But do not do so unless absolutely necessary. It would be better for you, much better, to avoid all difficulties. And to return here for your reward.'

'That's what I intend to do, Sir Theodore.' Spandrel closed the flap of the satchel and laid his hand on it. 'You can rely on me.'

'Let us hope so,' said Sir Theodore unsmilingly.

Spandrel left Hanover Square in a daze. After months of hand-to-mouth misery at Cat and Dog Yard, he was suddenly riding through London in a well-sprung carriage, with money in his pocket and a liveried driver at the reins. He knew it was too good to be true. But he consoled himself that some things were good *and* true. Maybe this was one of them.

Maria Chesney was certainly another. His most recent encounter with the Chesneys' talkative footman, Sam Burrows, in Sam's favourite Sunday watering-hole, had yielded the information that Maria was still not engaged to be married. Spandrel had taken this to mean that her heart still belonged to him, which had only deepened his gloom at the time, since there was no way in the world that Maria's father would let her marry a debtor. But he might not be a debtor for much longer. Maybe, with Sir Theodore's grateful help, he could finish the map and make a commercial success of it. And maybe old Chesney could then be induced to approve of him as a son-in-law.

Unwise though he knew it to be, Spandrel let such thoughts fill his head. He had drunk his fill of despondency. For the moment, he could not resist the flavour of a sweeter brew.

Jupe delivered Spandrel's letter to his mother promptly, if peremptorily. Beyond assuring Mrs Spandrel that her son would be out of the Middlesex magistrates' jurisdiction throughout his absence and therefore not liable to arrest, he told her nothing and was gone almost before she had read the few lines William had written. They likewise told her nothing, other than not to worry, which naturally she did, especially when Annie Welsh expressed her certainty that Jupe was the man who had called there on Friday morning. William had been planning this since then at least, possibly longer. That much seemed clear. But nothing else was. And, until it became so, she would do little *but* worry. 'For that boy's sake,' she gamely informed Annie Welsh, 'I hope he's got a good excuse for leaving his old mother in the lurch.'

Whether his mother would regard his excuse as good or bad did not figure in Spandrel's thoughts as Sir Theodore's skiff nosed in to the dock at Deptford and drew alongside the *Vixen* beneath a gun-metal noonday sky. His confidence had already faded in the sobering face of a journey down the Thames during which the boatmen

27

had said not a word to him, though they had exchanged many meaningful looks and mutters. He was cold and hungry and would soon be far from home. What was in the box? He did not know. He did not want to know. If all went well, he never would. And if all did not go well . . .

Why *had* Sir Theodore chosen him? And why had he not sent him by the Harwich route? There were questions, but no answers. Except one: he had to go through with it; he had no choice.

That would probably still have been Spandrel's conclusion had he been aware of the other sea crossing being made that day by a recent visitor to the house of Sir Theodore Janssen. Robert Knight was also on his way out of the country, boarding a private yacht at Dover by prior arrangement for the short voyage to Calais. When the Committee of Inquiry reconvened at South Sea House on Monday morning to continue his examination, it was going to find itself without an examinee.

Chapter Four

The Mapmaker's Journey

In other circumstances, Spandrel would probably have enjoyed his journey to Amsterdam, a choppy crossing on the *Vixen* proving, somewhat surprisingly, that he did not suffer from sea-sickness. Anxiety was a different matter, however. Once he had delivered the box to de Vries, he would be able to relish the sights and sensations of foreign travel. Until then, he could only wish the days and miles away.

He tried to keep himself to himself, but a loquacious tile merchant from Sussex called Maybrick wore down his defences in the passenger cabin of the *Vixen* and insisted on accompanying him from Helvoetsluys, where they landed on Monday afternoon, as far as Rotterdam. For Maybrick's benefit, Spandrel claimed to be what he would so like to have been: a mapmaker thinking of applying his talents to the cities of the United Provinces.

He could not complain too much about Maybrick, though, since the fellow took him to an inn in Rotterdam that was comfortable as well as cheap and told him how sensible he had been to avoid the Harwich run on account of the grasping ways of Essex innkeepers.

Spandrel was nevertheless relieved to continue on his own the following morning, by horse-drawn *trekschuit* along winding canals through flat, winter-stripped fields. Rain of varying intensity, ranging from drizzle to downpour, fell out of the vast grey dome of sky and the *trekschuit* kept up a slow if steady pace. It finally delivered its passengers to Haarlem nine hours later, in the chill of early evening, bone-weary and, in Spandrel's case, fuddled by spending all bar a few minutes of those nine hours inhaling other people's pipe smoke in the cramped cabin.

But Haarlem was only three hours from Amsterdam. Next morning, washed and refreshed, Spandrel felt his fragile confidence return. Before the day was out, he would have done what Sir Theodore had asked of him. Nothing was going to stop him. And nothing was going to go wrong.

The rain persisted. The Haarlem to Amsterdam *trekschuit* seemed draughtier and damper than the one Spandrel had travelled on the day before. Or perhaps it was simply that his tolerance was diminishing. The vast stretches of water between which the canal ran through a scrawny neck of land created the illusion that they were voyaging out to an island somewhere in the Zuyder Zee, well enough though he knew Amsterdam's location from his father's collection of maps.

At length they arrived, the canal running out into the moat that surrounded the city wall. Above them, on the wall, windmills sat like sentinels, their sails turning slowly in the dank breeze. It was early afternoon and Spandrel was eager to press on to his destination. Spending money with a liberality he reckoned he could easily accustom himself to, he hired a coach from the city gate to take him to the de Vries house. '*Ik heb haast*,' he told the driver, using a phrase he had picked up from merchant Maybrick. 'I'm in a hurry.' It was nothing less than the truth.

The houses of Herengracht were elegant and uniform, their high, narrow frontages lining the canal in a display of prosperity that convinced Spandrel he was entering the very heart of the city's mercantile community. The de Vries residence, which the coachman had seemed to know well, looked very much like its neighbours, a broad staircase leading up to a loftily architraved entrance at mezzanine level. Gazing up from the street, Spandrel noticed the hoist-beams jutting out above its topmost windows. Every house had such devices. His eye followed them round the curve of the canal. Suddenly, and unwelcomely, he thought how like a row of Smithfield meat-hooks they looked, waiting for a carcass. Then he thrust the thought aside and climbed the steps.

An elderly manservant answered the door. He had an unsmiling air of truculence about him, as if he sensed that Spandrel was not so important as to merit any show of respect. The fellow communicated by grimaces and hand signals, presumably because he spoke no English. He admitted Spandrel no farther than the marbled hall and left him to wait on a low chair literally overshadowed by a vast oriental urn on a plinth.

Five minutes passed, precisely timed for Spandrel by the long-case clock he was sitting opposite. Then a tall, dark-eyed man of about Spandrel's own age appeared. He had an intent, solicitous expression and was immaculately if plainly dressed. But there was also a languor about him, an impression of unstated superiority. And in those sea-cave eyes there was something else which disturbed Spandrel. He could not have said what it was. *That* was what disturbed him.

'Mr Spandrel,' the man said in perfectly enunciated but accented English. 'My name is Zuyler. I am Mijnheer de Vries's secretary.'

'Is Mijnheer de Vries at home?'

'I regret not.'

'I must see him. It is a matter of some urgency.'

'So I understand.' Zuyler cast a fleeting glance at the satchel. 'You are expected. But the time of your arrival was unknown. And Mijnheer de Vries is a busy man.'

'I'm sure he is.'

'My instructions are to ask you to wait here while I fetch him. He is at the Oost Indisch Huys. It is not far. But I cannot say how . . . involved in business . . . I may find him. Nevertheless . . .'

'I'll wait.'

'Good. This way please.'

Zuyler led him towards the rear of the house and into what was clearly de Vries's library. Well-stocked bookcases lined the walls and the windows were shaded against the depredations of sunlight, an unnecessary precaution, it seemed to Spandrel, in view of the grey weather he had travelled through. Sure enough, more light was coming from the fire burning in the grate than from the world beyond the windows.

'I will return as soon as I can,' said Zuyler. And with that he was gone, slipping silently from the room with disconcerting suddenness.

Spandrel looked around him. Busts of assorted ancients were spaced along the tops of the bookcases. Lavishly framed oil paintings of less ancient subjects – Dutch burgher stock, for the most part – occupied the space between them and the stuccoed ceiling. Above the mirror over the fireplace was a painting of a different order, depicting a castle of some sort in a tropical setting, palm trees bending in an imagined breeze. An armchair and a sofa stood either side of the fireplace. There was a desk in front of one of the windows and a wide table adjacent to a section of bookcasing given over to map drawers. Spandrel was tempted to slide the drawers open and see what they contained, but he resisted. He did not want to complicate his presence in the house in any way. He wished, in fact, to know as little as possible about its owner; and that owner, in turn, to know as little as possible about him.

But that was easier thought than adhered to. There was a clock in this room too, ticking through the leaden minutes. Spandrel sat down in front of the fire, stood up and inspected the paintings, sat down again, stood up again. And all the while he kept the satchel in his hand.

Twenty minutes slowly elapsed. Spandrel had little hope that de Vries could be swiftly extricated from his place of business. He stood glumly in the centre of the room, examining his reflection in the mirror. It was a clearer and fuller version of himself than he had seen for many months and the hard times he had lived through during those months had left their mark – there was no denying it. He looked older than his years. He had acquired a faint sagging of the shoulders that would become a permanent stoop if he did not mend his posture, which he thereupon did, to encouraging effect. But it was only that: an effect. It could not last. As if admitting as much, he let his shoulders relax.

At which moment the door opened behind him and a dark-haired young woman in a blue dress entered the room. 'Excuse me,' she said, her accent sounding genuinely English. 'I did not realize . . .'

'Your pardon, madam.' Spandrel turned and mustered a bow. 'I was bidden to wait here for Mijnheer de Vries.'

'You may have a long wait, sir. My husband is at East India House. I am not expecting him back before six o'clock.'

Spandrel registered the disconcerting fact that this woman was de Vries's wife. She could not be much above twenty-five, but Sir Theodore had described de Vries as a man of about his own age, so Mrs de Vries had to be more than thirty years his junior. To make matters worse, she was quite startlingly attractive. Not classically beautiful, it was true. Her nose was too long, her brow too broad, for that. But she had a poise and an openness of expression that overrode such considerations. Her blue dress set off her hair and eyes perfectly. There was a curl of some nascent smile playing about her lips. Her eyebrows were faintly arched. Around her neck she wore a single string of pearls, at her breast a white satin bow. Confined for so long to the female company of Cat and Dog Yard, Spandrel had forgotten how intoxicating close proximity to a well-dressed and finely bred woman could be. And even Maria Chesney had lacked something that Mrs de Vries quite obviously possessed: a confidence in her own womanhood that made her marriage to the crabbed old miser Spandrel had suddenly decided de Vries must be less a mockery . . . than a tragedy.

'Have you come far to see my husband, Mr . . .'

'Spandrel, madam. William Spandrel.'

'From England, perhaps?'

'Indeed.'

'It is always a pleasure to hear an English voice. You will have guessed, of course, that I am only Dutch by marriage. My husband speaks excellent English. So do most of the household. But . . .' She trailed into a thoughtful silence.

'I met Mr Zuyler.'

'Well, well, there you are. A fluent example, indeed. But fluency is not quite authenticity, is it?' She smiled.

'No,' Spandrel said hesitantly. 'I suppose not.'

'Where is Mr Zuyler now?'

'He has gone to fetch your husband.'

'To fetch him? With the expectation that he will wish to be fetched, I assume. You must be an important man, Mr Spandrel.'

'Hardly.'

'Has no-one offered you tea?'

'Er . . . no.'

'Then let me do so.' She moved past him to the bell-pull beside the fireplace and tugged at it. 'When did you arrive in Amsterdam?'

'This afternoon. By barge from Haarlem.'

'Then tea you will certainly need.'

'Thank you.' Spandrel smiled cautiously. 'It would be most welcome.'

'Please be seated.'

'Thank you.' Spandrel was aware of repeating himself. He sat down in the armchair and self-consciously lowered the satchel to the floor beside him.

Mrs de Vries sat on the sofa opposite him and seemed on the point of saying something when the door opened and a maid entered. There was a brief conversation in Dutch. The maid withdrew.

'How long,' Spandrel began, feeling the need to speak even though there was little he could safely say, 'have you lived in Amsterdam, Mrs de Vries?'

'Nearly three years, Mr Spandrel.'

'You speak the language . . . very well.'

'Not as well as I should. But Mr Zuyler has been as assiduous a tutor as his other duties will allow.'

'What part of England do you come from?'

'An obscure part. But your accent betrays you as a Londoner, I think.'

'You're correct.'

'How is the city these days?'

'The city is well. But the spirits of its citizens are generally low.'

'Because of the collapse in South Sea stock?'

'Indeed. I see you're well informed.'

'My husband is a man of business, Mr Spandrel. How should I not be? Besides, the South Sea Company has scarcely fewer victims here than in London. And those who have not thrown their money down that drain have consigned it to the pit of the Mississippi Company instead. Did London hold itself aloof from that?'

'I think not.' Spandrel had read various references to the Mississippi Company in the third- or fourth-hand newspapers that were his only informants on the world. It had been France's imitation of the South Sea scheme. Or was it the other way round? He could not rightly remember. 'But it seems . . . you know more about such matters than I do.'

'You would be unique among my husband's business associates if that were the case.'

'But I'm not his associate, madam. Merely the servant of one.'

'And would your master be Sir Theodore Janssen?'

Spandrel flinched with surprise. He had not expected to be seen through so easily.

'Forgive me, Mr Spandrel.' Mrs de Vries smiled at him reassuringly. 'The deduction required no great acuity on my part. Sir Theodore is my husband's oldest friend. My husband mentioned receiving a letter from him recently. Sir Theodore lives in London. You come from London. And Mr Zuyler hastens off to fetch Mr de Vries from the midst of his mercantile deliberations. You see? Simplicity itself.'

'Only when you explain it.'

'You flatter me.' Her smile broadened and Spandrel realized that flattery had indeed been his intention. Then there came a stirring of the latch. 'Ah. Here's Geertruid with our tea.'

Geertruid it was, somewhat out of humour to judge by the sighs that accompanied her arrangement of the cups, plates, spoons and saucers. A rich-looking cake had arrived along with the tea and, as soon as Geertruid had left, Mrs de Vries cut him a large slice and watched approvingly as he tasted it.

'Travel makes a man hungry, does it not, Mr Spandrel?'

'It does, madam, I confess. And this is . . . excellent cake.'

'Good. You must eat your fill. There is no need for a man to go hungry in this house. My husband's prudence in matters of business has served us well of late.'

'I'm glad to hear it.'

'There is a saying in Dutch he often quotes. "*Des waereld's doen en doolen is maar een mallemoolen.*" "The ways of the world are but a fool's merry-go-round." But, if that is the case, I often think, it begs the question: are we all fools, then? For we must all live in the world.'

'I'm not sure there can be an answer to such a question.'

'Not one we would wish to hear, at any rate. Quite so. Let us try another, then. How long have you been in Sir Theodore's service, Mr Spandrel?'

'Not long at all.'

'And before?'

'I am a mapmaker by profession.'

'Indeed? I wonder you do not pursue your profession.'

'Times are hard. And in hard times people decide they can live without maps.'

'But without a map, there is always the danger of going astray.'

'As many do.'

'How did you take up your profession?'

'From my father.'

'An eminent mapmaker?'

'A prosperous one – for a while.'

'My husband has a Mercator Atlas. Is that the sort of mapmaking of which we speak?'

'Not exactly. I map . . . closer to home.'

'Ah. Then you may be interested in this.' Mrs de Vries

rose and moved to the map drawers Spandrel had eyed earlier. She pulled one open, slid out a sheet and laid it on the table. 'A recent acquisition. Come and look at it.'

Spandrel set down his tea and joined her by the table. A map of London lay before him; one he well recognized as the work of a competitor.

'Is it good?' Mrs de Vries asked.

'It's . . . accurate. If a little . . . out of date.'

'Out of date?' Mrs de Vries laughed lightly. 'I shall look forward to teasing my husband with that remark.'

'All maps are out of date to some degree.'

'Then should we discard them, like an old newspaper?'

'They should be drawn so that you don't *want* to discard them.'

'Ah. Because of their beauty?'

'Yes.' He looked round at her to find that she was already looking at him. He was suddenly aware of her perfume enveloping him and of how close they were, the lace ruff at her elbow just touching his sleeve. 'Exactly.'

'So, your maps are works of art?'

'I only wish—'

The door opened abruptly, too abruptly for the arrival of a servant. And clearly the person who entered was nothing of the kind. He was a short, barrel-chested old man in russet greatcoat and black suit, the coat worn draped over his shoulders like a cape, the sleeves empty. His face was lined but mobile, broken veins reddening his sharp cheekbones beneath grey, wary eyes framed by a mane of his own snowy white hair. The absence of a wig and the way he had shrugged on the coat, presumably the more readily to shrug it off, conveyed at once a certain bluntness, if not brusqueness. Ysbrand de Vries, as Spandrel felt sure the newcomer was, lacked his old friend Sir Theodore Janssen's polish and perhaps also his subtlety. But he was the one of them who, according to his wife, had scorned

38

the lure of South Sea and Mississippi alike. He, Spandrel reminded himself, was the better judge of the two.

'Mr Spandrel,' the man growled unsmilingly. 'I am de Vries.'

'Your servant, sir. I've come—'

'Enough of that.' He glanced at his wife. 'You may leave us, madam. *Ga weg.*' It sounded like what it undoubtedly was: a dismissal verging on the curt.

'Goodbye, Mr Spandrel,' said Estelle de Vries, so unembarrassed by her husband's manner that Spandrel could only suppose it was what she was well used to. 'I hope you enjoyed your tea.'

'I did. Thank you.' Already, as he spoke, she was on her way out of the room. As the door closed behind her, he looked at de Vries and summoned a respectful smile. 'Mijnheer—'

'Janssen sent you?'

'Sir Theodore Janssen, yes.'

'With an article for safe-keeping.'

'Yes. But . . .' Spandrel retreated to the armchair and retrieved the satchel. 'I must take precautions, mijnheer. You understand?'

'What precautions?'

'I'm instructed to ask you to name the third member of the party on the occasion of your and Sir Theodore's first meeting.'

'Ha. *Spelletjes, spelletjes, spelletjes.* Janssen plays too much. You cannot always win.' De Vries pulled off his coat and tossed it over the back of the armchair. 'You liked the tea, Mr Spandrel? You enjoyed the . . . tart?'

'The cake was good.'

'The secret is in the spices.' De Vries scowled at him.

'No doubt.'

'Jacob van Dillen.'

'I beg your pardon?'

39

'The name you require . . . for Sir Theodore's game. Van Dillen.'

'Yes. Of course. I'm sorry.'

'So. The article. It is in the bag?'

'Yes.'

'Give it to me, then.'

Spandrel took the satchel to the table, laid it next to the map of London, opened the flap and slid out the despatch-box. De Vries's shadow fell across it as he did so, the old man's hand stretching out to brush the map aside.

'There were no . . . difficulties on your journey?'

'None, mijnheer.'

'That is good.' De Vries reached for the despatch-box and Spandrel noticed how swollen his knuckles were, how claw-like his fingers. He imagined them touching Estelle's soft, pale flesh and could not suppress a quiver of disgust at the thought. 'You are cold?'

'No. It's nothing.'

'Relief, perhaps.' De Vries slid the despatch-box towards himself. 'At a mission accomplished.'

'Perhaps.'

'You require a receipt?'

'Yes. Please. I do.'

De Vries smiled with half his mouth, then marched to the desk by the window and seized pen and paper. He did not sit down, but stooped to write, quickly, in a practised hand. Spandrel watched him, marvelling at how lightly his distorted fingers held the pen. Then he was done, and marching back to the table, holding out the receipt for Spandrel to take.

'Thank you, mijnheer.' Spandrel glanced down at the document and flushed at once with a sense of his own stupidity. 'But . . . it's in Dutch.'

'I *am* Dutch, Mr Spandrel.'

'I don't know what it says.'

'It is what you asked for. A receipt.' De Vries raised a wintry eyebrow. 'You doubt me?'

'I . . . must be sure.'

'Must you?'

'Yes. I think I must.'

'I think you must too.' De Vries gave another lopsided smile. 'I can also play games, you see? You write what you require.' He waved him towards the desk. 'I will sign it.'

Spandrel walked over to the desk, de Vries keeping pace behind him. He sat down, the old man looming at his shoulder, and wrote.

'Very good,' said de Vries when he had finished. 'But you have the date wrong. We are eleven days ahead of England here. And you are here, not there.' He took the pen, crossed out 25th January and wrote 5th February in its place. 'It is always better to be ahead than behind.' Then he added his signature. 'You are not an experienced traveller, I think.'

'No,' admitted Spandrel, shamed by his mistake.

'Dates can be confusing. It will still be January when you return to England. Those of us who make our profits and losses by the day' – he tapped his temple – 'keep such things in mind.'

'Yes. Of course.' Spandrel folded the receipt and slipped it into his pocket.

'Be sure not to lose that.'

'I will be.'

'When will you leave Amsterdam?'

'As soon as possible.'

'A pity, if this is your first visit. The city would repay a longer stay.'

'Sir Theodore will be anxious for confirmation of the box's safe delivery.' Spandrel stood up. 'I must go.'

'How will you travel?'

'The way I came. By barge.'

'You know the times?'

'I confess not.' Spandrel was once again brought up sharp by his own stupidity. He should have enquired about the return journey to Haarlem on arrival at the city gate. But, in his haste to reach de Vries's house, he had forgotten to do so. 'Do you, mijnheer, by any chance . . .'

'Keep them also in mind? No, I do not. But I employ someone who does.' De Vries strode to the door, opened it and bellowed into the hallway, 'Zuyler! *Hier! Onmiddellijk!*' Then, leaving the door open, he marched across to the table on which the despatch-box lay. But it was not the box he was looking at. 'Why did Estelle show you my map of London, Mr Spandrel?'

'She thought I would be interested.'

'Why?'

'Because I am a mapmaker by profession.'

'How did she know that?'

'I told her.'

'You tell too much.' De Vries turned and regarded him thoughtfully. 'It is a bad habit. You should—' He broke off at Zuyler's appearance in the doorway.

'Mijnheer?' There was a brief exchange in Dutch, then Zuyler nodded and looked at Spandrel. 'You are bound for Helvoetsluys, Mr Spandrel?'

'I am.'

'Your quickest passage would be by the overnight *trekschuit* direct to Rotterdam. It leaves at eleven o'clock, from the Oudezijds Herenlogement on Grimburgwal.' De Vries intervened in Dutch at this and Zuyler smiled faintly before continuing. 'Mijnheer de Vries suggests I take you there. He doubts you will find the way. The Herenlogement is an inn. You may wish to take a meal before your journey.'

'Thank you. I'm sure I can find it myself.'

'It would be my pleasure to escort you, Mr Spandrel.'

'In that case . . .' Spandrel glanced from one to the other of them, 'I accept.'

'Goodbye then, Mr Spandrel,' said de Vries. 'Tell Sir Theodore . . .'

'Yes?'

'Nothing.' De Vries looked at him unsmilingly. 'That is always best.'

Chapter Five

Into the Darkness

It turned out to be but a short walk from the de Vries house to Grimburgwal. Spandrel was nonetheless grateful to have a guide. The network of canals and bridges and alleys that comprised Amsterdam seemed designed to confuse the stranger, so similar was one part of the whole to another. He jokingly asked Zuyler if this were deliberate, but the Dutchman responded with dry seriousness that he thought not and had himself found London equally bewildering without being driven to suspect a plot against foreigners.

Zuyler, of course, had only a swift return to his secretarial duties to look forward to, whereas Spandrel, his task accomplished, was already anticipating the transformation in his circumstances that awaited him in England. The disparity in their levels of humour did not really surprise Spandrel. Indeed, having met Ysbrand de Vries, he could not help feeling sorry for anyone who had to work for him. An attempt to put this into words, however, fell as flat as his joke.

'I imagine Mijnheer de Vries is a demanding employer.'

'That is the nature of employment,' Zuyler replied. 'It makes demands of one.'

'Indeed. But—'

'And it seldom rewards imagination.' Zuyler pulled up and pointed to a handsomely pedimented building on the other side of the canal. 'That is the Oudezijds Herenlogement. The Rotterdam *trekschuit* will pick up from the landing-stage in front.'

'Well, thank you for showing me the way.'

'I hope you have a safe journey.'

'I'm sure I will.'

Zuyler gave him a faint little nod that hovered on the brink of becoming a bow but never did, then turned and walked away. Spandrel watched him for a few paces, then had to step beneath the awning over a hatter's shop while a coach drove by. It was mounted on sledge-runners, as if designed for harsher weather than the prevailing mild grey dismalness, but rattled across the cobbles briskly enough. When Spandrel looked in Zuyler's direction once more, he was nowhere to be seen.

The Oudezijds Herenlogement was as comfortable and congenial an inn as Spandrel could have wished for. The tap-room was full of smoke and warmth and chatter, even at this unpromising hour of the late afternoon. He ate a hearty stew, washed down with a mug of ale, and gleaned confirmation of the *trekschuit* departure time from the tapster. Then he smoked a pipe over a second mug of ale and considered how best to fill the evening he had at his disposal. Darkness had fallen over the city and he knew better than to stray far from the inn, for he would be certain to lose himself. This was not London. He carried no map, on paper or in his head. Much the safer course of action was to stay where he was.

But even the Oudezijds Herenlogement held its hazards. As more and more customers arrived, Spandrel was joined at his table by three drinkers of genial demeanour, one lean, animated and talkative, the other two paunchy, dough-faced and content to puff at their pipes and quaff from their mugs while their companion chattered on. The chatterer soon tried to involve Spandrel in the conversation and, upon realizing that an Englishman was among them, gleefully revealed his knowledge of the language.

Spandrel was half-drunk by then, nestled in a smoky swathe of self-satisfaction. Jan, the chatterer, evinced nothing but a grinning eagerness to hear his description of London life, while the puffing and quaffing pair – Henrik and Roelant – set a stiff pace of consumption which he felt obliged to match. A few desultory hands of cards were played, although Spandrel found it difficult to distinguish the clubs from the spades. Toasts were drunk to good health and fellowship. A venture to the jakes demonstrated to Spandrel that he was becoming unsteady on his feet, though he persuaded himself that a few lungfuls of night air aboard the *trekschuit* would cure the problem, ignoring the fact that the *trekschuit* was not due to leave for another few hours. Then he and Jan became embroiled in a comparison of Englishwomen and Dutchwomen that led to a fateful challenge. Jan knew a nearby *musico*, as he called it, where particularly delectable young women could be had at reasonable rates. Let Spandrel sample one and he would be bound to admit their superiority to anything London had to offer. Tea with Estelle de Vries had undeniably whetted Spandrel's sexual appetite, just as ale with Jan, Henrik and Roelant had fuddled his judgement. Assured by Jan that he would be back long before eleven o'clock, he accepted the challenge.

He knew it was a mistake as soon as he left the inn. Far from clearing his head, the night air administered a chill shock which set it reeling. That and the enveloping darkness disoriented him at once. Jan led the way, Spandrel several times needing Henrik's or Roelant's assistance to keep track of him through the cobbled gulfs of blackness between the few street-lamps, confusingly reflected as they were in the adjacent canal.

Then they left the canal behind, turning first right, then left, then right into a narrow alley lit only to the degree that it was less dark at its far end. Spandrel decided he had had enough. Lust had entirely deserted him. He hurried to catch Jan up, asking him to stop at the same time.

'I'm not sure about this, Jan. I don't feel—'

Suddenly, he tripped, on what he had no idea. He fell heavily to the ground and rolled into the central gutter, then struggled to his knees, looking around for assistance. But he did not receive assistance. Instead, he received a boot in the midriff that drove the breath from his body and was followed by a wave of nausea. A second boot added a sharp, disabling pain to the nausea. Then something blunt and heavy struck him round the side of the head. He fell helplessly into the gutter, his senses grasping little beyond fear and the impossibility of escape. He had been taken for a fool and he had acted like one. They were thieves and probably murderers too. He was done for.

He must have vomited at some point. He dimly saw a pale smear of it on one of their sleeves and heard the owner curse him. It was Henrik. Or Roelant. He could no longer tell. It earned him another cuff to the head and a deepening of the blear through which his brain struggled to understand what was happening. The ale he had drunk dulled his pain but sapped his ability to think or to act. He was dragged into a doorway and hauled into a sitting position. Then they began rifling through his pockets. One by one they were emptied, till finally his money-bag was pulled out, tearing off the button fastening the pocket it was in with such force that it bounced back onto his face from the wall next to him. '*Snel, snel*,' he heard Jan say. '*Het zand.*' Something else was being put in to replace the money-bag – something heavy and bulky. Whatever it was, the same was being thrust into his outer pockets. Then he was dragged upright and carried along the alley, held by his arms across Henrik's and Roelant's shoulders, his feet scuffing the cobbles.

He glimpsed lamplight to left and right and the vague outline of a bridge. They must be near a canal. That fact was as much as he had grasped before he was abruptly released and found himself falling. He managed to brace his arms in front of him to take the impact. But it was not the cobbles he hit.

The water was cold and darkly turbid, a soundless world that wrapped its muddy coils around him and held him fast. He could not swim, but even had he been able to he would probably have been helpless, so heavy did he feel, so resistant did the water seem. He recognized the end that he now confronted: a drowned drunkard, far from home. He struck out against it. He saw a shimmer of lamplight, refracted through the water. He was close to the surface, but not close enough. He sank back, abandoning the effort and with it himself to the oblivion that folded itself around him.

Then something caught at his shoulder and lifted him bodily through the water. He broke surface and gulped in the air, coughing convulsively. There were stone stairs at his back, leading down from the street into the canal. A boat-hook was being disentangled from his coat as he was dragged up the lower steps. Somebody was behind him, hands beneath his shoulders, knees braced at his side. 'Push yourself up,' said a voice he vaguely recognized. 'Push, damn your eyes.'

Spandrel did push, but it was the other man who did most of the work. When they were both clear of the water, he lay back, panting from the effort.

'We can't stay here.' Now Spandrel knew who he was. 'They may come back.'

'Zuyler? Is that . . . you?'

'Listen to what I'm saying,' Zuyler hissed. 'We have to go. Quickly.'

'I can't . . . move.'

'You'll have to.' Zuyler struggled to his feet, pulling Spandrel half-upright as he did so. 'Get up, man.'

'I can't, I tell you.' Spandrel gave way to a bout of coughing. His clothes were saturated, the stench of canal mud rising in a plume around him. 'I feel so weak.'

'This will help.' Zuyler bent over him, pulled something bulky from his right-hand coat pocket, then from his left, and tossed the objects into the canal. 'Sand-bags,' he announced. 'To weigh down your corpse.'

'Oh God.'

'God will not help you, Spandrel. But I will. Now stand up.'

Afterwards the instinct for survival that lies dormant until it is most needed could alone satisfactorily explain to Spandrel how he was able to bludgeon his body into the action required of it that night. Quaking from the cold, and from the shock of what had happened, his clothes a chill, dripping weight around him, he somehow managed to follow Zuyler through a labyrinthine mile of alleys and canalsides to a chemist's shop, the meanly furnished basement of which constituted Zuyler's less than stylish residence.

Zuyler lit a fire for Spandrel to warm himself by, huddled in a blanket, his wet, mud-caked clothes discarded. A glass of schnapps and a bowl of soup slowly revived him, until he was able to offer the man who had saved his life some stumbling words of gratitude.

'You thank me,' Zuyler responded, puffing thoughtfully at his pipe before adding, with a rueful smile, 'and I curse you.'

'What?'

'I curse you, Spandrel. For presenting me with such a choice.'

'I don't . . . understand.'

'What do you think happened to you tonight?'

'I . . . fell into bad company.'

'Indeed you did. But why?'

'Because I was . . .' He broke off to cough. The pain in his side every time he did so had convinced him that at least one of his ribs was broken. But the throbbing ache in his head had the meagre merit of distracting him from the injury. 'I was foolish.'

'And that is all?'

'What else?'

'What else is what brought me to your aid. Cornelis Hondslager is not a—'

'Who?'

'Hondslager. The thin one.'

'He said his name was Jan.'

'No doubt he did. Aliases are a natural condition of his occupation.'

'And what is his occupation?'

'He is an assassin, Spandrel. A hired killer.'

'Hired?'

'To kill you. The other two I don't know. His regular assistants, I think we can assume.'

'To kill me?' Spandrel was having difficulty keeping pace with the implications of what Zuyler was saying. 'But that means . . .'

'It was arranged beforehand. Exactly.'

'How do you know?'

'I observed a meeting yesterday between de Vries and Hondslager. It was the purest chance. The coffee-house they chose for the purpose is not the kind of establishment where my employer is likely to be seen, in normal circumstances. That is actually why I sometimes use it. Well, clearly the circumstances were not normal. Another customer had alerted me to Hondslager's occupation some time ago. I could have little doubt as to the reason for their meeting and fell to asking myself who de Vries wanted to have killed. Your arrival this afternoon provided a possible answer. It could have been a coincidence, of course. De Vries has many enemies. He might have felt obliged to eliminate one of them, though frankly I doubted it. It is not the kind of sanction de Vries would wish to invoke against a business rival, for fear another rival might be inspired to use it against him. No, no. A stranger to the city and its ways seemed much the likelier target. Your arrival therefore seemed anything *but* coincidental.'

'Why didn't you warn me?'

'Because you don't pay my wages, Spandrel. De Vries does, albeit reluctantly. My interests are not served by obstructing his affairs.'

'But you obstructed them this time.'

'Yes.' Zuyler took an irritated swig of schnapps. 'You can thank my conscience for that.'

'I do. Believe me.'

'Which will profit me precisely nothing. But there it is. What's done is done. After de Vries had finished with me this evening, I decided to call at the Oudezijds Herenlogement on my way home to see that you had come to no harm. But you were already in Hondslager's company, too drunk to notice me or indeed the trap that was closing around you. Where did you think you were going, by the way?'

'A *musico*.'

'Much as I thought. Well, you could say Hondslager's done you a favour, Spandrel. At least you won't have a dose of pox to remember Amsterdam by.'

51

'It's a great consolation.'

'There was nothing I could do while you were in their hands. They'd have made short work of me. Fortunately for you, however, they didn't linger after pushing you into the canal. They must have thought the sand-bags would keep you under. And they would have done if I hadn't been standing by with the boat-hook. I'd guessed what they were planning for you. Drowning's so much easier to explain than a knifing, especially for a newcomer to the city. *If* your body had ever been found, that is, which I doubt. There must be more than a few murdered men rotting in the mud at the bottom of our canals. So, I borrowed the hook from a barge moored round the corner and tried my hand at fishing you out.'

'You're a good fisherman, Zuyler. I'll say that.'

'Thank you. It's not often a mere secretary has the chance to save someone's life.'

'If saving me's what you had in mind, I'm afraid your work's not done yet.'

'How so?'

Spandrel sighed. His thoughts were ordered enough now to reveal the bleakness of his plight. He was alive. But, in many ways, he might just as well be dead. De Vries could have had no reason to commission his murder other than as a favour for a friend – his oldest friend, Sir Theodore Janssen. Janssen had wanted Spandrel to deliver the box to de Vries. But he had not wanted him to return with proof that he had done so. That was clearly not part of his plan at all.

'Spandrel?'

'The letter Sir Theodore sent ahead of me to de Vries.' He looked sharply at Zuyler. 'Did you see it?'

'No.'

'So you don't know if, in that letter, Sir Theodore

asked his good friend Ysbrand to ensure I didn't leave Amsterdam alive.'

'Do you think he did?'

'What else am I to think?'

'Why would he do that?'

'Because he required the services of a discreet and reliable courier.' Now Spandrel knew why he had been chosen for the mission, rather than Jupe or some other lackey. He was easily suborned and eminently expendable; he was the perfect combination. 'You understand, Zuyler? There's no more discreet kind of courier . . . than the dead kind.'

Chapter Six

Plot and Counter-Plot

Spandrel slept little that night. He and Zuyler sat talking by the sputtering fire into the small hours, and even when Zuyler had retreated to his bed in the back room, leaving Spandrel to find what rest he could on the cot beside the chimney-breast, sleep proved elusive. His ribs pained him and there was no position he lay in that did not chafe a tender spot.

None of that would have kept him awake, however, so physically weary did he feel. It was the whirl of thoughts in his head that would give him no peace. It was the compulsive gaze of his mind's eye into the uncertainty of his future.

He was alive. De Vries, and hence soon Sir Theodore Janssen, must think him dead. But he was not. That represented his one advantage over them. Unhappily, it was outweighed by more profound disadvantages. He had delivered the despatch-box, but the receipt de Vries had signed for it had been stolen, along with all his money. He could not ask de Vries for a replacement without exposing himself to the danger of a second attempt on his life. But he could not return to England and demand Sir Theodore honour their bargain without such a replacement. Not that he supposed Sir Theodore *would* honour their bargain, under any circumstances. His debts were not going to be cancelled. The map was not going to be finished.

What to do, then? He had no money with which to pay for safe passage out of the city. He scarcely even had clothes to his back, those in which he had been dragged from the canal being so badly soiled by mud and dirty water that it was doubtful he could wear them again, save in dire emergency. Zuyler had lent him a night-shirt, but he could hardly be expected to offer him the run of his wardrobe.

Zuyler had, in truth, already done enough. He had seemed, on first encounter, to be an arid, unbending sort of fellow. But his actions had spoken louder than his cautious words. The account he had given Spandrel of himself had revealed that they were alike in many ways. Educated above his station by a clever but impecunious father, Pieter Zuyler had learned English from the many English students attending the university in his home town of Leiden. He had befriended one of the more prosperous of them, who had offered him employment as a clerk in his father's shipping office in Liverpool. Zuyler had spent three years there before his talents had come to the notice of Ysbrand de Vries through a recommendation from the Dutch East India Company's Liverpool agent. The opportunity to return to the country of his birth had proved irresistible. But he had come to regret seizing that opportunity.

'De Vries is a hard man,' Zuyler had said, his tongue loosened by schnapps. 'Who expects anything else? Not me. But there's hard and hard. De Vries is granite, through and through. Also mean, vicious and cunning. As you've found out.'

'What manner of life does that mean Mrs de Vries leads?'

'I don't know. She never complains. Not to me, at any rate. She behaves as the model wife. And he parades her on his arm as a trophy, to make his rivals hate him the more. I comfort myself with the thought that he would not wish his trophy to be' – Zuyler had cast Spandrel a meaningful glance – 'damaged.'

'You think him capable of that?'

'I think him capable of anything.'

'A formidable enemy, then.'

'Extremely.'

'How can I hope to elude him?'

'By fleeing. And fleeing far. There is no other way.'

'I have to consider my mother.'

'It seems from what you tell me that you'll have to let her think you're dead. Janssen would be sure to hear of any communication between you.'

'Is that what you would do in my position?'

Zuyler had stared long and hard into the fire before replying. 'No. I confess not.'

'Then what *would* you do?'

'There comes a time, my friend, when a man must turn upon his enemy. I cannot say if that time has come for you. But, for me, in your shoes . . .'

'It would have done.'

'Yes.' Zuyler had nodded at him. 'I think so.'

And that was what Spandrel thought too as he lay on the cot and gazed sleeplessly into the darkness. If he fled, he fled from everything. There was nothing he could take with him, not even his past. And his future would be a blank sheet, a mapless void. This was his fate at the hands of powerful men. This was as much as he could hope for. Unless . . .

It was a drizzly dawn in Amsterdam. Spandrel saw the grey sheen of it on the pavement as he looked up through the basement window. He had found a twist of coffee and brewed it in a pot. The aroma woke Zuyler. They sat by the remains of the fire, drinking it, strangely shy of talk at first, perhaps because each of them was waiting for the other to

56

mention the topic they had wrestled with so unavailingly a few hours before.

'I must be gone soon,' said Zuyler eventually, through a thin-lipped smile. 'De Vries does not appreciate lateness.'

'I should be gone soon myself.'

'Take any clothes that you need. Mine are all of a muchness. And all likely to be a little long in the arm and leg for you. I can't help that, I'm afraid. You could do worse than ask my landlord to bandage your ribs.' He nodded upwards. 'Barlaeus is a kindly sort. And a better doctor than many who call themselves doctors. I could spare you a guilder to see you on your way.'

'My way to where?'

'Far from Amsterdam is the only suggestion I can make.'

'You made a different suggestion last night.'

'It's true. I did. Have you decided to act upon it?'

'Yes.'

The two men looked at each other, coolly and soberly acknowledging the momentousness of Spandrel's answer.

'What should I do, Zuyler? How am I to strike back at him?'

'Are you sure you want me to tell you?'

'Oh yes. I'm sure.'

'Very well.' Zuyler leaned forward, an eagerness for intrigue lighting his features. 'Your only chance, as I see it, is to retrieve the box you delivered and find out what it contains. Then you will know why it was deemed necessary to have you killed. And with that knowledge . . . you may be able to bring down your enemies.'

'De Vries *and* Janssen?'

'I think they stand or fall together in this.'

'But how am I to lay hands on the box now? De Vries will have it under lock and key.'

'Indeed he will.'

'Well, then?'

'It would be impossible, without the help of someone close to him.'

'Such as his secretary, you mean?'

'Exactly.' Zuyler grinned at him.

'You've risked enough for me already. I can't—'

'You misunderstand, Spandrel. The extreme measures taken against you convince me that the contents of that box can be used to break Mijnheer de Vries. To bring him down. To ruin him. Do you think, after all I have endured as his . . . creature . . . that I would baulk at a few small risks to bring about such a satisfying result?' Zuyler's grin broadened. 'Your salvation, my friend. And my pleasure. What say you to that combination?'

Spandrel said yes, of course, as he was bound to. And so Pieter Zuyler and he became co-conspirators. Zuyler had no doubt where the despatch-box was. De Vries kept all his most valuable – and secret – possessions in an iron chest in his study. The key to the chest never left his person, clipped as it was to his watch-chain. It would be necessary to break the chest open. But that was the beauty of Zuyler's plan.

'Tomorrow night,' he gleefully disclosed, 'Mijnheer and Mevrouw de Vries are attending a concert. De Vries wishes to be regarded as a music lover, even though the only music he really enjoys is the chink of coins in his purse. They will be gone from eight o'clock until midnight at least. They will probably go on to a supper party afterwards. De Vries likes me to stay at the house when he's not there. He doesn't think the servants are capable of dealing with any emergency that might arise. Though he's never spoken of it, I suspect burglary is what he truly fears. So, I'll oblige him . . . by supplying a burglar.'

'Me?'

'Exactly. You will enter at the rear. I can arrange for the

gate next to the coach-house to be unlocked. I can also arrange for one of the library windows to be unfastened. There's a ladder in the shed next to the coach-house. You can use that to reach the window. The study is the room directly above the library. You'll have little to fear from the servants. They'll take the opportunity of de Vries's absence to huddle over the fire downstairs and complain about him. On this occasion, I think I'll join them. It would be as well for me to have witnesses to my whereabouts at the time of the burglary.'

'How strong is the chest?'

'I'm not sure.' Zuyler smiled. 'I've never tried to break it open. But by the look of the hasp . . .' He plucked the poker from the fireplace and weighed it in his hand. 'Not strong enough.'

To avoid evidence being turned up later of complicity between them, the two men agreed that they should part straight away. Zuyler lent Spandrel a suit of clothes, along with enough money to pay for overnight lodgings. He directed him to a discreetly located tavern, the Gouden Vis, where they would meet after the event to examine the contents of the despatch-box. They left separately, Spandrel first, with a farewell handshake to seal their agreement.

Spandrel walked slowly away from Barlaeus's shop that damp winter's morning, his ribs jarring at every step. He would have to buy a bandage for them from some other chemist. But already the pain seemed less intense, dulled as it was by the contemplation of something he would never have expected to be able to inflict on the likes of Sir Theodore Janssen and his very good friend, Ysbrand de Vries: revenge.

Spandrel assumed – as why would he not? – that Sir Theodore was still comfortably installed at his house in

Hanover Square, perhaps at that moment perusing his morning newspaper over a cup of chocolate, smug in his certainty that the courier he had chosen to carry the despatch-box and its so very important contents to Amsterdam was dead, his lips sealed for good and all.

Sir Theodore's situation was, in truth, rather different. Robert Knight's failure to appear before the Committee of Inquiry at South Sea House on Monday had led to a convulsion of righteous indignation in the House of Commons and the forced attendance there of those directors of the South Sea Company who were also Members of Parliament, followed shortly afterwards by their committal to the Tower pending further investigations by the committee, now vested with full executive powers. By the following day, the net had been widened to include all directors and officials of the company.

That morning, therefore, found Sir Theodore confined in an admittedly commodious but scarcely elegant chamber in the Tower of London. He had a view from his window of the traffic on the Thames and the wharves of Bermondsey, but the smell of the river at low tide was a heavy price to pay for such a prospect. The furnishings of the chamber might have been described as generous by someone not as accustomed as Sir Theodore was to the best. Happily, he had always possessed a pragmatical disposition and age had taught him patience if nothing else. Chocolate tasted the same wherever it was drunk, even if the Governor did exploit his monopoly on prisoners' supplies to charge scandalous amounts for portage. And though Brodrick and his fellow inquisitors might think they had him at their mercy, Sir Theodore was confident that they would eventually find it was quite the other way about.

There had been no objection to his valet waiting upon

him in his altered place of residence and it was certainly a relief to Sir Theodore that he could begin each day with an expert shave. But Jupe's tonsorial talents, though considerable, were not those his employer valued most highly. Jupe's grasp of events was what Sir Theodore wished to call upon, every bit as much as his steady hand with a razor.

'Who is still at liberty, Jupe?' Sir Theodore accordingly enquired as his barber-cum-newsmonger slid the blade over the crown of his head. 'I'm told there are a dozen of us here.'

'That would be correct, sir. And more are sought. I believe there is not yet a warrant out for Deputy Governor Joye, however. The committee must expect to find him particularly helpful.'

'When does he go before them?'

'Today. Along with Sir John Blunt.'

'Blunt will tell them whatever he thinks will serve him best. And that, I suppose, will be nearly everything.'

'But not *quite* everything, sir?'

'They would need to speak to Knight for that.'

'As they would assuredly like to.'

'Do they know where he is?'

'Brussels has been mentioned.'

'An obvious choice. The Austrian authorities are unlikely to bestir themselves to do the committee's bidding.'

'But the King's bidding, sir?'

'A different matter – should it arise.'

'Rumour has it that the Duke of Wharton means to hire a hearse and drive it through the streets today in a mock funeral procession for the company.'

'The Duke of Wharton is a fool. He and his fellow Jacobites no doubt see this crisis as a gift from the gods. Well, well. Let them stage their funeral. Let them have their fun. What of the Government?'

'Lying low, I rather think, sir. Aislabie is said to be finished and Walpole to be certain of succeeding him as Chancellor.'

'Ah, Walpole. There *is* a man we must watch.'

'There is as yet' – Jupe cleared his throat – 'no word from Amsterdam, sir.'

'Too soon, Jupe.' Sir Theodore permitted himself a faint smile. 'Just a little too soon.'

Chapter Seven

Breaking and Entering

The Gouden Vis was a small, well-run, brightly painted tavern near the Montelbaanstoren, a disused harbour-side watchtower to which a previous generation of Amsterdam's city fathers had added a clock, a decorative spire and a mermaid wind-vane. Spandrel had a good view of the tower from his room, as well as of the harbour, into which the Montelbaanswal canal ran past the front of the tavern. He watched the shipping plying back and forth, the comings and goings from the warehouses on the other side of the canal, the light silvering and fading over the city. He had little else to do for two whole days and a night, while he awaited his chance to turn the tables on Ysbrand de Vries and Sir Theodore Janssen. He could not wander the streets for fear of a chance encounter with the dreaded Hondslager or indeed with de Vries himself. Nor could he while away his time in the tap-room. He could not trust himself when in his cups. That was clear, painfully so, as his ribs and assorted other aches frequently reminded him. Not that he had the money with which to drink away the hours. The loan from Zuyler was strictly for necessary expenditure. And Spandrel's necessities – bed and board, a hammer and chisel to break open the chest in de Vries's study and a dark-lantern to find his way by – had consumed the greater part of it. There was nothing for it but to sit and wait.

63

Idleness, however, encouraged his mind to wander, even if his feet could not. What was in the despatch-box? What was the secret his death had been intended to conceal? De Vries and Janssen were old men as well as old friends. The answer might lie decades in the past. Or it might rest firmly in the present. Janssen's part in the South Sea disaster came irresistibly to mind. Did that have something to do with it? If so, Spandrel might be about to become involved in matters with which the likes of him should have no dealings.

But he was already involved. He had been from the moment he accepted Sir Theodore's offer. There was no way out – unless it was by plunging further in. His father would have told him to leave well alone. But then his father was partly responsible for the predicament in which he found himself. Dick Surtees, by contrast, would have urged him on. Spandrel had not thought of his harum-scarum schoolfellow in months, nor seen him in years; not since, in fact, Dick had thrown up the apprenticeship Spandrel had persuaded his father to offer him on the grounds that surveying was 'devilish tedious' and declared his intention of going abroad in search, he had told Spandrel, 'of adventures'. But Spandrel, he had added, should stay where he was. 'You're just not the adventuring kind, Billy. Take my word for it.'

Spandrel smiled at the memory. The joke was on Dick now. Adventures, it seemed, were not restricted to the adventuring kind. Anyone could have them. Even, perhaps especially, when they did not want to.

The weather changed during Friday afternoon, a stiffening breeze thinning and then clearing the cloud. The city changed with it, glowing in the sparkling light reflected from the harbour. When the sun set, it did so as a swollen scarlet ball, glaring at Spandrel across the Amsterdam rooftops. He knew then that his waiting was nearly at an end.

When the clock on the Montelbaanstoren struck nine, he went down to the tap-room and drank two glasses of brandy. Dutch courage, they called it, and he had need of some. But two glasses were as much as he risked. Then he went back to his room to collect the hammer and chisel, concealed in a sack. He lit the lantern and set off.

The night was cold. The breeze of the afternoon had strengthened to a bone-chilling wind. There were few people on the streets and those who were did not dawdle. Nor did Spandrel. He followed the route Zuyler had said was the easiest, even if it was not the quickest, along the Montelbaanswal to the Amstel. He crossed the river by the first bridge to the west and traversed a deserted market-place. From the far corner of the market-place a narrow street led off between the rear walls of the houses on the Herengracht and the frontages of humbler dwellings. This, according to Zuyler, would take him to de Vries's coach-house entrance, which he would be able to recognize by the lamp-bracket on the coach-house door, worked as it was in the form of a monkey. The lamp would be lit, in readiness for the coach's return. If not lit, it could only mean that de Vries had not gone to the concert for some reason, in which case the attempt would have to be abandoned.

But it *was* lit. And there was the cast iron monkey beneath, grinning at him, it seemed, in the flickering glow of the lamp. Spandrel closed the shutter on his lantern, withdrew into the shadows and waited for the clock Zuyler had assured him was within earshot to strike ten, by which time Zuyler was confident the servants would all be in the basement, digesting their supper and regurgitating familiar complaints about their master.

It was a cold and nervous vigil that probably lasted

no more than ten minutes but felt to Spandrel like so many hours. He half-expected the coach to return, or Hondslager to leap at him out of the darkness. Less fancifully, he feared a passer-by would notice him and become suspicious. But there were no passers-by, save one savage-looking cat carrying a mouse in its jaws, who paid Spandrel no attention whatever. Only the stars watched him. Only the night listened. Eventually, the clock struck.

The narrow door in the wall beside the coach-house entrance opened with barely a creak. Spandrel stepped through into a short alley leading to the garden. It appeared as a gulf of blackness between him and the house, where lights shone dimly in the basement. Otherwise all was in darkness. He opened the shutter on his lantern and made his way along the coach-house wall until he reached the lean-to shed at its far end. He raised the latch and eased the door open. There was the ladder, just inside, standing among the hoes and rakes. He took the hammer and chisel out of the sack and wedged them in his pockets in order to free a hand for the ladder, then set off across the garden with his burden, holding the lantern at arm's length in front of him to light the path.

He was breathing heavily by the time he reached the terrace, sweating despite the cold. He glanced down into what looked like a pantry, into which light was spilling meagrely from a room beyond. Mercifully, there was no-one to be seen. Nor, when he paused to listen, could he hear any voices. The coast was clear.

Telling himself to go slowly and carefully, he propped the ladder against the sill beneath the farthest window of the library – the one Zuyler had said he would leave unfastened – and clambered up. There was a moment's resistance from the sash. Then, with a squeak, it gave. He pushed it halfway up, hung the lantern from one of the handles on the frame and scrambled in.

He was back in the room where Estelle de Vries had plied him with tea and Ysbrand de Vries had taken his contemptuous measure of him. He imagined them sitting next to each other at the concert, Estelle relishing the music while Ysbrand relished only the envy of other men that the sight of her would inspire. Spandrel wondered if she would be secretly pleased by what he was about to do. He could not help hoping she would. Maybe it would somehow set her free. If so—

Angry with himself for wasting time on such thoughts, he turned and pulled the ladder up after him. Leaving it in position would be to invite discovery. He laid it on the floor, then retrieved the lantern and closed the window. Silence closed about him as he did so, a silence broken only by the ticking of a clock. He looked round the room, at the bookcases and the paintings and the classical busts. They, like Estelle, were emblems of de Vries's wealth and power. He had no other use for them. They meant no more to him than did anything or anyone else.

Spandrel crossed the room, listened for a moment at the door, heard nothing, then turned the handle. The door opened onto the unlit hallway. The servants must have shut themselves in downstairs. Otherwise he would surely be able to see a glimmer of light in the stairwell. But there was none.

He closed the library door carefully behind him and stood still for a second, his senses straining. Clocks ticked. The wind mewed. He could detect nothing else – no sound, no movement. His luck, their luck, was holding. He moved to the stairs and started up them, avoiding the middle of the treads for fear of creaks.

The door to the study, located directly above the library, was to his left as he reached the top of the stairs. Hurrying now in spite of himself, he strode across to it and opened it just far enough to slip inside. Then caution reasserted

67

itself. He inched the door shut without letting go of the handle and slowly released it as the snib engaged. Then he turned and raised the lantern, his eyes casting about for the chest.

There it was, stowed against the far wall, between the fireplace and the window: a stout, brass-bound iron chest, fastened with a padlocked hasp. Spandrel walked over to it, ignoring the desk whose shadowy bulk he was aware of beneath the window to his right. He knelt down in front of the chest and tested the hasp with his hand. Zuyler was right, as he had been about everything else. It could be forced readily enough. There would be some noise made in the process. That was the biggest problem. But the servants were far from zealous. That was clear. Zuyler would no doubt be able to persuade them that any noise they did hear came from elsewhere. Spandrel set the lantern on the floor and took out the hammer and chisel.

As he did so, he noticed, out of the corner of his eye, some strange discrepancy in the shadow of the lantern. He turned and saw a dark, liquid patch on the floorboards and on the rug laid in front of the desk. He picked up the lantern and raised it, directing the beam of light towards the patch.

It was blood, inky black in the lantern-light. And on the floor next to the desk lay a human figure. Spandrel caught his breath at the sight of Ysbrand de Vries's snowy white hair and at his own immediate certainty that the old man was dead. He had not gone to the concert after all. He had gone to meet his maker instead.

Spandrel stood slowly up and stepped towards the desk. He could see de Vries's face now, distorted by the agony of his death. There was blood on his chest and a thick pool of it beneath him where he lay. The toe of Spandrel's shoe touched something. Looking down, he saw a knife lying on the rug, its blade glistening. He looked back at de Vries, at the fixed grimace of his lips, at the staring blankness of his eyes. He tried to think what he should do, how he should react. It was the last thing he had expected, the very last. Whatever secrets the despatch-box contained, they could not hurt de Vries now.

Suddenly, the door was flung open. Light flooded into the room. Spandrel spun round to see the elderly manservant who had admitted him to the house on Wednesday standing in the doorway, holding a candle-lamp. The fellow's jaw dropped open as he took in the scene. Then Zuyler appeared at his elbow, holding a lamp in his left hand – and a pistol in his right. He moved towards Spandrel, his face expressionless, the weapon raised.

'You've killed him, Spandrel. You've murdered Mijnheer de Vries.'

'What? No. What are you—'

The truth silenced Spandrel in the instant that it burst upon his mind. The friendship unlooked-for; the ingenious plan; the unguarded house: they were all part of a plot in which he was a victim along with de Vries. He had been taken for a fool once again. And this time no-one was going to come to his rescue.

He made a lunge for the door, but it was too late. Even as he moved, Zuyler clapped the pistol to his head, halting him in mid-stride.

'Stay exactly where you are, Spandrel,' said Zuyler, cocking the firearm as he spoke.

'But for God's—'

'Shut your mouth.'

The muzzle of the pistol was boring into Spandrel's temple, forcing him back against the edge of the desk. Zuyler's eyes were in shadow, but Spandrel could sense they too were boring into him.

Zuyler flung a volley of Dutch over his shoulder. The old

fellow nodded and hurried away, his footsteps pattering down the stairs. 'I've sent him to alert the watchman,' Zuyler said, the tone of his voice altering now they were alone. 'They'll call out the Sheriff for this. The murder of an eminent citizen in his own home is a grievous thing. But it could be worse. At least the murderer didn't escape. Of course, he may still try. In which case, I'd have no choice . . . but to shoot him.'

'You're mad.'

'Far from it. I'm appalled and indignant at the slaughter of my cherished employer. Now, put the lantern on the desk.' Spandrel did so. 'Drop the hammer and chisel.' Again, he obeyed. They thumped down onto the rug. 'Walk over to the body.'

The pressure of the pistol relaxed just enough to let Spandrel move. He took three halting steps, shadowed by Zuyler, until they were both standing over de Vries.

'Kneel down.' Spandrel lowered himself to his knees. He felt the dampness of the blood seeping through his breeches. 'Lay your palms in the blood.' Spandrel hesitated for no more than a second, but it was enough to bring the pistol prodding at his temple. 'Do as I say.' The calmness in Zuyler's voice told Spandrel clearly that defiance was useless. With a shudder, he flattened his hands on the floor in front of him. 'Now, smear them across your chest.'

Spandrel did as he had been told, glancing up at Zuyler as he plastered the blood over his shirt and coat. 'Why did you kill him?' he asked, almost pleadingly.

'The question, Spandrel, is why *you* killed him. Stand up.'

'If you mean to shoot me, you may as well have done with it.'

'I'm not going to shoot you unless you force me to. I'd rather you were taken alive. Now, stand up.'

Spandrel began to rise, wondering if this was his best chance of springing at Zuyler. He had to do something before the Sheriff and his men arrived and convinced themselves of his guilt. He might be able to overpower Zuyler, perhaps even force the truth out of him. He braced himself on one knee, then lunged at Zuyler's midriff.

The pistol went off with a crack, deafeningly close to Spandrel's right ear. But the shot was wide. Spandrel's weight threw Zuyler off his feet. The two men fell together, the lamp rolling away and adding a tangle of shadows to their struggle. Zuyler had lost hold of the pistol as he struck the floor. Seeing it bounce clear, Spandrel made a grab for it, intending to use it as a club. But as he grasped the barrel and swung back towards Zuyler, he glimpsed too late the hammer in the Dutchman's hand, arcing up to meet him.

Chapter Eight

The Arms of the Law

When Spandrel came to his senses, he thought for a moment that he was back in the Fleet Prison. All the ingredients were in place: the subfuscous light filtering down from a high, barred window; the coarse straw mattress he lay on; the coughs and oaths of his cellmates; the stale rankness of confined humanity. Then his mind began to piece together the truth of his situation, which was worse by far than it had been during his miserable days in the Fleet. He was not wherever he was because he could not pay his debts. He was there because he was suspected of murder. And not just any murder. Ysbrand de Vries was dead. Somebody would have to pay for that – with their life.

He sat up and was at once aware of a jolt of pain in his head so intense that he thought for a moment he had been struck with an axe. Then he remembered the hammer in Zuyler's hand, swinging towards him. He reached gingerly up and winced as his fingers touched the source of the pain. His hair was stiff with clotted blood. He did not know how bad the wound might be, but he was alive and capable of coherent thought. Looking around and catching the baleful eye of one of the other occupants of the cell, he reckoned that was the sum total of his blessings.

There was an exchange in Dutch between the man who had noticed Spandrel and another, gravely voiced fellow in the shadows on the farther side of the cell who seemed to be called Dirk. Dirk then shuffled into clearer view, revealing himself as a gaunt scarecrow of a man, dressed in sewn-together rags that had surely never been clothes. There was a glint in his eye that made Spandrel think of a weasel peering from its hole.

'English, guard said. I speak bit.' He gave a toothless smile.

'I'm English, yes.'

'What you do, Englishman? What they have you for?'

'I did nothing. It's all a mistake.'

'Hah! Mistake. *Ja.* Right.' Dirk winked at him. 'All of us too.'

'I'm telling you the truth. I'm innocent.'

'*Ja, ja.* Who cares? You here. What *for?*'

'Murder,' Spandrel admitted bleakly.

'You kill?'

'So they say.'

'Who?'

'A merchant called de Vries.'

'De Vries? Ysbrand de Vries?'

'Yes. But—'

'De Vries dead?'

'Yes. He's dead.'

Dirk let out an eerie whoop of triumph and clapped his hands together. Most of the other half-dozen or so prisoners turned to look at him. 'You kill well, Englishman. De Vries a good man to kill. Very good.'

'I didn't do it.'

Dirk shrugged and grinned helplessly. 'Tell the executioner. Then you tell me what he says.' With that he sat down on the mattress at Spandrel's feet and winked again. 'You kill de Vries. Now . . .' Dirk mimed the looping of a noose around his neck and the jerking of a rope above his head. 'They kill you.'

*   *   *

Spandrel would have preferred to ignore Dirk, but no-one else spoke English and a few scraps of information were there to be gleaned amidst his alternately morbid and exultant ramblings. They were in a cell beneath Amsterdam's Stadhuis – the Town Hall. Spandrel had been brought in the previous night. The guards' reticence about his offence was now explained by the eminence of his alleged victim. They might expect a meal of stale bread and sour ale around noon. And Spandrel might expect to be questioned before the day was out. He was important, after all. At any rate, his crime was. Dirk was just a humble pickpocket, their cellmates little worse than vagrants. Some of them had been there for weeks, awaiting trial. When they had been tried – and found guilty, of course – a flogging or branding or both would follow. Spandrel would be dealt with in the same way, though perhaps more expeditiously; the authorities would not wish to be accused of dragging their feet in such a case. Only the end would be different. And, for Spandrel, it would be the end in every sense.

It was early evening when they came for him. Two guards marched him out of the cell and along a narrow passage lined on one side by the doors of neighbouring cells and on the other by a blank wall. They reached a large, high-ceilinged room, lit by candles at one end. In the shadowy reaches at the farther end, he thought he could make out the shape of a rack.

A long table stood beneath the chandelier in front of the empty grate. It was colder than in the cell, Spandrel's breath misting in the air. Three men sat at the table, one equipped with pen and paper. A fourth man stood by the shuttered window, smoking a pipe. He was older than the others and seemed to take no interest in Spandrel's arrival. The guards

74

led Spandrel to a chair facing the table and gestured for him to sit. Then they shackled one of his legs to a large wooden block chained to the floor and left.

The two men at the table without pen and paper conversed briefly in Dutch, then one of them – a skinny, sallow-faced fellow with a squint that his narrow, bony nose seemed only to emphasize – said slowly in English, 'Your name is William Spandrel?'

'Yes.'

'This is your examination on the charge of the murder of Mijnheer Ysbrand de Vries. Do you admit the crime?'

'No.'

'You were caught in the act, Spandrel. You cannot deny it.'

'I can explain.'

'Do so.'

Spandrel had already decided that his only chance, and that a slim one, of escaping from the trap Zuyler had lured him into was to tell his inquisitors the truth – the whole truth – and to hope they could be persuaded to doubt Zuyler's version of events. He did not know precisely what that version of events was, of course, but he had little doubt that it painted him in the blackest of colours. He told his story from the beginning, therefore, and held nothing back. He could not judge how convincing it sounded. He was met only by the blankest of faces. When he had finished, there was a discussion in Dutch, then a brief silence, broken by a question he thought he had already answered.

'What did the despatch-box contain?'

'I told you. I don't know.'

'Where is it now?'

'I don't know. If it's not in the chest in Mijnheer de Vries's study, then Zuyler must have taken it.'

'Why would he do that?'

'I don't know.'

The man by the window barked a sudden intervention. The English-speaker reacted with no more than a rub of the brow, then said, 'You are an agent of the Marquis de Prié, Spandrel. This is known.'

'Who?'

'You told Mevrouw de Vries that you had come from London by way of Brussels. Why visit Brussels unless it was to attend on the Marquis for instructions?'

'I've . . . never been to Brussels in my life.' A sickening realization clogged Spandrel's thoughts. Estelle de Vries had lied. And that could only mean that she and Zuyler were in this together. 'You must believe me.'

'How can we? The Marquis's intelligence is faulty. Cornelis Hondslager was killed in a tavern brawl several weeks ago.'

'Zuyler must have lied to me about him too.'

'You are the liar, Spandrel. Admit it. Spare yourself a great deal of suffering.'

'I've told you the truth.'

'We will give you time to think. Then you will be re-examined.' The man rose, crossed to the doorway and shouted something in Dutch. One of the guards appeared and there was a murmured conversation.

'Zuyler killed him,' Spandrel shouted in desperation. 'Don't you understand?'

'We are moving you to a cell on your own,' came the un-ruffled reply. 'You may be able to think better there. For your sake, I hope you do.'

Solitary confinement made Spandrel yearn for the company of Dirk the garrulous pickpocket. A despair, blacker than the night beyond the small, barred window set high in the wall, closed around him. And daybreak did not dispel it. His head ached less and his ribs seemed to be

76

healing well, but that only cleared his mind of a precious distraction from the bleakness of his plight. He had told the truth, but it had done him no good. Sooner or later, torture, or the threat of it, would force him to change his story. Then his guilt would seem to be confirmed and punishment would swiftly follow. Such was the cruel logic of the law in every land. He would admit he was the agent of a man he had never heard of. He would admit to a murder he had not committed. Then they would have done with him.

Why had Estelle de Vries lied? Only one answer made sense to Spandrel. She and Zuyler must be lovers. Now, she could inherit de Vries's wealth and marry the younger man. Yes, that had to be it. Spandrel was the unwitting means to their happy end.

And the three men who had tried to kill him? Were they really agents of de Vries? Or was all of that a piece of play-acting, commissioned by Zuyler? If so, Sir Theodore Janssen might have meant to honour their bargain after all. In that case, Spandrel need only have left Amsterdam when he had the chance and he could even now be contemplating a future free of debts and rich in opportunities.

Instead, he was contemplating four damp walls, a lousy palliasse and an early death. He had seen enough hangings at Tyburn to know how it would be. Whether men went bravely to the gallows, or quaking in terror, made no difference. Hanging was not beautiful. It was twitching limbs, loosened bowels, bulging eyes and frothing lips. It was a thing many were glad to watch, but none to experience, a just penalty for the guilty, occasionally visited upon the innocent.

Monday – morning or afternoon, he was not sure – brought a visitor. At first, Spandrel thought his examination was about to resume, but the guards made no attempt to remove him from the cell. Instead, they shackled him and chained him to a hook on the wall, then made way for his visitor.

He was a blond-wigged, dapper young man in a fawn-coloured coat, which he clutched close about himself, either because he was cold or because he was worried, not unreasonably, that the cloth might be soiled by brushing against something. A kerchief was bundled in his hand and he seemed to be restraining himself with some difficulty from holding it to his nose. There was an anxious frown on his face to complete the impression of someone who found himself where he had no wish to be with no intention of remaining one minute longer than he had to.

'You're Spandrel?' he said in a genuinely English voice.

'Yes.'

'Cloisterman. British vice-consul.'

'Have you come to help me?'

'The only help I can give you is to urge you to tell the Sheriff everything.'

'I have done that.'

'He seems to think otherwise. Why were you in Brussels, for instance?'

'I wasn't. Mrs de Vries is lying.'

'An unfortunate accusation to level at a grieving widow. She will be at her husband's funeral today. The Consul will also be there, seeking to make some manner of amends for the disgrace you have brought on the British community in Amsterdam.'

'De Vries was killed by his secretary, Mr Cloisterman: Pieter Zuyler. Mrs de Vries knows that full well. She probably helped him.'

'Why should she have done that?'

'For the money she'll inherit, I suppose. The money they'll share.'

78

'But she won't inherit, Spandrel. Not much, at all events. De Vries had a son by an earlier marriage, now a V.O.C. officiary in Java.' By V.O.C. Cloisterman meant the Dutch East India Company – the Verenigde Oostindische Compagnie. Spandrel had learned that much from Zuyler. 'The younger de Vries, not the charming widow,' Cloisterman went on, 'is made rich by what you've done.'

'But I didn't do it. I didn't do anything. The Sheriff accused me of being in league with some marquess . . .'

'The Marquis de Prié.'

'Yes. But I've never heard the name before in my life, far less met him. Can you at least tell me . . . who he is?'

'You seriously claim not to know?'

'I tell you, sir, as God's my witness, I've no idea.'

'Well, well. This is a pretty turn-about, I must say.' Cloisterman seemed so struck by the notion that Spandrel might actually be innocent that he forgetfully released his coat and placed a thoughtful finger on his chin. 'The Marquis de Prié is Minister Plenipotentiary to the Governor-General of the Austrian Netherlands. He might have his reasons for wishing de Vries dead.'

'What reasons?'

'Who can say with certainty? I gather the Marquis favours the creation of a Flemish East India Company to rival the V.O.C., presumably to enrich the Flemish mercantile classes and so warm them to their masters in Vienna whom de Prié loyally serves. The V.O.C. has done all it can to prevent that happening. De Vries was a native of Flanders, with many friends in Antwerp and Brussels. He may have wielded considerable influence to that end.'

'I know nothing about any of this. I never went to Brussels. I brought a package from London on behalf of Sir Theodore—'

'Janssen. Yes. Also of Flemish stock. Another wielder of influence. But Sir Theodore, as you must know, is a man

79

in severely straitened circumstances. His present situation is indeed faintly comparable to your own.'

'How so?'

'When do you claim to have left London?' Cloisterman asked, ignoring Spandrel's question.

'A week ago . . .' Spandrel thought hard. 'A week ago yesterday.'

'Sunday the twenty-second of January, in the Old Style?'

'Yes. That's right. Sunday the twenty-second.'

'Would it surprise you to know that Sir Theodore was arrested by order of Parliament on Monday the twenty-third and consigned to the Tower?'

It did surprise Spandrel – very much. 'The Tower. Why?'

'Because the chief cashier of the South Sea Company, Mr Knight, fled the country the same day that you left: Sunday the twenty-second. It's all up with the South Sea. And with its directors. Mr Knight, incidentally, is reported to have fled . . . to Brussels.' Cloisterman gave a wan smile. 'These are deep waters, Spandrel. And the currents are treacherous. A man could easily drown in them.'

'I *am* drowning.' Spandrel reached out instinctively to clasp Cloisterman's sleeve, but Cloisterman stepped smartly back and the chain snapped taut. They looked at each other warily across three feet of fetid cell-space. 'Is there nothing you can do to help me, sir?'

'Very little.'

'But even a very little . . . might be enough.'

'I doubt it.' Cloisterman's expression softened marginally. 'Yet I will' – he gave a little nod that seemed intended to afford Spandrel some small comfort – 'see what I can do.'

With the proverbial celerity of bad news, word of his old friend's demise had already reached Sir Theodore Janssen. All the other reverses he had suffered in recent weeks had been anticipated and, in one way or another, allowed for. This, by contrast, was a blow he had not expected to receive. Death might call on men of his and de Vries's age at any time, of course. But murder, in the supposed safety of his own home? It could scarcely be credited. Yet it had happened. The report was not to be doubted. Ysbrand de Vries was dead. And amidst the sorrow Sir Theodore felt at the loss of the very last of his youthful contemporaries, he was gnawed also by an anxiety he dared not fully explain even to his loyal valet and prime informant, Nicodemus Jupe.

Today was the anniversary of the execution of King Charles I. As a mark of respect, Brodrick's Committee of Inquiry was not sitting. But tomorrow they would resume their work, fortified by whatever Blunt and Joye had told them. Sir Theodore's judgement was that by now they knew the worst. But knowledge was not proof. They might find that commodity rather more elusive. Nor were they alone in that. The news from Amsterdam had left the hunters and the hunted on dismayingly equal terms. And the news from Amsterdam was about to become more dismaying still.

'It's been confirmed, sir,' said Jupe. 'Mijnheer de Vries's killer was Spandrel.'

'It stretches credulity that the man should be capable of such a thing.'

'Yet it seems he was.'

'And this happened on Friday evening?'

'Yes, sir. At about ten o'clock. The weapon was a knife. Spandrel broke into the house and slew Mijnheer de Vries in his study.'

'I have lost a good friend, Jupe. I wish to know why.'

'Perhaps Spandrel isn't the fool he seemed to be.'

'But still a big enough fool to be caught in the act. There is something wrong here. Very wrong.'

'Do you wish me to make any specific inquiries . . . about the despatch-box?'

'No. That is . . .' Sir Theodore thought for a moment. 'How is the committee expected to proceed?'

'Rumour has it that Mr Brodrick will tomorrow set a date for them to report to the House of Commons. Within a fortnight, it's believed.'

'So soon?'

'A stiff wind's blowing, sir, no question.'

'Then we must take in sail. I want you to go to Amsterdam, Jupe. As soon as possible. Establish the facts – the *true* facts – of Ysbrand's death. And find the despatch-box. It must not fall into the wrong hands.'

'And whose are the right hands, sir?'

'Pels's Bank is a safe lodgement for the time being. But you understand, Jupe?' Uncharacteristically, Sir Theodore grasped his valet's wrist. 'It must be found.'

'Yes, sir.' Jupe's eyes met his master's. 'I understand.'

Chapter Nine

Meetings and Messages

Evelyn Dalrymple, chargé d'affaires at the British Embassy in The Hague, regarded the visitor to his office with measured caution. He had learned by occasionally bitter experience to hear out all those who claimed his attention on matters affecting the dignity of the Crown. Most were time-wasters, naturally. But the few who were not were unlikely to be correctly identified by his subordinates. Some, indeed, might be deliberately turned away in an attempt to embarrass him. In the Ambassador's absence on extended leave, Dalrymple had to be on his guard. The doubters and the enviers were ever alert for some slip on his part, however minor, that could be exploited to discredit him.

Kempis, the fellow sitting on the other side of his desk, was an especially difficult case to assess. He was a tall, dark-haired Dutchman in his middle to late twenties, smartly though soberly dressed, who spoke the perfect English of a well-educated man, but nonetheless had about him a suggestion of humble origins. What he did and where he came from were subjects he had declined to expand upon. In one sense, this had pleased Dalrymple, since it suggested they would come rapidly to the purpose of the visit. In another sense, however, it had worried him. The reticent, he had generally found, were more troublesome in the long run than the loquacious.

'What can I do for you, mijnheer?' Dalrymple ventured. 'An urgent matter, my secretary tells me, affecting' – he added a lilt of incredulity to his voice – 'the good name of the King.'

'King George is Governor of the South Sea Company, I believe,' Kempis said.

'Honorifically, yes.' Dalrymple's heart had sunk at the mention of the South Sea. He had lost enough money of his own on that foredoomed enterprise to need no reminding of it. So had many Dutchmen, who had insisted on dragging their consequent resentments to his door. If Kempis were another, this was likely to be a painful discussion, best cut short. 'But that is the full extent of His Majesty's involvement.'

'As far as you're aware.'

'You claim closer knowledge of the subject?'

'Some detailed information has come into my possession, certainly. Believe me when I say, Mr Dalrymple, that its wide dissemination would have consequences of the utmost gravity for your political – and your royal – masters in London.'

'I must take leave to doubt that, mijnheer.'

'Please do. I am not trying to convince you. I only want you to communicate my request to the appropriate person.'

'And what *is* your request?'

'In return for the surrender of the article I have come by, I require the payment of one hundred thousand pounds in high denomination Bank of England notes.'

Dalrymple could not suppress a flinch of astonishment. 'I beg your pardon?'

'One hundred thousand pounds, Mr Dalrymple. A round plum.'

'Very amusing.' Kempis's dark-eyed gaze did not encourage the notion that he was joking, but Dalrymple felt obliged to pretend that he thought he was. 'This is not the kind of request I can—'

'Tell them I have the Green Book.'

'What?'

'The green-covered ledger, lately in the keeping of the chief cashier of the South Sea Company. I have it.' Kempis leaned forward. 'And I know what it contains. I know everything.'

'There, mijnheer, you have the advantage of me.' Like a duck on the waters of the Hofvijver, which he could see if he turned and looked out of the window, Dalrymple was now engaged in strenuous efforts to remain afloat, efforts he could not allow to disturb the placid surface of his remarks. He knew that Robert Knight was presently in Brussels, taking his ease at the Hôtel de Flandre. He suspected that the Embassy there would already have applied for a warrant to arrest him. The Austrian authorities, however, could be expected to drag their feet about issuing one. They owed Britain no favours. Dalrymple knew nothing of green-covered ledgers, but he thought it safe to assume that Knight would have taken good care of his most sensitive documents. They were unlikely to be in the hands of an importunate young Dutchman. But he knew too little to be certain of that. The South Sea affair was riddled with many unlikelihoods, of which this would not be the most remarkable. Prevarication was therefore his only recourse. 'How, may I ask, did you arrive at your valuation of this information?'

'By asking myself what I would pay for its suppression were I the King's loyal minister.'

'I cannot imagine why you persist in mentioning His Majesty in this regard.'

'Then do not trouble to imagine. Simply convey my terms.'

'As they stand at present, mijnheer, I feel sure they would be dismissed out of hand.'

'That is because you do not know what the Green Book contains. But I do know. And so, of course, do those recorded in it. One could hardly forget such matters. I have some experience of book-keeping. The tale this book tells is clear and damning.'

'Perhaps you would care to show it to me.'

'Do you think me so foolish as to have brought it with me?'

'You are surely not implying that it would have been unsafe to do so, are you, mijnheer? This is the British Embassy, not a den of thieves.'

Kempis smiled, as if amused by the distinction. 'Mr Dalrymple,' he said steadily, 'will you present my request to your government?'

'Such as it is, I will.'

'That is all I ask. I will return here – shall we say one week from today? – for their answer. At that time I will specify how the exchange is to be made.'

'Exchange?'

'Of book for money. Time and place. Conditions. And so forth. It will have to be carefully managed.'

'If it is to be managed at all. I must say you seem remarkably confident of what answer you will receive.'

Kempis nodded in cool acknowledgement of the fact. 'Yes,' he said. 'I am.'

Somewhat against his better judgement, but adhering to the sound principle that it is wise to defer to other people's judgement in difficult cases, Dalrymple at once set about preparing a despatch for urgent transmission to the Secretary of State's office in Whitehall. It would take two days to arrive and another three or four days for a reply to reach him. A week should suffice for Kempis to have his answer. The nature of that answer would satisfy Dalrymple as to whether the man was an impertinent knave or an ingenious schemer. He could not for the moment decide which. And he would not have cared to bet on the outcome. He decided to take Kempis's advice and not trouble to imagine.

Imagination was one of the few indulgences left to William Spandrel, in his cell beneath the Stadhuis in Amsterdam. The days slipped slowly by, measured in the drift of light across the wall, in its strengthening and its weakening. Cloisterman did not return. Nor was Spandrel called for re-examination. It was as if he had been forgotten by all save the guards. His wounds healed, but the meagre diet of bread and ale sapped his strength. Only his thoughts roamed freely, back into his past and out across his uncharted future. Always they returned to the two questions he could not begin to answer. What was in the despatch-box? And why had de Vries been killed? Not for his money, it seemed. But there was a reason. There had to be. Spandrel's only hope of finding out what it was rested in other people. And that was hardly any hope at all.

Nicholas Cloisterman was perhaps the person upon whom Spandrel was relying the most. He had, after all, promised to see what he could do. Alas for Spandrel, he had decided in the days following his visit to the Stadhuis cells that what he *should* do, even if it was less than what he could do, was nothing. He was inclined to believe Spandrel's plea of innocence, but to involve himself in such a tangled affair unnecessarily would surely be folly. One did not thrive in the consular service by annoying the local authorities. If the Sheriff wished to persuade himself that Spandrel was an agent of the Marquis de Prié, so be it. Spandrel was a person of no consequence. Nobody would care if he lived or died; nobody, at all events, who might ever call Cloisterman to account. Reluctantly, therefore, though not *very* reluctantly, he dismissed him from his thoughts.

Such a dismissal did not prove as simple a matter as he had supposed, however. Friday morning found him, as was his wont, lingering over a cup of chocolate and a quiet pipe in Hoppe's coffee-house at the western end of the Spui canal, perusing a fortnight-old copy of *Parker's London News*. He was several paragraphs into a chronicle of the latest outrages of highwaymen on Finchley Common when an ostentatious throat clearance drew his attention to a lean, lugubrious fellow who was standing by his table and looking at him critically down an eagle's beak of a nose.

'Can I help you?' Cloisterman snapped.

'I hope you may be able to, sir. My name is Jupe. I am in the service of Sir Theodore Janssen.'

'Janssen, you say?' Cloisterman closed his newspaper. 'That's odd.'

'Why, sir?'

'Never mind. What can I do for you?'

'I was told I might find you here. May I . . . join you?'

'Very well. But I . . .' He drew out his watch. 'I have very little time to spare.'

'Of course. We are all pressed.' Jupe sat down. 'You are Mr Cloisterman, the vice-consul?'

'Yes.'

'I wonder if you can help me. I am making inquiries on Sir Theodore's behalf, concerning . . .' Jupe lowered his voice. 'Mijnheer de Vries.'

'Mijnheer de Vries is dead.'

'Indeed, sir. Murdered, so I understand. By a fellow-countryman of ours. William Spandrel.'

'I know little of the matter, Mr . . .'

'Jupe, sir. Did I not say? Nicodemus Jupe.'

He had said. And Cloisterman had not forgotten. But he did not wish to imply that he was paying as much attention to this grave-faced emissary of the deep-dealing Sir Theodore Janssen as in truth he was. 'An Englishman called Spandrel is in custody, I believe.'

'I am told you have visited him in his place of confinement, sir.'

'You seem to have been told a good deal, Mr Jupe.'

'But not enough to satisfy Sir Theodore as to the circumstances of his old friend's death.'

'It is gratifying to know that Sir Theodore is able to spare a thought for a murdered friend in the midst of all his other . . . difficulties.'

'They were *very* old friends, sir.'

'And business partners of long standing, I'll warrant.'

'Since you mention business, sir, there's a matter on which I'd value your advice.'

'Oh yes?'

'Spandrel was engaged by Sir Theodore to deliver an article of some value to Mijnheer de Vries. Sir Theodore is naturally anxious to establish the whereabouts of that article.'

'Spandrel told me about the package. I wasn't sure whether to believe him.'

'You may believe him about that, sir. The question is: did he deliver it?'

'So he claims. If you're in doubt, ask de Vries's secretary – a fellow called Zuyler.'

'I would, sir, if I could. But Zuyler has left Amsterdam. As has the widow de Vries.'

'Really?' Cloisterman tried not to appear surprised. The fact remained, however, that he was. Spandrel had flung accusations of murder at Zuyler, mendacity at Estelle de

Vries and conspiracy at the pair of them. Cloisterman had been inclined to regard this as the desperate talk of a desperate man. Now, he was not so sure. 'How long have they been gone?'

'I don't know, sir. The staff at the house were not very forthcoming.'

'Did they go together?'

'There again . . .' Jupe shrugged. 'Their destination was likewise not disclosed to me.'

'Do you think they took the package with them?'

'It's possible, sir.'

'No doubt you feel unable to disclose to me its contents.'

'They have not been disclosed to *me*, sir.' Was Jupe lying? Cloisterman's instincts told him that, if not actually lying, he was at least dissembling. Whether he had been told or not, he knew what the package contained. 'Sir Theodore entrusted the package to Mijnheer de Vries. Mijnheer de Vries is dead. Sir Theodore therefore requires the return of the package. He is entitled to insist upon it.'

'Then let him come here and insist.'

'That is not presently possible.'

'Quite. Let us turn, then, to what is possible. Spandrel has told all who will listen that Zuyler murdered Mijnheer de Vries and conspired with de Vries's wife to incriminate him. The Sheriff prefers to believe that Spandrel murdered de Vries, acting on behalf of a hostile foreign power.'

'Spandrel is no assassin, sir.'

'He does not seem to have the makings of one, does he? And now the two people he accused have left Amsterdam, with, you believe, the package he delivered to de Vries.' Cloisterman paused, expecting Jupe to confirm this last point. When no confirmation came, he frowned at the other man and said, 'What is the package worth, Mr Jupe?'

'Worth, sir?'

'Yes. *What is it worth?*'

'I have no way of knowing, sir.'

Cloisterman gave an exasperated sigh. 'In that case, neither you nor I can say whether Spandrel's accusations are likely to have any substance.' He picked up his newspaper and reopened it with a flourish. 'And there would appear to be nothing more I can do for you.'

In London, that same Friday morning, Dalrymple's despatch reached the desk of James, Earl Stanhope, His Majesty's Secretary of State for the Northern Department. It did not find his noble lordship in a receptive mood. Recent weeks had been a trial for him. He had known little and understood less of the whole South Sea affair, preferring to leave financial matters to the management of his principal political ally and First Lord of the Treasury, the Earl of Sunderland, while he concentrated his endeavours on the creation of a new and stable order of relations between the European states. All his achievements in that regard were now imperilled, however, by the embarrassment, bordering on disgrace, that the failure of the South Sea scheme had brought to the Government.

Brodrick's committee, it was rumoured, had extracted evidence from Joye and Blunt of corruption extending to the most senior of ministers, including Aislabie, the Chancellor of the Exchequer, Craggs, the Postmaster-General, and Stanhope's own cousin, Charles, who as Secretary to the Treasury had personally conducted most of the negotiations leading to the South Sea Company's generous offer, as it had seemed at the time, to take over the lion's share of the National Debt. Some of the more alarmist rumour-mongers suggested that Sunderland himself was tainted. If so, the lease on power Stanhope had shared with Sunderland for the past four years might be about to expire. Sunderland could not be persuaded to tell him how great the danger was, but tomorrow, when the House of Lords was due to examine Blunt, it would surely become apparent.

These were nerve-testing times, therefore, for Lord Stanhope. As the responsible minister, he had instructed the Embassy in Brussels to secure Knight's arrest as soon as his whereabouts became known. Latest reports suggested that this was imminent. Stanhope was aware, however, that there was a constitutional objection in Brabant, within whose jurisdiction Knight had placed himself, to the extradition of criminal suspects, an objection the Austrian authorities could not readily override. He had pointed this out to Sunderland at their last meeting, only for Sunderland to reply enigmatically, 'That may be no cause to shed tears.'

What did the fellow mean by that? It was hard to resist the conclusion that Knight confined somewhere abroad, out of the committee's reach, was an outcome Sunderland distinctly approved of. But even if matters did resolve themselves in that way, it would not still the tongues of their accusers. And sooner or later those accusers would have to be answered. If ministers were forced to resign, especially if Sunderland was one of them, the King would be obliged to reconstruct the Government. Walpole was already talked of as Aislabie's successor at the Exchequer. The Treasury might soon be within his grasp. Then where would Stanhope's precious new continental polity be? Walpole was a narrow-minded Norfolk squire. He knew nothing of Europe. He would ruin everything Stanhope had worked so long and assiduously to bring about.

The threat of such ruin galled Stanhope the more because it had arisen from the greed and stupidity of other people. He was personally blameless. Yet it seemed he could not escape punishment. It was enough to drive a man mad. And it was certainly sufficient to fray his temper as he perused Dalrymple's urgent communication.

£100,000? For *what*? Dalrymple must be losing his reason. Perhaps it was time to send Cadogan back to The Hague if this was the measure of the man representing British interests in the United Provinces. It must surely be obvious, even to Dalrymple, that if the ledger spoken of by his mysterious Dutch visitor were truly a compendium of Knight's deepest secrets, it would not have left his side. Dalrymple seemed to suppose that the mere mention of what he semi-fabulously described, with breathless capitals, as 'The Green Book' would somehow justify his effrontery in passing on such a request. But Stanhope would show him his error. Kempis was clearly a mountebank. And mountebankery could only work its magic on fools. Stanhope had been visited by troubles enough on account of the foolishness of others. This was one instance where he could bear down hard upon it.

Stanhope seized his pen, dipped it in the ink-well, and began to write. Dalrymple would not have to wait long for his answer. He would have it short, but far from sweet.

Nicholas Cloisterman, meanwhile, was also composing a letter. His conversation with the odious Jupe had persuaded him that there were sinister ramifications to the murder of Ysbrand de Vries. The package Spandrel had delivered to de Vries on behalf of Sir Theodore Janssen contained something worth killing for, something connected with the fugitive Robert Knight and the failed South Sea Company. Cloisterman did not know what it was and in many ways was happy not to. But clearly he could no longer keep the little he did know to himself. Dalrymple, chargé d'affaires at the Embassy in The Hague, would have to be told. Let him make of it what he pleased. Cloisterman would have done his duty. At least, he would be seen to have done it. And that, he had tended to find, was more important in the long run.

Chapter Ten

Hell to Pay

Evelyn Dalrymple, chargé d'affaires at the British Embassy in The Hague, regarded the visitor to his office with suppressed apprehensiveness. Kempis had come for his answer. And Lord Stanhope had made it very clear what that answer should be. Indeed, he had made it very clear that Dalrymple should not have needed to be told how to respond to such a demand. But Stanhope had not met Kempis. Staring into the Dutchman's wine-dark eyes, Dalrymple detected no weakness, no lack of confidence in the terms he had set. He did not look like a man whom it was wise to dismiss out of hand.

Dalrymple was also troubled by various pieces of information that had lately come his way. From the Embassy in Brussels he had received notification that on Friday last, the day on which Stanhope had written to him, Robert Knight had been arrested while trying to leave Brabantine territory and removed to the citadel at Antwerp. No mention had been made of any papers found in Knight's possession. Dalrymple could only assume that any so found would by now be on their way to London and Stanhope's desk in Whitehall. Oddly, however, Cloisterman, the vice-consul in Amsterdam, seemed convinced that some vital South Sea document was now in the possession of the errant secretary and widow of a murdered V.O.C. merchant called de Vries. He had written to Dalrymple, warning him to be on his guard, but failing, typically, to suggest what he should be on his guard against.

Matters were further complicated by a report that had reached him from London that very morning of the House of Lords debate of Saturday evening. Sir John Blunt, it seemed, had refused to tell their assembled lordships what he had confided to Brodrick's committee. Proceedings had been acrimonious and inconclusive. Lord Stanhope, it was stated, had been 'taken ill' in the midst of a furious exchange with the Duke of Wharton. His exact condition was not known.

Taken all in all, Dalrymple did not rightly see how he could be less comfortably placed. Knight's papers were in transit. Stanhope was ill. Cloisterman was on – or up – to something. And Kempis required an answer. Dalrymple tended, in these circumstances, as in so many others, to favour procrastination. But he doubted it would carry him through.

'If you insist upon an answer at this time, mijnheer—'

'I do.'

'I should not recommend you to, I really should not.'

'I will take my own advice, thank you, Mr Dalrymple.'

'As you please.'

'Are my terms accepted?'

'As I say, this really is not—'

'*Are they accepted?*'

Dalrymple took a long, calming breath. 'No, mijnheer. They are not.'

'Not?' Kempis cocked one eyebrow. He seemed not so much angry as incredulous. 'I cannot have heard you correctly.'

'His Majesty's Secretary of State for the Northern Department—'

'*Who?*'

'Lord Stanhope. The relevant minister.'

'Very well. What does he say?'

Dalrymple glanced down at Stanhope's letter and decided against direct quotation as likely only to prove inflammatory. 'He rejects your demands.'

'He does *what*?'

'He declines to entertain them, mijnheer. He is quite . . . unequivocal . . . on the point.'

'You did tell him what I told you . . . about the Green Book?'

'I did indeed.'

'Then he cannot say no to me.'

'But he has.'

'That is his last word on the matter?'

'I do not say that. The situation is somewhat volatile at present. Wait a while and it is poss—'

'*Wait*?' Now Kempis *was* angry. He jumped from his chair and glared across the desk at Dalrymple, his eyes flashing. 'You expect me to dally here while Lord Stanhope's agents come in search of me – and what I hold? You must think me mad, sir. Your masters have had time enough. If they won't pay me, someone else will.'

'Who might you have in mind, mijnheer?' Dalrymple asked, exerting himself to sound unflustered.

'Oh, I think I know where I will find a ready buyer, never fear. You may tell Lord Stanhope that the King will not thank him when he realizes who that buyer is. Or exactly what he has bought. Be it on his head. And on yours, Mr Dalrymple. Good day to you, sir.'

The discussion had gone as well, Dalrymple afterwards concluded, as it could have been expected to. Nobody would be able to reproach him. He had done what he had been bidden to do. And he had taken one significant precaution, instructing Harris, his secretary's clerk, to follow Kempis upon his departure from the Embassy. Harris was quick-witted and fleet-footed enough to trail Kempis to his lodgings. But he returned less than half an hour later with disappointing news.

'I think he must have been expecting something of the kind, sir. He walked to Prinsessegracht and I kept behind him, out of his line of sight, all the way. But a coach was waiting for him there. They took off at a tearing pace, I can tell you. I thought I glimpsed a woman in the coach. I couldn't get close enough to see any more. They crossed the canal at the next bridge and headed east.'

Kempis had eluded him. That too, Dalrymple felt, was to have been expected. All he could hope now was that he would hear no more from him – or even about him.

But Dalrymple's hopes were to be dashed that very evening. A reception at the Swedish Embassy promised only the blandest of entertainment, but an appearance by him, however brief, was inescapably called for. No sooner had he arrived, late and in unsociable humour, than other guests were sympathizing with him on a loss to his nation of which he was embarrassingly unaware. Lord Stanhope, it rapidly transpired, was dead.

Dalrymple's shock at the news seemed generally to be interpreted as grief for a fallen leader. In truth, grief had nothing to do with it. The excuse that he had only been following orders in turning Kempis away was an excellent one, so long as the giver of those orders remained alive. Now, the excuse would ring alarmingly hollow.

The Swedish Ambassador expressed his entire understanding of Dalrymple's need to leave early and the condolences of the gathering accompanied his departure. He hurried the short distance to the British Embassy, intending to roast any clerks still on the premises for not bringing the news to his door earlier in the evening. He found Harris in his outer office and was on the point of peppering him with abuse when he noticed a stranger warming himself by the fire.

He was a glower-faced ox of a man, with bulging eyes, a nose that would have done justice to a prize-fighter and a prominent scar on his forehead. His black hair, streaked with grey, was tied back in a pigtail. His clothes were old and dusty, but of good quality. Dalrymple had jack-a-dandyish tendencies and could tell fine cloth by its cut, even when it was frayed and travel-stained. He could also tell a fighting man by the hang of his sword. And this was a fighting man by temperament, even if he was perhaps too old to see much action.

'You're Dalrymple?' the fellow growled, with no pretence of civility. There was a Scots twang to his voice, which Dalrymple took as ample explanation of his abruptness.

'I am, sir. Who is this . . . gentleman, Harris?'

'McIlwraith,' the other said, before Harris could so much as open his mouth. 'Captain James McIlwraith.'

'And what can I do for you, Captain McIlwraith?'

'General Ross sent me.'

'Who?'

'General Charles Ross, M.P. A member of the House of Commons Committee of Inquiry into the failure of the South Sea Company. He's been deputed by the committee to secure the records of chief cashier Knight. I'm here on his behalf.' McIlwraith pulled a piece of paper from his pocket and held it out for Dalrymple to read. 'You're called upon to give me all necessary assistance.'

'Am I?' Dalrymple perused the document. It carried the House of Commons seal, Ross's signature and the countersignature of Thomas Brodrick, chairman, as Dalrymple well knew, of the committee in question. There appeared no reason to doubt its authenticity, other than

McIlwraith's lowly rank and uncouth demeanour. 'Well, well. It would seem I am.'

'I'll thank you for a word in private.'

'Leave us, Harris.' Harris obeyed, with what looked like alacrity. Dalrymple moved to the desk and assumed what he judged to be a patrician pose beside it. 'You're personally acquainted with General Ross, Captain?'

'I served under him.'

'In the late war?'

'I had that honour.'

Dalrymple now had the measure of his man. Eight years had passed since the end of the War of the Spanish Succession, more like ten since any serious fighting. But still they were to be found in every tavern, these scarred, bemedalled survivors of shot and shell who dreamed of being under fire as others might dream of paradise. McIlwraith had no doubt struck terror into the enemy at Blenheim and Ramillies and Marlborough's various other blood-soaked victories. He could never have become an officer in peacetime and a mere captaincy suggested he had been a pretty truculent one in wartime. But General Ross trusted him, doubtless with good cause. He had his orders and would stick at nothing to carry them out.

'They have Knight locked up in the citadel at Antwerp,' said McIlwraith. 'I was there last night.'

'Should you not have remained there, Captain? If his . . . records . . . are what you—'

'Where's Kempis?'

'Who?' Dalrymple asked softly, trying hard to disguise his surprise.

'Kempis. The man you wrote to Lord Stanhope about.'

'My correspondence with the Secretary of State can be no business of a House of Commons committee.'

'Oh, but it can. When the subject of that correspondence is a green-covered ledger.'

'You seem to know a great deal, Captain.' (More, in truth, than was good for Dalrymple's peace of mind.) 'How did you come by such information, may I ask?'

'Never you mind. But Stanhope's dead. You know that, don't you?'

'Yes. I do. Sad tidings, indeed.'

'If you say so. Apoplexy, or something of the kind. Though whether brought on by the goadings of the Duke of Wharton in the House of Lords debate on Saturday or the prodigious quantity of Tokay he's said to have drunk at the Duke of Newcastle's the night before is uncertain.'

'He'll be greatly missed,' Dalrymple insisted stubbornly.

'By you, perhaps. Not by all.'

'By all men of feeling.'

'Feeling, is it? Why, I've a—' McIlwraith broke off and ran a hand over his chin and down his neck. Dalrymple heard with distaste the rasp of the stubble against his palm. 'I haven't the leisure to bandy words with you, Dalrymple. Where is Kempis?'

'I have no idea.'

'But you've seen him this very day, according to your clerk.'

'I'm really not at liberty to discuss my dealings with Mijnheer Kempis, or anyone else. I answer to His Majesty's ministers, not the House of Commons.'

'I wouldn't be too sure of that. Do you really want your name to go in the committee's report as a damned obstructive jack-in-office?' McIlwraith stepped closer. His voice dropped. 'I know what Kempis was trying to sell. And for how much. I also know what Lord Stanhope instructed you to do: send Kempis away with a flea in his ear. Which I've no doubt you obediently did. It's a stroke of bad luck for you Stanhope's dead, meaning his instructions are so much waste paper you'd have done better to use as kindling for your fire. But there's good luck

101

for you as well. Information will aid me more than your head on a platter. So, *where* is Kempis?'

'I don't know.'

'You surely can't mean you just let him walk away?'

How predictable it was that Harris had failed to mention his own part in the day's proceedings. 'He gave us the slip,' Dalrymple admitted through gritted teeth.

'I don't suppose he found that so very difficult.' McIlwraith stepped closer still, raking Dalrymple with a contemptuous glare. 'You must have something on him, man. For pity's sake.'

Dalrymple found himself wishing fervently that he did have something; anything, indeed, however insubstantial. And at that point his memory came to his rescue. 'I suspect his real name is Zuyler,' he said, enjoying the sight of contempt giving way to surprise on McIlwraith's face. And there was something else to relish in the moment. Cloisterman was going to regret that unhelpful memorandum. 'Perhaps our vice-consul in Amsterdam can assist your further inquiries.'

Spandrel knew nothing of such far-off events as the death of Lord Stanhope and the arrest of Robert Knight. His life had shrunk to the dingy confines of his cell and an occasional, much cherished walk in an enclosed courtyard. The guards did not know, or if they did would not reveal, why he had not been re-examined. The answer to this and all Spandrel's other questions being so consistently unhelpful, he stopped asking and lapsed into a strange, numb torpor in which his mind grew as empty as his days. He wondered if his mother would ever learn what had become of him, but no longer worried how anxious she might be. She and all the other people he knew were slowly becoming part of a dream he often had: a dream of maps and streets and clear, unwalled horizons. But waiting for him when he woke was the dim, dank reality of the cell. Through its high, barred window came snatches of sound from the city around him: hoofbeats, footsteps, the rumbling of cart-wheels, the shrieking of gulls. He listened to such sounds for hours at a stretch. He watched the movement of shadows on the wall and tried to guess what cast them. He held long, rambling conversations with his father in which he took both parts. Slowly, little by little, thoughts of the future left him. He asked nothing of the guards. Soon, he would ask nothing of himself. And then . . .

One winter's morning which Spandrel had no way, in his confinement, of distinguishing from any other, but which most inhabitants of Amsterdam knew to be Friday 21st February in the New Style, saw the customary tumult of commerce on the Dam, the square in front of the Stadhuis. Barges were loading and unloading at the wharf-side. Merchants from the nearby Exchange were clustering round the Weigh-House. At the fish and vegetable markets, business was brisk.

Nobody was minded, therefore, to pay much attention to the man striding about impatiently at the foot of the steps that led up to the main entrance of the Stadhuis. And a fleeting glance at his face – scarred and balefully forbidding – was enough to discourage prolonged scrutiny. It was evident that whenever he paused to stare up at the columned and pedimented frontage of the Stadhuis, he was not doing so to admire the statues representative of Prudence, Justice and Peace, but to look at the clock on the dome above them.

The clock showed it to be eight minutes after ten when a figure rounded the north-eastern corner of the building and hurried to meet him. The newcomer was breathless and irritably flustered, softer-faced and sleeker than the first man. Neither of them looked pleased by their meeting. There was no handshake, far less a bow, but a curt nod on one part and a scowl of greeting on the other.

'Captain McIlwraith?'

'Aye. And you, I take it, are Cloisterman.'

'I am.'

'You're late.'

'I cannot order my affairs to suit your sole convenience. Had you arranged to call on me at my office, I dare say—'

'I've had enough of offices, man. There are no keyholes in the open air for clerks to listen at. The Amsterdammers seem to do their share of business here. It should be good enough for you.'

'Well, I'm here, am I not?'

'I was assured of your full assistance.'

'Then you'd best tell me what I can assist you with.'

'Spandrel. The fellow they have in there' – McIlwraith crooked a thumb towards the Stadhuis – 'for the murder of de Vries.'

'I'm aware of the case.'

'An assassin in the pay of the Austrians, do you think?'

'I do not.'

'A dupe, then? A pawn in a deeper game?'

'Perhaps.'

'If so, shouldn't you be doing something to help him?'

'It's a matter for the Sheriff.' Cloisterman shrugged. 'Spandrel's a person of no consequence.'

'But the reason he came here *is* of consequence. It's crammed with consequences. And I'm here to unravel them.'

'I wish you luck.'

'I want more than your wishes, man. Zuyler stole the package Spandrel delivered to de Vries. He's been to The Hague trying to sell it to that booby who supposedly represents our nation's interests there.'

'You mean Mr Dalrymple?' Cloisterman looked un-ruffled by the disparaging reference to his superior.

'I mean the simpering clothes-horse who goes by that name, aye. He turned Zuyler away. But Zuyler's not returned here. Nor has the widow de Vries. They've gone in search of a buyer elsewhere. And some servant of Sir Theodore Janssen's called Jupe has gone after them.'

'Has he?'

'Oh, I think so. And I think I can guess where Zuyler and Mrs de Vries are heading just as readily as friend Jupe.'

'Where might that be?'

'Never mind. What concerns me is that I've never met Zuyler *or* Mrs de Vries. But Spandrel has.'

'Well, yes.'

'*And* he's had sight of the contents of the package he delivered to de Vries.'

'Presumably.'

'Why has the Sheriff not brought him before the magistrates for trial?'

'Who can say?' Cloisterman gave another shrug. 'The wheels of justice turn but slowly.'

'Not when a man of de Vries's standing in the community is murdered in cold blood by a foreigner.'

'Even so . . .'

'Why the delay, man? You must have some idea.'

'I could only guess.'

'Then do it.'

'Well, the sudden departure from the city of Zuyler and Mrs de Vries goes a little way towards supporting Spandrel's contention that they murdered de Vries. Only a very little way, it's true, but it may be sufficient to have persuaded the Sheriff that he should await their return before proceeding.'

'He'll have a long wait.'

'You think so?'

'And all the while poor wee Spandrel will moulder in gaol.'

'Inevitably.'

'Inevitably, is it? I don't think so.' McIlwraith clapped Cloisterman round the shoulder, sending him staggering to one side. 'Time you were bestirring yourself, Mr Vice-Consul, on behalf of a fellow-countryman in distress.' McIlwraith grinned crookedly. 'High time.'

Chapter Eleven

Dogs on the Scent

The Secretary of State is dead; long live the Secretary of State. That same Friday, dated eleven days earlier in England, was the first day in office of Lord Stanhope's successor as Secretary for the Northern Department. Charles, Viscount Townshend, had good reason to be pleased with himself as he sat behind Stanhope's desk in the Cockpit building off Whitehall. Four years previously, Stanhope and his great ally Sunderland had succeeded in ousting him from the very same post by playing on the suspicions of the King that he and the then First Lord of the Treasury, Robert Walpole, had deferred overmuch to the Prince of Wales during one of the King's sojourns in Hanover. Walpole, who happened to be Townshend's brother-in-law as well as his best and oldest friend, had resigned along with him. Now, thanks to the grievous inundations of the South Sea, they were back.

Walpole, it was true, had presently to be content with the post of Paymaster-General of the Forces. But he was certain to succeed Aislabie as Chancellor of the Exchequer in due course and, if the Brodrick Committee unearthed damning evidence against Sunderland, as it well might, he could soon be in sole dominion at the Treasury. Their partnership would then be fully restored. Yes, on the whole, Townshend had every reason to be delighted. An ill wind had blown much good to a deserving pair of plain-mannered Norfolkmen.

But much good was not all good. The Paymaster-General was, as it happened, presently slumped in the chair on the other side of the desk, chewing at an apple and scratching his stomach through the gap between two straining buttons of his waistcoat. The smile he often wore was absent. He had not even been cheered by the news Townshend had just conveyed to him that the Secretary for the Southern Department, James Craggs the younger, Stanhope's supposedly brilliant pupil, was mortally ill with the smallpox. Something was clearly amiss.

Townshend knew only too well what it was. The reason for the prevailing glumness was to be found amongst the papers scattered across the desk between them. Or rather, it was not to be found there. Its absence *was* the reason.

The slew of papers comprised Stanhope's most recent correspondence. Among the material that had arrived since his death was a bundle of documents sent post-haste from Brussels after their confiscation from Robert Knight following his arrest near the Brabantine border. They did not include a certain green-covered ledger by which so many set such very great store. And without that what they did include was of little significance. Bar one disturbing communication from chargé d'affaires Dalrymple at The Hague.

With a sudden oath, Walpole plucked what remained of the apple from his mouth and flung it into the fire, where it buried itself sizzlingly among the coals. 'Dalrymple should be grateful he's out of my reach,' he growled. 'Otherwise I'd be tempted to roast him on a spit for what he's done.'

'He was following orders, Robin,' Townshend ventured.

'As he wastes no time in pointing out. What can Stanhope have been thinking of? To reject Kempis so . . . bluntly . . . was madness.'

'Stanhope took him for a rogue. It's understandable. We all assumed Knight would have the Green Book about him.'

'I assumed nothing. I hoped. That is all. Kempis should have been kept dangling till we knew for certain.'

'Stanhope seems to have been in no mood to temporize. Perhaps he was already unwell when he wrote to Dalrymple.'

'More likely Sunderland didn't trust him enough to explain how important the Green Book is.'

'I'm not sure I understand that myself.'

'None of us will, Charles.' Walpole paused to prise a fragment of apple skin from his teeth. 'Until we see for ourselves.'

'In that case, wasn't Stanhope right to rebel at the very notion of paying a hundred thousand pounds for it?'

'A hundred thousand may come to seem like a bargain.'

'Surely it could never be that. Unless—' Townshend broke off and eyed Walpole thoughtfully. 'Well, you always knew more of such matters than me, Robin.'

'The less you know the better.'

Walpole shaped a smile that failed to reassure his brother-in-law, but succeeded in deterring him from further enquiry. It occurred to Townshend that there was a distinct similarity between his own relative ignorance and that in which Sunderland had evidently kept Stanhope. The only difference was that Sunderland was a shifty and self-serving manoeuvrer, whereas Walpole, his boon companion and dear wife's loyal brother, would never betray him. Of that he felt certain.

'The question now,' said Walpole, slapping his thighs for emphasis, 'is what's to be done?'

Cloisterman had several reservations about the course of action he had embarked upon. The most serious of these was the impossibility of deciding what his masters in Whitehall, whoever they were following Stanhope's death, would later declare they had wanted him to do. Should he be helping McIlwraith, or obstructing him? Dalrymple had committed nothing to paper on the subject, presumably so that later he could either take credit for Cloisterman's actions or disown them, according to which way the wind blew. There was no way of extracting specific guidance from Dalrymple. Cloisterman knew better than to try. And the Consul had eagerly delegated full responsibility to him. 'I always leave dealings with the Sheriff to you, Nick. You have a sure hand in these matters.'

Cloisterman could only hope the Consul was right. A sure hand he certainly needed to play. Fortunately, Sheriff Lanckaert was a cautious and patriotic man, who could be expected to resist consular representations on behalf of the prisoner Spandrel. McIlwraith's suggestion, which Cloisterman had agreed to pass on, was that Spandrel should be given the chance, under close escort, to locate the chemist's shop beneath which, he claimed, Zuyler had lodgings, lodgings, indeed, where Spandrel said he had passed the night following the alleged attempt on his life. Zuyler had vanished before he could be questioned on the point, but de Vries's servants all said Zuyler lived in the house and had no outside lodgings. Nor was a chemist called Barlaeus known to anyone. But lies so easily nailed were scarcely worth the telling. It made no sense for Spandrel to make such things up. Perhaps, therefore, he had not made them up. Perhaps Zuyler had taken secret lodgings as part of the deception and given Spandrel a false name for his landlord just as he had for the hired assassin. If a chemist of some other name could be found who had recently let his basement to someone matching Zuyler's description, matters would be turned upon their head and Spandrel might be released – into McIlwraith's waiting arms.

But Cloisterman did not expect that to happen. He did not expect Lanckaert to agree to any part of the exercise. And if Lanckaert should confound his expectation, he did not foresee the result McIlwraith anticipated. Implicating Zuyler in de Vries's murder would not exonerate Spandrel. Spandrel might as easily have been his accomplice as his dupe, the lies he had told, if lies they were, merely desperate attempts to talk his way out of trouble.

From Cloisterman's point of view, Lanckaert's likely intransigence was a godsend. He would have assisted General Ross's representative as best he was able, without that assistance altering events in any way that could subsequently be laid at his door. McIlwraith would charge off in pursuit of Zuyler and Mrs de Vries, leaving Cloisterman in peace, with a ready answer to any criticism, readier still should that criticism emanate from the slippery Dalrymple.

It was thus with no apparent reluctance but very little enthusiasm that Cloisterman presented his request to Lanckaert's English-speaking deputy, Aertsen, in his cramped office beneath the eaves of the Stadhuis that Friday afternoon. Aertsen and he were occasional combatants in closely fought games of chess at Hoppe's coffee-house and pursued their official discussions in a similar vein, with every allowance for each other's tactical acumen. They had both questioned Spandrel and formed their views on the case. But their views were irrelevant and so they wasted no time on them. Lanckaert's judgement was all that mattered. And there Aertsen had a surprise for Cloisterman.

'An interesting proposition, Nicholas. I rather think it may commend itself to Mijnheer Lanckaert.'

'You do?'

'You look surprised.'

'I am. Are you sure?'

'I cannot be sure. But I am optimistic.'

'Why?'

'Because Mijnheer Lanckaert wishes to discover an Austrian conspiracy. Indeed, he *needs* to discover one. The V.O.C. expects it of him.'

'I'm asking for Spandrel to be given an opportunity to exonerate, not incriminate, himself.'

'You cannot have one without the other.'

Zuyler's flight had marked him down as Spandrel's co-conspirator, perhaps the arch-conspirator. That, Cloisterman clearly saw, was how it was. And now he had volunteered to help the authorities prove their point. Freedom would be dangled like a carrot in front of Spandrel, only to be snatched away once he had led them far enough in pursuit of it. It was the way of the world. It could not be helped. Certainly not by Cloisterman. He shrugged. 'So be it.'

'I will speak to Mijnheer Lanckaert as soon as possible.' Aertsen smiled, which had the disquieting effect of exaggerating his squint. 'And we shall see if I read him aright.'

But as to that there was no doubt. Aertsen was no more likely to advance an unfounded opinion than an undefended pawn. Cloisterman already had his answer. And it was not the one he wanted.

When, the following afternoon, the guard he knew as Big Janus opened the door of his cell, the last thing Spandrel expected him to say – the last thing he would have dared to hope – was that he had a visitor. Big Janus seemed to sense this and went so far as to smile. 'Mijnheer Cloisterman,' he announced, as if genuinely pleased on Spandrel's account. He jangled the keys in his hand, then seemed to decide that manacling Spandrel was unnecessary. He stepped back, holding the door open for Cloisterman.

'Mr Cloisterman,' Spandrel said, struggling to control the surge of hope that had overcome him. 'Thank God.'

'Good afternoon.' Cloisterman's gaze revealed nothing. 'Are you being well treated?'

'Well treated?' Spandrel caught Big Janus's eye over Cloisterman's shoulder. 'I . . . have no complaints.'

'I'm glad to hear it.'

'I thought . . . I'd been . . .'

'Forgotten? Nothing of the kind, I assure you. I've been doing my very best for you.'

'Thank you.' Spandrel would have fallen at Cloisterman's feet had he thought the gesture likely to be appreciated. 'Thank you, sir.'

'And I have secured for you a significant concession.'

'Thank you. Thank you so much.'

'Do you think you could lead us to Zuyler's lodgings?'

'His . . . lodgings?'

'Yes. Where you went after he rescued you from the canal.'

'The canal.' Spandrel's mind grappled unfamiliarly with the process of connected thought. 'Of course. Zuyler's lodgings. Beneath the chemist's shop.'

'Exactly. Could you lead us there?'

'Yes. I . . . think so. I . . . I'm sure. I would know the way from . . . the tavern.' For the life of him, Spandrel could not remember the name of the tavern where he had spent the night before his ill-fated return to the house of Ysbrand de Vries. But he would eventually. It would all come back to him in time. 'I could do it, Mr Cloisterman. I could.'

'I believe you. And you're to have the chance.'

113

'When?'

'Monday.'

'And when is . . .' Spandrel tried to calculate how many days had elapsed since he had last heard the church bells ringing for the sabbath. Was it five, or six? He shook his head helplessly.

'It's the day after tomorrow,' said Cloisterman, taking pity on him.

'Thank you. Of course it is. The day after tomorrow. And this . . . will help my case?'

'It may do.' Cloisterman hesitated, then said, 'We'll find out, won't we? On Monday.'

Although the Paymaster-Generalship of the Forces was a relatively lowly office, it enjoyed certain significant privileges. The most lucrative of these was custody of the Army pay-roll, which was handed over by the Treasury at the beginning of each year and gradually disbursed, the balance being invested by the Paymaster for his personal benefit until it was called upon. In time of war, when the Army was so much bigger, this practice could make a man fabulously wealthy. The Duke of Chandos, Paymaster-General during the War of the Spanish Succession, had been desperately trying to find ways of spending his money ever since and was rumoured to have lost £700,000 on South Sea stock without batting an eyelid. In time of peace, the riches that accrued to the fortunate incumbent did so at a slacker pace, but accrue they nonetheless did. This was Walpole's second spell in the post and he was now what careful husbandry of his Norfolk estate could never have made him: a man of considerable means.

He was also in occupation of the Paymaster's official residence, Orford House, attached to the Royal Hospital at

Chelsea. It was a residence entirely suited to the dignity and pre-eminence he had resolved should be his and he had no intention of surrendering it when he assumed a more senior role in government. Indeed, as he took his Sunday morning ease there, strolling on the lawns that ran down to the Thames in sunshine warm enough for spring, he was already turning over in his mind ways of annexing more of the hospital's buildings and grounds for his private use. His wife had expressed a wish for an aviary and he himself thought a summer-house would look rather fine on the terrace where a few pensioners were currently taking the air. Yes, changes there would be, here and in Norfolk, when he came into his own.

His pleasing reverie was interrupted by the arrival of a visitor, someone he had been expecting and whom he needed to speak to. But it was nevertheless with a certain sinking of the heart that he watched the visitor approach across the lawn from the rear of the house. Colonel Augustus Wagemaker was not a man Walpole or anyone else looked forward to meeting.

He was a thick-set, bustling figure, with a head patently too large for his body, but a face that made this feature more menacing than ludicrous. There was something of the battering-ram in his jutting jaw and prow-like nose and something harsher still in his eyes: a dead, flat, shark's glare of hostility that even his deference to Walpole could not quite extinguish. He had been recommended for special services by Lord Cadogan after tirelessly hunting down remnants of the Earl of Mar's Jacobite army in the wake of the Fifteen and had shown himself to be reliable in all circumstances. He was also a man of notoriously few words and Walpole valued his reticence almost as much as his ruthlessness.

'Good morning, Colonel,' said Walpole. 'A fine day.'

'Lord Townshend has told me what you want of me, sir,' Wagemaker replied, the reference to the weather seeming to have passed him by. 'I'm anxious to be off.'

'Of course. And I'll not detain you long. But I wished to have a private word with you before you left. I trust Lord Townshend explained our difficulty.'

'He did, sir.'

'The item must be recovered. I cannot exaggerate the importance of your mission.'

'I understand, sir.'

'A great deal depends upon your success. A very great deal.'

'I don't intend to let you down, sir.'

'No. I'm sure you don't. And with that in mind . . .' Walpole placed an amiable hand on Wagemaker's shoulder. 'Bring this off for me, Colonel, and you'll be richly rewarded. I shall soon have many valuable offices at my disposal. To take but one example, I anticipate that the Rangership of Enfield Chase will shortly fall vacant. I could imagine you occupying that position with considerable distinction.'

Wagemaker nodded. 'So could I, sir. Since you mention it.'

'It is to me that you should deliver the item. Not Lord Townshend. You follow? To me personally.'

'I follow, sir.'

'And to me that you should then look for advancement.'

'Yes, sir.'

'Which you will not do in vain.'

'*If* I recover the item.'

'Exactly.'

'Would you really consider appointing a mere colonel to a rangership, sir?'

'Well . . .' Walpole smiled. 'Perhaps a general would be more appropriate.'

'Perhaps so, sir.' For a moment, Walpole thought Wagemaker might break into a smile himself. But there was only the faintest softening of his expression to indicate his eagerness for the prize that could be his. 'I'd best be on my way now, sir. I have work to do.'

Chapter Twelve

Out of the Frying-Pan

Cloisterman had rarely felt less at his ease than during the journey he undertook on Monday morning. It led from the cells of the Stadhuis to the Goudene Vis tavern on Montelbaanswal and thence, by a circuit of initially wrong but eventually correct turnings, to the chemist's shop where Spandrel claimed to have been accommodated overnight in Zuyler's lodgings.

Cloisterman's unease was the result of a bad conscience. He had long believed his conscience to have been extinguished by the dulling effects of his vice-consular duties. To find that it could still be pricked and hence still existed was deeply disturbing and accounted in part for his distracted mood throughout the proceedings. The false nature of those proceedings was what troubled him. Spandrel believed that, if he could prove his claimed association with Zuyler, he would thereby prove his innocence. This belief could be seen shining in his pale and haggard face like a candle behind a mask. But he was wrong, as Cloisterman well knew. All he could achieve, if successful, was to prove his guilt in the eyes of the Sheriff.

They travelled in Aertsen's coach, Cloisterman and Aertsen sitting next to each other opposite Spandrel and his guard, the aptly nicknamed 'Big' Janus, to whom Spandrel was handcuffed. Spandrel's hands were also manacled together and Aertsen had supplied a constable to ride escort for them. A single glance at the prisoner suggested that these precautions were excessive, to say the least. Thin and weak from his confinement, Spandrel did not look capable even of trying to escape. Not that he was likely to, of course. He was in truth pitifully eager to do exactly what the Sheriff wanted him to do, though not, sadly, for the same reason. Cloisterman could hardly bear to look at him, knowing what he did. It was a rotten business and the sooner it was over the better.

The principal obstacle to its swift conclusion lay in Spandrel's uncertainty about the route he had followed from the chemist's shop to the Gouden Vis and the added complication of tracing it in reverse. Cloisterman wondered if there would ever be an end of trailing up one canal and down another, while Spandrel leaned out of the window of the coach, giving directions that then had to be translated by Aertsen for the benefit of the driver. Eventually, however, he saw true recognition dawn on Spandrel as they headed south along the Kloveniersburgwal. 'Stop, stop,' the poor deluded fellow shouted. 'This is it.'

They were indeed outside a chemist's shop, similar in appearance to dozens of others around the city, including the one where Cloisterman went for headache cures and condoms. The name of the proprietor was not displayed. A sign bearing the single word *Apotheek* hung above a grimy window filled with dusty jars. Steps led up to the shop doorway, while others led down to a shuttered basement. It would be in Spandrel's best interests, Cloisterman knew, for there to be nothing to connect Zuyler with these premises. He found himself hoping that such would be the case. But he was aware that Spandrel would do everything he could to substantiate his claim. And the sly half-smile on Aertsen's face suggested he would offer him every encouragement to that end. 'I think,' Aertsen said, 'that we should go in, don't you, Nicholas?'

Cloisterman's consent was hardly needed and Aertsen did not wait for his answer. The party disembarked from the coach and entered the shop, Aertsen instructing the driver and escorting constable to remain where they were. 'This is Barlaeus's shop,' chirruped Spandrel as he and Big Janus made their entangled ascent of the steps like a pair of reluctant and ill-matched dancers. 'I'm certain of it.'

But Spandrel's certainty only took them so far. The proprietor, a thin, stooped fellow in a skull-cap, did not answer to the name of Barlaeus and displayed no flicker of familiarity with the name of Zuyler either. Aertsen insisted that he close the shop, then questioned him for some minutes, too quickly for Cloisterman's grasp of Dutch, before reporting what he had said. 'He is Balthasar Ugels. He has traded from these premises for nearly twenty years and says he has never had a lodger. He lives here with his wife and daughters. He says the rooms below are used for storage only. The family lives above. He says he is famous for his gout cure. Have you heard of the Ugels gout powder, Nicholas?'

'I do not happen to suffer from gout, Henrik,' Cloisterman replied with a measured sigh.

'Nor I. But it is perhaps—' Aertsen broke off at the appearance from the rear of the premises of a plump young woman with raven-black hair and eyes to match. 'One of the daughters, I presume.' Aertsen turned to Ugels and asked him in Dutch to confirm this, which the fellow did, adding something Cloisterman failed to catch. Whatever it was caused Aertsen to chuckle.

'Care to share the joke?'

'He says she knows nothing. But nothing about what? The denial betrays him, I think.'

'It does nothing of the kind.'

'Excuse me, sir,' put in Spandrel. 'Surely if—'

'Be silent, man,' snapped Cloisterman. 'Let me deal with this.'

'But—'

'*Silent, I said.*'

Everyone was struck dumb for a moment by the force of Cloisterman's words. Looks were exchanged. Ugels nervously licked his lips. The daughter began to tremble. Aertsen took a few slow steps towards her. 'Juffrouw Ugels?' he gently enquired. She nodded mutely in reply. He went on, asking her slowly and simply enough for Cloisterman to understand whether anyone had lodged in the house recently and whether the name Zuyler meant anything to her.

'*Nee,*' she said each time. '*Nee.*' But her face coloured as she spoke and she could not meet Aertsen's gaze. There was no doubt about it. She was lying. Cloisterman watched a tell-tale bead of sweat trickle down her father's brow.

'We will visit the store-rooms, I think,' said Aertsen. 'And see exactly what is being stored there.'

Ugels received this announcement with twitching anxiety and the implausible objection that he had mislaid the key. Aertsen let him babble on for a moment, then told him coldly and abruptly that he would be arrested and thrown into gaol if he did not do as he was told. With that, the key was found.

Ugels led the way to the front door and opened it. Cloisterman followed Aertsen out, expecting him to carry on down the steps. But he stopped dead on the landing at the top of them, so suddenly that Cloisterman collided with him. Before he could protest, however, he saw what had halted Aertsen in his tracks.

The coach was gone. So was the constable. They had been told to wait. It was unthinkable that they should have disobeyed. Yet gone they were. *'Wat betekent dit?'* said Aertsen irritably. 'What does this mean?' It was a good question.

Suddenly, it was answered. A figure burst out from beneath the steps and rushed up towards them. Cloisterman barely had time to recognize McIlwraith before he also realized that the Scotsman was carrying a double-barrelled pistol in each hand. 'Get back,' McIlwraith shouted, clapping one of the pistols to Aertsen's head and pointing the other at Cloisterman.

They stumbled back into the shop. Cloisterman heard the girl scream. Then McIlwraith kicked the door shut behind him. 'Tell her to be quiet,' he said in Dutch to Ugels, who whimpered some plea to his daughter that reduced her screams to sobs. 'That's better,' he declared in English. 'Now, I'm sorry to interrupt the pantomime, gentlemen, but I can wait upon the law no longer.'

'McIlwraith, are you mad?' asked Cloisterman disbelievingly.

'Far from it. Simply in a hurry. These pistols are primed and cocked. The longer we stand here debating my state of mind, the greater the danger I'll forget myself and blow Mijnheer Aertsen's head off. Is that understood?'

'It is understood,' said Aertsen in a wavering voice.

'I want Spandrel. Tell the big fellow to release him.'

Aertsen turned slowly round, the twin muzzles of the pistol pressing into his head as he did so. His face was fixed in a grimace of fear and there was a sheen of sweat on his upper lip. He murmured an instruction to Big Janus. The guard hesitated. He spoke again, more loudly. Now the guard responded and began sorting through the keys that hung at his waist.

'Be quick about it,' said McIlwraith. A glance over his shoulder through the window of the shop suggested he was more nervous than the steadiness of his tone implied.

Perhaps he was worried that the constable might return. How he had got rid of him and the coachman in the first place Cloisterman could not imagine.

'What's happening, sir?' Spandrel whispered. 'I don't understand.'

'Just do as he says.'

There was a metallic clink as the handcuffs opened. 'The manacles too,' said McIlwraith. But Big Janus had anticipated that and was already working on them.

'I don't want to escape,' said Spandrel stubbornly. 'I'm not trying to.' But in the next moment the manacles were off him. Whether he desired it or not, liberty – of a sort – was his.

'Come over here, Spandrel,' McIlwraith ordered. 'Move, man.'

'I can't. I have to stay.'

'I'm offering you your only chance of freedom. I suggest you grab it with both hands.'

'No. I can prove my innocence. Here. Now.'

'You've gulled him good and proper, haven't you?' McIlwraith glared at Cloisterman. 'Well, it's time for a little enlightenment. Tell him the truth, Mr Vice-Consul.'

'The truth?' Incomprehension was written across Spandrel's face.

'You cannot prove your innocence, Spandrel,' said Cloisterman, perversely aware at some level far below his fear of what might be about to happen that he welcomed the course of action McIlwraith had forced upon him. 'If Zuyler can be shown to have lodged here, it will be taken as proof that you and he conspired together to murder de Vries.'

'What?'

'Once that's been proved to the Sheriff's satisfaction, you'll be prevailed upon to admit it.'

'And by "prevailed upon" he doesn't mean by weight of

reasoned argument,' said McIlwraith with a grim smile. 'Understand?'

Spandrel did understand. He looked at Cloisterman, who nodded towards the door in as open a gesture of approval as he dared risk. The girl was whimpering, but nobody else made a sound. Aertsen caught Cloisterman's eye and held his gaze for a moment. There was going to be some form of reckoning for this. And it was not going to be pleasant. But that lay in the future. In the present, Spandrel took several hesitant steps towards the door.

'De sleutel,' said McIlwraith to Ugels. 'Snel.' The key to the door was proffered in a trembling hand. 'Take it from him, Spandrel.' Spandrel did so. 'We'll lock the door behind us, gentlemen. I advise you to be in no hurry about breaking it open. I'll not scruple to kill any man who follows us.'

'We will not follow,' said Aertsen. 'You have my word.'

'For what that's worth, mijnheer, I'm only a very little obliged. But thank you anyway. Open the door, Spandrel.' Spandrel obeyed. 'Your servant, gentlemen.' McIlwraith backed out onto the landing and nodded for Spandrel to follow. 'Close it, mijnheer. If you please.'

Aertsen stretched forward and pushed the door shut. McIlwraith and Spandrel were now visible only as blurred shadows through the frosted glass of the window. There was a click as the key turned in the lock. Then the shadows vanished.

No more than a second of silence and immobility followed. Then Aertsen rounded on Cloisterman, anger supplanting his fear. 'I hold you responsible for this.' He was ashamed. Cloisterman could see that. His parting assurance to McIlwraith – 'We will not follow' – had been a craven and probably unnecessary surrender. 'You encouraged this . . . this madman.'

'Henrik—'

'And you'll answer for it, I assure you.'

Cloisterman summoned a smile. 'Do I have your word on that?'

Aertsen stepped closer. 'What does he intend to do?'

'At a guess, I'd say he intends to go after Zuyler and Mevrouw de Vries. He needs Spandrel to identify them and the article he delivered to de Vries, which McIlwraith believes them to be carrying.'

' "At a guess". That is all, is it? Just a guess.'

'What are you suggesting?'

'If I find any evidence that you knew what he was planning . . .'

'Shouldn't we be taking steps to catch them rather than arguing about who's to blame? There'll be a back door out of here, I've no doubt. Unless, of course . . .' Cloisterman looked Aertsen in the eye without flinching. Normally, he deferred to the judicial authorities in all matters. Now, however, the time had come to show a little defiance – a little, it occurred to him, of the spirit of McIlwraith. 'Unless you intend to honour your promise. And let them get clean away.'

Chapter Thirteen

Over the Water

'We'll be walking away from here as calmly as two professors on a promenade, Spandrel,' said McIlwraith, uncocking the pistols and slipping them into the pockets of his greatcoat. 'If you attempt to break away, however, I'll shoot you down without a moment's hesitation. Be in no doubt of that. I have need of you, but my need's not so pressing that I'll brook any resistance. And you're an escaped prisoner, remember. I'd probably be rewarded for my pains. We have a little way to go to a place of safety. Once there, I'll explain what I want from you. Until then, you'll keep your mouth shut and your ears open. Now, walk straight ahead.'

The simplicity of these instructions was strangely welcome to Spandrel. Who – or what – McIlwraith was he had no idea. But the fact remained that he was no longer in a cramped cell beneath the Stadhuis, nor were manacles chafing his wrists. He was free – up to a point. And, to judge by what Cloisterman had said, not a moment too soon. There was treachery everywhere. No-one could be trusted. But, for the present, he was walking the streets of Amsterdam and breathing the clear, sunlit air. It was enough. It was, in truth, all he had recently longed for.

The route they followed led through a busy market-place, then steadily north, by a series of alleys and canalside streets, to the harbour. As they reached the bustling waterfront, a view opened up between the rooftops to the east of the Montelbaanstoren. But they headed west, along the wharves and over the canal bridges. Slowly, Spandrel lost his sense of conspicuousness. Nobody knew who he was and nobody cared. By rights, he should have tried to flee the city. But out on the long straight roads through the flat fields of a country he did not know he really would be conspicuous. The city that had been his prison was also his only refuge.

At length, they entered a quieter district at the western end of the harbour. The warehouses here were mostly shuttered and unattended. A windmill loomed ahead atop a seaward bastion of the city wall. Some way short of it, McIlwraith directed Spandrel down an alley between a high wooden fence on one side and a row of warehouses on the other. Sawing and hammering could be heard from over the fence, but they had the alley to themselves. The far end was a wharf on some inlet of the harbour. A barge drifted by in the distance as they walked.

'This is far enough,' McIlwraith announced suddenly. They stopped by the doors of a warehouse that looked to Spandrel just like all the others to left and right. The number 52 and the word SPECERIJEN were stencilled over the lintel. McIlwraith took out a key and opened the wicket, then motioned for Spandrel to enter.

The interior was dark and cold as a tomb, but dry, the dust scented with sweetness. McIlwraith lit a lantern that hung from a beam, but its circle of light stretched no further than a nearby jumble of upturned boxes and a bench, on which stood a wicker hamper. Spandrel was left to imagine how far off the rear wall might be. There were patterings and scurryings from the darkness.

'We'll be here till nightfall,' said McIlwraith. 'There's coal and a brazier somewhere, so we'll not freeze to death. And . . .' he crossed to the bench and unstrapped the hamper 'the rats haven't gnawed through this yet, so we'll not starve either.' He raised the lid. 'Bread. Cheese. Ham. A flagon of ale. And some tobacco. Plenty of everything. Just what you'll be needing after a couple of weeks on prison rations.'

'Why are you doing this?'

'Not because I'm sorry for you, Spandrel, if that's what you were hoping. My help comes with a price.'

'I have no money.'

'But you can pay me back, nonetheless.'

'How?'

'Eat something, man. You need to build your strength up.' McIlwraith kicked a box into position next to the bench and gestured for Spandrel to sit. He pulled a hunk of bread off a loaf and passed it to him with some thick slices of ham. Then he uncorked the flagon and stood it on the bench near Spandrel's elbow. 'Good?'

The bread was fresh and doughy, the ham lean and succulent. Their flavours surged through Spandrel. He coughed and took a gulp of the ale, then looked up at McIlwraith. 'Good,' he announced.

'Don't bolt it or you'll bring it up no sooner than you've got it down. There's plenty of time.' McIlwraith stowed his pistols away, then lit a pipe and sat up on the bench while Spandrel ate and drank more slowly. 'I'm Captain James McIlwraith. Acting on behalf of General Ross for the House of Commons Secret Committee of Inquiry into the South Sea Company. The Brodrick Committee, as it's known. Heard of it?'

'Yes. I think so. But what—'

'All in due course, Spandrel. Just listen, there's a good fellow. I have a House of Commons warrant authorizing me to do whatever's necessary to carry out the committee's wishes and requiring any British subject I encounter to assist me. Consider your assistance called upon. I've taken this warehouse on a short let. As far as the owner's agent is concerned, I need it to handle a consignment of cinnamon. But we're the consignment. You and me. And we're leaving rather than arriving. Aertsen will expect us to make for Rotterdam. His men will ride a stableful of horses into the ground chasing our shadows. They'd have overtaken us if we'd gone that way, no question. You'd have slowed me down too much to outrun them. As it is, we're leaving by ship. The *Havfrue* is a Danish vessel. It sails for Christiania tonight. We'll be on it. The master's agreed – for a generous consideration, naturally – to convey us to the eastern shore of the Zuider Zee. We'll be put off at Harderwijk. That's in the province of Gelderland. Be grateful for these Netherlanders' constitutional niceties, Spandrel. You can't be arrested outside Holland without all manner of swearing and affidaviting, for which there wouldn't be time even if Aertsen guessed our destination. And he's not likely to do that. We'll buy horses at Harderwijk and make for the border.'

'But why? Where are we going?'

'Lord save us, do you understand nothing, man? Isn't it obvious?'

'No. Not in the least.'

McIlwraith sighed. 'You delivered the Green Book to de Vries, didn't you?'

'I delivered something.'

'You must have seen what it was.'

'No. It was sealed in a despatch-box. I saw the box. Nothing more.'

At that McIlwraith loosed a guttural laugh that echoed in the rafters above them. 'I was hoping you'd know it by sight. That was one of my reasons for heezing you out of gaol. You *would* know Zuyler and the winsome widow by sight, wouldn't you?'

'Yes. Of course.'

'Then I'd best be grateful for small mercies. That pair have the Green Book, Spandrel. They tried to sell it to the Government – *our* Government – for a hundred thousand pounds.'

'*How much?*'

'A hundred thousand. And they'd likely have been paid it, but for numskullery in high places.'

'A hundred thousand . . . for a book?'

'Not just any book. The *Green* Book. The repository of the South Sea Company's darkest secrets. Who was bribed. When. How much. All the names. All the figures. Everything.'

'That's what I delivered?'

'It seems so. It wasn't with Knight when he was arrested. And Knight's known to have visited Janssen just before leaving England. It's what the committee's been looking for since it started work last month: the only true record of the company's dealings. The audited accounts were just a bundle of false figures and fictitious names. But even bribers need to keep tally. To root out the guilty men, high and low, the committee needs that book. And I mean to procure it for them.'

'How?'

'By catching up with Zuyler and his *amorosa*. It's clear they murdered de Vries and left you to take the blame. I'm not sure if Zuyler or de Vries was behind the attempt on your life – if that's what it was – and it doesn't much matter now anyway. According to Cloisterman, de Vries's money goes to his son. The widow doesn't even get her proverbial mite. Maybe the old man cut her out of his will for fear she might otherwise have a good reason to hasten his exit from this world. If so, he'd have made sure she knew that, which can't have filled her head with warm, wifely thoughts. Soon Zuyler was showing her what a younger man has to offer and they talked of running away together. But they needed money. And the Green Book offered them a way of getting more than they could ever hope to squeeze out of de Vries. They must have known it was on its way before you arrived. Between them, they must have weevilled into every one of de Vries's secrets. Oh, they've been clever. No question about it. But cleverness has a habit of foundering on simple bad luck. Our Embassy at The Hague's in the charge of a brainless popinjay. And the Secretary of State he answered to – the late, unlamented Lord Stanhope – had kept himself so calculatingly ignorant of the South Sea escapade that he didn't understand what Zuyler was offering for sale. So, the offer was rejected. How sad, how inconvenient, for our flitting pair of love-birds.' McIlwraith clapped his hands together. 'But how very fortunate for us.'

'Fortunate?'

'Aye, man. Fortunate for both of us. For me because, if the sale had been completed, the Government would have the Green Book. And we can safely assume too many ministers are named in it for them to allow it ever to see the light of day. Sunderland, for one. Why, if the committee could nail his dealings to the barn-door . . . Well, I still have a chance now of enabling them to do just that.'

'And me?'

'You? It's even better for you, Spandrel. You're out of gaol. And you'll stay out if you stick by me. The committee will be in your debt if we deliver them the Green Book. That means the Government will be in your debt, because it's certain we'll have a whole sparkling new set of ministers once the truth about the existing lot's known. No fear of being sent back here to face trial then. No need to hide from your creditors. The most eminent of them will likely be facing trial himself.' McIlwraith's tone turned suddenly sombre. 'That's if you help me, of course. Decide it's safer to run for it and you have my word you'll have to run for ever. I'll make sure you can't go home to England without being arrested and handed over to the Dutch authorities. You'll be back where you started – and where you'd have stayed but for me.' Then his tone softened again. 'But there's no question of that, is there? We're in this together.'

'All you want me to do is help you find Zuyler and Estelle de Vries?' It sounded simple, though Spandrel knew it was unlikely to be so. But what choice did he have? McIlwraith was right. They *were* in this together.

'That's all, my bonny fellow.'

'Then I'll do what I can. Though for the life of me I don't see *how* you hope to find them.'

'By putting myself in their shoes and using what God gave me to think with. Zuyler told Dalrymple – the popinjay at The Hague – that he knew where to find another buyer. And that the King wouldn't thank him and Stanhope when he learned who that buyer was. Those were his very words. Which he may come to regret uttering. Who would pay most dearly to disgrace His Majesty's Government in the eyes of his people? Who but one who would be King himself – who thinks he already is, by rights?'

'The Pretender.'

'You have it, Spandrel. They mean to try their luck with the Jacobites. They'd find a nest of them in Paris. But their dealings with Dalrymple and Stanhope will have left them wary of negotiating through intermediaries. I reckon they'll go to the court of James Edward Stuart himself.'

'In Rome?'

'Aye. But don't worry.' McIlwraith grinned. 'We'll catch up with them long before they set foot in the Eternal City. That's a promise.'

Spandrel still had no idea how McIlwraith meant to keep his promise when they boarded the boat sent for them by the master of the *Havfrue* at a nearby wharf early that evening and headed out across the moonlit harbour to where the ship was waiting for them at its anchorage beyond the boom. He was both more frightened and more excited by what had happened than he wanted McIlwraith to realize. His new-found companion might be his saviour – or a devil in disguise. There was no way to tell. Nor could Spandrel hazard the remotest guess at how, or where, or when, their journey would end. He had feared he might never leave Amsterdam and had hoped only for a safe return home. Now, instead, he had embarked on a voyage into the unknown. He was further from home than ever. And he could not turn back.

Chapter Fourteen

Cold Pursuit

The days following 'the abduction of the prisoner Spandrel', as the incident at Ugels's shop was drily described in Aertsen's formal report, were difficult ones for Cloisterman. He had to rebut any implication that he had connived with McIlwraith to spirit Spandrel away, but he could not do so as forcefully as he might wish in case Aertsen felt his own position was threatened. In that event, he would probably defend himself by persuading Sheriff Lanckaert to recommend that Cloisterman be declared *persona non grata* and sent back to England in disgrace. Cloisterman enjoyed life in Amsterdam and his courtship of the daughter of a wealthy tobacco merchant was at a promising stage. Banishment would spell disaster for all his plans and had to be fended off.

The only way he could see of doing this was to tread lightly where the issue of Spandrel's guilt or innocence was concerned. It was now obvious that Zuyler had murdered de Vries and manoeuvred Spandrel into taking the blame. To state that openly, however, would be to question the competence of the Sheriff and hence of his deputy. He refrained from raising the matter, therefore, and hoped that Aertsen would reciprocate his restraint.

In this regard, the authorities' failure to recapture Spandrel and to seize his abductor was actually quite satisfactory, since it meant that the issue need not be confronted. Spandrel's escape from custody was embarrassing, but not as embarrassing as an admission that the real guilty party had long since slipped through their fingers. It was also noticeable that Aertsen did not press the matter of McIlwraith's status as an agent of the Brodrick Committee. To do so might precipitate a formal complaint by the States of Holland to the House of Commons, with consequences too serious to contemplate for all concerned. Officially, therefore, McIlwraith was an anonymous confederate of Spandrel and, so long as he was not apprehended, that is what he would remain.

Cloisterman was obliged, of course, to report a reasonably accurate version of events to Dalrymple. He calculated, however, that Dalrymple, like Aertsen, would favour the line of least resistance. It had to be assumed that McIlwraith, with Spandrel as his willing or unwilling travelling companion, was no longer in the United Provinces. And it was unlikely that the pair would ever return. In that sense, they were no longer the concern of vice-consuls and chargés d'affaires. Let McIlwraith do his worst and leave others to worry about the consequences. Cloisterman's memorandum to Dalrymple on the subject bore the imprint of this agreeable urging between every reticent line.

It did not, though, yield the response Cloisterman expected, which was either silence or a testy but essentially approving little note. Instead, Cloisterman received by return of post a summons to The Hague. 'I should be obliged,' Dalrymple wrote in an abominable hand that suggested haste, perhaps even desperation, 'if you would wait upon me here at the very earliest juncture available transport will permit.' It did not augur well. In fact, it augured ill.

* * *

The urgency of the summons had the meagre advantage of justifying Cloisterman in the minor extravagance of travelling by coach rather than *trekschuit*. The journey nevertheless took the better part of a day and he was tempted to put off reporting to the Dalrymplian presence until the following morning, weary as he was and in need of supper and a bath. Reckoning, however, that he would find the chargé long since departed, he made his way to the Embassy and announced his arrival.

Dalrymple had indeed already gone home, but his secretary's clerk, Harris, was still there, instructed to remain, it transpired, with a late arrival by Cloisterman specifically in mind. 'Mr Dalrymple's anxious to see you, sir. Very anxious, I should say. I'm to escort you to his residence without delay.'

Dalrymple's residence was, in fact, only a short walk away. The simplest of instructions would have sufficed for Cloisterman to find it unescorted. Harris's company seemed intended, Cloisterman could not help but feel, to guard against his turning back rather than losing his way. The auguries were growing worse all the time.

A musical entertainment of some sort was under way when Cloisterman was admitted to the house. A snatch of jaggedly played Handel wafted out behind Dalrymple from the drawing-room. A disagreeable and faintly disturbing smile was hovering around the chargé's moist lips and Cloisterman hardly supposed it was because he was pleased to see him. Harris was told to wait in an antechamber, while they retired to the privacy of Dalrymple's study, where the smile rapidly faded.

'When did we last have the pleasure of seeing you here, Cloisterman?'

'The farewell reception for Lord Cadogan, as I recall.'

'As long ago as that?'

'It was, yes.'

'Well, well. Perhaps it's fortunate for you that it's me rather than his lordship you have to answer to. He was a hard taskmaster and wouldn't have been amused by your mishandling of recent events.'

'I afforded Captain McIlwraith every assistance,' said Cloisterman steadily. 'As you instructed me to.'

'My instructions did not include helping him to abduct a prisoner.'

'I didn't help him.'

'No? I'm not sure Sheriff Lanckaert would agree with you.'

'My report was detailed and accurate. If you've read it, you'll—'

'I've certainly read it. And a sorrier chronicle of mismanaged affairs I've seldom been obliged to peruse.'

'I'm sure I'd be diverted by your exegesis of what I should have done.'

'I haven't time to give lessons in adroitness, Cloisterman. It's lucky for you the Dutch don't seem disposed to make a fuss about it.'

'That's not entirely a question of luck.'

'Really?' Dalrymple eyed Cloisterman sceptically. 'How you've made your peace with the Amsterdam authorities I prefer not to know. I've not called you here for the purpose of recrimination. Circumstances do not afford me the leisure for such an exercise.' This, Dalrymple's expression implied, was something he regretted. 'Do you realize the degree of uncertainty that hovers over all our futures under the new Secretary of State?'

'Lord Townshend is clearly not the same man as Lord Stanhope.'

'He is not even his own man, Cloisterman. Walpole tells him what to think and do. And he will tell many more what to think and do before long. Brodrick's committee was due to report to the House of Commons today. Did you know that?'

'I confess not.'

'Their charges, whatever they are, will only strengthen Walpole's hand. It is his tune we must dance to now. You understand? We cannot allow him to doubt our loyalty.'

'I'm sure he will have no cause to.'

'In that case, you will be glad to learn that you have an opportunity to demonstrate your loyalty to the new order.'

'Oh yes?' Cloisterman did not feel glad. Quite the reverse. He felt an apprehensiveness amounting almost to dread. 'What manner of opportunity?'

'A special emissary of Lord Townshend – and hence Walpole – is waiting for you at the Goude Hooft. It's an inn not far from here. Harris will show you the way. The emissary's a military man. Colonel Augustus Wagemaker. A straighter sort than McIlwraith, but just as tough, I should say.'

'And he's waiting for *me*?'

'Yes. You know more about this whole damnable business than anyone else. You're the obvious choice.'

'For what?'

'Wagemaker will explain his requirements to you. You will do your best – your very best – to comply with them.'

'Can you give me no idea what they are?'

'Onerous, I shouldn't wonder. Though well within your compass. You're going on a journey, Cloisterman.' Dalrymple's smile had crept back out from its hiding place. 'And it could be a long one.'

The contents of the Brodrick Committee's report, at which Dalrymple could still only guess, were by now already known to the House of Commons in London. It had taken four hours for the document to be read, by Brodrick until his voice gave out and then by the Clerk of the House. The complexities and obscurities of the tale it told were formidable but, so far as the Government was concerned, the charges were horribly simple. Bribes, in the form of free allocations of South Sea stock which could be sold later at a guaranteed profit, had been paid to certain ministers to ensure that they turned a blind eye to glaring irregularities in the National Debt conversion scheme, irregularities that had left the Company with liabilities for the year ahead of £14,500,000 to be set against income from the Exchequer of £2,000,000: insolvency, in other words, on a grand, not to say grotesque, scale. The ministers named as recipients of bribes were, as expected, Chancellor of the Exchequer John Aislabie, Postmaster-General James Craggs the elder, Secretary to the Treasury Charles Stanhope and, as less confidently anticipated . . . the First Lord of the Treasury and Groom of the Stole, Charles Spencer, third Earl of Sunderland.

How the House would proceed in the light of such a damning report was still unclear when it adjourned for the evening. Impeachment of the named ministers was the obvious course, but that would mean entrusting verdict and punishment to the Lords. Many favoured trying them, peers and all, along with the directors, in the Commons. The decision on that would have to wait for another day.

Some matters would not wait, however. The report had accused the Secretary of State for the Southern Department, James Craggs the younger, not of accepting a bribe himself but of negotiating bribes for the Duchess of Kendal and her so-called nieces. The Duchess, born Ehrengard Melusina von der Schulenburg, was none other than the King's openly acknowledged mistress. The King's wife had been confined in a German castle for the past twenty-seven years after being divorced on grounds of non-cohabitation following an affair with a Swedish count. The Duchess's 'nieces' were in reality her daughters by the King. Their corruption, if proved, would creep close to the person of the King himself. Craggs could not be interrogated on the point. Smallpox held him in its mortal grip. And his fellow Secretary of State, Viscount Townshend, had nothing to answer for. But one awkward duty did devolve upon him: that of explaining to his fretful monarch how the royal ladies' reputations were to be protected.

Thus it was that at an unheard-of hour for such summonses, Lord Townshend found himself being ushered into the royal closet at St James's Palace by the Turkish Groom of the Chamber, the notoriously inscrutable Mehemet. The scarcely less inscrutable Earl of Sunderland was already present. He had a narrow, skewed face that seemed forever suspended between a smile and a frown. His eyes were close-set and evasive. He greeted Townshend with his customary coolness, clearly unabashed by being accused in the Commons earlier that evening of accepting £50,000 worth of South Sea stock as virtual hush-money.

But if Sunderland was calm in the face of the storm, the King was not. He had always been a difficult man to read, what with his stilted English, his immobile features and his unsociable temperament, but it was apparent to Townshend that the committee's traduction of his beloved mistress had hit a tender spot. 'They had not the right to say these things,' he complained through gritted teeth. 'Mr Craggs was helping to the Duchess. What is wrong with that?'

'I'm sure Lord Townshend doesn't think there was anything wrong,' said Sunderland.

'Indeed not, Your Majesty,' Townshend swiftly rejoined. 'And I'm confident the purchase of shares by the Duchess is not what will occupy the House in its consideration of the report.' (She had not purchased them, of course, but it was as well to subscribe to the fiction that she had.)

'The purchase of shares by *anyone*,' said the King with heavy emphasis, 'is out of their business.'

Townshend glanced at Sunderland. What – or rather whom – did the King mean by 'anyone'? It was a certain bet that his Groom of the Stole knew the answer. 'I fear, sir, that they will make it their business.'

'Perhaps your brother-in-law could dissuade them from doing so,' said Sunderland, with more of his smile than his frown.

'He did dissuade them from printing the report.'

'Printing?' The King's face was briefly lit by horror. 'We want no printing.'

'And there will be none, sir.'

'His Majesty is concerned about Mr Knight's . . . papers, Townshend. How is it that your department has failed to secure all of them?'

'Knight took steps to keep some of his more . . . sensitive . . . records from us. But we're on the track of them.'

'Track?' queried Sunderland. 'You speak literally?'

'Where is it?' the King put in, adding in an explanatory growl, '*Das Grüne Buch*.' He was apparently unable to bring himself to describe the article in English.

'We're doing everything we can to find it, sir.'

'We?' Sunderland's eyebrows twitched up.

'My department,' said Townshend levelly.

'Assisted and advised, no doubt, by your brother-in-law.'

'The Paymaster-General does what he can.'

'So he does. But you should beware. The robin is by nature a solitary bird.'

'In the present circumstances, Spencer, I should have thought you had more to beware of than me.'

'The report? It's nothing.' Sunderland flapped a dismissive hand. 'They can't touch me.'

'Without the Green Book, you mean?'

'I mean—' Sunderland broke off, apparently deciding that what he really meant was better not disclosed. 'They wouldn't have the nerve,' he eventually added. 'I made most of them. And I can break the rest.'

'Break them,' the King said suddenly, rousing himself from the reverie into which he had sunk while his two ministers bickered. '*Ja*. That is what you must do.'

'With the greatest respect, sir,' said Townshend, 'the Commons are not to be broken. But they may be controlled. With young Mr Craggs so ill and his father and Mr Aislabie accused of serious lapses, it is as well for us all that Mr Walpole is there to defend your Government. And that, I assure you, he is doing tirelessly.' Sunderland sniffed derisively but, holding the King's eye, Townshend went on. 'There is only so much that Lord Sunderland and I can accomplish in the Lords, sir. This will be settled by the Commons. Mr Walpole is trying his very best to hold them in check. If anyone can do it, he is the man.'

'Walpole,' said the King musingly. 'Can we trust him?'

'I trust him,' Townshend replied.

'And it seems,' Sunderland put in, 'that the rest of us will have to.'

Walpole was in truth a harder man to trust than Townshend cared to admit. He was so warm, so amiable, so vastly confiding. Townshend had been to Eton and Cambridge with him, had married his sister, had dined and hunted and argued and caroused with him down the years; yet still did not know, most of the time, what was in his mind. Beyond Walpole's many confidences, there were always other purposes he was set upon serving.

One such had taken him from the House of Commons that night to the Tower of London, a journey of which

142

Townshend knew, and was to know, nothing. Walpole had been confined there once himself and wished for no reminder of that nadir of his political fortunes. But Sir Theodore Janssen could hardly be summoned to Westminster. And Sir Theodore he had to see.

'This is a surprise,' the elderly financier admitted when his visitor was shown in. 'And an honour, I suppose.'

'We must talk, Janssen,' Walpole said brusquely. 'And we must do so to the point. If I want to thrust and parry, I shall hire a fencing master.'

'And what is the point, Mr Walpole?'

'You know Brodrick's committee reported to the Commons today?'

'Of course. A pretty scene, no doubt. And a distressing one, I should imagine, for several of your fellow ministers. The Governor will soon be running short of accommodation here.'

'I don't care about my fellow ministers, Janssen. I care about myself. I suppose *you* care about *yourself.*'

'Naturally.'

'This is no state for a gentleman of your age and distinction to find himself in.' Walpole glanced around the chamber. 'Now is it?'

'I'm forced to agree.'

'I want the Green Book.' Walpole smiled. 'And I have no time for shilly-shally.'

'So it would appear.'

'What do *you* want, Sir Theodore?'

'To live the years that remain to me in freedom and comfort.'

'Not likely, as things presently stand.'

'Alas no.'

'Where's your valet, by the by? I'm told he no longer visits. Who shaves you now I don't know, but, by the look of your chin, he's no barber.'

'The comings and goings of servants are surely beneath your concern.'

'Nothing is beneath my concern.' Walpole lowered his voice. 'Where is Jupe?'

'I wish I knew. As you're so kind to point out, I have need of him.'

'But I suspect he's serving those needs. Even if you don't know his whereabouts. I'll put it simply for you. Knight gave you the Green Book for safe-keeping. But you've lost it. And Jupe has gone in search of it.'

'That is the most—'

'Don't deny it. It would be a waste of your time as well as mine. Some weeks from now, the Commons will decide how to punish you for your part in this catastrophe. You'll need powerful friends then to escape imprisonment or penury or both. But you have none. They're all dead or fled or in the same boat as you. Your only hope is me. I can help you, Sir Theodore. And I will. If you help me.'

Several seconds of silence followed while the two men looked at each other. Then Sir Theodore said, 'What do you want?'

'I've told you. The Green Book.'

'I don't have it. Nor do I know where it is.'

'But that may change. If it should, I want to be the first to hear.'

'Very well. I agree.'

'You do?'

'What choice do I have?'

'You have the choice of thinking you may be able to deceive me. Knight gave you the book so that it could be removed to a place of safety and used to bargain for clemency. There can have been no other reason. You may suppose that can still be done. But you would be in error. I cannot be forced to help you. I can only be persuaded.'

'Then I must try to persuade you.'

'So you must.'

'Persuasion is a two-edged sword, though. I have opened the book. I know what it contains.'

'I felt sure you did.'

'Do you?'

'How could I?'

'How indeed? But there's the strangest thing. I have the impression, you see – the very distinct impression – that you know exactly what the book contains. If so, you'll also know that prevailing on the House of Commons to treat me leniently would be a trifling price to pay for keeping those contents secret.'

'Trifling to me, perhaps.' Walpole winked. 'But everything to you.'

'Everything may be exactly what's at stake.' Sir Theodore rubbed his ill-shaven chin. 'If the book should fall into . . . the wrong hands.'

'It's certainly a pity you didn't take better care of it.'

'A pity, you say?' Sir Theodore summoned a defiant smile. 'As to that, Mr Walpole, it's a pity a great many people – a great many *grand* people – didn't take better care.'

As one conversation was ending at the Tower of London, so another, bearing on the same subject, was beginning at the Goude Hooft inn in The Hague. Cloisterman had found Colonel Wagemaker waiting for him in a balconied booth above the cavernous tap-room and had instantly formed a less favourable impression of Lord Townshend's emissary than the one given him by Dalrymple: 'A *straighter sort than McIlwraith, but just as tough.'* That was true as far as it went, but it did not capture the spine-shivering balefulness of the man. There was a flint-hard edge to him, but no spark of passion.

Cloisterman was surprised to find himself thinking fondly of McIlwraith as he falteringly met Wagemaker's icy gaze.

'You travel light, Mr Cloisterman,' Wagemaker said. 'That's good.'

'As a matter of fact, Colonel, I don't travel light. An overnight journey from Amsterdam to The Hague is scarcely the Grand Tour.'

'Nor's the journey we'll be undertaking. But it may last as long.'

'Mr Dalrymple said something of the kind. I should appreciate—'

'You know what this is all about?'

'Knight's ledger. Yes, I know.'

'And you're skilled in the consular arts, I'm told.'

'I like to think so.'

'I can't afford to be held up. I'm a soldier, not a politician. But I may need to be a politician to win through. That's when you'll earn your keep.'

'I've no wish to "earn my keep", as you put it. I have duties in Amsterdam I'd be happy to return to.'

'You'll not see Amsterdam again in a hurry. We're heading south.'

'South?'

'That's where Zuyler and Mrs de Vries will have gone. I'm told you know Mrs de Vries by sight.'

'I've met her a few times in company with her late husb—'

'Good enough. You also know Spandrel.'

'Yes.'

'And Jupe.'

'Well, yes. Captain McIlwraith, too, if it comes to—'

'*I* know McIlwraith, Mr Cloisterman. Of old.' For the first time, there was a spark of some emotion in Wagemaker's eyes. And it was not friendship. 'You can leave him to me.'

146

'When you say south . . .'

'Zuyler and Mrs de Vries will try to sell the ledger to the Jacobites. It's obvious.'

'You mean they'll take it to the Pretender? In Rome?'

'They'll try. But we must overtake them before they reach their destination and retrieve the ledger. We must also overtake McIlwraith and Jupe. They're all ahead of us. But not so far ahead that they can't be caught. Any of them.'

'This sounds distinctly . . . perilous.'

'There'll be difficulties. There may be dangers. That's to be expected.'

'Not by me. I have no experience of such endeavours. I am *not* a soldier, Colonel.'

'You don't need to tell me that.' Wagemaker ran a withering eye over him. 'But it seems you're the best I'll get.'

Cloisterman did not sleep well that night. Wagemaker meant to leave at dawn and, reluctant though he was, Cloisterman would be leaving with him. He cursed Dalrymple for volunteering his services, suspecting as he did that they were a handy substitute for Dalrymple's own. He cursed his luck as well. Amsterdam had turned out to be the right place at the wrong time. Hard riding and harsh dealing lay ahead and he was not sure which he was worse equipped for. Yet there was no way out, short of resigning his post and returning to England to face an uncertain and impecunious future. There was not much sign of a way *through* either. It was the very devil of a business. But it was the devil he was bound to serve.

Chapter Fifteen

The Road South

The pace McIlwraith set was predictably stiff. Spandrel, who had not ridden in over a year and had never done so regularly, was saddle-sore and weary before they left Dutch territory. He was sustained to that point by fear of recapture. Once they were on the winding high road of the Rhine Valley, however, he began to protest and plead for a day's rest. He was wasting his breath, of course. McIlwraith's hopes of overhauling Zuyler and Estelle de Vries rested on the likelihood that they were not naturally fast travellers and had no particular reason to fear pursuit. They were not fools, though. The Green Book was a slowly wasting asset and a dangerous article to possess. The sooner they reached Rome and sold it the better.

At the Grau Gans, Cologne's principal coaching inn, McIlwraith gleaned the first confirmation of their route. An English couple by the name of Kemp, the husband an excellent speaker of German, had stayed at the inn a week before. They had been travelling by chaise, but seemed embarked on a journey calling for a more robust vehicle. A wheelwright had been needed to replace some splintered spokes. And they had asked the landlord to recommend other inns on the road to Switzerland.

This discovery put McIlwraith in high good humour. He drank more, and talked more, in the tap-room that evening than he had at any time since leaving Amsterdam.

Spandrel drank his fill as well and was soon too fuddled to follow what was being said. He retained a vague memory of McIlwraith reminiscing about the number of men he had killed in battle and an occasion on which, apparently, the Captain-General himself, the Duke of Marlborough, had sought his tactical advice. There was something too about secret missions behind enemy lines. But here Spandrel's memory grew vaguer still. As perhaps did McIlwraith's reminiscences.

The captain showed no ill effects of his over-indulgence next morning, rousing Spandrel before dawn and insisting on an early start. Spandrel, for his part, had a thick head that a few hours on horseback transformed into a ferociously aching one, the spot where Zuyler had hit him with the hammer throbbing to eye-watering effect. When he complained, McIlwraith suggested he should treat it as a useful reminder of the Dutchman's treachery, which he now had the chance to avenge.

But vengeance was far from Spandrel's thoughts. The simple joy of freedom had given place to a nagging fear that he was simply wading deeper and deeper into a morass. If his experiences since leaving London had taught him anything, it was that humble folk should never meddle – nor even allow themselves to become remotely involved – in the affairs of the great. Yet, here he was, straying still further into them. Green Books and Jacobites could easily be the death of him. If they were, he would have no-one to blame but himself. And no-one else would care anyway. But what was he to do? McIlwraith had him where he wanted him: by his side. And that was where he was bound to remain. Until . . .

When? That was the question. If the Kemps *were* Zuyler and Estelle de Vries, they were a week ahead of them. That could amount to three hundred miles. Spandrel did not see how such a gap could be closed, however hard they rode. Much the likeliest outcome, it seemed to him, was that it would *not* be closed. They would reach Rome too late to prevent the sale of the book. In some ways, he hoped he was right. There would be nothing they could do, but he would have done what was required of him and might hope for some modest reward. In other ways, he knew that to be a fool's counsel. If they failed, there would be no reward for him, other than abandonment far from home.

It was better than imprisonment in Amsterdam, of course. Compared with what had seemed to lie in wait for him only a few days previously, this journey was a gift from the gods. It was just that with nothing but un-certainty waiting at the end of it and a cold head wind seeming to blow down the valley whenever a sleety drizzle did not descend from the mountains, a gift could soon feel like a curse.

'Don't look so long-faced, man,' McIlwraith upbraided him over supper that night, which they spent at an inn near Coblenz where the Kemps had not been heard of. 'I feed and horse you. I even think for you. Ah . . .' He pointed at Spandrel with his fork, on which half a gravy-smeared potato was impaled. 'That's it, isn't it? You've been thinking on your own account. You don't want to get into that habit. It's not a bit of good for you.'

Good for him or not, though, Spandrel continued to think – and to worry. About what would happen if and when they overtook their quarry. And about what would happen if they never did.

Spandrel might have been even more worried had he realized, as McIlwraith certainly did, that they were also being pursued. Their surreptitious exit from Dutch terri-tory had necessitated an indirect and time-consuming route as far as Cologne. Their original lead had thus

150

been pared down to barely a day. Wagemaker and Cloisterman spent that night at the Grau Gans, where they too heard about the English couple in the chaise – and about the pair of travellers who had expressed an interest in them the previous night.

It had been a physically exhausting and mentally wearing two days on the road for Cloisterman since their departure from The Hague. Wagemaker was a taciturn and unsympathetic travelling companion, who seemed to think Cloisterman's command of German and his ability to recognize several of the people they were looking for compensated for his poor horsemanship and lack of stamina – but only just. Cloisterman resented this, but had been poorly placed to do much about it. Revived and emboldened by the Grau Gans's food and wine, however, he decided to hit back in the only way he could, by questioning Wagemaker's tactics.

'We may be close to McIlwraith and Spandrel, Colonel, but we're all of us a long way behind the two people who actually have what we're trying to retrieve. I fail to understand how you hope to catch up with them.'

'I reckon we will.'

'And on what is your . . . reckoning . . . based?'

'It's based on the fact that when Zuyler and Mrs de Vries reach Switzerland, they'll have a hard choice to make. To cross the Alps? Or to take a boat down the Rhône to Marseilles, then look for a sea passage to Naples, say, and hope to travel up to Rome from there?'

'They can't go down the Rhône,' said Cloisterman, suddenly beginning to follow Wagemaker's reasoning.

'Why not?'

'Because of the outbreak of plague in Marseilles last summer. The port's still closed. There's no traffic on the Rhône. Most of Provence is reported to be in a state of chaos. Nobody in their right mind would try to go that way.'

151

'So I hear too. Which way will they go, then?'

'Over the Alps. They have to.'

'At this time of the year? I'd think twice about doing it alone. With a woman . . . it's asking for trouble.'

'What choice do they have?'

'They could wait for milder weather.'

'But that could mean waiting for a month or more.'

'So, they won't wait. But I don't think they're equal to it. I think they'll try the crossing and abandon the attempt when they realize how difficult and dangerous it is. And by then . . .' Wagemaker's right hand closed around an imaginary throat. 'They'll be within our reach.'

'And within McIlwraith's.'

'Yes. Jupe's as well. But if it had been easy . . .' Wagemaker unclenched his hand and stared at his palm. 'They wouldn't have sent me.'

The death from smallpox at the age of thirty-five of Secretary of State James Craggs the younger did not distract the House of Commons for many moments from its pursuit of the ministers named in the Brodrick Committee report. Walpole's recommendation of impeachment before the Lords was ignored, though whether this displeased him or not was hard to tell. Instead, the Commons voted to hear the cases themselves, which happened to mean that Walpole would be able to play a full part in the trials and influence their outcomes . . . one way or the other.

'The taking in, or holding of stock, by the South Sea Company for the benefit of any member of either House of Parliament or person concerned in the Administration (during the time that the Company's Proposals or the Bill relating thereto were depending in Parliament) without giving valuable consideration paid,' the House resolved after several days' debate, 'were corrupt, infamous and dangerous practices, highly reflecting on the Honour and Justice of Parliament and destructive of the Interest of His Majesty's Government.'

The charge was laid. Now, those accused would have to answer to it.

The trial of the first of those accused, Charles Stanhope, was still pending when McIlwraith and Spandrel crossed the Swiss border just outside Basle, one long and gruelling week after crossing the Dutch border nearly five hundred miles to the north. They had been detained at Heidelberg for the best part of a day by the need to obtain certificates of health from a hard-pressed doctor appointed by the local magistrate. Without them, Swiss customs officers were sure to turn them back on the grounds that they might be plague-carriers who had crept into the Palatinate from France. Another wrangle over certification had followed at Freiburg, where they had strayed into the Austrian enclave of Breisgau. McIlwraith had raged against these delays and pressed ever harder on the road to compensate for them. Spandrel's memory was of bone-weary rides in seemingly permanent twilight along frozen tracks through the snow-hushed fringes of endless forest. Travel, he had learned, was not the exhilarating experience he had dreamed it might be when gazing at his father's maps as a child.

Of Zuyler and Estelle de Vries there had been intermittent news suggesting that they were now only a few days ahead. Spandrel consoled himself with the thought that they were unlikely to be enjoying the journey any more than he was. Of Jupe, however, there was no trace, which had prompted Spandrel to suggest he might have given up. But McIlwraith had poured scorn on this idea. 'He's had the good sense to travel alone, man. That's all it is. I wish I'd followed his example, instead of hoppling myself with someone who rides like a nun on a donkey *and* never stops complaining.'

Despite the frequency of such insults, Spandrel had grown strangely fond of his companion. McIlwraith seemed to be just about the only person he had met since leaving England to have told him the truth, uncomfortable though it sometimes was. It was not so much that Spandrel trusted him, as that he felt safe with him. There was a reassuring solidity of body and purpose to the man. He had driven Spandrel hard, but nothing like as hard as he had driven himself.

In Switzerland, it seemed clear, their journey would reach its crisis. With the Rhône closed, the only route to Italy lay over the Alps. And in late winter, the only pass worth considering was the Simplon. McIlwraith expected the chase to end there. How it would end he did not say. Perhaps he did not know. Or perhaps, Spandrel reflected, he did not think it wise to disclose.

They left Basle early next morning and crossed the Jura ridge in fine, dry, cold weather. Spandrel had anticipated that the Alps would be craggier and perhaps snowier versions of the Black Forest peaks they had passed. When he first saw them massing on the horizon ahead, however, vast and white and forbidding, he realized just what kind of a barrier they represented and could hardly imagine that there was a way through them.

'They strike fear into your heart, don't they, Spandrel?' said McIlwraith. 'But remember. They'll do the same for our soft-bred Dutchman and his lady love. We have them now. Like rats in a trap.'

They descended from the ridge into the Aare valley and followed its winding course south as far as Berne. The city occupied a steep-banked lobe of land jutting out into a deep eastward loop of the river. They arrived at dusk, entering by one of the gates in the defensive wall on the western side. It was, for Spandrel, just one more in a succession of tired, travel-stained, twilit arrivals. Berne appeared no different from anywhere else they had been. The gateman recommended an inn: the Drei Tassen. They made their weary way to it along ill-lit, cobbled streets. They took a room, stabled the horses and went to the tap-room in search of food and drink. It was a routine they had followed in half a dozen other cities.

After the meal, McIlwraith lit his pipe and gazed broodily at the fire. This too was his custom. There had been no repetition of the drunken reminiscences he had permitted himself in Cologne. Spandrel was warm and replete now. Soon, he was having difficulty keeping his eyes open. He hauled his aching limbs out of the settle and announced he was off to bed. McIlwraith nodded a goodnight to him and stayed where he was. Spandrel knew it could easily be another couple of hours before the captain turned in. But he would still be up again before dawn. Sleep was not something he seemed to need much of.

Spandrel, on the other hand, needed every hour he could snatch. He paused in the passage leading to the stairs, then turned and headed for the yard at the rear of the inn. Cold as it was outdoors, a visit to the jakes before he crawled between the sheets could not be avoided.

A few minutes later, he was on his way back across the yard, hugging himself for warmth. As he neared the inn door, a figure stepped into his path from the darkness beyond the reach of the lantern that burned above the lintel.

'Spandrel.'

The voice came as no more than a whisper. Even so, Spandrel knew at once that he recognized it. He could not

155

put a name to the voice, however. Stopping just before he collided with the man, he squinted at him through the shadows cast by the lantern.

'What are you doing here, Spandrel?'

'Who's there?'

'Don't you know me?'

'I . . . I'm not sure.'

The man stepped back, allowing the light from the lantern to fall across his face. Now Spandrel saw him plainly for who he was.

'You.'

'Yes.' The man nodded. 'Me.'

'What do you want?'

'An answer to my question. You're supposed to be in prison in Amsterdam, awaiting trial for murder. So, what are you . . . and your new-found friend . . . doing here – exactly?'

Chapter Sixteen

A Handful of Air

'I thought you were away to bed,' said McIlwraith, frowning up at Spandrel from his fireside chair. Then he looked across to the man who had accompanied Spandrel back into the tap-room. 'Who's this spindle-shanks?'

'I am Nicodemus Jupe, sir.'

'Sir, is it? I like the sound of you more than the look of you, Jupe, I'll say that. I suppose we were bound to tread on your coat-tails before long. But I didn't expect you to call on us to pay your respects. What do you want?'

'He thinks we should—'

'Let him speak for himself,' barked McIlwraith, cutting off Spandrel's explanation. 'Well?'

'Could we find somewhere a little more private?' Jupe glanced around. 'I'm sure you won't want our affairs widely known, sir.'

'*Our* affairs?' McIlwraith grunted. 'There's a reading-room of sorts on the other side of the passage. With no fire lit, we should have it to ourselves. The chill will keep you awake, Spandrel, even if Jupe's conversation fails to enthral. Lead the way.'

A few moments later, they were in the reading-room, with the door closed behind them. There were desks and chairs spaced around wood-panelled walls. A large bookcase held an assortment of atlases, almanacs and Bibles. A single copy of a Bernese newspaper lay on the table in the centre of the room, beneath a chandelier in which barely half the candles were lit. It was, as McIlwraith had predicted, breath-mistingly cold.

'Say your piece,' growled McIlwraith, propping himself against the table to listen. 'You can begin with how you knew we were here.'

'Apparently, the gatemen always recommend this inn, sir. No doubt the landlord makes it worth their while.'

'Are you staying here?'

'No, sir.'

'Then you were looking for us?'

'I knew someone would follow. It was inevitable. I've been . . . keeping my eye open.'

'But lodging elsewhere. Why's that?'

'I'll explain that in a moment, sir.'

'Stop calling me sir. You're not in my troop, thank God.'

'Very well . . . Captain.'

'How much has Spandrel told you?'

'Only that you're an agent for the Brodrick Committee. I was afraid you might represent the Government.'

'What do you care who I represent?'

'I care a good deal, Captain. We want the same thing. The Green Book.'

'Which your master did his best to put out of the committee's reach. The same thing? Aye. But not for the same reason.'

'Circumstances have changed. Our reasons now coincide.'

'How do you reckon that?'

'Sir Theodore's best hope of lenient treatment by the committee is to help them. By surrendering the Green Book to them rather than the Government. He and Mr Knight originally planned to force the Government to protect them by threatening to publish the contents of the book. You see I tell you so quite openly. I'm concealing nothing.'

'And poor Spandrel here was to die to make sure that threat could be safely made.'

'It seems so. But that wasn't my fault. I only did what Sir Theodore told me to do.'

'And no doubt you're still doing his bidding.'

'Sir Theodore instructed me to retrieve the book and prevent it falling into the wrong hands. There'll be a Government agent not so very far behind you and I can't risk him succeeding where you or I might fail. My chances of securing the book alone are slim. I need your help.'

'But do we need yours, Jupe? That's the question.'

'You do. Because I know where the book is.'

'Oh, you do, do you?' McIlwraith pushed himself upright and took a step towards Jupe. 'Well, why don't you tell us?'

'May I see your House of Commons warrant first, Captain?' Jupe stood his ground unflinchingly. 'I need to be sure you're what Spandrel says you are.'

'Hah!' McIlwraith laughed, as if impressed by Jupe's steadiness of nerve. He plucked the warrant out from his pocket and handed it over. 'Satisfied?' he asked after a moment.

'Perfectly.' Jupe handed the warrant back. 'Your intention would be to deliver the book to General Ross in London?'

'Or Mr Brodrick. It makes no matter. But that *is* what I mean to do.'

'And you'd be willing to afford me safe passage back to London with you?'

'I could see my way to doing that, aye.'

'It's all I ask.'

'Consider it done. *If* you lead us to the book.'

'I can do that very easily.'

'How?'

'Zuyler and Mrs de Vries arrived here yesterday.'

'They're in Berne?'

'Yes. They've made no move to leave as yet. I've taken a room in the lodging-house they're staying in. They don't know me, of course. But I know them. Mr and Mrs Kemp, they call themselves. The Drei Tassen was obviously too popular for their liking. They preferred somewhere quieter. But not quiet enough. It didn't take me long to find where they're hiding. They've not been out much. When they do leave the house, they lock their door securely. But I expect they take the book with them wherever they go, so there'd be no point forcing an entrance when they're not there. And when they are there . . .' Jupe shrugged. 'Mijnheer de Vries's fate suggests Zuyler would be quite prepared to kill anyone trying to wrest the book from them.'

'Which is why you haven't tried to do so single-handed.'

'It is. I admit it.'

'Why haven't they headed on south?'

'Gathering their strength for the crossing of the Alps, perhaps. Making inquiries as to the best way to go about it. Who knows? You could ask them yourself, though. This very night.'

'So I could.' McIlwraith smiled. 'And so I believe I will.'

It was late now, but the taverns remained busy and a few hardy chestnut-mongers were still stooped over their braziers at the corners of the streets. They headed east along the main thoroughfare of the city, past a squat clock tower and on between tall, arcaded housefronts. A chill mist thickened as they neared the river, blurring the light from the lanterns that hung between the arches.

Whether McIlwraith had any doubts about the wisdom of what he seemed set upon doing Spandrel did not know.

The captain was armed, of course, and had loaded his pistols before they set off. For his part, Spandrel felt torn between an eagerness to share in the humiliation of the two people who had happily let him take the blame for their crime and a suspicion that things could surely not fall out as simply as they promised to. Jupe had explained himself logically enough. And to take them unawares was the tactic most likely to succeed. Yet Spandrel could not rid himself of a nagging doubt. This silent march through empty streets reminded him of the night he had broken into the de Vries house in Amsterdam. His expectations had been confounded then. And, for all he knew, they might be again.

A slender church spire stretched up into the night sky behind them as they started to descend to the river, then was blotted out by the mist. Jupe led them down a narrow side-street and stopped at a door above which a lantern burned, illuminating the sign *Pension Siegwart* over the bell. He looked up at the windows on the upper floors, then pressed a cautionary finger to his lips.

'There's a light in their room,' he whispered.

'No matter,' McIlwraith replied, his own whisper sounding like a file scraping on rough wood. 'We'll take them as we find them.' He closed the shutter on the lantern he had been carrying and handed it to Spandrel. 'Open up, Jupe.'

Jupe slipped the pass-key from his pocket, unlocked the door and pushed it carefully open. There was a single lamp burning in the hall. More light – and a burble of voices – seeped up from the basement. They stepped inside and Jupe closed the door. 'Their room is the first floor front,' he said in an undertone. 'The best in the house.'

'Well, that'll save us a clamber up to the attics, won't it?' said McIlwraith. 'Lead on, man.'

161

Jupe set off up the stairs. McIlwraith signalled for Spandrel to follow and brought up the rear himself. There were a few creaks from the treads as they climbed, but Spandrel still caught the ominous click of a pistol being cocked behind him. He wanted to stop and ask McIlwraith if he was sure he was acting for the best. Above all, he wanted to slow the pace of events. But he knew it made no real sense to do so. McIlwraith was the hardened soldier and was well aware of the advantage of surprising the enemy. It was not an advantage he had any intention of letting slip.

But surprise comes in many guises. They reached the landing and doubled back to the door at the far end. A wavering line of light could be seen beneath it. And a moving shadow, as of someone pacing up and down between the lamp and the door. Then, as they drew closer, Spandrel caught the distinct sound of a sob. The voice, he felt sure, was female.

'A lovers' tiff, perhaps,' McIlwraith whispered in his ear. 'That could suit us well.' He moved past Spandrel to Jupe's shoulder. 'They lock the door when they go out, you said. What about when they're in?'

'I don't know.'

'Then try it, man.' McIlwraith stepped back and raised one of his pistols. 'Now.'

Jupe reached out, turned the handle and pushed.

The door opened and McIlwraith strode into the room. Over his shoulder, Spandrel saw Estelle de Vries turn and stare at him in astonishment. 'Cry out and it'll be the last sound you make, madam.' McIlwraith pointed the pistol at her and glanced around. 'Where's Zuyler?'

The best room in the house amounted to a sparsely furnished chamber boasting a four-poster bed that seemed to belong in more spacious surroundings, a single chair, a chest of drawers and a rickety dressing-table. There were no doors to other rooms and Zuyler was nowhere to be seen. Estelle de Vries was wearing a plain dress and shawl. Her hair was awry, one strand falling across her cheek. Her face was pale and drawn, her eyes red and swollen. As she pushed back the wayward strand of hair with a shaking hand, Spandrel saw that there was a bruise forming over the cheekbone. 'You,' she murmured, her shock turning to a frozen look of horror as their eyes met. 'Oh, dear God.'

'Where's Zuyler?' McIlwraith repeated.

'Not . . .' She shook her head. 'Not here.'

'Close the door, Jupe. Is the key in the lock?'

'Yes.'

'Turn it. We'll need warning of Zuyler's return.'

'Mr Spandrel,' said Mrs de Vries in a fluttering voice. 'How . . . did you . . .'

'Escape from the trap you set for me?' Spandrel hoped he sounded more bitter than he felt. She deserved every reproach he could fashion. Yet finding her as she was – distraught, deserted for all he knew – he could not help feeling a pang of sorrow for her. 'Why should you care?'

'It was thanks to me,' said McIlwraith, uncocking the pistol. 'Captain James McIlwraith, madam. Special representative of the House of Commons Secret Committee of Inquiry into the South Sea Company.'

'The . . . what?'

'This is Jupe,' he went on. 'Valet to Sir Theodore Janssen. You may have seen him before. He's been following you. As have we.'

'I don't understand.'

'I think you do. We want the Green Book.'

'Book? What book?'

'Come, come, madam. You and your paramour tried to sell it to the British Government. And now you're on your way to Rome to hawk it round the Pretender's court. It's useless to pretend otherwise.'

'Useless?' She looked at McIlwraith, then at Spandrel, then back at McIlwraith.

'Utterly.'

'And who did you say you represent?'

'The House of Commons Secret Committee of Inquiry into the South Sea Company.'

'You mean the Government?'

'No, madam. The House of Commons. You're English, for pity's sake. You must know the difference.'

'Of course. I . . . I thought . . .' She put her hand to her brow and squeezed her eyes briefly shut, then fingered away some tears from their edges. 'May I sit down?'

'By all means.' McIlwraith pulled the chair back for her with a flourish. She sank into it. 'Where is the Green Book?'

To Spandrel's amazement, she laughed, then took her handkerchief from her sleeve and dabbed at her eyes. 'Forgive me. It is . . . almost funny.'

'I pride myself on my sense of humour,' said McIlwraith, placing a heavy hand on the back of the chair. 'But I regret to say the joke has eluded me. Where's the book?'

'I don't have it.'

'Does Zuyler?'

'No.'

'Then what's become of it?'

'It's gone.'

'Gone where . . . exactly?'

'Into the river.'

'What?'

'I threw it into the river.'

'You destroyed it?' put in Jupe.

'Yes.' She nodded. 'I did.'

'We don't believe you,' said McIlwraith.

'I don't blame you. I hardly believe it myself. But it's true.'

'You threw it into the river?'

'Yes. I walked out onto the bridge down there' – she

164

gestured towards the river – 'and tossed the book over the parapet. Then I watched it being borne away in the current. The river's in spate. It bobbed along like a piece of driftwood, until the water soaked into the pages and weighed it down. Then it sank. Or I lost sight of it in the turbulence. It makes no difference. Ink and paper don't fare well in water. There's a sodden lump of something on the riverbed a few miles downstream, I dare say. But for the only purposes you care about, it's gone.'

A brief silence fell. There had been such a ring of truth in what Estelle de Vries had said that the three men were momentarily struck dumb. Had she really done it? If so, only one question mattered. And it was McIlwraith who posed it. 'Why?'

'Because some things matter more than money. Such as love. Or the loss of it.' Her head fell. 'Pieter and I . . .'

'Fell out?'

'Everything I did was for him. For us. Our future.'

'Such as murdering your husband?'

'Have you ever been in love, Captain?'

'Aye. For my pains, I have.'

'But you're a man. You cannot love as a woman does. Not just with her heart. But with every fibre of her being. You do not understand.'

'Make me understand.'

'Very well. I adored Pieter. I worshipped him. I did whatever he said we had to do to escape . . .' She shuddered. 'From de Vries. Yes, I helped Pieter kill him. And I lied to blacken Mr Spandrel's name.' She turned and looked at Spandrel. 'For that I am truly sorry.'

'Not as sorry as I am,' said Spandrel, wondering if she grasped the doubleness of his meaning.

'All de Vries's money goes to his son,' she went on.

'We know,' said McIlwraith. 'But why should that worry someone who loves with every fibre of her being?'

165

'It didn't. But Pieter . . . said we had to have money if he was to keep me in the manner he wished to. He could not bear the thought of me living in poverty. And with the Green Book . . .'

'There was no need to see whether your love would thrive in adversity.'

'No. Exactly. We were greedy, of course. I don't deny it.'

'That's as well.'

'It wasn't all greed, though. Not for me.'

'But for Zuyler?'

'Perhaps.' She gave a crumpled little smile. 'When we arrived here yesterday, he told me that he would have to go on alone. That the Alpine crossing would be too much for me. I assured him it would not. But he insisted. He would leave me here, travel on to Rome alone and then return to fetch me when he had sold the book. But in his eyes I could see the truth. He wasn't coming back for me. It had all been for the money. And he didn't mean to share it. He didn't love me. He never had. I'd merely been the instrument of his enrichment. We argued. But he didn't change his mind. There was, of course, no possibility that he would. He had made it up a long time ago. He went out then. He had already arranged to sell the chaise, apparently, needing the proceeds to hire a guide for the crossing. While he was out, I took the book down to the bridge and threw it into the river. It was the last thing he had anticipated. Otherwise he would have taken it with him. He did not understand, you see, how deeply I loved him. And how little the money mattered once he was lost to me. But if I could not have him, he could not have his reward. It seemed very simple to me. And I was glad to do it, glad to hurt him as he had hurt me. When he returned, I told him at once what I had done.' She shook her head. 'He searched the room, you know. He didn't believe me. He thought I'd hidden it somewhere. When he realized the

166

truth, he grew angry.' Her fingers moved to the bruise on her cheek. 'Very angry.'

'And then?'

'He left. I imagine he's in some tavern now, cursing my name and drowning his dreams of the wealth that won't now be his.'

'Nor yours.'

'Nor anyone's.' She looked from one to the other of them. 'Aren't you going to look for it? You surely won't take me at my word.'

McIlwraith sighed. 'No. I fear we can't do that.' He turned to Jupe and Spandrel. 'You both know what you're looking for. I suggest you set about it.'

'We're not going to find it,' said Spandrel. 'Are we?'

'Probably not. But look anyway.'

It did not take long. The chest of drawers contained only clothes and there were few places where such an object could be hidden. Jupe pulled a travelling bag from beneath the bed and opened it. Inside was the despatch-box. But it was empty, as Spandrel had known it would be. Then Jupe rolled aside the rug covering half the floor and crouched over the boards with the lantern, looking for some sign that one of them had been lifted. But there was none.

'Congratulations, madam,' said McIlwraith, when the search had come to its predictable conclusion. 'The Government will be grateful to you.'

'Why?'

'Because the Green Book's destruction serves them well. The guilty go free and—' He chopped the air with the edge of his hand. 'Love conquers all.'

'We should find Zuyler,' said Jupe grimly.

'Aye. So we should.'

'What will you do to him?' asked Estelle.

'I don't know.' McIlwraith looked at her. 'Whatever it is, I doubt it'll compare to what you've already done to him.'

167

'Tell him . . .'

'What?'

'That he's lost something more valuable than the Green Book.' She gazed into the guttering fire. 'And there will come a time when he regrets it.'

'Did you believe her, Spandrel?' McIlwraith asked as they walked away from the house a few minutes later.

'Yes.'

'Me too. Jupe?'

'She may be lying. She may be more cunning than you think.'

'You have no soul, man. "Heaven has no rage, like love to hatred turned, nor Hell a fury, like a woman scorned." Mr Congreve had it right, I reckon.'

'I'm a mere servant, Captain. What would I know of a playwright's moralizing?'

'Enough. If you wanted to. But to business. I doubt we'll have to look far for our despondent Dutchman.'

He was right. They found Zuyler in the third tavern they tried, a loud, smoke-filled establishment that was clearly as much a brothel as a drinking den. Zuyler seemed to have availed himself of both of the commodities on offer. He was leaning back in his chair at a corner table, with a girl on his knee and two bottles, one empty, one nearly so, in front of him. His left hand held a goblet, while his right was cradling one of the girl's ample breasts, barely concealed by her bodice.

'A charming scene, don't you think, gentlemen?' McIlwraith declared, dragging the girl to her feet and telling her to be on her way, which she promptly was. 'Mijnheer Zuyler!' Zuyler looked around in slack-jawed confusion, apparently uncertain where or why the girl had gone. 'Perhaps you prefer to be called Kempis. Or Kemp.'

'Who . . . are you?' Zuyler slurred.

'Surely you know Spandrel here.'

'Sp-Spandrel?' Zuyler gaped at him, his eyes visibly struggling to focus. 'That can't . . .' He tried to rise, then slumped back. 'No,' he said. 'You're not . . .'

'Oh but he is. Why don't you tell him what you think of him, Spandrel?'

'What would be the point?' Spandrel shook his head dismally.

'Maybe you're right,' said McIlwraith. 'An enemy in his cups is a contemptible thing. We have a message for you, Zuyler. From Estelle.'

'Estelle?' Zuyler spat. '*Die zalet-juffer.*'

Suddenly angry, Spandrel stepped forward and hauled Zuyler out of his chair. Then, staring into the eyes of the man who had all but condemned him to death, he realized how empty the prospect of revenge was. He pushed Zuyler away and watched him fall against the chair, then slide to the floor, toppling the table as he went.

'What did he call her?' asked McIlwraith, as the bottles rolled to rest at his feet.

'I don't know,' said Spandrel. 'And I don't care.'

'Is that so? For a moment, I thought you did. We'll forget the message, then, shall we?'

'He would.' Spandrel looked down at Zuyler where he lay, spilt wine dripping onto his face from the table. 'Even if we delivered it.'

They walked down to the river gate. McIlwraith tipped the gateman to let them through the wicket and they made their way to the middle of the bridge. The river was lost in mist and darkness, but they could see it spuming round the cutwater by the light of the gatehouse lanterns at either end and could hear the roar of it as it swept on round the bend to the north.

'This isn't how I'd expected the chase to end,' said McIlwraith. 'And it's far from what my superiors will want to hear. But hear it they must.'

'I'm still not convinced,' said Jupe. 'They may have lodged the book at a bank and be waiting for us to give up before retrieving it and carrying on to Rome.'

'You said yourself, man, that they've hardly set foot outside the house since arriving. So, they couldn't have known Spandrel and I were here. Are you suggesting they contrived all this just *in case* we came calling?'

'No,' Jupe admitted. 'I suppose not. But I shall keep my eye on them till their intentions are clear, nonetheless.'

'A wise precaution, no doubt.'

'I've been away from the house too long as it is.'

'Don't let us detain you.'

'I shan't. This is all very . . . unsatisfactory, you know.' There was a reproachful edge to Jupe's voice.

'Aye, aye. Life often is.'

'I'll bid you good night, then. You know where to find me.'

'And you us.'

McIlwraith and Spandrel watched Jupe walk away along the bridge until he had vanished into the shadow of the gatehouse arch. Several more moments passed with nothing said. The river rushed on below them. Then Spandrel asked plaintively, 'What are we to do now?'

'Now?' McIlwraith clapped him on the shoulder. 'Isn't it obvious?'

'No.'

'There's only one thing to do in a situation like this.'

'What's that?'

'We follow Zuyler's example. And get roaringly drunk.'

As McIlwraith and Spandrel walked up through the mist-filled streets of the city towards the Drei Tassen inn

170

and the lure of its tap-room, Jupe was climbing the stairs of the Pension Siegwart. His room was on the third floor. But his climb ended at the first. There he paused, as if pondering some course of action, before heading along the landing to the door of the room taken by the couple known to the landlady as Mr and Mrs Kemp, where a light was still burning.

He knocked at the door with three soft taps. A moment later, it opened and Estelle de Vries looked out at him.

'Mr Jupe,' she said, with no inflexion of surprise. 'You're alone?'

'Yes, madam.'

'McIlwraith and Spandrel?'

'Have gone.'

'Do you think they were fooled?'

'Oh yes.' Jupe nodded. 'Completely.'

Chapter Seventeen

Blood and Vanishment

The mist had all but gone by morning. The sun was up in an icy blue sky, glinting on the giant horseshoe of the Aare, within which were clustered the spires and turrets and jumbled rooftops of Berne. Spandrel looked down at the river from a high, buttressed terrace behind the cathedral. A line of broken water marked the course of a weir linking the southern bank to a landing-stage and dock away to his left. Smoke was rising from a mill adjoining the dock and the sound of sawing from a woodyard carried up to him through the clarified air. A man with a fowling-piece under his arm was walking across a field on the opposite shore, a dog trotting beside him through the patches of snow. The world went on its way. And so did the people in it.

The thoughts filling Spandrel's head were not those he would have expected in the wake of his confrontation with the two people who had saddled him with the blame for a murder. Many times, languishing in his cell in Amsterdam, he had wondered what he would do if he ever set eyes – or laid hands – upon them. And never once had it occurred to him that he would simply walk away and leave them to their own devices. But what else could he do? They had worked his vengeance out for him. They had undone themselves. Estelle de Vries he now saw as beyond condemnation, Pieter Zuyler as beneath contempt. They hated each other more than he could contrive to hate either of them.

For Estelle he felt in truth no hatred whatever, rather a perverse kind of admiration. To risk all – and to lose all – in the name of love was somehow magnificent. Spandrel did not care that she had destroyed the Green Book. He faintly approved of the action. And he could not help worrying what its consequences would be for her. Zuyler's capacity for violence might yet cost her dear. She should leave Berne without delay. She should return to England and put behind her the follies and the evils Zuyler had tempted her into.

Whether she would he did not know. It had seemed to him, listening to her account of herself in that mean little room at the Pension Siegwart, that he could almost taste the blackness of her despair. She had abandoned her old life and now her new life had abandoned her. What would she do? 'She might drown herself,' McIlwraith had said at some late and drunken stage of the previous night, 'before Zuyler does it for her.' This suggestion, half-jest though it was, had lingered in Spandrel's mind, till he had convinced himself that something of the kind was horribly possible, that it might, indeed, have already happened.

It was to shake off the depression that this idea had plunged him into that he had left McIlwraith breakfasting morosely at the Drei Tassen and walked aimlessly about the streets of the city as it stretched and yawned and came to its Saturday morning self.

But he had not succeeded. The depression remained. And gazing down at the river, on which a barge had just now put out from the dock, he realized that there was only one way to be rid of it. He would have to return to the Pension Siegwart. And make some kind of peace with Estelle de Vries.

*   *   *

The door was answered by a twinkle-eyed butter-ball of a woman whom Spandrel took to be Frau Siegwart. Her command of English was evidently little greater than his of German and he did not help his cause by asking for Mevrouw de Vries. Once he had laughed that off and specified Mrs Kemp instead, there was a glimmer of understanding and he was invited to enter.

The stairs shook under Frau Siegwart as she led Spandrel up to the first floor and she was panting by the time they reached the door of the best room in the house. She knocked at it briskly, then more briskly still when there was no response. *'Ich verstehe nicht,'* she said with a frown. *'Wo sind sie?'* She listened, knocked again, then tried the handle.

The door was not locked. Frau Siegwart pushed it open and peered into the room. There was no-one there. Glancing in over her shoulder, Spandrel noticed at once what a sharp intake of the landlady's breath suggested she too had noticed. The drawers in the chest beneath the window were sagging open. And they were empty.

For a moment, while Frau Siegwart mumbled to herself and looked around, Spandrel struggled to understand what had happened. Where was she? Where were *they*? If Estelle had fled, as she well might have done, she would surely not have taken Zuyler's possessions with her. Unless, of course, they had fled *together*.

'Jupe,' he said aloud. 'Where's Jupe?'

'Wie bitte?'

'Jupe. He's staying here. *Mr Jupe.'*

'Der Engländer?'

'Yes. That's right. He's English too. Jupe.'

Grasping apparently that her other English guest might be able to shed light on the disappearance of Mr and Mrs Kemp, Frau Siegwart clumped off towards the stairs. Spandrel followed.

Another two flights took them to a low-ceilinged landing at the top of the house. Frau Siegwart, breathing now like a bellows, rapped at one of the doors. There was no response. She tried again, with the same result. Then she grasped the handle and turned it.

Jupe's door was also unlocked, which somehow surprised Spandrel. But his surprise on that account was rapidly overborne by the shock of what he and Frau Siegwart found themselves looking at through the open doorway.

Jupe and Zuyler lay next to each other at the foot of the bed. There had been a struggle of some kind. The dressing-table had been overturned and the rug was bunched and ruckled beneath them. A pool of congealed blood extended across the rug and the floorboards around it. There was no movement, no sign of life. Both men, Spandrel realized at once, were dead.

'*Mein Gott,*' said Frau Siegwart, crossing herself as she spoke.

Spandrel stepped cautiously past her into the room and leaned forward, trying to see and understand what had happened. Zuyler was lying on his side, his face partly concealed by a fold of the rug. But enough of it was visible for there to be no doubt that he had died in agony. His eyes were bulging, his tongue protruding. There were splinters of wood scattered around him. One of his knees was sharply raised and the heel of his boot had gouged at the boards. He was wearing the greatcoat Spandrel had seen tossed over the back of the chair next to him in the tavern the night before. He did not seem to have been stabbed. There was blood beneath him, but no sign of a wound. The cause of his death looked to be the narrow leather strap wrapped around his neck. It was loose now, but there was a deep red line beneath to show where it had been drawn tight.

The blood belonged to Jupe. He lay on his back, staring sightlessly up at the ceiling. A knife was buried to the hilt in his chest and his coat was sodden with blood. His left hand held the knotted loops of the strap, trailing in his stiffening fingers. It looked as if he had strangled Zuyler, who had managed to stab him with the knife as he did so. The wound had proved fatal, but not quickly enough to save Zuyler. Even as his life's blood had drained away, Jupe had finished what he had set out to do.

But why? What had they fought about? Spandrel's gaze moved to a knapsack lying open by the chest of drawers, with a bundle of clothes beside it. They were Jupe's, presumably. Had he been packing for a journey? If so, he would not have thrown his clothes on the floor. If he had stowed them in the knapsack, however, in readiness for his departure, and someone else had then pulled them out in search of something concealed beneath them—

'*Herr Jupe*,' Frau Siegwart wailed, suddenly realizing who the dead pair were. '*Und Herr Kemp.*' She clapped her hands to her cheeks. '*Fürchterlich.*'

'You should call for help,' said Spandrel.

But a different thought had struck Frau Siegwart. '*Wo ist Frau Kemp?*' Then she forced out the words in English. 'Where . . . Mrs Kemp?'

It was a good question. Indeed, it was a better question than Frau Siegwart could possibly know. Where was Estelle de Vries? And what did she have with her? Spandrel looked down at the two dead men. 'I don't know where she is,' he said, truthfully enough, though he could have hazarded a good guess at where she might be going. 'I don't know anything.'

'We've been a pair of fools, you and and I,' said McIlwraith an hour or so later, when Spandrel had finished describing to him the gruesome scene at the Pension Siegwart. 'You see what this means, don't you?'

'I think I do,' said Spandrel. 'Estelle de Vries didn't destroy the Green Book.'

'No more she did. But we'd have gone on believing her tearful little story save for something a sight more reliable than our judgement. Greed, Spandrel. That's what's undone them.'

'*Them?* Jupe was on their side, not ours?'

'You have it. He saw us arrive here, then went to Zuyler and his lady love and convinced them that, without his help, they'd not escape us. Remember her confusion about who I represented – the Government or the House of Commons? Jupe must have told them I was a Government agent. A natural enough assumption, in the circumstances.' McIlwraith pounded a fist into his palm. 'Jupe was the sceptical one, wasn't he? "I'm still not convinced." "I shall keep my eye on them." He overplayed his hand and we still didn't see the cards up his sleeve.'

'He hid the book in his room?'

'Aye. Then they performed their touching masquerade in the hope that we'd give up and go away, leaving them to go on to Rome and sell the book, sharing the proceeds among the three of them.'

'What went wrong?'

'It sounds as if Zuyler caught Jupe in the act of decamping with the book. I don't suppose they trusted one another for an instant. It was an alliance of necessity. Realizing that there'd probably be a Government agent coming after them in due course as well must have cast its own shadow.'

'Will there be?'

'Aye, man, of course. You don't think we have the field to ourselves, do you?'

'You never told me that.'

'Did I not? Well, perhaps I didn't think you needed to worry your head over it. And no more you do.' But there, though he did not say so, Spandrel begged to differ. 'Nor about Zuyler and Jupe, now they've done for each other. There's only one person we need to consider.'

'Estelle de Vries.'

'The very same. She must have gone to Jupe's room when Zuyler didn't return and found them dead. Whether she shed a real tear for her lover to add to the false ones she sprinkled over us last night we'll never know. What we do know is that she took the book from Jupe's knapsack and—'

'We can't be sure she did.'

'You said you searched the room.'

'Yes. After the landlady rushed off to raise the alarm.'

'And the book wasn't there.'

'No. But—'

'For pity's sake, man. Why else would she leave without raising the alarm herself?'

'No reason, I suppose,' Spandrel reluctantly admitted. 'It must be as you say.' But it was such a cold-blooded thing to have done. Even now, he could hardly bring himself to believe it of her.

'She's gone and the book's gone with her,' said McIlwraith. 'The question is: where?'

It was not an easy question to answer. Even if she had lied to them about Zuyler selling the chaise, she could hardly have driven it away herself. She might have hired a driver, of course, but she would surely have realized it could not be long before they learned Jupe and Zuyler were dead and drew the correct conclusions. To attempt to outrun them on the road was futile. So, McIlwraith reasoned, she would prefer to travel by the first available public coach and set off for the Simplon Pass from wherever the coach took her.

The Drei Tassen happened to be the principal coaching inn of the city. Enquiries revealed that no services had left for any destination since the previous afternoon. At noon, however, the Basle and Interlaken coaches were both due to leave. She would hardly head back to Basle. Interlaken, lying forty miles to the south-east, was the obvious choice. Rather too obvious, however, for McIlwraith's liking.

And so it proved when they stood in the inn yard at noon and watched the coaches load and depart. There was no sign of Estelle de Vries. By then, word of the murders at the Pension Siegwart was abroad. The consensus of tap-room wisdom was that you could never tell with foreigners. It was at least a blessing that this pair had killed each other and left the locals unmolested. Old Frau Siegwart should choose her guests more carefully.

By dusk McIlwraith and Spandrel between them had visited just about every inn, stable and boarding-house in the city. No unaccompanied Englishwoman, or Dutchwoman come to that, was to be found. Nor was there any word of such a person hiring transport or even asking how it might be hired.

'Where can she be?' asked Spandrel, as they made their way back to the Drei Tassen through the darkening streets.

'She may be lying low,' said McIlwraith. 'Privacy can be bought, like most things.'

'Could she have persuaded some traveller to take her with him?'

'She could. There aren't many who'd refuse a woman like her . . . well, near enough whatever she wanted.'

'Then she could be anywhere.'

'Or on the road to it. Aye. But where do they say all roads lead? She won't give up now, Spandrel. Sooner or later, she'll turn south. It has to be the Simplon Pass. That's where we can be sure of catching her. She might be hiding here somewhere. But I'll waste no more time and boot leather looking. We'll leave in the morning.'

Nothing, Spandrel knew already, despite the brevity of their acquaintance, changed McIlwraith's mind once it was made up. He was a man of firm will and fixed decisions. But even firmness can be pushed aside by a greater force. There is no decision, however fixed, that cannot be out-decided.

As they walked along the passage towards their room at the Drei Tassen, a door ahead of them some way short of theirs slowly opened, the light from a lantern beyond the windows at the rear of the inn falling unevenly across a figure that stepped out into their path. McIlwraith pulled up at once and sucked in his breath. He knew who the man was. And Spandrel sensed that he did not like him.

'I saw you coming,' the man said. He was a squat, burly fellow, with a head too large for his body. His face was in shadow, but there was menace enough simply in his posture. Spandrel felt suddenly cold. 'You should be more careful.'

'Colonel Wagemaker,' said McIlwraith quietly. 'What brings you here?'

'The same wind that's blown you in.'

'Is that so?'

'I'm in the King's service, McIlwraith. I outrank you. In more ways than one.'

'I can only think of one, Colonel. And that wasn't always the case.'

'Where's the widow de Vries?'

'I don't rightly know.'

'Nor would you tell me if you did.'

'True enough.'

'But she does have the book, doesn't she?'

'Book?'

'Don't try to play blind-man's-buff with me, McIlwraith. Jupe and Zuyler are dead. But *she* slipped through your fumbling fingers, didn't she? Cloisterman's at the Town Hall now, trying to—'

'Cloisterman's with you?'

'He is. And that's Spandrel you have skulking beside *you*, isn't it? So, we have our seconds ready-made for us, don't we?'

'Seconds? You surely don't mean to—'

'Kill you? Most certainly. Unless you kill me. I told you that if we ever met again I'd finish it between us. Well . . .' Something in the tone of Wagemaker's voice revealed the smile that Spandrel could not see. 'We meet again.'

Chapter Eighteen

Old Scores

'Quite a turn-up, eh, Spandrel?' said McIlwraith, as he sat by the window of their room at the Drei Tassen and gazed out at the blank Bernese night. By the flickering light of the single candle, Spandrel saw him raise his whisky flask to his lips and sip from it. 'Just what we didn't need. Just what *I* didn't want.'

'You're really going to fight him?'

'I have no choice. Despite appearances, I lay claim to be a gentleman. Colonel Wagemaker demands satisfaction. And I must give it him. Tomorrow, at dawn.'

'This is madness.'

'A form of it, certainly.'

'What's it about? Why does he hate you?'

'He blames me for his sister's death.'

'And are you to blame?'

'Aye. I am. But so is he. We share the blame. I believe that's what he can't stomach.'

'How did she die?'

'It's not a story I'm fond of telling. But since we need to consider the possibility that I may not be alive tomorrow to correct the cholerical colonel's version of events . . .' McIlwraith chuckled. 'As my second, you come close to being my confessor, Spandrel. You know that?'

'I haven't agreed to be your second.'

'You'll do it, though. I know you well enough by now.

We may despise the forms of this world, but we observe them nonetheless. It'd be as cowardly for you to refuse to stand by me as for me to refuse to stand against him.'

'And, if so, I'm entitled to know why.'

'Aye. So you are.' McIlwraith took another sip of whisky. 'It goes back to the war. Like so much else in my misdirected life. Glorious days and grievous: they were the way of it. But we didn't mind. Not while Marlborough led us. A hard man. And a harder one still to read. But a leader, in his heart as well as his head. You'd have followed him into the fissures of Hell. Blenheim, Ramillies, Oudenarde, Malplaquet. I was at all of them. And proud to be. Then the politicians did him down, as good soldiers always are done down by backstairs intrigues and closet bargains. The Government changed its hue. The Captain-General was dismissed. Peace talks began. We surrendered in all but name. Most of the British troops went back to England, while the negotiations dragged on through the spring and summer of 1712. I was with Albemarle's Allied division during those months. Nobody knew what we were supposed to be about. Most of the officers were Dutch or German. There were precious few British left. And precious little spirit left either. The French seized their chance, crossed the Scheldt and attacked us at Denain. Seventeen battalions were lost. I was one of the many taken prisoner. We were sent to Valenciennes and confined there until a truce could be agreed. I fell in with an English officer from the garrison at Marchiennes, which the French had also captured. He was badly wounded and our captors made little effort to treat him. Before the truce was concluded, he was dead. His name was Hatton. Captain John Hatton. He was a good fellow. He made me promise to carry a letter he'd written to a young lady in England to whom he was engaged. His beloved Dorothea. You already know her surname.'

'Wagemaker.'

'The very same. The Wagemakers owned land in Berkshire. Still do, I dare say. When I was released and sent to rejoin what was left of my regiment, I was immediately discharged on half-pay. The country was done with us fighting men. Our time was over. I had no notion of what to do or where to go. I certainly had no wish to return to Scotland. I burned my boats there a long while ago. I had it in my mind to go back to what I knew best: fighting. There's always an army somewhere in the world that wants a recruit. But before I set to thinking about that, I had to deliver Hatton's letter to his betrothed. I wrote to her, warning her of my visit, then travelled to the Wagemakers' house, Bordon Grove, on the edge of Windsor Forest.'

'Was Colonel Wagemaker there?'

'He was. Though he was only a lieutenant then. Reduced to half-pay, like me, and cooling his heels at home. Our Augustus saw himself as head of the family, following his father's recent death, though his brother Tiberius had the running of the estate, such as it was. As for Dorothea, she was the pick of the bunch, as she'd have been of many another. Not merely beautiful, but sweet-natured and altogether lovely. A young woman of such breeding that you couldn't help wondering how she'd acquired so ill-bred a pair of brothers. A lamb to their wolves. She thanked me for my condolences and for bringing the letter. She urged me to stay awhile. And so I did. I stayed, indeed, too long. Brother Tiberius offered me the rent of a folly on the estate. Blind Man's Tower, it's called, on ironical account of the staircase to the top being on the outside of the building, open to the elements, with neither guard nor rail. But the ground floor's as cosy as a cottage. I took it just for the winter. By spring, I planned to be on my way.'

'And were you?'

'I was. But much had happened by then. What

Wagemaker and I are to duel over was already done. I grew to know the family too well. That was my mistake. A soldier needs a billet. But he should never think he's found a home. The Wagemakers were pressed for money. Their father had been a poor manager of their interests and Tiberius wasn't the man to repair them. A loose-tongued aunt who lived with them and kept their invalid mother company muttered to me more than once about debts hanging round their necks. No doubt that explains why Tiberius was willing to rent me Blind Man's Tower. Any income was useful. And it also explains why he and Augustus weren't at all sorry that poor Hatton was dead. They never made any pretence that they were, speaking slightingly of him on several occasions, until they saw it tried my temper to do so and guarded what they said. They had a different, wealthier, husband in mind for Dorothea: Esmund Longrigg, owner of a neighbouring and better founded estate. Longrigg held the office of chief wood-ward or somesuch in the Forest hierarchy, which carried with it an enviable load of perquisites. He and Dorothea were put much together at balls and musical evenings that Christmas and Longrigg liked what he saw. But Dorothea didn't. I couldn't blame her for that. I didn't like the look of Longrigg myself. Tallow to her beeswax. But moneyed. To her brothers, that was all that mattered. They en-couraged her to accept his proposal if, or, as they saw it, when it came. And come it did.' McIlwraith sighed and drank some more whisky. 'She asked for time to think. Then she turned to me for advice. She detested Longrigg. But she knew how important it was to the family's future that she marry him. Yet still she detested him. Her life with him would be a misery. What was she to do?'

'What did you tell her?'

'To refuse him.' McIlwraith looked across at Spandrel, his face wreathed in shadow. 'If her brothers were so

185

concerned about the family's future, by which they meant their own comfort, they should bestir themselves to secure it, rather than mortgage their sister's happiness.' He seemed to smile at the recollection of his words. 'Such was my advice.'

'Did she take it?'

'She refused him, right enough. Which displeased them mightily, as you can imagine. The more so because they knew she'd been to see me before giving Longrigg his answer and suspected I'd put her up to it. Nobly, she denied it. But when they accused me nonetheless, I chose not to deny it. I didn't care to be summoned to the house and cross-questioned like some tenant caught poaching. Longrigg was with them. The brothers seemed to think they had the right to tell me what to do simply because I was living on their property. Harsh things were said. Tempers were lost. Longrigg had the gall to suggest I was harbouring dishonourable intentions towards Dorothea. Then Augustus went further, implying they might not just be intentions. I demanded he withdraw the slur. He refused. So, I called him out. There was nothing else for it.'

'*You* challenged *him*?'

'Aye. But the duel was never fought. Dorothea was being held a virtual prisoner by then. I wasn't permitted to see her. But she knew what had happened. She smuggled a letter to me by her maid pleading with me not to fight her brother. She said she couldn't bear the thought of either of us dying on her account. I replied, saying it was a matter of honour and I had no choice but to fight, unless Augustus took back the remark, which I knew he wouldn't. Even then, he was too stubborn for that. And too brave. He'd deliberately provoked the challenge. He *wanted* to fight me. And I wanted to fight him, God forgive me. But we never did fight. Till now, anyway. A day and time were

186

fixed for us to meet. The night before, Dorothea implored her brother to apologize to me. When he refused, she calmly said good night to him, walked up to the top floor of the house and threw herself over the balustrade into the stair-well.'

Spandrel caught his breath. 'She killed herself?'

McIlwraith nodded grimly. 'It was all of a sixty-foot drop to the stone-flagged hall. Certain death. And the only certain way she knew to prevent the duel. She had my letter, my pompous resort to honour as a justification for refusing to withdraw the challenge, concealed in the sleeve of her dress. Augustus found it, of course. He's a diligent searcher, if he's nothing else. And finding it somehow enabled him to forget his own responsibility for what she'd done. He laid it all at my door. The duel was called off, naturally, as a mark of respect, as Dorothea had known it would be. As far as Augustus was concerned, though, it was only a postponement, until after the funeral.'

'But not as far as you were concerned.'

'No. I couldn't go through with what Dorothea had laid down her life to avert. I withdrew the challenge.'

'What did Wagemaker do then?'

'He issued one of his own. Which I declined, on the tenuous grounds that a junior officer cannot challenge a senior. The actual grounds were rather different, of course. And seemingly beyond his comprehension. As it appears they still are. Now, however, he's no longer my junior. I cannot decline to meet him.'

'What will happen?'

'One of us will die. He hasn't waited eight years to content himself with a shot into the air. He's a man of his word. And he's given it.'

'But his sister's memory . . .'

'Is more likely to stay my hand than his.'

'But it won't, will it? You don't mean . . .'

'I don't know what I mean, Spandrel. It's late. And whisky inclines me to mawkishness. I'll tell you this for what it's worth, though. I lost no time in quitting Blind Man's Tower after the funeral and taking off on my travels. The Danish army found a use for me in its war against Sweden. That's how I came to learn enough of their language to be able to negotiate our passage aboard the *Havfrue*. I wasn't the Danes' only British mercenary, of course. There were a good many. And among them was one who'd met Lieutenant Augustus Wagemaker while serving in Ireland. He'd been a notorious duellist there, apparently. Quick to take offence. Determined to seek satisfaction for it. And never known to miss.' McIlwraith drained the whisky flask. 'I think Dorothea knew full well that it was far more likely to be me she was saving than her brother.' He sighed. 'There's a thought to ponder when we reach the standing-place tomorrow. If I'm right, Wagemaker knows it as well as I do. Perhaps she loved me a little. Perhaps more than a little. If so, that's really what he hates me for. And why he means to kill me.'

No candle burned in the room a few doors down the passage that Colonel Wagemaker was sharing with Nicholas Cloisterman. But only one of its occupants was still awake. Cloisterman lay on his bed, eyes wide open, staring anxiously into the darkness. From the other side of the room came the steady rise and fall of Wagemaker's slumbering breaths. How a man could sleep so soundly on the eve of a duel Cloisterman could not imagine. He had studiously avoided such affairs of honour himself, preferring any number of apologies and humiliations to the prospect of sudden, painful and, as he saw it, pointless death. He had never served as a second either and had no wish to do so now, but Wagemaker had insisted, deploying the ingenious argument that this was a heaven-sent opportunity to eliminate a dangerous rival in their pursuit of the Green Book and that Cloisterman was therefore obliged to assist him.

The possibility did not seem to have crossed Wagemaker's mind that he, rather than McIlwraith, might be eliminated by the morning's exchange of fire. He seemed, indeed, blithely confident of the outcome. 'McIlwraith's as good as dead,' had been his dismissive remark on the subject. As to the reason for the duel, which Cloisterman felt entitled to know if he was to stand as a second, about that too Wagemaker had been sparing with his words. 'He brought about my sister's death. Now he must pay for her life with his.'

If these two irascible old warriors were determined to take pot-shots at one another, that, so far as Cloisterman was concerned, they were welcome to do. He certainly could not prevent them. It was also undeniable that it would be easier to wrest the Green Book from Estelle de Vries, whom they would surely overtake before she reached the Simplon Pass, without McIlwraith trying to do the same. None of these considerations eased his mind, however. He did not like Wagemaker and he did not trust him. He did not subscribe to the colonel's notion that this would be a quick, clean kill, an old score settled and a present problem solved, free of consequences, devoid of penalty. In Cloisterman's experience, life was never that simple and nor was death.

A particularly disturbing thought was that he had no idea what the attitude of the Swiss was to duelling. For all he knew, it might be forbidden by some ancient cantonal law. If so, the seconds as much as the duellists would be in breach of it. During his visit to the Town Hall, he had represented himself to the Sheriff's officer with whom he had discussed the deaths of Zuyler and Jupe as a reputable and accredited agent of the British Government. How the Sheriff would react to such a personage involving himself in a duel he did not care to contemplate. But Wagemaker was Walpole's man. And Walpole seemed likely soon to be the arbiter of all their fates. Cloisterman had no choice but to do as he was bidden.

He did not have to like it, however. He especially resented his inability to think about anything else. There was surely much to ponder in the singular circumstances that had led to the fatal struggle at the Pension Siegwart. Zuyler and Jupe had killed each other and Estelle de Vries had fled with the Green Book. That seemed clear. But where had she fled to? The Simplon Pass was so obvious a destination that Cloisterman feared it might be too obvious. Mrs de Vries had shown herself to be a cool-nerved and resourceful woman. Just how resourceful he was not sure they yet knew. But he could not seem to concentrate on the clues to her intentions that he felt certain were scattered amidst the sparse facts of her behaviour to date. Instead, his mind was clogged with the brutal absurdities of a dawn duel between two men he scarcely knew over a long dead woman he had never known at all. It was a miserable scrape to find himself in. And somehow it seemed more miserable still because one of the duellists was sleeping like a baby in the same room where Cloisterman knew he was destined to toss and turn till the long night ended. Whereupon . . .

'Damn you, Dalrymple,' he muttered under his breath. 'I didn't deserve this.'

But deserving, as he was all too well aware, had absolutely nothing to do with it.

Chapter Nineteen

The Wages of Honour

The roofs of Berne rose above them like those of some dream city, floating, girding mountains and all, on the mist that shrouded the river.

It was a still, chill, breathless dawn in the sloping, snow-spattered meadow where the four men assembled, between the mist-line and the Interlaken road. Few words were spoken at first and most of those were in the form of a stumbling effort by Cloisterman to call the duel off, to which Wagemaker responded with a grunted refusal and McIlwraith with a fatalistic shrug. Spandrel and Cloisterman were shivering and clearly ill at ease, whereas the two men who were about to hazard their lives were icily calm. They took off their greatcoats, then Wagemaker opened the pistol-case he had brought and offered McIlwraith his choice of the matched pair. They loaded the weapons themselves, apparently concluding, without the need of saying so, that their seconds were unequal to the task.

'We should toss a coin to see who has the right to fire first,' said Cloisterman, fishing one from his pocket. 'Unless . . .' But, with a shake of the head, he abandoned his last attempt at mediation.

'No need,' said Wagemaker, holding McIlwraith's gaze with his. 'Ten paces each, then turn and shoot. Agreed?'

'However you please,' said McIlwraith. 'Since you want this so badly, you may as well have the ordering of it.'

'Agreed, then. You can put your money away, Mr Cloisterman.'

'May I at least count the paces for you?' Cloisterman asked through pursed lips.

'You may,' said Wagemaker. 'Shall we get on?'

'One thing,' put in McIlwraith. 'Before we do.'

'Well?'

'Dorothea wouldn't have—'

'Don't mention my sister by name, sir. I don't choose to give you the right to.'

'What you *choose* to do is to defile her memory.'

'By God, you have a nerve. Now let's see how steady it is. Are you here to talk or to fight?'

'I'm here to give you satisfaction, Colonel. As I'm bound to. But we should be clear. Dorothea sacrificed her life to prevent us doing just this eight years ago.'

'Is that true?' asked Cloisterman.

'It's no business of yours whether it's true or not,' barked Wagemaker. 'Step back and let's be doing.'

'Very well.' Cloisterman retreated, signalling for Spandrel to follow.

When they were thirty yards or so away, Wagemaker cocked his pistol and McIlwraith cocked his. They nodded to one another, then took up position, back to back.

'Oh God,' groaned Cloisterman. 'This really is going to happen.'

'Did you think it mightn't?' asked Spandrel.

'I hoped.' He sighed, then shouted, 'Ready?'

'Ready,' came Wagemaker's reply.

'Ready,' McIlwraith confirmed.

'One,' Cloisterman called. And at that they started walking.

*　　*　　*

Duelling was no part of life in Spandrel's bracket of society. It was to him a strange and exotic indulgence of the upper classes, to which army officers, however humble their origins, also had habitual recourse. He had witnessed one once, thanks to Dick Surtees overhearing the arrangements being made in a coffee-house by the seconds and suggesting they go along and take a look at 'two pea-brained sparks using each other for target practice'. It had been a bloodless affray in Hyde Park, the 'pea-brained sparks' in question missing their targets by a country mile, looking heartily relieved to do so and departing arm in arm, like the best of friends. Spandrel found himself wishing there could be a similar outcome to the second duel he was ever about to witness. But he knew in his heart there could not be. Blood would be shed at the very least. A life – Wagemaker's or McIlwraith's – was likely to be lost in the exchange that now lay only a few seconds in the future. He fervently hoped it would not be McIlwraith's. But he greatly feared that it would. At the count of ten, he held his breath.

The two men were about twenty yards apart when they turned. Wagemaker spun on his heel, raised his arm and took aim a fraction of a second more swiftly – more naturally – than McIlwraith. The Scotsman's arm was still just short of the horizontal when Wagemaker fired. The loud crack of the pistol shot broke the silence that had followed Cloisterman's count of ten, only to be swallowed in a cawing rise of rooks from the mist-blurred trees further down the meadow. For a frozen instant, Spandrel did not know what had happened. There was no answering shot. The two men stood perfectly still, framing the city behind them, the cathedral tower seeming to mark, like a raised finger, the point from which they had measured their paces.

Then McIlwraith groaned and took one stumbling, sideways step. His arm dropped. His other hand moved to his chest. He seemed about to fall. Wagemaker slowly lowered his pistol. 'He's done for him,' said Cloisterman, stepping forward. 'As he swore he would.'

But McIlwraith did not fall. With a cry more like that of a beast than a man, he wrenched himself upright. Spandrel could see his chest heaving with the effort. He was hit, perhaps fatally, but something stronger than lead shot was holding him on his feet. He took one lurching step back to the position from which he had stumbled, his racing breath pluming into the air around him. Then he raised his pistol once more.

'He means to fire,' said Cloisterman, pulling up sharply.

'You're a dead man, Captain,' Wagemaker called to his opponent. 'You can't even stand straight, let alone shoot straight.' With that he threw his pistol to the ground. 'This is—'

There was a second pistol shot. Wagemaker's head jerked violently back as bone and blood burst out of it. He swayed for a moment, then fell backwards, hitting the frosted turf with a thud. There was no other movement. He lay where he fell, like a puppet whose strings have been cut, still and lifeless.

'Good God,' murmured Cloisterman. 'Good God Almighty.'

McIlwraith let his pistol fall to the ground. Then, slowly, as if stooping to pray, he slipped to his knees. Spandrel began running towards him. As he ran, he saw the captain topple over onto his side, his body convulsed by a series of spluttering coughs. Then he lay still.

'Captain?' Spandrel bent over him and touched his elbow. There was blood on McIlwraith's waistcoat, oozing through the fingers of the hand he had clasped to the wound and darkening the frost-white grass beneath him. 'Can you hear me?'

'I can . . . hear you,' McIlwraith replied through clenched teeth. 'Wagemaker?'

Spandrel looked across at Cloisterman, who had hurried to where the colonel was lying and was stooping over him. Hearing the question, he looked over his shoulder and said, 'Quite dead, Captain, I assure you.'

'But he still has the . . . advantage of me.' McIlwraith seemed to be smiling. 'At least he died . . . cleanly.'

'You're not going to die,' said Spandrel.

'I wish you were right. But as usual . . . you're wide of the mark. Unlike . . . Wagemaker.'

'I'll fetch a doctor,' said Cloisterman. 'As fast as I can. Stay here, Spandrel. And go on talking to him. It may help.'

The two men exchanged nods, then Cloisterman took off across the field in a loping run, the tails of his coat flapping out behind him. He was heading towards the houses clustered around the bridge by which they had left the city, the bridge from which Estelle de Vries claimed to have thrown the Green Book into the river. Since she had uttered that claim, no more than thirty hours or so ago, Zuyler and Jupe and Wagemaker had all met their deaths, suddenly and violently, when they were least expecting to. And now McIlwraith seemed likely to join them.

'Has he gone?' McIlwraith's voice was hoarse and strained.

'Yes. Don't worry. He'll—'

'Stop jabbering and listen to me, Spandrel. I don't have long. I'm dying, man.'

'No. No, you're not.'

'Don't contradict me, damn you. I've seen enough death . . . in my time . . . to know what it's like. *Just listen to me.*'

'I'm listening, Captain.'

195

'Good. This is . . . important. You must leave here. Now.'

'I can't do that.'

'You must. Take my pouch. It's in my coat. There's money. Guineas. Louis d'or. And sequins. You'll need those for Rome.'

'Rome?'

'You have to go on . . . without me.'

'I can't leave you like this.'

'There's . . . no choice. I've been here before. Not to Berne. But to Switzerland. I know their ways. This is a Calvinist canton. They come down hard on . . . Catholic indulgences. That's what they see duelling as. You and Cloisterman will be arrested . . . as soon as the Sheriff hears what's happened. Do you want to go back . . . to prison? Maybe even a Dutch one? A warrant naming you as a suspected murderer . . . could find its way here from Amsterdam . . . while you're in custody. Do you . . . want that?'

'Of course not.'

'Then go. While you still can.'

'I won't leave you until the doctor's arrived.'

'There'll be nothing for him to do.' McIlwraith winced. 'An undertaker, now. He could be . . . useful.'

'Don't say that.'

'I'm only . . . facing facts, man. You should . . . do the same. You mustn't be here when Cloisterman returns. He's for the Government, remember, and . . . well capable of handing you over to the authorities . . . in exchange for his own freedom. I don't want him . . . spending the committee's money.'

'He wouldn't do that.'

'Wouldn't he? You're too trusting, Spandrel. That's your . . . big weakness. So, trust me . . . for once.'

'I do.'

'Good. In that case . . .' McIlwraith twisted round and

clasped Spandrel's arm in a disconcertingly strong grip. 'For God's sake, go.'

Another half an hour had passed by the time Cloisterman returned to the meadow, accompanied by a doctor none too pleased to have been summoned from his breakfast-table and two of his manservants, equipped with blankets and a litter. McIlwraith was unconscious, though still breathing. But of Spandrel there was no sign. He had draped the captain's greatcoat over him and added Wagemaker's to keep him as warm as possible. And then . . .

'Where have you gone, Spandrel?' Cloisterman muttered, gazing suspiciously into the distance. 'What game are you playing?'

'This man is near death, mein Herr,' said the doctor, interrupting the drift of his thoughts. 'We must take him to my house.'

'Very well.'

'There has been . . . a duel?'

'Yes.'

'But it is Sunday. The sabbath. Have you no . . .' The doctor frowned at him. '*Verachtenswert.*'

'What?'

'We must go. We will not save him. But we must try.'

They loaded McIlwraith onto the litter, strapped him in and set off at a brisk pace across the meadow. Cloisterman made no move to follow.

'Come with us, mein Herr,' the doctor called back to him. 'There will be questions.'

'*Natürlich.*' Cloisterman made after them, quickly enough at first to catch up, then more slowly. Questions. Yes. There would be. A great many questions. And not enough answers. He stopped and looked across at Wagemaker's body, the face white beneath the shattered

197

brow, the clotted blood black against the frozen grass. He remembered the colonel's steady, sleeping breaths of the night before. So much certainty, so much strength, undone in an instant.

'Mein Herr!' The doctor's voice carried back to him through the cold, clearing air. 'We will send someone for the other. *Einen Leichenbestatter. Kommen Sie!*'

'I'll follow. In a moment.'

What should he do? Spandrel had fled. That was obvious. And who could blame him? Not Cloisterman. He was inclined to do the same himself. He had been told to assist Wagemaker. But Wagemaker was dead. Dalrymple had said nothing about trying to complete Wagemaker's mission in the event of the colonel's demise. Strictly speaking, Cloisterman's duties were at an end. He could not be blamed for returning to The Hague and reporting the dismal facts as they stood. He *would* be blamed, of course. But he could bear that a good deal better than having to answer to the Bernese authorities for the havoc he might be accused of wreaking in their peaceful city – on the sabbath, as the doctor had pointed out. The doctor, however, did not know his name and was presently preoccupied with McIlwraith. There was an opportunity for Cloisterman to slip away. But it would not last long. If he did not take it, he might come to regret it. And, so far, he had come to regret just about everything that had happened since his departure from Amsterdam. It was time to think of himself.

'Excuse me, Colonel,' he said under his breath as he turned towards the road. 'I really must be going.'

Chapter Twenty

Chances and Choices

The trial before the House of Commons of Charles Stanhope, Secretary to the Treasury, was closely argued and narrowly decided. The evidence presented seemed damning, but Walpole spoke vigorously for the defence and rumours abounded that the King had pleaded with certain Members to abstain. Abstentions, indeed, were what ultimately saved Stanhope. Three members of Brodrick's own committee left the House before the vote was taken, the aptly named Sloper among them. Stanhope was eventually acquitted by 180 votes to 177.

The public reaction to thus being cheated of a prime victim was predictably querulous. A mood of simmering riot prevailed for some days afterwards. Once more, it was widely and plausibly asserted, the politicians had spat in the eye of Justice.

To avoid inflaming the situation still further, it was decided that the funeral of James Craggs the younger, lately deceased Southern Secretary, should be held at night. Under the cover of darkness, therefore, late in the evening of the day following Stanhope's acquittal, many of the great and the good of Augustan England – or the greedy and the grasping, according to taste – filed into Westminster Abbey to pay their obsequial respects to one for whom death had forestalled many reproaches.

Near the front of the sombrely clad gathering, Viscount

Townshend found himself awkwardly seated between Walpole and the Earl of Sunderland, between the coming man in the political firmament and its fading force.

For one whose power was draining away almost by the hour, however, Sunderland contrived to seem remarkably unconcerned by the difficulties that confronted him. 'Carteret will be confirmed as Craggs' successor within days, I believe,' he casually ventured. 'You think you will find him pliable, Townshend?'

'He has not been recommended for his pliability, Spencer.'

'Has he not? For his ability, then? Ability can be a dangerous thing.'

'Except in oneself,' Walpole muttered.

'Oh, quite, quite,' said Sunderland. 'And securing Stanhope's acquittal undoubtedly suggests ability of a high order . . . in someone.'

'It certainly augurs well for those yet to answer to the case,' said Walpole with a sidelong smile.

'His Majesty would be pleased if all his traduced ministers could be acquitted,' said Sunderland. 'Preferably by handsomer majorities.'

'That may be asking for too much.'

'The prerogative of kings, Walpole. If you don't understand that . . .' Sunderland shrugged and flipped open his prayer-book, then closed it again and tapped the cover. 'What of the other matter so much on His Majesty's mind?' He smiled. '*Das Grüne Buch*, as he coyly refers to it.'

'In hand.'

'But not *in our hands*.'

'Not yet.'

'Soon?'

Walpole curled his lip. 'I trust so.'

'You sent Wagemaker, didn't you?' Townshend did his best not to look surprised by this disquieting evidence that

200

Sunderland's information network was functioning as efficiently as ever. 'What if he should fail – or fall by the wayside?'

'Don't worry, Spencer,' Walpole replied. 'Whatever happens, we shan't ask you for advice.'

'No? Well, here's some anyway. You should—'

Before Sunderland could let fall his pearl of statesmanly wisdom, the funeral drum sounded and a noise from behind them of shuffling feet and clearing throats signalled the arrival of the coffin. The three men rose, along with those to right and left of them. There was a second drum-beat. Then, in the instant before the dirgeful music began in earnest, Sunderland leaned towards Townshend and finished what he had been saying, though in too hushed a tone for Townshend to think that Walpole would be able to catch the words.

'Always assume the worst.'

Assuming the worst had become second nature to Nicholas Cloisterman since his departure from The Hague in the company of the late Colonel Wagemaker. Nothing had gone right and almost everything had gone wrong. Wagemaker was dead, the Green Book was probably already on the other side of the Alps and Cloisterman's own recent conduct, he could not but admit to himself, bore no close inspection. He had fled Berne with a singular lack of vice-consular dignity and no clear plan other than to return to Amsterdam and face down any criticism that Dalrymple threw at him.

The lapse of days had made that plan seem less and less prudent, however. At Burgdorf he had sold his horse, being no natural horseman, in favour of travelling by *post-wagen*, a slow but reliable mode of transport that had taken him first to Lucerne, then Zürich, then the spa town of Baden, where he had thought to sample the waters in the hope that they might have some tonic effect on him, before heading north to the Rhine and seeking a passage downstream. It was at Baden, on the evening of Craggs' funeral in London, the waters as yet unsampled, that he finally realized it would not do; it simply would not do.

He reviewed matters over a mournful pipe as he paced the chill and empty promenade by the banks of the Limmat. Turn it over how he might, his situation was even less appetizing than the meal he had just consumed at the Rapperswil inn. But sometimes it was as necessary to confront uncomfortable truths as it was to swallow unpalatable food. He would be expected to have done more than he had. Ultimately, he served the same master as Wagemaker. And that master would be satisfied by nothing less than retrieval of the Green Book. Failure would only be excused if it could be shown that no effort had been spared in the attempt. Thus far, Cloisterman's efforts did not look unstinting so much as grudging, if not minimal. He was going to have to do better.

He stopped and gazed soulfully down into the river. This sort of business did not suit him. It really did not. Yet it was business he would have to attend to. As from tomorrow. He sighed, turned up his greatcoat collar and started back towards the inn. There was an early call to be arranged.

An early call did not figure in William Spandrel's intentions for the following day. His flight from Berne had been far from the aimless retreat Cloisterman had contrived to make, but had yielded strangely similar results. Feeling unable to risk returning to the Drei Tassen for his horse, he had walked south along the Interlaken road to the first post-house, where he had used some of McIlwraith's money to have himself driven on to Thun. There he had stayed overnight, heavy-hearted and lonely, before boarding a southbound coach early the following morning. Many jolting hours later, he had discovered that what the Thun innkeeper meant by south was not the Simplon Pass but Lake Geneva. He had finished his second day on the road at Vevey, as far from his destination as he had begun his first.

Naturally, he had intended his stay at Vevey's Auberge du Lac to be brief, but he had been woken in the night by the onset of a violent ague that kept him abed for the next two days, too ill even to think of leaving his room, let alone the inn. It was, according to the not unsympathetic landlady, Madame Jacquinot, 'La grippe; c'est partout.' There was nothing to be done but to sweat it out. The evening of Craggs' funeral in London and of Cloisterman's about-turn in Baden found Spandrel decisively out of action.

Some semblance of normal health began to return to him the following day. By the afternoon he felt well enough to sit by the window of his room and watch the comings and goings of ferries and barges from the quay below the inn. The sun sparkled on the lake and warmed him through the glass. There was a springlike bloom to the weather. But for anxiety born of the knowledge that he had accomplished precisely nothing towards fulfilling his promise to McIlwraith to hunt down Estelle de Vries, he might have been able to summon a degree of contentment as he surveyed the scene.

He thought of McIlwraith more wistfully then than at any time since leaving him to die in that snow-patched meadow outside Berne. It was not only that he missed him more acutely than he would ever have expected. It was also that it had been so easy to let him decide what to do and when to do it. Now, Spandrel had to think and act for himself. Tomorrow, he would set off for the Simplon Pass.

If Estelle had gone that way, she was almost certainly beyond the Alps by now, perhaps even beyond Milan, although his grasp of Italian geography was far too insecure to guess where she might be, or how long it might take her to reach Rome. He should have paid more attention to McIlwraith's references to the journey that lay ahead while he had the chance. As it was, he would have to rely on whatever information he could glean along the way.

Luck would be bound to play its part, of course. So far, he did not seem to have enjoyed his share of it. But luck, he reflected as he watched an elegant pink-sailed yacht nose in towards the quay, always turned in the end, one way or the other.

And there below him, as the yacht tied up and the passengers disembarked, it did so, in that instant, just for him.

There were three passengers: two men and a woman. The men were both wearing plush hats, beribboned wigs and extravagantly swag-cut greatcoats, flapping open to reveal frilled stocks and brocaded waistcoats. They were of about the same age – mid to late twenties – and clearly neither lacked for funds, at any rate to lavish on expensive tailors. Physically, they could hardly have been more different, however. One was tall and cadaverously thin, with a narrow, pale, bony face to which his fruitily feminine lips seemed scarcely to belong. He struck a pose with every step, flourishing a cane as counterpoint to his daintily flexed ankles. The other was short and fleshy, poised between youthful plumpness and middle-aged corpulence, with puddingy features set in a smirking face, the high colour of which suggested a toping disposition. He clumped along the quay in what was presumably intended to be a confident swagger.

204

They were both English. Spandrel could hear their braying tones from where he sat, though he could not make out more than the odd word. Their female companion was also English. This he knew, even though she was saying nothing as far as he could tell. Nor was it her taste in clothes that gave her away. The sky-blue dress visible beneath the mushroom-grey travelling coat was undeniably fetching, but also curiously anonymous. What settled the issue beyond doubt was that he recognized her very well. She was Estelle de Vries.

Spandrel put on his boots and coat so quickly that the exertion induced a coughing fit, from which he had barely recovered when he left his room and hurried downstairs. Estelle and her new-found friends had been ambling along the quay when last glimpsed, admiring the view of the lake and the snow-capped mountains beyond. But Spandrel was convinced he would find them nowhere in sight or already going back aboard the yacht. The chance that fate had handed him was a fleeting one. He had to seize it, though how to do so was still unclear to him as he reached the hall and turned towards the front door.

But he need not have hurried. There they were, in front of him, being ushered into the dining-room by Madame Jacquinot, no doubt attracted, as he had been, by the Auberge du Lac's freshly painted air of welcome. Estelle glanced along the hall at him as they went. He saw her catch her breath and look quickly away. Then she stopped and said something to Madame Jacquinot. It seemed to be a request of some kind. The two men moved ahead into the dining-room. But Madame Jacquinot led Estelle further down the hall. Spandrel moved back up the stairs out of sight. A door opened below him. He glimpsed a wash-stand and mirror in the closet it led to. 'Merci, madame,' said Estelle. She stepped inside and closed the door. Then Madame Jacquinot bustled off to attend to the men, whose laughter could be heard echoing in the low-ceilinged dining-room.

Spandrel moved cautiously to the closet door. It opened as he approached and Estelle stepped out to meet him. 'Mr Spandrel,' she said. 'This is . . . a surprise.' And not, her expression suggested, a pleasant one.

'There's a small garden.' Spandrel nodded towards the rear quarters of the building. 'We can talk there.'

'I can't be gone long.'

'I don't know who those two preening ninnies are, Mrs de Vries, but I'd wager they know nothing of the murdered husband you left in Amsterdam, not to mention the dead lover in Berne. In the circumstances, I think you can be gone as long as you need to be. Shall we?'

'You don't look well,' she said, as they reached the daylight and turned to face each other.

'You, on the other hand, look uncommonly well.' It was true. Perhaps it was the lake air, or the thrill of the chase, that had given a heightened colour to her cheeks. She did not seem at all frightened. She seemed, indeed, utterly calm, inconvenienced by this turn of events, but un-dismayed.

'Where is Captain McIlwraith?'

'Dead.'

She frowned. 'That I am sorry to hear.'

'A Government agent caught up with us. There was a duel.'

'And the agent?'

'Also dead.'

'So much death. I am sorry, Mr Spandrel. Though I don't suppose you believe me.'

'Why should I? You lied *about* me in Amsterdam. You lied *to* me in Berne.'

206

'Those lies seemed . . . necessary.'

'You still have the Green Book?'

'It's in a safe place.'

'Where?'

'A bank. In Geneva.'

'Why didn't you make for the Simplon Pass when you left Berne?'

'I'm not sure. I was confused. Pieter's death was so violent, so . . . stupid. I could scarcely think for the shock of what had happened. They killed each other, he and Jupe. You know that?'

'I saw their bodies. Left by you for someone else to discover.'

'I couldn't remain. You must understand how it was.'

'Oh, I do.'

'You think me very callous, don't you?'

Spandrel nodded. 'Yes.'

'I suppose I must seem so. But it isn't—' She glanced back towards the door by which they had left the building. 'I shall be missed soon.'

'Who are they?'

'Mr Buckthorn and Mr Silverwood are two young English gentlemen sent abroad by their fathers to improve their minds. I met them in Geneva and persuaded them to add me to their party. We are due to set off for Turin in just a few days. I gather the Mont Cenis Pass is scarcely more formidable than the Simplon.'

'Why did you go to Geneva?'

'Because I could not hope to complete my journey unaided and alone. Geneva was the closest city where I was likely to find the sort of help I needed.'

'And you weren't disappointed.'

'What brought you to Vevey?'

'Chance. *Mis*chance, so far as you're concerned.'

'I would deny anything you told them.'

'Would your denials suffice?'

'Perhaps. Perhaps not. I would prefer . . .' She looked at him with a faint, self-mocking smile. 'Not to find out.'

'You don't have to.'

'Are you proposing a partnership, Mr Spandrel?'

'Either I go with you. Or you don't go at all.'

'The Green Book?'

'We share the proceeds of the sale.'

'What of Mr Buckthorn and Mr Silverwood?'

'Tell them I'm your cousin. Tell them whatever you think they're likeliest to believe. But persuade them to let me join the party. Do you think you can do that?'

'Probably.'

'And will you?'

'It seems I must.' She arched her eyebrows at him. 'Does it not?'

Chapter Twenty-One

Between the Covers

Estelle Plenderleath, only daughter of Josiah Plenderleath, led a comfortable if not cosseted childhood amidst the rural quietude of Shropshire, untroubled – because no-one could bear to tell her – that the family estate was entailed and would pass to a male cousin when her father died. This the hale and affectionate Squire Plenderleath did not seem likely to do for many years. But a riding accident plucked him inconsiderately away, obliging his widow to explain the sombre consequences to Estelle and the pair of them to take refuge with relatives in London, while the cousin took prompt and unceremonious possession. The Spandrels were as welcoming as the constraints of space and money would permit, but those constraints were far from negligible and Estelle's mother encouraged her to seek a moneyed husband who could rescue both of them from their sadly reduced circumstances. A Dutch merchant called de Vries, whose dealings with Mr Spandrel in connection with his mapmaking business led to an encounter with Estelle, became instantly and fortuitously enraptured. There was a significant difference in age, it was true, but de Vries showed himself to be a good man and Estelle could scarcely allow her heart to rule her head. They were married and, for several years thereafter, Estelle lived quietly and dutifully with her husband in Amsterdam, while her mother, supported by an allowance from de Vries, retired to Lyme Regis. Then, quite suddenly, de Vries died. Estelle, now a wealthy widow, decided that the time had at last come to enjoy herself. De Vries had often promised to show her the wonders of Rome, but had always been too busy to take her. Now, she would take herself. When news of her departure reached her mother, the old lady was thrown into a state of high anxiety by the thought of a vulnerable young woman undertaking such an arduous and hazardous journey on her own. The Spandrels were persuaded to send their son William after her to afford such protection and assistance as he could. William was not to know, of course, that when he found Estelle he would not find her alone, but enjoying the solicitous attentions of two excellent young gentlemen whose path had crossed hers in Geneva: Giles Buckthorn and Naseby Silverwood.

Spandrel was given no cause to doubt, during the days following his addition to the travelling party, that Buckthorn and Silverwood believed this version of events. (It was not a question of Buckthorn *or* Silverwood; the two men were as similar in their opinions and modes of expression as they were *dis*similar in appearance.) Why should they not believe it? The account of themselves to which Estelle and Spandrel had agreed to subscribe at the conclusion of their hasty negotiations in Vevey contained enough of the truth to disguise that which was not true. The exact proportion was unknown to Spandrel. Had Estelle ever been Miss Plenderleath, the demure Salopian lass? He was inclined to think not. But since, as Estelle at one point remarked, the secret of successful lying was to invent as little as possible, perhaps she really had been.

What was undeniable was the dexterity with which she accommodated Spandrel in the tale she had already told Buckthorn and Silverwood, a tale that grew around him in the telling and wove their separate pasts into an interdependent present. There were times, posing as Estelle's cousin, when he actually believed that was what he was. Certainly, he could not afford to do other than consistently pretend he was. The fiction, once agreed upon, had to be maintained – for both their sakes.

Fortunately, Buckthorn and Silverwood were an incurious pair, at least so far as Spandrel was concerned. They were not interested in him at all. They affected, indeed, to ignore him. Their attentions were devoted to Estelle and not, even then, to the circumstances that had thrown her into their company, but to the alluring possibilities that arose as a result. Amidst all their exaggerated courtesies and languid drolleries, it was obvious that they were as besotted with Estelle as she had intended them to be. They were just down from Oxford, bored, idle, vain and arrogant, acquainted, if they were to be believed, with a legion of great men and beautiful women. But they had never met anyone like Estelle de Vries. Of that Spandrel felt certain.

Spandrel, for his part, was obliged to simulate a degree of cousinly familiarity with Estelle, as she was with him. This sharing of secrets was undeniably exciting. It was all too easy to dream of a future more delectable than any he had previously envisioned. But tempting prospects, he well knew, made bad guides. Their partnership was not likely to be an enduring one. He reminded himself of his intention to wrest the Green Book from her at the first possible opportunity and deliver it to the Brodrick Committee in accordance with McIlwraith's dying wish.

But no such opportunity presented itself during the three days the party spent in Geneva. Estelle argued, not unreasonably, that the book was best left where it was – in a safe at Turrettini's Bank – until their departure. Buckthorn and Silverwood believed it was a jewel-box she

211

had deposited there. And why would they not, since that was what she had told them? As to the Alpine crossing, they favoured a delay until after Easter, but Estelle was keen to proceed at once, purportedly on account of her thirst for a sight of those Roman antiquities her late husband had evocatively described to her. Spandrel was rather pleased with himself for settling the issue by suggesting that Buckthorn and Silverwood had been taken in by blood-curdling travellers' tales of ravening wolves in the mountain passes at this time of the year. Their fear of personal discomfort, let alone danger, was only surpassed by their fear of losing face before Estelle. A departure upon the morrow was instantly agreed.

That afternoon, Estelle asked them to escort her to the bank so that she might collect her jewel-box. They were clearly delighted that this honour was conferred upon them rather than Spandrel. And Spandrel had no choice but to give every appearance of feeling slighted by being passed over for such a duty. What he actually felt was a growing suspicion that opportunities of laying his hands upon the Green Book during the journey to Rome were going to be few and far between. Estelle, indeed, had probably already resolved that he would have none. But, as to that, she might yet be surprised.

If Spandrel believed himself capable of surprising such a woman as Estelle de Vries, he failed to allow for the probability that she would spring a greater surprise on him. That evening, when the ill-matched party of four met for supper at the Clé Argenté, the comfortable inn near the cathedral where they had been lodging, Buckthorn and Silverwood proposed an evening of cards and music at the house of the tirelessly hospitable Monsieur Bouvin, whose acquaintance they had recently made. Estelle excused herself on grounds of a headache and retired to her room.

Spandrel claimed to have a letter to write. After some grumbling about the unsociability of their companions, Buckthorn and Silverwood headed out into the night.

Spandrel had no letter to write, of course. He left the inn a short time afterwards and sought out a humble tavern where he could drink and smoke at his ease and not mind his manners and turns of phrase, as he felt obliged to do while playing the part of Estelle's cousin. An hour or so later, feeling less fretful and altogether more himself, he made his way back to the Clé Argenté.

As he entered his room, he noticed something pale lying on the dark boards at his feet. It was a note, apparently slipped under the door in his absence. He held it up to read by the light of the lamp he was carrying.

I must see you tonight. Come to my room. E.

She was waiting for him, seated by a well-stacked fire, wearing some kind of loosely belted dressing-gown in which threads of gold glimmered in the firelight. A bottle of brandy and two glasses stood on a small table beside her chair.

'What can I do for you . . . cousin?' Spandrel began.

'Sit down. Join me in a glass.'

Spandrel fetched the upright chair from its place by the dressing-table and set it down on the other side of the hearth from her, then poured them both some brandy. He felt wholly unsurprised by her masculine taste in liquor.

'Where have you been? Not to Monsieur Bouvin's, I assume.'

'No.' Spandrel seated himself and sipped some brandy. 'Not to Monsieur Bouvin's.'

'We should trust each other, William,' she said. 'Really we should.'

213

The only response Spandrel could summon was a rueful smile.

'I'm perfectly serious.'

'I'm sure you are.'

'We have a long journey ahead of us. Too long, I think, to be spent in watching each other for signs of impending treachery.'

'How's that to be avoided?'

'By putting what unites us before what divides us.'

'The Green Book unites us. And the money it's worth. Nothing else.'

'Nothing? Come, William. Why do you think we've been able to convince Mr Buckthorn and Mr Silverwood that we are cousins?'

'Because they're easily convinced . . . by you.'

'And by you. We seem like cousins. There's a similarity, a . . . kinship. Fate has handed us this chance to transform our lives. We must take the chance. Together.'

'Is that what you told Zuyler?'

'Pieter was greedy. But you are not. You are in truth rarer than you look. You are a good man.'

'And an easily flattered one, you seem to think.'

'Not at all. Do you think me beautiful?'

He looked at her in silence for a moment, then said, 'Yes. I do.'

'Is that flattery?'

'It's the truth.'

'Exactly. The truth. The book is in a case in the dressing-table drawer, William. Would you like to see it? I think you should.'

He frowned at her in puzzlement, then rose and carried the lamp he had brought from his room across to the dressing-table. He stood it on the table and slid open the drawer. A red, padded-leather jewel-box lay within. This he lifted out and set down by the lamp.

'It's not locked,' said Estelle from behind him. 'In ordinary circumstances, it would be, of course. But these are not ordinary circumstances.'

Spandrel released the catches and raised the lid. There was the book: a plain, green-covered ledger, with leather spine and marbled page edges. For this, and what it contained, men had died. He had nearly been one of them. Yet now, here it was, in his grasp. He hooked a finger under the cover and opened it.

The pages were ruled in columns. In the middle were listed names, on the left and right amounts at dated intervals, paid in and paid out. But for most of the names nothing had been paid in, only out. And the sums involved were massive: £10,000 here, £20,000 there. The transactions on the page he was looking at dated from about a year before. Each was recorded in the same hand, the initials of the writer, R.K., added in minute script above each entry. Spandrel turned to the next page, then the next. Thousands more, in a forest of zeros, met his gaze. He turned back to the beginning and ran his eye down the names. Then he caught his breath.

'Are you surprised?' Estelle's voice was scarcely more than a whisper. She was standing beside him now, her shadow, cast by the fire, flickering across the page. 'So many of them. The proud and the mighty. All that they took, down to the last farthing.'

'But . . . I never thought . . .'

'That there would be so many? Or that they would have taken so much? Some paid for less than they received. Others paid nothing at all. Every one of them was, and is, a bought man. And what men they are. Dukes, marquesses, earls, Members of Parliament, courtiers, ministers, persons of distinction. Abundant largesse, showered on the great and the wealthy, while the seaside widows and the humble shopkeepers scraped together their pennies to buy stock these people were made a gift of. Do you wonder that Pieter asked a hundred thousand pounds for this book?'

'No. I don't.'

'The book you carried from London to Amsterdam . . . for how much?'

'The promise of hardly anything, compared with . . .' He nodded glumly at the ranks of figures.

'Where we're going . . . we might reasonably ask for more than a hundred thousand.'

'Might we?'

'I think so. See . . .' She turned the page and pointed to an entry. 'Here.'

Spandrel stooped for a clearer view. On the line where Estelle's finger rested was written, *Rt. Hon. J. Aislabie, on behalf of H.M.*

'The Chancellor of the Exchequer,' said Estelle. 'On behalf of His Majesty. The King.' Her finger moved to the right. 'One hundred thousand pounds' worth of shares. That is why Pieter fixed on the figure. And how much paid for them?' Her finger moved to the left. 'Twenty thousand pounds. Just twenty. Then the whole allocation was sold back to the company, when the price was near its zenith, at a colossal profit. What do you think the London mob would do if they knew?'

'I think they might do almost anything.'

'Exactly. Which means the Pretender will pay hand-somely for possession of this book – our book.'

'Why didn't the King pay handsomely, when he had the chance?'

'The message must have gone astray. Pieter dealt through intermediaries. We won't make that mistake.'

'Won't we?'

'We won't make any mistakes. Trust me.'

'That word again. *Trust.*'

'It comes in many guises. And pledges come in different forms. Not just words, William.'

'What else?'

'Can you not guess?'

Spandrel felt a slither of something soft and silken across his hand. He turned towards Estelle and saw that she had released the belt of her gown. It hung open. Beneath, she wore only the thinnest of shifts. His mouth was dry, his mind aswarm with competing instincts. A good man? There she was surely mistaken. He wanted her, even more than he wanted the money. But it seemed he could have both. They were his for the asking.

Estelle slipped off the gown. It fell about her feet. The firelight behind her revealed the outline of her body through the shift. Desire engulfed Spandrel. He had to have her. What he would not even have dreamt to be possible when they had met in the library at her husband's house in Amsterdam was suddenly and deliriously about to happen. He reached out. She grasped his hand and slowly led it to her breast, full and soft beneath the shift. The warmth of her thrilled through him.

'Estelle—'

'Don't say anything.' She drew him closer. 'Whatever pleasure I can give . . . is yours to take.'

Chapter Twenty-Two

Over the Mountains

There were times – most of them when he was swaying in a strange kind of litter on the shoulders of four mountain porters with nothing but their sureness of hand between him and a sheer drop into a chasm of pure white snow and stark black rock – when Nicholas Cloisterman came seriously to doubt that he would survive the Alpine crossing. He remembered his Classics master at King's, Canterbury, pondering the puzzle of which route Hannibal had taken, elephants and all, back in 218 B.C. and was now quite certain on one point: it could not have been the Simplon Pass.

Arriving at Brig after a three-day journey from Baden, Cloisterman had joined a small party of travellers bound for Milan, happy as they were to accept his share of the cost of hiring guides and porters. The journey that followed was occasionally awe-inspiring, so vast and majestic were the Alps in their late winter grimness. But it was more often bone-numbingly cold and hair-raisingly hazardous. For Cloisterman the relief that he felt as they descended to Lake Maggiore was tempered only by the awareness that he would have to come back this way, though not, it was true, in late winter.

As to what season it would be, spring or summer, he had no way to tell. There had been no word at Brig of a lone female traveller. His enquiry on the subject had yielded nothing beyond the suggestion that, at this time of the year, he had to be joking. Nor did the British Consul at Milan, an amiable sinecurist called Phelps, prove any more helpful. Of Estelle de Vries there was no trace. Where she was remained a mystery. But where she was going was certain. And Cloisterman would have to follow.

'Business in Rome, is it?' remarked Phelps. 'I don't envy you, I must say. Concerns the Pretender, does it?'

'What makes you think so?' Cloisterman responded warily.

'Nothing else seems to take Government men that way. You know the wretched fellow has a son and heir now?'

'Of course.' News of the birth of a male to the Stuart line a couple of months previously had travelled fast.

'Horribly healthy, I gather.'

'How pleasing for his parents.'

'But not our employers, eh? Well, I wish you luck, whatever your business.' Phelps grinned. 'I expect you'll need it.'

A man in still greater need of luck than Cloisterman was Chancellor of the Exchequer John Aislabie, whose trial commenced at the House of Commons in London on the very afternoon of Cloisterman's unilluminating conversation with Consul Phelps in Milan.

Alas for Aislabie, luck did not come his way. The consequences of another acquittal following Charles Stanhope's evasion of justice were too serious to be contemplated. Walpole said nothing in defence of Aislabie, whose explanation that he had burnt all records of his dealings in South Sea stock because they were of no importance once settled was not well received. Small wonder, since those dealings had netted him a profit of £35,000. He was convicted, expelled from the House and consigned to the Tower, there to languish until occasion could be found to anatomize his estate and decide how much of it, if not all, should be forfeit.

Celebratory bonfires were lit across London as the news spread. Public anger was appeased. 'Sometimes,' remarked Walpole, watching the flames light the night sky from Viscount Townshend's Cockpit office, 'a sacrifice there has to be.'

'Will Aislabie be enough for them?' asked Townshend.

'I'd happily give them Sunderland as well. But the King's uncommonly fond of the fellow. And the King expects me to persuade the House to spare him.'

'Will you be able to?'

'I think so. Just so long as no new evidence turns up.'

'Such as the Green Book? I worry about it, Robin, I really do.'

'So you should. If it fell into the wrong hands . . .' Walpole cast his brother-in-law a meaningful look. 'They might be lighting bonfires for us as well.'

The four English travellers who arrived in Turin the day after Aislabie's conviction in London had a no less arduous Alpine crossing than Cloisterman to look back on. The vertiginous scramblings of their porters over the wind-scoured Mont Cenis Pass had caused Estelle de Vries no apparent alarm, however. It had therefore been necessary for her male companions to affect a similar unconcern, their true feelings concealed behind devil-may-care quips and high fur collars.

The performance of Buckthorn and Silverwood in this regard had scarcely wavered, although Buckthorn had mentioned wolves often enough to suggest a pre-occupation with the subject and Silverwood had manifestly not been amused by the porters' discontented mutterings about his weight.

Spandrel for his part had found it easy to assume an uncharacteristic jauntiness of manner. The frozen beauty of the Alps was something he had never expected to experience. Nor, for that matter, was the sexual favour of such a woman as Estelle de Vries. He had entered a new world in more ways than one and his elation left little space for fear, nor indeed for the thought that Estelle did not and could not love him. She had used the act of love to bind him to her and she had succeeded. The memory of their night together in Geneva was sometimes clearer to Spandrel than the events taking place around him. Like a white flame of refined pleasure, it burned within him. He was hers, completely. And she was his, reservedly. He was aware of the disparity, what it meant and why it existed. He knew the promises he was breaking and the dangers he was ignoring. But he also knew that what she had given him he could not resist.

The cramped accommodation available to Alpine travellers had prevented any immediate repetition of their night of passion. Buckthorn and Silverwood could be given no hint of how matters stood between them. It was one more secret for them to share – the darkest and most delicious of all. At a spacious inn of the sort the Savoyard capital might be expected to boast, however, that secret might both be kept and enjoyed.

But Estelle did not agree. 'We must be careful,' she counselled during a few snatched moments of privacy. 'If Mr Buckthorn and Mr Silverwood should learn that we are lovers, they would be consumed by jealousy. They might also come to doubt that we have given them a true account of ourselves. They are not above spying at corners and listening at keyholes. We must give them nothing to spy upon.'

'We don't need them any more,' Spandrel protested. 'Let's go on alone.'

'It was agreed that they would accompany me to

Florence. I cannot spurn them now. To Florence we must go – together.'

'And after Florence?'

'You'll have me all to yourself.'

It was a promise and a lure. Florence was the better part of a week away. Until then . . .

'Don't spoil what we have, William. There's so much more to come. Very soon.' She kissed him. 'Trust me.'

He did not trust her, of course. He could never do that. But he did adore her. And he was not sure that he would ever do otherwise.

'Mr Walpole,' the Earl of Sunderland announced in a tone of mock geniality as he stepped into the Paymaster-General's office at the Cockpit the following morning. 'I'm a little surprised to find you here, I must say.'

'No more than I'm surprised to see you here,' growled Walpole.

'I only meant that so many posts are said to be within your grasp – more I sometimes think than are not – that it's a touch disconcerting to realize that in truth you're still only' – Sunderland looked about him and smiled – 'the Army's wages clerk.'

'What can I do for you, Spencer?'

'It's what *I* can do for *you* that brings me here, my dear fellow.'

'Good of you to think of me when you've so much else on your mind.'

'The trial, you mean? Next week's . . . grand entertainment.'

'*Your* trial.'

'We all have trials. Some bear them better than others.'

'Some have more to bear.'

'Indeed.' Sunderland plucked his snuff-box from his coat pocket and took a pinch, as if needing to clear his

222

nose of some unpleasant smell. 'I have . . . disappointing news for you. I'm sure you'll . . . bear it well.'

'What news?'

'A Secret Service report, the contents of which I thought it kinder to convey to you personally than . . . through the normal channels.'

Soon, very soon, Walpole consoled himself, the Secret Service would be reporting to him, not Sunderland. Then he would be the one doling out their nuggets of intelligence to those he judged fit to hear them. Then *he* would be master. But for the moment, Sunderland still stood above him, albeit on a crumbling pedestal. 'Kind of you, I'm sure.'

'As to kindness, you might not think it so when you hear what I have to tell you.'

Walpole leaned back in his chair and scratched his stomach. 'Well?'

'Colonel Wagemaker. Your . . . agent.'

'Is that what you think he is?'

'It's what I think he *was*. Until he was killed in a duel at Berne on the twenty-sixth of last month.'

Walpole summoned a grin to cover his discomposure. 'Wagemaker? Dead?'

'As the mission you sent him on.'

'How's this . . . said to have happened?'

'A duel of some sort. Details are sparse. But dead he undoubtedly is. It seems you did not choose wisely. As for Townshend's assurances to the King that you and he would soon have the Green Book under lock and key . . .' Sunderland cocked his head and treated Walpole to a look of distilled condescension. 'What are they worth now?'

'I never put all my eggs in one basket, Spencer. Any more than you do.'

'A hard policy to follow, when the basket is so distant.'

Walpole shrugged. 'Hard, but prudent.'

223

'Prudent, but unlikely.' Sunderland propped himself on the corner of the desk and held Walpole's gaze. 'Your eggs are smashed, Mr Paymaster. Every last one.'

'I doubt it.'

'Of course you do. Doubt's your stock-in-trade. I'll send you a copy of the report. That should still a few of those doubts.'

'I'm obliged.'

'Obliged to me. Yes. I'm glad you understand that.' Sunderland stood up. 'And I'd be gladder still if you remembered it.' He moved towards the door, then stopped and looked back. 'The King accepts that Aislabie had to go. But he wishes it to end there. He wants no more ministers led away to the Tower.'

'No more than you do, I'm sure.'

'If you aim to win his favour, you'd do well not to disappoint him.'

'I'll see what I can do.'

'If you'll take my advice . . .' Sunderland's gaze narrowed. 'You'll make sure you do enough.'

The gloom of a London winter seemed far away amidst the balmy pleasantries of a Tuscan spring. Relaxing in the walled garden of the British Consul's Florentine palazzo beneath a sapphire sky, warmed by good food, fine wine and mellow sunshine, Nicholas Cloisterman felt that his journey from Amsterdam was at long last beginning to yield some rewards. His host, Percy Blain, was an intelligent cynic after Cloisterman's own heart and his hostess, Mrs Blain, was proof that cynicism might be a sure guide to many things but not to womankind. After but two nights beneath their roof, he felt that he was among friends.

Nor was friendship the only gift the Blains had bestowed upon him. Blain, in whom he had confided all but the exact nature of the book he was so earnestly seeking on the British Government's behalf, had suggested a precaution they might take, there in Florence, to reduce the likelihood of that book's arrival in Rome.

The precaution depended on the co-operation of the Tuscan authorities and it was the securing of that co-operation which Cloisterman and Blain were now toasting over a glass of excellent local wine beside a plashing fountain and a table still bearing the remnants of a splendid repast.

'How were you able to bring it off?' Cloisterman asked, still unclear on the point. 'The Dutch authorities would have sent me away with a flea in my ear if I'd ever put such a request to them.'

'But the Dutch are a powerful and independent people,' replied Blain. 'What is the Grand Duchy of Tuscany but a pawn on the great powers' chessboard? The Grand Duke is an old man, his son and heir a childless degenerate. The treaty with Spain our late Lord Stanhope spent so much time and effort negotiating cedes Tuscany to the Spaniards when the Medici line fails, which it surely soon will. But Stanhope is dead. New ministers mean new policies. Treaties can be *re*-negotiated. That is the Grand Duke's hope. And that is why *his* ministers are so keen to oblige us.'

'Every customs post will be on the look-out for Mrs de Vries?'

'Any Englishwoman *or* Dutchwoman, travelling alone *or* in company, whatever name she gives, will be stopped and searched. Believe me, the customs men need no encouragement to perform such a task with the utmost diligence.'

'She might not pass through Tuscany.'

'It is a considerable diversion to go round. And from her point of view surely an unnecessary one.'

'True,' Cloisterman conceded. Estelle de Vries would head for Rome by the most direct route. That was certain. And that was indeed the one problem Blain could not solve for him. 'But by the same token . . .'

'She may already have passed through.'

'Yes. She may.'

'My enquiries suggest not. But it's possible, of course. I can't deny it.'

'I shall have to press on, then.'

'A pity. Lizzie and I have enjoyed your visit.'

'So have I.'

'As for what awaits you in Rome . . .' Blain smiled. 'The Pretender's so-called court is a warren of squabbling Scots. We have one of them in our pay, of course. More than one, I dare say. Our masters in Whitehall don't trust me with all their secrets. Colonel Lachlan Drummond is a name I *can* give you, though. I shouldn't rely on him overmuch. But he's there to be used. As for—' Blain broke off at the sight of his wife hurrying out to them from the deep shade beneath the loggia at the rear of the palazzo. 'What is it, my dear?'

'A message from Chancellor Lorenzini.' She handed him a note and smiled across at Cloisterman. 'I thought you'd wish to see it at once, in case it had some bearing on your discussions.'

'Let's hope he hasn't had second thoughts about granting your request,' said Cloisterman.

'Surely not.' Blain tore the note open and looked at it, then frowned. 'Well, I say . . .'

'What is it?'

'The Pope is dead.' He passed the note to Cloisterman for him to read. 'It seems you'll find Rome in the fickle grasp of an interregnum. I was just about to tell you that His Holiness keeps the Pretender on a tight rein. But now, it seems . . .' Blain shrugged. 'The reins are off.'

*　　*　　*

If Cloisterman had known that Estelle de Vries was at that moment not in Rome, more than a hundred miles to the south, but in Genoa, more than a hundred miles to the north, he would no doubt have remained in Florence, contentedly waiting for the Tuscan authorities to seize his prey for him. But he did not know. And ignorance can sometimes be a useful ally.

The journey from Turin to Genoa along mud-clogged roads had been neither fast nor agreeable. Along the way, an idea had formed in Spandrel's mind, an idea that had taken him down to Genoa's bustling harbour on the very afternoon of the party's arrival in the city. There he had chanced upon the British merchantman *Wyvern*, bound for Palermo by way of Orbitello and Naples. It was a two-day voyage to Orbitello, the master's mate told him, and a day by coach from there to Rome, a much quicker route to his destination than overland all the way; and paying passengers could be readily accommodated. A deal was thereupon struck.

It was a more fortuitous deal than Spandrel knew, for Orbitello lay in the tiny Austrian enclave of the Presidio, sandwiched between Tuscany and the Papal States. By this route, he and Estelle would never set foot on Tuscan territory; Cloisterman's trap would never be sprung.

Spandrel would no doubt have rubbed his hands in satisfaction had he been aware of this happy consequence of his negotiation of a swift coastal passage south. But he was not aware. And yet rub them he nonetheless did, as he left the *Wyvern* and hurried back towards the *albergo* where he and his companions had taken lodgings. Silverwood had complained of sea-sickness on the placid waters of Lake Geneva. The Mediterranean would surely be too much for him to contemplate. Besides, Orbitello was closer to Rome than Florence. And it was Florence that

Silverwood and Buckthorn had proclaimed as their destination from the start. No, no. Only two passengers would be leaving aboard the *Wyvern* in the morning. Estelle had promised him he would soon have her all to himself. And now he would – even sooner than she had expected.

But Spandrel's reckoning was awry. Giles Buckthorn had no intention of allowing his friend's sea-sickness to separate them from Estelle.

'The arrangement is an excellent one, Mr Spandrel. So excellent that we will come with you. I'm sure the *Wyvern* can accommodate two more passengers.'

'Oh, I don't—'

'Leave it to me. I'll cut down there now and hire a berth for us.'

'But Mr Silverwood's clearly no sailor.'

'Nonsense. It was because Lake Geneva was a millpond that he felt it. The ocean wave is just what he needs.'

'And this will keep you from Florence.'

'No matter. We will simply turn our itinerary about and take Florence after Rome. Ah, *la città eterna*. With a veritable Venus for company. What could be better?' Buckthorn struck a classical pose, arm outstretched, and gave Spandrel a fruity-lipped grin. 'Nothing, I rather think.'

Chapter Twenty-Three

Whither all Roads Lead

The trial by the House of Commons of the First Lord of the Treasury, Charles Spencer, third Earl of Sunderland, was fixed, by fateful chance, for the Ides of March. Legally, the event was without precedent, a peer of the realm being traditionally answerable only to the House of Lords. The fact that the trial was to be held in the absence of the accused, Sunderland not even deigning to watch from the gallery, added piquancy to the uniqueness of the occasion, while rumours that Walpole had been making free with bribes to save his old enemy's neck rumbled darkly in the background.

The debate, when it came, was fast and furious. The accusation that Sunderland had received £50,000 worth of South Sea stock without paying a penny for it was stark, but by no means simple, with neither chief cashier Knight nor his infamous account book on hand to settle the issue. That rested instead on votes, some freely given, some expensively bought. In the end, as many had predicted, Sunderland was acquitted.

The public were outraged, but unsurprised. And, as the dust settled, the delicacy of Walpole's judgement became apparent. Sunderland had survived, but the margin of votes by which he had done so – 233 to 172 – was too narrow for him to claim exoneration. He had escaped the

Tower. But he could not remain at the Treasury. His days were numbered. His era was over. While that of Walpole was about to begin.

Unless, of course, there was something even Walpole had failed to foresee.

The following morning saw a solitary and travel-weary Englishman present himself at the Porta del Popolo, northernmost of the gates set in the ancient wall surrounding Rome. It was a hot, glaringly bright spring day that would have been considered a fine adornment to high summer in Amsterdam, let alone London. Harassed by the customs officer into administering a bribe, Nicholas Cloisterman was at length allowed to pass through into the piazza on the other side, where he paused to admire, despite his fatigue, the Egyptian obelisk standing at its centre. Beyond this haughty finger of Imperial plunder from times long gone by, three streets led off into the city like the prongs of a trident. Cloisterman was bound for the right-hand prong, the Via di Ripetta, and, some way along it, the Casa Rossa, an *albergo* recommended to him by Percy Blain. Anglo-Papal relations being as cool as they were, the British Government had no consular representation in the city. Cloisterman was on his own. But he did not expect that to prove a problem. Early communication with the Government's spy at the Pretender's court, Colonel Drummond, would establish whether or not Estelle de Vries had already reached Rome. If not, Cloisterman could safely return to Florence and let Blain and the Tuscan authorities do what needed to be done. If she had, on the other hand . . . But Cloisterman was too tired to confront that issue unless and until he needed to. Succumbing to the importunate blandishments of one of the many *servi-*

tori di piazza, he engaged a fly and bade the driver take him directly to the Casa Rossa.

If Cloisterman had lingered in the Piazza del Popolo until late afternoon, he would have been taken aback to witness the arrival in Rome not just of Estelle de Vries, but also of William Spandrel, in the company of two Englishmen, one shaped like a bean-pole, the other like a water-butt – Giles Buckthorn and Naseby Silverwood. The latter pair administered as many loud complaints as lavish bribes before progressing beyond the customs-house, while Mrs de Vries and her supposed cousin attracted little attention. Buckthorn and Silverwood had it on good authority, so they declared, that the best accommodation was to be found in or near the Piazza di Spagna. By strange chance it was the very same fox-faced *servitor* who had earlier obliged Cloisterman who now earned another fee by leaping aboard their carriage and directing its driver to their destination.

The light was fading fast as they drove along the Via del Babuino, the sky turning a gilded pink. Spandrel saw the alternately grand and dilapidated buildings to either side as purple-grey monuments to a world he had never expected to experience – ancient, exotic and mysterious. He should have felt exhilarated. Instead, the bile of regret and resentment lapped at his thoughts – regret for the promise he had given McIlwraith and was now busily breaking; resentment of Buckthorn and Silverwood for forcing Estelle to maintain a seemly distance from him. His only consolation was that they had finally arrived where their bold project of enrichment could be enacted. Once the book presently nestling in Estelle's travelling-case was sold, Buckthorn and Silverwood could be forgotten, along with everything else comprising their past. Only the future would matter then. And it was the future that seemed to glitter in Estelle's eyes as she glanced across at him. Nothing would be denied him then.

The Palazzo Muti, Roman residence of the self-styled King James III of England and VIII of Scotland, was a handsomely columned and pedimented gold-stuccoed building at the northern end of the Piazza dei Santi Apostoli, close to the heart of the old city. The Pretender had spent all but the first six months of his life exiled from the country he claimed the right to rule. The failure of the Fifteen had led to a still more humiliating exile from France and the past four years had found him sheltering in Rome, further than ever, both metaphorically and geographically, from where he wanted to be. Yet those four years had also seen his marriage, to the beautiful Polish princess, Clementina Sobieski, and her obliging production of a bonny baby boy. With the British Government mired in unpopularity, half its ministers on trial and the other half scrabbling for position, the Pretender's prospects did not currently seem as negligible as they often had.

Surveying the Palazzo Muti from the *trottoir* on the other side of the piazza, the lanterns flanking its entrance newly lit against the encroaching dusk, Cloisterman reflected that, grand though it was, it was far from grand enough for a king. Nor were its surroundings – narrow, rubbish-strewn streets rank with mud and *merda* – in any way flattering to James Edward Stuart's dignified view of himself. All in all, the Pretender's home-from-home looked what it was: a tribute to his past failures. But they would not matter if he could achieve one crowning success. And for that, Cloisterman suspected, the Green Book might be enough.

He moved away then, walking smartly towards the other end of the piazza. Before reaching it, he turned right, back towards the Corso, middle and longest of the three streets leading south from the Piazza del Popolo. He crossed the Corso, headed up it a little way, then turned off along a narrow street consumed by the shadows of unlit buildings, before stepping through a low arch into a dank courtyard, where he felt his way to a doorway and rang three times at the bell.

A minute or so passed, then the sound of shuffling feet and the glimmer of a candle seeped around the door. It creaked open and a small old woman with no more flesh on her than a sparrow squinted out at him. '*Si?*'

'For Colonel Drummond,' said Cloisterman, thrusting a letter into her ice-cold hand. 'You understand?'

'Colonel Drummond,' she repeated, comprehendingly enough. '*Si, si.*'

'It's important.' He raised his voice. '*Importante.*'

The candlelight made a shadowy chasm of her toothless grin. There was the rattle of something that might have been a laugh. '*Si, si. Sempre importante.*' Then she closed the door in his face.

Circumstances had meanwhile conspired to smile on the wishes and desires of William Spandrel. The Piazza di Spagna was a broad concourse, centred on a fountain fashioned in the likeness of a leaking boat, separating the Spanish Embassy from a muddy, cart-tracked slope, at the top of which stood the twin bell towers of the church of Trinità dei Monti. The *servitor* who had accompanied them from Piazza del Popolo persuaded Buckthorn and Silverwood that the most charming lodgings in the area were to be found in the Palazzetto Raguzzi, at the northern end of the piazza. Buckthorn and Silverwood were indeed charmed by the two first-floor rooms that were available, though chagrined to discover that the whole party could not be accommodated under the same roof. After much courteous proposing and chivalrous disposing, it was agreed that Estelle had to be given the benefit of one of the rooms and Spandrel that of the other, while Buckthorn and Silverwood contented themselves with rooms at the Albergo Luna in Via Condotti, just off the piazza.

The Palazzetto Raguzzi was well named so far as Spandrel was concerned. His room, like Estelle's, was palatially proportioned, with high windows overlooking the piazza, and was richly furnished. Such odd stains and frays as there were did not prevent it being just about the grandest lodgings he had ever secured. But grandeur was something he was already looking forward to becoming accustomed to. And meanwhile there was a priceless pleasure to be enjoyed.

After dinner with Buckthorn and Silverwood at the Albergo Luna, they retired early to the Palazzetto on grounds of fatigue following the long day's journey. Fatigued they certainly were. But for Spandrel that counted for nothing compared with his four days' worth of pent-up longing for Estelle. She seemed as delighted as he was to end their self-denial. An evening of irksome attendance on Buckthorn and Silverwood's by now all too familiar vapidities gave way to a night of physical release in which the joy Spandrel had felt in Geneva bloomed anew. It was a joy he knew at the back of his mind he should not make the mistake of supposing that Estelle shared. But by morning, suppose it he nonetheless did.

By morning also their thoughts had turned to the purpose for which they had come to Rome. 'We must deposit the book at a bank this morning,' said Estelle, as they lay in bed together at dawn. 'Mr Buckthorn and Mr Silverwood will be eager to show me some of the antiquities I have assured them I am equally eager to see. I propose you complain of some minor illness and absent yourself. They will not question your absence.'

'I reckon not.'

'In fact,' said Estelle with a smile, 'they will be rather pleased by it.'

'And won't hide their pleasure well.'

'Exactly. At all events, while I am yawning my way round some ruin or other, you will go to the Palazzo Muti and seek an audience with the Pretender's secretary.'

'What if he won't see me?'

'If you are persistent, he will. It may take a little while. We must be patient. When you tell him what we have to sell, he will understand its significance. And he will pay what we ask to gain possession of the book. For the Pretender, it will promise an end to exile.'

'Is that truly what the Green Book means, Estelle? Revolution in our homeland? A Stuart king back on the throne?'

'Who knows? And who cares?' Estelle inclined her head to look at Spandrel. Her eyes were deeper shadows amidst the shadows of the room. The scent of her flesh was all about him, the cunning and the daring of their scheme wreathing itself around his intoxicating memories of the night before. 'This is for us, William. Us and no-one else.'

'I wish you could come with me.'

'So do I. But such negotiations are best conducted by a man. It is the way of the world.'

'Who'd have conducted them for you if we hadn't met in Vevey? Buckthorn? Or Silverwood?'

'Neither.'

'But you just said—'

235

'Enough.' She silenced him with a kiss. 'We met. We made our pact.' She stretched out her hand to touch him beneath the sheets. 'Now we look forward. Not back. Ever again.'

Chapter Twenty-Four

Skinning the Bear

'Mr Spandrel, is it?' said James Edgar, as he looked up from his desk.

It was the late afternoon of the following day. The glaring Roman light of noon had faded to a purpling pink in the sky and to a blackening grey in the office of the private secretary to King James VIII and III, as Mr Edgar would undoubtedly have described himself. He was a spare, round-shouldered, bespectacled man who looked, though he probably was not, much older than the thirty-two-year-old king-in-exile whom he served. Mr Edgar was the dry-as-dust inky-fingered quintessence of a Scottish solicitor, transplanted with no apparent change of habit to the land of dead Caesars and dissolute cardinals.

Spandrel had waited many hours to see Mr Edgar. He had been left to cramp his haunches during those hours on a narrow chair in a draughty passage near the main stairway of the Palazzo Muti, while a contrasting assortment of whispering clerics, grumbling Scots and pinch-mouthed servants passed him heedlessly by. He had waited as patiently as he could, bearing Estelle's prediction of delay in mind. The Green Book was now safely lodged at the Banco Calderini, while Estelle was being shown the wonders of the Pantheon and the Campidoglio by the ever attentive Buckthorn and Silverwood. It was Spandrel's demanding lot to await his opportunity of a conversation

237

with the dour Mr Edgar and to ensure that the opportunity, when it came, was not wasted.

'My name is Spandrel, yes. May I come straight to the purpose of my visit?'

'I'd be grateful if you did. I'm a busy man, Mr Spandrel. And we have more than our fair share here of uninvited visitors. I can't afford to waste my time hearing all their stories.'

'I'm obliged to you for seeing me, then.'

'I was told you gave no sign of meaning to leave.'

'I've come too far to do that without explaining myself . . . to someone close to . . .'

'The King?'

Spandrel shrugged. 'Yes. The King.'

Edgar smiled thinly. 'You don't sound like a true believer, Mr Spandrel.'

'My beliefs don't matter.'

'Do they not? How far *have* you come, by the by?'

'That doesn't matter either. It's what I've come *with* that's important.'

'And what is that?'

'The secret account book of the chief cashier of the South Sea Company.'

Edgar raised one sceptical eyebrow, but seemed otherwise unmoved. 'The Green Book?'

'You've heard of it?'

'I've *heard* of many things. The King's loyal friends in England make sure I do. The South Sea disaster is a judgement on those who let in a German prince and his greedy minions to rule the Stuart domain. I'm aware of all the highways and byways of the affair. But I'm not aware of a single reason why I should suppose that a . . . man like you . . . might have charge of the errant Mr Knight's sin-black secrets.'

'It's a long story. Chance and treachery are about the sum of it.'

'As of many a story.'

'I have the book, Mr Edgar. Believe me.'

'Why should I?'

'Because you can't afford not to. It represents a heaven-sent opportunity for you.'

'You don't look like a heavenly messenger to me.'

'The Green Book lists all the bribes paid to secure passage of the South Sea Bill last year. Exactly how much. And exactly who to.'

'Tell me, then. *Exactly* how much was it?'

'I'm no accountant. It would certainly take one to tease out the pounds, shillings and pence. Many hundreds of thousands of pounds is as close as I can get. More than a million, I'd guess.'

'Would you, though?' Edgar's gaze was calm but penetrating. He looked neither disbelieving nor con-vinced. 'And *exactly* who received this money?'

'I can give you some names.'

'Do.'

'Roberts; Rolt; Tufnell; Burridge; Scott; Chetwynd; Bampfield; Bland; Sebright; Drax.'

'Members of Parliament to a man.'

'You'd know them better than me, Mr Edgar. They're all listed.'

'Who else?'

'Carew; Bankes; Forrester; Montgomerie; Blundell; Lawson; Gordon—'

'Sir William Gordon? The Commissioner of Army Accounts?'

'Sir William Gordon, yes.' Estelle had insisted he memo-rize some of the names and now he realized how right she had been to. Edgar's expression was softening. His doubts were receding. 'And various peers.'

'Which ones?'

'Lord Gower; Lord Lansdowne; the Earl of Essex; the Marquess of Winchester; and the Earl of Sunderland.'

'Sunderland?'

'Yes.' Spandrel looked at Edgar with the confidence of knowing that what he said was absolutely true. 'The First Lord of the Treasury's isn't the most eminent name in the book.'

'No?'

'Far from it.'

'Whose is, then?'

'His master's.' Spandrel paused for effect. He was beginning to enjoy himself. 'The King.'

'The King?' Edgar smiled. 'I take it you are referring to the Elector of Hanover.'

'I beg your pardon.' Spandrel felt himself blushing at his mistake. In the looking-glass world of the Palazzo Muti, it was important to remember who was notionally a king and who was not. 'I do mean the Elector of Hanover. Of course. But whatever we call him . . .'

'He is listed.'

'Yes.'

'To the tune of what?'

'An allocation of one hundred thousand pounds in stock for a payment of only twenty.'

'When was the allocation made?'

'The fourteenth of April.'

'Then it signifies nothing. That was when the First Money Subscription opened. Twenty per cent would have been a normal first instalment.' Edgar shook his head. 'Dear me, Mr Spandrel. You seem to be just another bearskin jobber, of the kind the Stock Exchange always has in plentiful supply.' Seeing Spandrel's uncomprehending look, he added, 'You are trying to sell me the bear's skin before you have killed the bear.'

'No, no. You must let me finish. The K—' Spandrel gulped back the word. 'The Elector of Hanover,' he continued slowly, 'sold the stock back to the company on

240

the thirteenth of June at a profit of sixty-eight thousand pounds. He never paid any more instalments.'

'No more instalments?' Edgar queried softly.

'None.'

'Sold back . . . and treated as fully paid?'

'Yes.'

Edgar pursed his lips. 'Were any other members of the Elector's family similarly treated?'

'Yes. The Prince of Wales. That is, I mean—'

'Let it pass. I know who you mean.'

'Also the Princess.'

'Aha.'

'As well as the Duchess of Kendal and her nieces.'

'As one would expect.'

'And the Countess von Platen.'

'Both mistresses. What a considerate lover the Elector is.'

'I should also mention . . .' Spandrel hesitated. He knew from what McIlwraith had told him of the political situation at Westminster that the name he was about to let fall was in many ways the most significant of all. 'Walpole.'

'*Robert* Walpole?'

'Yes.'

Edgar looked straight at him. 'You're sure of that?'

'I'm sure.'

'How much?'

'I can't say.'

'Why not?'

'Because . . .' Spandrel had employed Estelle's tactics faithfully and was not about to stop. He had told Edgar enough. Now it was time to name their price. 'We need to agree terms, Mr Edgar.'

'Terms?'

'For your purchase of the book.'

'You are not making a gift of it to the cause, then?'

'No.'

'You are merely a thief, seeking to sell what he has stolen.'

'Do you want to buy it . . . or not?'

'How much did Walpole receive?'

'How much are you willing to pay to find out?'

'*How much*, Mr Spandrel' – Edgar let out a long, slow breath – 'are you demanding?'

'One hundred thousand pounds.'

'Absurd.'

'I don't think so.'

'The King hasn't the resources to pay such money.'

'It's not so very much . . . for a kingdom.'

'For a kingdom?' Edgar leaned back in his chair and rested his hand thoughtfully on the papers strewing his desk. A moment of silence passed. Then he looked up sharply. 'Why are you offering this to us instead of to the Elector? He'd pay handsomely to retrieve the evidence of his own corruption.'

'I lost all the money I spent on South Sea stock. Every penny. I was cheated. I want the people who cheated me to suffer for what they did.'

'Revenge, is it?'

'Partly.'

'But mostly greed.'

'Call it what you will. The price is a fair one.'

'The price is extortionate. But . . .' Edgar drummed his fingers. 'I will apprise the King of your proposition.'

'When can I have an answer?'

'Return here at noon tomorrow. By then, I should have something for you, be it an answer or no.'

'The Green Book blasts the reputation of every man in it, Mr Edgar. It can topple a throne. You'll never have—'

'I know what it can do. *If* what you say is true.'

'It's true.'

'Then be patient, Mr Spandrel.' Edgar nodded towards the door. 'Until noon tomorrow.'

Colonel Lachlan Drummond must once have cut an imposing figure. He was broad-shouldered and square-jawed enough to have led many a man into battle and many a woman into bed in his time. But that time was gone. Exiled in Rome with his make-believe king, he had sought consolations where he could find them. Now, bloated and bedraggled, his mind fuddled and his words slurred by drink, he slumped at a table in a private booth at the rear of L'Egiziano, a coffee-house just off the Corso, gazing blearily across at Nicholas Cloisterman, while a smile hovered complacently on his lips.

'The King's been entertaining no Dutch widows, my friend. You can be sure of that. The Queen would scratch out the eyes of any woman who—'

'You seem deliberately to misunderstand, Colonel. Mrs de Vries is no courtesan.'

'Whatever she is or isn't, she hasn't shown her face at the Palazzo Muti.'

'Is there anything to suggest that valuable information might have reached your master? Talk of another rising, perhaps?'

'There's always talk.'

'A recent change of mood. Anything.'

'We've been drinking Prince Charlie's health for the past three months. The birth of a son and heir has put everyone in good spirits. I don't know about anything else. There's some . . . nervousness . . . now the Pope's up and died. But that's to be expected.'

'What I'm referring to would be known only to a few.'

'Aye. But I'm one of the few, d'you see?' Drummond tapped his nose. 'There's not a whisper in a corridor I don't

243

get to hear in due course. Your Mrs de Vries is a bird that hasn't flown into our parish.'

'I wish I could be sure of that.'

'You can. She's not been here, my friend. She's not been near.' Drummond leaned forward, the brandy on his breath wafting over Cloisterman. 'Do you mean to wait in case there's sign of her?'

'I haven't decided.'

'Either way, vigilance doesn't come cheap.'

'You don't, Colonel, certainly.' Cloisterman lifted a purse from his pocket and slid it across the table. 'I'll bid you good afternoon,' he added, rising to his feet.

'Good afternoon to you, my friend.'

Leaving Drummond to count his money, Cloisterman hurried from the booth and threaded his way between the settles and tables in the main room of the coffee-house. Blain had assured him of Drummond's reliability as an informant, though whether Blain had ever met the fellow Cloisterman did not know. It was difficult to place much confidence in the good colonel's self-proclaimed vigilance. The only reassurance Cloisterman had obtained for his money was that the Green Book – and the havoc it might wreak – was not the talk of the Palazzo Muti.

The likelihood, Cloisterman consoled himself, was that Estelle de Vries had not yet reached Rome. It was therefore also likely, given the precautions Blain had taken for him in Florence, that she never would. Telling himself to feel more satisfied with his afternoon's work than he did, he stepped from L'Egiziano into the chill onset of a Roman night and strode down the street to its junction with the Corso, intending to cross the thoroughfare and make for his lodgings at the Casa Rossa.

A lantern illuminating a sign on a tobacconist's shop at the corner was all that saved him from a collision with a man hurrying along the Corso. As Cloisterman pulled sharply up, the man headed on across the side-street, apparently unaware of what had happened.

Cloisterman, for his part, stepped back to the wall of the shop and leaned against it for support, his heart racing. He had caught a clear sight of the man's face in the light of the lantern and had recognized him immediately. He could still do so, in fact, by the set of his shoulders as he pressed on into the shadows.

'Spandrel,' Cloisterman whispered incredulously to himself. 'What are you doing here?' Instinctively, he started after him.

As he did so, another man brushed past him, heading in the same direction as Spandrel. He was short, thin as a whippet and almost as fleet-footed. Something in the angle of his head and the intent, forward tilt of his body told Cloisterman at once what he was about. He was following Spandrel too. There were others, it seemed, who wanted to know what the bankrupt English mapmaker was doing in Rome.

James Edward Stuart, Pretender to the thrones of Scotland and England, was nothing if not assiduous in his pretensions. He addressed himself seriously to every stray chance and frail hope of the restoration of his dynasty. In his dedication to the cause, however, stood revealed his weakness. He was a king by birth and upbringing, who clung to the title because it was the only thing he knew. Long-faced and lugubrious, he was no-one's vision of the ideal monarch. As to whether he had the heart of a king, or his newly born son had for that matter, only time would tell.

But time was suddenly of the essence, as James Edgar's unaccustomed urgency of manner made clear. It was early evening at the Palazzo Muti and the king whose kingdom its walls comprised had intended to visit the nursery before dinner to dandle his celebrated infant. Instead, he found himself closeted with his secretary in earnest discussion of a potentially earth-shaking development.

'How important might this book be to us, Mr Edgar?'

'It proves the Elector of Hanover, his son, his daughter-in-law, his mistresses and most of his ministers, past and present, to be self-serving scoundrels.'

'Surely we knew that already.'

'But this *proves* it, sir. The nation is on its knees, brought low by the South Sea fraud. If your subjects understood how the prince who rules them had profited from their ruin, I believe they would rise against him and demand the return of their true king. I believe, in simple fact, that this book represents a surer prospect of success than any you or your father before you have ever enjoyed.'

'Then we must have it.'

'Indeed, sir. So we must.'

'How is it to be obtained?'

'This fellow Spandrel demands a sum of one hundred thousand pounds for its surrender.'

'So much?'

'I will persuade him to accept a lower figure. I have had him followed, naturally, but I feel sure he will not have the book about him. Some payment will probably be necessary. But if I may speak freely, sir . . .'

'Please do.'

'Our friends say London is in a ferment. Stanhope's acquittal has outraged the populace. Sunderland will doubtless have been acquitted by now as well, with Walpole's connivance. They are all in it together. And the Green Book will damn every one of them. Whatever we have to pay for it . . . will be a bargain.'

*   *   *

While in Rome the Pretender and his secretary contemplated the sudden opening of a host of attractive vistas, in
London the Postmaster-General, James Craggs the elder,
foresaw only ruin on the eve of his trial before the House
of Commons. Beset by grief for his son and a keen knowledge of the truth of the charges laid against him, he
resolved the matter by taking a fatal dose of laudanum.
The last of the trials of senior ministers implicated in the
South Sea scandal was thus over before it had begun.
While in Rome other forms of trial were just about to
begin.

Chapter Twenty-Five

Bend or Break

Where was Estelle? It was nearly ten o'clock, yet still she had not returned to the Palazzetto Raguzzi. Spandrel was growing anxious. He had called at the Albergo Luna earlier on his way back from the Palazzo Muti, intending to claim a partial recovery from the illness that had supposedly prevented him accompanying Estelle on her afternoon tour with Buckthorn and Silverwood, but neither they nor she had been there. Perhaps they had decided to dine before returning to their lodgings. Perhaps Rome by night had proved as diverting as Rome by day.

This Spandrel doubted. Estelle would be as eager to hear how he had fared at the Pretender's court as he was to tell her. She would have found some way to prevail upon Buckthorn and Silverwood to that end. But clearly something had prevented her. What could it possibly be?

He had waited long enough. Another visit to the Albergo Luna would relieve his anxiety to some degree. For all he knew, Buckthorn and Silverwood might by now have arrived there with Estelle. He flung on his coat, extinguished the lamp and made for the door.

Cloisterman had spent several chill hours lurking in the shadows of the Piazza di Spagna, waiting for Spandrel to emerge from the Palazzetto or for Estelle de Vries to enter. So far, neither had. The whippety fellow likewise

248

dogging Spandrel's trail had vanished. The night had deepened. Cloisterman had grown cold and bored and less and less certain of what he should do.

Now, as ten o'clock struck in the tower of Trinità dei Monti, palely lit by the moon on the hill above the piazza, he decided to try his luck at the Albergo Luna, where Spandrel had called briefly on his way along the Via Condotti. Perhaps that was where Estelle was hiding. Certainly he did not doubt that she was somewhere close at hand.

Pulling his hat down over his eyes and his greatcoat collar up to meet it, he turned and hurried away across the piazza.

A few minutes later, Spandrel emerged from the Palazzetto Raguzzi and set off across the piazza, following unwittingly in Cloisterman's footsteps.

As he turned into the Via Condotti, he was surprised to see that a small crowd had gathered outside the Albergo Luna, which lay a hundred yards or so ahead. A coach had pulled up in front of the inn and there were shouts and whistles from the crowd. As Spandrel drew nearer, he saw that the coach was not one of the low-slung gilded conveyances he had already become accustomed to seeing on the streets, but was darkly painted and soberly styled, with shutters at the windows.

Then he stopped dead in his tracks. From the inn emerged two tall, black-greatcoated figures, holding between them a shorter, slighter man, whose hat toppled from his head as he was marched out and loaded into the coach to reveal a blond wig and a pale, disbelieving face. It was the face of Nicholas Cloisterman.

'The Romans do so savour every little drama of life, don't they?' The voice came from behind Spandrel as the coach door slammed and Cloisterman was driven away.

249

Spandrel turned to find Buckthorn standing virtually at his shoulder, smiling blandly. 'Do you happen to know the poor fellow they've arrested?'

'Arrested?'

'Looks like it to me.' Buckthorn's gaze drifted towards the departing coach, then moved back to Spandrel. 'So, do you know him?'

'Of course not.'

'Really? That's odd. He's been keeping watch on the Palazzetto Raguzzi for the past few hours. Now he strolls down to the Luna and gets himself dragged off to the clink. *Deuced* odd, I'd say.'

'I know nothing about him. Where's Estelle?'

'With Naseby.'

'And where is he?'

'Not at the Luna. And just as well, it seems.'

'What do you mean, Buckthorn?'

'Don't be testy, old man. I'll be happy to explain.'

'Why not just tell me where they are?'

'Because it's not as simple as that. Let's go back to the Raguzzi. We can talk there.'

'We can talk here.'

'And be overheard? I'd really rather not take the risk. You'll agree a few precautions are in order when you hear what I have to say. And if the lovely Estelle's welfare is at the forefront of your concern – which as an ever-attentive cousin I'm sure it is – you'll indulge me on the point.' Buckthorn's smile broadened. 'Come along, do.'

It took them no more than five minutes to reach Spandrel's room at the Palazzetto Raguzzi. Nothing was said on the way, but in the silence Spandrel could read more than was good for his peace of mind. Buckthorn had changed from the rich, dunderheaded young wastrel he had seemed to be. He was somehow older, subtler, worldly-wiser. Or perhaps that was what he had been all along. Perhaps Giles Buckthorn, the spoilt and shallow Grand Tourist, was nothing but an artful impersonation. If so, Naseby Silverwood, his similarly minded friend, probably was as well. In which case . . .

'How are the beds here?' Buckthorn enquired, as Spandrel lit the lamps. 'Soft enough?'

'The accommodation's very comfortable.'

'I'm sure it is.'

'Do you mind telling me where—'

'Your cousin is? Haven't the vaguest, old man.'

'But you just said Estelle—'

'Estelle? Oh, is that who you mean? Sorry. I thought we'd dropped that pretence. Let's be honest. She's no more your cousin' – he smiled – 'than Naseby and I are chums from Oxford.'

'Where is she?'

'Somewhere safe and secure.'

'What do you mean by that?'

'I mean she's our prisoner. And she'll remain so until our business is concluded.'

'Your . . . *prisoner*?'

'Quite so. And in case you doubt me, here's something to convince you we're keeping a very close eye on her.' Buckthorn took something from his pocket and tossed it across to Spandrel.

Spandrel caught it in his right hand and gazed down in astonishment at what he saw nestling in his palm: a blue silk garter, of the kind, if it was not the very same, that he knew Estelle wore; that he knew oh so well.

Rage flooded into him. He made to lunge at Buckthorn, but the other man was too quick for him. A punch to the pit of the stomach doubled him up, then Buckthorn was behind him, pulling him half-upright. He saw the blade of a knife flash in the lamplight. Then it was at his throat. He felt the edge of it pressing against his skin.

'We'll kill her if we have to, Spandrel,' Buckthorn rasped in his ear. 'You too.'

'What do you want?'

'Those jewels of hers she's so prudently lodged at a bank in every town we've stopped in. Not that we think they are jewels, of course. But treasure. Yes. Treasure they certainly are, of some kind, at any rate, which your anxiety to reach Rome suggests is worth more here than anywhere else. That's why we let you get this far.'

'I don't know what you're talking about.'

'But you do. You must do. You see, you're named on the Calderini receipt along with Estelle.' So he was. Estelle had insisted on a joint receipt. She was to keep it in case he ran into trouble at the Palazzo Muti. But both their signatures were required to reclaim what the receipt described as a *scatola di gioielli rossa*: a red jewel-box, containing a green book; *the* Green Book. 'Tell me one more lie, Spandrel, and I'll slit your throat.' Buckthorn's voice was as hard and sharp as the knife in his hand. 'Do you understand?'

'Yes.'

'Good. Now, what's in the box?'

'A book.'

'What kind of book?'

'An account book. It belongs to the chief cashier of the South Sea Company. It records all the bribes the company paid last year to get their bill through Parliament.'

'Does it, indeed? Whom did they bribe?'

'Members of Parliament. Government ministers. The royal family.'

'Hence Rome. You're trying to sell it to the Pretender, aren't you?'

'Yes.'

'What's your asking price?'

252

'One hundred thousand pounds.'

'Estelle does fly high, doesn't she? Well, I doubt you'd ever have got that much. But never mind. Who's the fellow we saw being marched out of the Albergo Luna?'

'Cloisterman. British vice-consul in Amsterdam.'

'Whence he followed you and Estelle, presumably. Who was de Vries?'

'A merchant there, entrusted with the book by one of the directors of the company.'

'I take it de Vries didn't meet with a natural death.'

'No.'

'So, you're murderers as well as thieves. Well, I'm sorry to have to disappoint you, I really am. Your efforts were all in vain. What are your arrangements with the Pretender?'

'I'm to meet his secretary, Mr Edgar, at noon tomorrow.'

'The arrangements have changed. I'll be going in your place. At eleven o'clock tomorrow morning, you'll meet me at the Banco Calderini, where you'll withdraw the box and surrender the contents to me. We'll already have persuaded Estelle to countersign the receipt and to give us the key to the box, so there'll be no difficulty. In exchange, I'll tell you where you can find her, alive and relatively unharmed. At that point, our business will be concluded. Should we meet again thereafter, it'll be the worse for you. For both of you. You follow?'

'I follow.'

'And you agree?'

'Yes.'

'I thought you would. Strictly between you and me, I'm not sure Estelle would, if your positions were reversed. But that's women for you, isn't it?' Suddenly, the knife was whipped away from Spandrel's throat. Buckthorn was in front of him now, backing towards the door, the knife held defensively before him. 'A piece of parting advice, Spandrel. *Always* look a gift-horse in the mouth. Oh, and don't try to follow me. You're simply not up to it.' He opened the door behind him. 'Good night,' he added. Then he stepped out into the passage and closed the door.

Spandrel raised a hand to his throat. He stared at the smear of blood on his fingers, then moved unsteadily across to the bed and sat down. He heard his breathing as if it were that of someone else, slowly returning to normal. His thoughts did so at the same pace, settling bleakly on the certainty that Buckthorn was right. He was no match for them. This was the end of his fond dream of wealth. As for Estelle, all he could do now was whatever it took to save her life. And then . . . But no. He could not look so far ahead. He could not bear to.

Cloisterman's ride in the shuttered black coach was a short one, so short that he was still struggling to understand what had happened when a change in the note of the horses' hoofbeats told him they were passing beneath a covered gateway into a courtyard of some kind. There he was bundled out and up some steps into a large, lamp-lit building. His guards marched him along an echoing, high-ceilinged corridor, then up a winding, stone-flagged staircase, finally delivering him to a first-floor room of some magnificence, decorated with frescoes, tapestries and a pair of opulent chandeliers in which every candle was burning.

In the centre of the room, behind a desk as large as many a banqueting-table, sat a corpulent, heavy-lidded, goatee-bearded man of advanced age, dressed in the red robes and cap of a cardinal. He cast Cloisterman a darting, reptilian glance, but said nothing. Then Cloisterman looked towards the only other occupant of the room: a brawny, bright-eyed priest with cropped black hair and a cherubic flush to his cheeks, who was standing at one end of the table. He fixed Cloisterman with a twinkling gaze and said, in Irish-accented English, 'Good evening, Mr Cloisterman. Welcome to the Quirinal Palace. I am Father Monteith. This is His Excellency the Pro-Governor of the City of Rome, Cardinal Bortolazzi. He speaks no English, so you'll pardon me if I . . . articulate his thoughts.'

'What the devil is going on here, sir?' demanded Cloisterman, summoning as much outraged dignity as he could. 'Why was I dragged from the Albergo Luna like some . . . common criminal?'

'Because you were enquiring after a Mrs de Vries and had already displayed an interest in her travelling companion, Mr Spandrel.'

'What's that to you?'

'The Pro-Governor is responsible for the maintenance of peace and order in the city.'

'I'm threatening neither.'

'What are you here for?'

'To see the antiquities.'

'Come, come. That won't do. You've not been near the Colosseum, have you? But you have been near the Palazzo Muti. You've conferred with a notorious spy at King James's court. And Mr Spandrel has been in discussion with the King's private secretary.'

'I know nothing about any spy. Or what Spandrel may or may not have been doing.'

Monteith sighed. 'These denials are futile, Mr Cloisterman. If the Pro-Governor is so minded, you can be consigned to a dungeon at the Castel Sant'Angelo for the rest of your life, with neither charge nor trial. You are not in the United Provinces now.'

'How did—' Cloisterman broke off, instantly regretting the admission.

'A guess, based on the Dutch ring to Mrs de Vries's name. But it's unimportant. Where you've come *from* does not concern us. Why you've come *here* does.'

'I'm the British vice-consul in Amsterdam.' The mention of dungeons had settled the issue in Cloisterman's mind. He could not continue trying to brazen his way out of whatever he was in. 'My Government—'

'Is no friend of His Holiness the Pope.' Monteith rounded the table and moved closer. 'As I'm sure you're aware, however, there is no pope at present. His Holiness Clement the Eleventh was gathered unto the Lord last week. Several more weeks are likely to elapse before his successor is elected by the College of Cardinals. When he is, he will no doubt wish to be assured that he finds his temporal realm in good order. The Pro-Governor is determined to ensure that he does.'

'So,' Cloisterman ventured, believing he had at last caught the priest's drift, 'the Pro-Governor's prime concern is to maintain the affairs of state . . . *in statu quo nunc.*'

'Indeed it is.' Monteith's head bobbed like that of a bird pecking at seed. '*Exactly* as they are now.'

'A sudden enhancement of the prospects of a restoration of the Stuart line to the British throne would not therefore be—'

'Any more compatible with that policy than their sudden extinction.'

'I see.'

'I'm glad you do. Now, the Pro-Governor does not wish to know what Mr Spandrel has been hawking around the Palazzo Muti. But he does wish to know whether your presence in Rome indicates that the consequences for your Government of His Majesty King James's acquisition of . . . whatever the article is . . . would be – how shall I put it? – disastrous.'

'That would be to put it lightly.'

'Would it, now?'

'I'm afraid so.'

'Well, well.' Monteith frowned. 'As bad as that.' Then his expression brightened. 'We shall just have to see what we can do.' He beamed at Cloisterman. 'Shan't we?'

Spandrel was still lying on his bed at the Palazzetto Raguzzi an hour later, staring sleeplessly into the darkness above his head, when he heard a noise at one of the windows. He sat up. The noise returned. It was surely that of a pebble striking the glass. He rose from the bed and crossed to the window. He had not bothered to close the shutters earlier and now had a clear view down into the moonlit piazza. A man was standing below him, preparing to throw another pebble. As he raised his head to aim, Spandrel recognized him. And froze in astonishment.

Chapter Twenty-Six

Lie Ledger

The Banco Calderini occupied the ground floor of a middling-sized palazzo near the Ponte Sant'Angelo. From the pavement in front of the bank, there was a clear view across the bridge of the Castel Sant'Angelo, the papal fortress that loomed above the Tiber. But Spandrel did not so much as glance towards it. In a deep shadow cast by the razor-sharp Roman sun, he waited, head bowed, as eleven o'clock struck on unseen church towers all around him.

Before the clocks had finished striking, his waiting ended. Buckthorn, dressed to the nines as usual, sauntered round the corner of the building and bade him an icy-smiled good morning. Spandrel said nothing, for nothing needed to be said. He led the way into the bank.

The marble-floored, high-ceilinged interior was cool and echoing, murmured consultations and shufflings of paper joining above them like the rustling of bats' wings. As they moved towards the counter, Buckthorn took something from his pocket and passed it to Spandrel. 'Duly countersigned,' he said softly. It was the receipt. 'And lo, what do we have here?' He jiggled the key to the jewel-box in his gloved palm.

The first clerk they approached spoke no English. There was a delay while a bilingual clerk was found. Then a further delay while he descended to the vault to fetch the

258

jewel-box. Spandrel fell to studying Estelle's two signatures on the receipt. There was no discernible difference between them, no sign of suffering at the hands of her captors.

'She is well enough,' said Buckthorn, as if reading his thoughts. 'We have treated her better than she treated her husband.'

'Where is she?'

'All in good time. The book first.'

The clerk returned, carrying the scarlet jewel-box. He placed it on the counter and invited Spandrel to confirm that it had not been tampered with.

'Let's open it and see,' said Buckthorn. He unlocked the box and raised the lid. A green-covered book lay within. 'Is this a ledger which I see before me?' He chuckled, then closed the box. 'Sign for it, Spandrel.'

The clerk, who had displayed no reaction whatever on seeing what the jewel-box contained, offered Spandrel a pen. Spandrel countersigned the receipt and passed it to the clerk, along with two sequin coins: the agreed storage fee. '*Grazie, signore,*' said the clerk. The transaction was at an end.

Buckthorn gathered up the box and started towards the door. Spandrel took several hurried steps to catch up with him. He wanted to ask once more where Estelle was, but something held him back.

He was still hesitating when they reached the street. There Buckthorn stopped and turned to him with a smile. 'Your meek compliance is much appreciated, Spandrel. If I were you, I'd try some other kind of work. You're not equal to this kind. Nor, to speak candidly, are you equal to Estelle. But you'll be wanting to know where she is, nonetheless. And you'll be needing this.' He handed him a key – larger and heavier than the one that had opened the jewel-box. 'Go to the Theatre of Marcellus. Look for a door with the letter E on it: E for Estelle. This is the key to the door. She'll be waiting for you inside.'

'But where is . . . the Theatre of Marcellus?'

'You'll find it, I'm sure. And now I really must be going. Naseby will be growing anxious, which isn't good for him. And we have an appointment at noon we really can't afford to miss.' He patted the jewel-box. 'Goodbye, Spandrel. It's been a pleasure.'

No sooner was Buckthorn out of sight than Spandrel hastened towards the Ponte Sant'Angelo. At the side of the road adjoining the bridge stood a calash, its driver seated and holding the reins, as if expecting a passenger. Spandrel climbed smartly aboard.

'*Dove?*' queried the driver.

'The Theatre of Marcellus,' Spandrel replied.

'*Si. Il Teatro di Marcello. Andiamo.*' The driver geed up the horses and they started away.

The Theatre of Marcellus stood close to the Tiber a mile or so to the south, where the river divided round the Isola Tiberina. It was an ancient Roman amphitheatre, atop which some later generation had added two storeys of their own to form a strange, hybrid palazzo. This too was now in decay, at a faster rate, it seemed, than the ruin it had squatted on. The lower arches of the amphitheatre had also been filled in, to form workshops and store-rooms. Business was being conducted in some, but most were closed, their heavy wooden doors firmly shut on whatever lay within.

Telling the driver to wait, Spandrel jumped down from the calash and began running round the curve of the building, shading his eyes as he trained them on the doors. Then he saw what he was looking for: a large E, crudely daubed in yellow paint.

He turned the key in the lock and pulled the door open. Sunlight flooded into a narrow, windowless chamber in which dust swirled, but nothing else moved. There was a table to one side, with a lamp standing on it. Otherwise the room was empty. Then, as his eyes adjusted to the gloom that lay beyond the sun's reach, he saw another door, in the middle of the rear wall. There was a barred vent above it, and through the vent came a voice from the space beyond. 'Is someone there?' It was Estelle. 'Help me. Please.'

'It's me,' Spandrel called. 'William.' Then he strode to the door, pulled back the bolts and flung it open.

She was crouched on a mattress that was actually too big for the floor it lay on and curled up against the wall at either end. The air was damp and fetid. Her face was smudged with dirt, her hair streaked with dust, her once-lovely pink moiré dress creased and stained. 'Thank God you found me,' she said, rising unsteadily to her feet. 'What has—' She swayed slightly and Spandrel stepped forward to support her.

'You're safe now. My God, Estelle, I thought they might have killed you.' He tried to put his arm round her, but she pushed him away.

'I'm sorry,' she said, squinting into the sunlight behind him. 'I can't bear to be touched while I'm so filthy.'

'That doesn't matter. At least you're alive.'

She stumbled past him into the outer room. 'Where are Buckthorn and Silverwood? Where are they, William?'

'I don't know. Possibly at the Palazzo Muti.'

'You didn't—' She looked round at him sharply. 'You didn't give them the book?'

'Not exactly.'

'Then where is it?'

'I'll explain later. We must get away from here.' He gathered up her cape, which lay crumpled on the mattress, and tried to put it round her, but she shook it off.

261

'Explain now.'

'It'll be better if—'

'*Now.*'

'Estelle—'

'Tell me, William.' Her gaze was stern, her ordeal forgotten, it seemed, in the face of what she deemed far more important. 'Where is the Green Book?'

'Gone.'

'Gone where?'

'Back to England. With Cloisterman.'

'What?' She stared at him disbelievingly.

'Buckthorn and Silverwood have a green-covered ledger filled with gibberish. Whether they realize that before, during or after their meeting with the Pretender's secretary at noon is in the lap of the gods. Whenever it is, though, they'll come looking for us, quite possibly with a pack of angry Highlanders at their backs. That's why we have to leave here. Now.'

'I'm going nowhere until you explain what's happened.' Estelle's voice was as cold and implacable as her face. Already, moments after being rescued, she was thinking more about what she had lost than about what she might have gained.

'Buckthorn and Silverwood must have told you what they meant to do.'

'Of course they told me. I was trusting you to find some way to outwit them.'

'How could I? They had your countersignature on the receipt.'

'I had to sign. They held a pistol to my head.'

'I feared for your life, Estelle. Buckthorn gave me . . . proof that they were holding you captive.'

'The garter. Is that it? Were you afraid they might rape me?'

'Yes.' Why the answer sounded foolish Spandrel could not tell. Yet, strangely, it did. 'Of course I was.'

'As they meant you to be. Poor credulous William. You agreed to their demands?'

'Yes. And I'd have given them what they wanted. But Cloisterman changed my mind.'

'How?'

'He came to me late last night and told me how matters stood. Apparently, the authorities know everything that happens at the Palazzo Muti. They weren't willing to let the sale of the book proceed in case the new pope didn't approve of the consequences. So, we had to be stopped. But without the Pretender realizing who'd stopped us. Cloisterman was to take the book back to the British Government. If we refused to let him and tried to sell it, we'd be arrested. When I told him about Buckthorn and Silverwood, he suggested giving them a fake ledger. The authorities instructed the bank to open the jewel-box with one of their skeleton keys. The real ledger was then impounded and handed over to Cloisterman. He's been given safe-conduct to the Tuscan border.'

'That book would have made us rich.'

'Not here, Estelle. Not in Rome. It wasn't destined to be.'

'And what is destined to be?'

'I've agreed we'll go south. To Naples. There's a trader sailing from the river-port at two o'clock. It's expecting to take on two passengers. I've packed our belongings. They're on the calash.'

'And what will we do in Naples?'

'I don't know.'

'No.' She looked at him sadly, almost pityingly. 'Exactly.'

Nothing was said as the calash bore them across the bridge onto the Isola Tiberina, then over the next bridge to the west bank of the Tiber and down to the vast riverside hospital of San Michele, beyond which lay their destination: the Porto di Ripa Grande, principal river-port of the city.

They found the trading ketch *Gabbiano* tied up and loading at the embankment steps. All they had to do was go aboard. But when their driver made to take their bags off the calash, Estelle told him to leave them where they were. The fellow looked helplessly at Spandrel, clearly unsure whose orders he should obey.

'We can't stay, Estelle,' reasoned Spandrel. 'You must understand that.'

For answer she merely sighed and began slowly pacing to and fro along the embankment, staring up into the blue vault of the sky and smoothing her hair as she walked. Tangled though it still was, it shimmered in the sunlight. A memory of running his fingers through those dark tresses came to Spandrel with a jag of pain, as of something precious that he had already lost.

'It's nearly one o'clock. They'll be looking for us by now. They're bound to be. We should be below decks – out of sight.'

'Hiding?' She stopped and tossed the word back at him.

'Yes.'

'And fleeing?'

'We have no choice.'

'*I* have a choice.'

She had never looked more beautiful than in that moment, standing on the embankment above the jumble of boats and masts and furled sails, her hair awry, her dress stained, her eyes wide and accusing. It was futile. There was nothing she could do to retrieve the book. And yet it was magnificent. There was nothing she could *not* do. 'We have to go,' said Spandrel. 'I gave my word.'

'Your word. Not mine.'

'For God's sake, Estelle. Please.'

She looked at him long and coolly, then said, 'No. I will not go. Not this way.'

'Then how?'

'I'm going north.'

'You can't mean . . .'

'I'm not giving it up. I'm not letting *Mr* Cloisterman steal my future from under my nose.' She began walking towards the calash. 'You go to Naples, William. You keep your word. But don't ask me to go with you. I intend to be on the next coach north. Cloisterman can't be at the border yet. And even if he is—' She reached the calash, grabbed Spandrel's bag and heaved it to the ground, stumbling with the effort. Then she turned to the driver. '*Piazza del Popolo. Subito. Rapidamente.*'

Chapter Twenty-Seven

Every Man's Hand

Spandrel stared down at the busy scene of loading and making ready aboard the *Gabbiano*. Half an hour had passed since Estelle's departure, but still he had not moved from the embankment. He had never felt less certain about anything in his life. To go with Estelle in pursuit of Cloisterman was folly, to remain in Rome madness. Yet, as Estelle had said, what was there for them to do in Naples? What was there for *him* to do? McIlwraith's money would soon run out. With the Green Book gone, only destitution awaited him, in an unknown city far from home – destitution and despair.

He had done his best. He had played the cards fate had dealt him as adroitly as he could contrive. But there had always been those cleverer and more ruthless than him to steal the hand. It would have been Buckthorn and Silverwood but for Cloisterman's intervention. 'You've thrown in your lot with a murderess,' Cloisterman had said to him the night before. 'You should be grateful to be let off so lightly.'

Grateful? No. He was not that. But lonely and homesick, riddled with guilt and self-pity, he most certainly was. He knew why he had thrown in his lot with a murderess, if that was what Estelle really was. Money was not the half of it. For as long as he had been her secret lover and co-conspirator, life had been a revel of dreams and sensations he had never expected to experience. It had been . . . glorious. And now the glory was done. He had been given much and promised more. But all he was left with was the little his existence had previously amounted to.

Then he understood at last. He had to follow her. What they would achieve by going after Cloisterman he did not know. But at least they would achieve it – or fail to – together.

He hired a fly that had just delivered a passenger to the hospital. The most direct route to the Piazza del Popolo lay back the way they had come, crossing the Tiber uncomfortably close to the Theatre of Marcellus. Loth to take such a risk, Spandrel told the driver to cross by the next bridge up.

No sooner had they set off than a curricle, hard-driven by the look of the dust-cloud it was raising, bore down on them from the direction of the city. Spandrel's driver had to pull in to avoid a collision. As the curricle swept past, Spandrel realized that Buckthorn and Silverwood were aboard. They were heading for the river-port. How had they known where to look for him? Had someone over-heard him talking to the calash-driver at the Theatre of Marcellus?

It hardly mattered now. Looking over his shoulder, Spandrel saw to his horror that they were reining in. They had seen him. And they would outrun the fly. There was no doubt of it. Even if they did not, what could he achieve by pressing on? He would simply endanger Estelle if he led them to the Piazza del Popolo.

The neighbourhood to his left was a warren of alleys and courtyards, where a man could travel faster on foot than by any carriage. His decision was made in the instant the thought came to him. He leaped from the fly, abandoning his bag, and began to run.

'Spandrel!' He heard Silverwood's piping voice from behind him. 'We want a word with you.'

He did not stop.

Spandrel was soon safe, at any rate from Buckthorn and Silverwood. Trastevere was an unfathomable maze of jumbled dwellings, where the poorest inhabitants of Rome lived in a seething squalor that made Cat and Dog Yard look almost desirable. The dull-eyed children and blank-faced women watched Spandrel plunge past them with indifference, but his peacock-clad pursuers would find themselves – not to mention their gold pocket-watches and silver snuff-boxes – the objects of considerable attention, once they had given up the curricle, as the narrow going would force them to.

Just as Spandrel could not be tracked through Trastevere, however, so he could not keep track of where he was. Whichever turn he took seemed only to lead uphill, away from the river and further from his destination. He could not turn back for fear of blundering into Buckthorn and Silverwood, so on he went, by crumbling steps and winding paths, till he suddenly emerged onto a wide road flanked by high-walled gardens. He was on the Janiculum Hill, commanding a view so extensive that he thought he could make out the twin domes of the churches that stood where the Corso reached the Piazza del Popolo. But what use was that – other than to tell him just how far he was from where he wanted to be?

There was nothing for it but to follow the line of the city wall round to the Vatican and hope to pick up a fly there. The afternoon was already well advanced. Every hour he lingered in Rome added to his peril. But the *Gabbiano* would have sailed by now. He had thrown away one chance and not yet grasped another.

His pace quickened.

*   *   *

Spandrel entered the Piazza di San Pietro as an ant might stray onto a beach: as one tiny, insignificant speck in a vast landscape. The colonnades seemed to circumscribe a space too huge for him to comprehend. The sunlight sparkled in the fountains and cast a stretched and minatory shadow of the central obelisk to meet him, while the pillars and dome of St Peter's itself soared shimmeringly above the steps on the farther side of the piazza. It struck him for a moment that he had never seen anything made by man more beautiful than this.

But he could spare no time to relish even unparalleled beauty. He headed towards the steps leading up to St Peter's, at the foot of which were gathered several carriages, some of which might well be for hire.

He was about halfway between the obelisk and the steps when he realized someone was keeping pace with him away to the right. Glancing towards him, he saw that it was Silverwood. He stopped. So did Silverwood. Then a twitch of the fellow's head told him where Buckthorn was: no more than twenty yards to Spandrel's rear, ostentatiously flicking back his coat to reveal the handle of the sword he was wearing.

Spandrel was outflanked and outmanoeuvred, his retreat cut off. They had either guessed where he would go in search of transport or had simply struck lucky; it hardly mattered which. His only hope now was the safety of holy ground. He ran to the steps and started up them. Silverwood rushed to intercept, but his rush was another man's dawdle. Buckthorn posed the greater threat and Spandrel could not afford to look back to see how close he was.

He reached the top of the steps and headed for the nearest door into the basilica. There were footsteps behind him now, pounding on the flagstones. Then a hand closed around his shoulder. 'Hold hard,' shouted Buckthorn, wrenching Spandrel round to face him. 'You'll answer to us before you do any praying.'

There was a knife in Buckthorn's hand. Spandrel had seen it before and knew how adept the fellow was with it. He moved instinctively away, but suddenly Silverwood was behind him, panting and swearing and pinning his arms at his back.

'Where's the Green Book, Spandrel?' Buckthorn feinted a lunge with the knife. 'Where is it, damn you?'

'I . . . don't have it.'

'Estelle must have, then. Where is she?'

'Out of your reach.'

'If that's true, I'll—'

Buckthorn never finished the sentence. Suddenly, the blunt end of a halberd struck his wrist and the knife clattered to the ground. Buckthorn cried out in pain. Then he and Silverwood were seized by tall, broadly built men in helmets and brightly striped uniforms. They were men of the Pope's Swiss Guard and Spandrel did not think he had ever been so pleased to see a soldier in his life.

'Take your hands off us,' bleated Silverwood. 'You can't treat English gentlemen like this.'

Clearly, however, the Swiss Guards believed they could. More probably, they neither spoke nor understood English and did not think people brandishing knives at the very door of St Peter's were at all likely to be gentlemen. They dragged the pair unceremoniously away.

'We'll come after you, Spandrel,' shouted Buckthorn. 'Don't think you've seen the last of us.'

A friar standing close by shook his head disapprovingly. '*Un coltello, qui,*' he said, to no-one in particular. '*Un sacrilegio.*' Sacrilege? Yes. Spandrel supposed what they had done could well count as that. And he also supposed sacrilege was something the papal authorities bore down on very hard indeed. On the whole, he reckoned he probably *had* seen the last of them.

He turned away and hurried back down the steps.

The Piazza del Popolo was empty. Not of people, of course. There was the normal assortment of *servitori*, tradesmen, travellers and idlers, the customary comings and goings through the gate. But of Estelle there was no sign. And to Spandrel, casting about him as he circled the piazza, it seemed that all he saw was emptiness.

More in hope than expectation, he approached a group of men sitting on the plinth at the foot of the obelisk. They were smoking and enjoying the afternoon sunshine. They looked as if they had been there some time. '*Parla inglese, signori?*' he ventured. But the only answer he received was a deal of squinting and shrugging. 'Has a coach left here for Florence? *Una carrozza? Per Firenze?*'

One of the men, the shortest and slightest built, stood up then and moved to Spandrel's elbow. 'Why should you want to know?' he asked, in a heather-soft Scottish accent.

Suddenly, the other men were on their feet as well, clustering round Spandrel. His arms were seized and held. 'Let go of me,' he protested. 'Who are you?' But he knew who they were. And he knew they were not going to let him go. There were no Swiss Guards to come to his aid here.

'There's a coach leaving this minute, Mr Spandrel. It's not going to Florence, I'm afraid. It's going to the Palazzo Muti. And you'll be riding in it.'

'A change of plan, Mr Spandrel?' said James Edgar, surveying him across his desk at the Palazzo Muti half an hour later. 'Where is the Green Book, pray?'

'I don't have it.'

'Did you ever?'

271

'Oh yes.'

'How did you come to lose it?'

'It's difficult to explain.'

'Really? I suggest you find a way to do so. And I suggest you adhere strictly to the truth while you're about it. Otherwise the Tiber will have another nameless corpse floating down it tonight.' Edgar frowned. 'You understand?'

Spandrel nodded. He understood. All too well.

The light was failing by the time Spandrel finished. It was the same chill point of late afternoon as when he had previously sat in Edgar's office, just twenty-four hours before. But everything had changed since then. He had nothing to sell and nothing to dream of. He did not even have any lies left to tell. And for that at least he was strangely grateful.

'Confession to a priest is seen in the true faith as a means of absolution, Mr Spandrel,' said Edgar, after a lengthy silence. 'A pity for you I'm not a priest.'

'I've given you what you asked for: the truth.'

'I believe you have. But it's not the truth I wanted to hear. Nor yet to carry to the King. The Green Book on its way to Tuscany with an escort of Swiss Guards. And treachery even in the Quirinal Palace. Cardinal Bortolazzi is a great friend of the Bishop of Osimo, who many believe will be the next pope. If the King cannot trust such people . . .' Edgar sighed. 'Some truths are better for kings not to know.'

'I'm sorry.'

'What use to me is your sorrow?'

'None, I suppose.'

'I'm glad you understand that.'

'But . . .'

'What's to become of you? Is that the question teetering on your lips?'

'Yes.'

'What's to become of any of us?' Edgar took an irritable swipe at the papers on his desk, then rose and strode to the window. He gazed out thoughtfully at the gathering dusk for several long moments, before turning round to face Spandrel once more. 'You are a lucky man, Mr Spandrel.'

'I am?'

'I have a proposition for you.'

'What is it?'

'Go before the King and tell him you never had the Green Book. Tell him you are an errant clerk of the South Sea Company, seeking to profit from the scraps of information you accumulated in the course of your work. Tell him that, as far as you know, the Green Book was seized from Mr Knight when he was arrested in Brabant and has been in the keeping of the Elector's ministers ever since.'

'But . . . that's not . . .'

'The truth? No. Exactly. It is a version of events that will make me look a fool and you a still more contemptible rogue than you actually are. But it will merely disappoint the King, not destroy him. And that is the most I can hope to gain from this sorry affair. For you, there is a reward.' Edgar smiled grimly. 'Survival.'

'You'll . . . let me go?'

'Not quite. I will persuade the King to spare you. And then I will send you away. There is a ship sailing from Cività Vecchia on Wednesday. The master is a friend of ours. A true friend. You will be aboard. The ship is bound for Brest. And there you will be delivered. What you do then – so long as you never return to Rome – is none of my concern.'

'If I refuse . . . to tell this tale?'

Edgar shrugged. 'The Tiber awaits.'

'I had hoped . . . to go to Tuscany.'

'Fashion a different hope.'

'Can I not—'

'No.' Edgar looked straight at him. 'You cannot.'

'I have no choice but to accept?'

'No sane choice, certainly.'

'Then . . .'

'You accept?'

Brest, or Naples. What difference did it make? What had he achieved by going after Estelle other than to lose her over again? Even the truth was forfeit now. He had no choice. Perhaps he had never had one. He had no hope. But he did have life.

'Mr Spandrel?'

'Yes.' He nodded. 'I accept.'

Interlude

April 1721–March 1722

Chapter Twenty-Eight

Ways and Means

At the beginning of April, 1721, the Earl of Sunderland bowed to the seemingly inevitable and resigned as First Lord of the Treasury. Robert Walpole succeeded him with immediate effect, combining the office with that of Chancellor of the Exchequer. The nation's finances were thus squarely under Walpole's control. So indeed was the nation's mail, since he at once appointed his brother Galfridus Postmaster-General, or Interceptor-General, as some suspicious letter-writers dubbed him.

Sunderland was not quite a spent force, however. He remained Groom of the Stole and the King's principal confidant, with control of the Secret Service. He was willing to lie low for a while, but not to accept defeat. There were Members, actual and prospective, to be bribed and blackmailed before the general election due to be held the following March. If more of Sunderland's bought men than Walpole's found a seat in the new Parliament, their fortunes might yet be reversed.

The South Sea Sufferers Bill had meanwhile to make its way through the old Parliament. It was intended to be the last word on the notorious Bubble, recovering as much as possible from the estates of the directors and other convicted parties to defray the company's losses. But the last word was a long time being uttered. Each director was allowed to offset certain inescapable liabilities against his declared assets, necessitating lengthy argument at every stage. Deals were done, bargains struck, favours rewarded. Aislabie, the disgraced former Chancellor, escaped with the bulk of his fortune intact. The heiresses of the deceased Postmaster Craggs were leniently treated. And Sir Theodore Janssen, when his turn came, was mysteriously allowed to keep more than any other director.

The public knew what all this amounted to, of course: corruption in its normal nesting-ground – high places. But what was to be done? Robert Knight remained locked up and incommunicado in the Citadel at Antwerp. (Though not if persistent rumours of his secret removal elsewhere were to be believed.) Of his most sensitive records there was no apparent trace. Walpole waited until most Members had slipped away to their country seats before bringing the matter to the vote early in August. Despite the audible protests of aggrieved creditors outside the House, the Bill was passed. Legally, the South Sea affair was closed.

In Rome, the Pretender continued to believe that discontent over the issue would lead to his restoration. As a plot-hatchery, the Palazzo Muti remained busy. But plots and risings, especially the successful kind, were not quite the same thing. The newly elected Pope Innocent XIII – the former Bishop of Osimo – assured James Edward of his full support, before giving a very good impression of forgetting about him altogether.

At the end of September came news of Knight's escape from the supposedly escape-proof Antwerp Citadel and his abscondence across the border into France. The Brodrick Committee's oft-repeated demands for his extradition had finally been answered, though scarcely in the fashion its members had hoped. Another deal had clearly been done. Before the year was out, Knight had established himself in Paris as a financial consultant. As the former chief cashier of a bankrupt company with debts of £14,500,000, his credentials for such a role were manifestly impeccable.

That portion of the British public still hoarding South Sea shares certificates and notes of credit bore such events in a mood of half-stifled fury. Out of pocket and humour alike, they came to hate Walpole even more than the delinquent directors who had bilked them. 'The Screenmaster-General', as they called him, had screened his enemies as well as his friends, leaving the poor and the innocent to pay the price.

They can hardly have been surprised when it became known that the presses used for printing the Brodrick Committee's reports had been smashed on the orders of Viscount Townshend. There were to be no second editions. Not that those reports contained more than a fraction of the truth, of course. Only a certain green-covered ledger could tell the whole story. And nobody seemed to know where that might be found, or indeed whether it still existed.

With a collective sigh of relief on the part of those who had lost less by it than they had gained, the sorry saga of the South Sea was consigned, if not to history, then at least to history's waiting-room, whence it was likely to be retrieved only in the most extraordinary circumstances. The political world's attention shifted back to more familiar ground: a struggle for power between two able and ambitious men, to be decided by that orgy of auctioned loyalty known as a general election.

Book Two

April–June 1722

Chapter Twenty-Nine

Death of a Statesman

Viscount Townshend hurried across St James's Square through a breezy spring morning. His destination was the London residence of the Earl of Sunderland and the circumstances were sufficiently extraordinary for him to feel disconcertingly torn between elation and apprehension. The election results were still arriving, in their customary dribs and drabs, and those so far received had left the issue between Sunderland and Walpole tantalizingly undecided. But those results had suddenly become irrelevant. The issue *was* decided. Sunderland was dead.

News had reached Townshend the previous evening of Sunderland's sudden and as yet unexplained demise. It had been conveyed to him by the Lord Privy Seal, the Duke of Kingston, considerably put out at being instructed by Walpole to secure all the dead Earl's papers at once, even if it meant breaking into his study to do so. Kingston had not cared much for the propriety of this move and nor had Townshend. But he had nevertheless told Kingston to proceed. His brother-in-law's instincts, though sometimes brutal, were always to be trusted.

It was undeniable that the long struggle with Sunderland had taught Walpole some unedifying lessons. He had become more secretive, more devious, more downright egotistical. He hid the traits well, beneath bonhomie and bluster, but they were there for those who

283

knew him best to detect. This latest turn of events was an example. With Sunderland scarcely cold in his death-bed, let alone his grave, Walpole was laying claim to documents that were technically the property of his family, trampling on the feelings of his pregnant widow and blithely incurring the wrath of his mother-in-law, the formidable Duchess of Marlborough. All this, moreover, he had embarked upon without troubling to consult Townshend.

A consultation of sorts was presumably what awaited Townshend at Spencer House. But it would be of the kind he was growing all too used to: one held after the event. Perhaps he should protest. 'Remember, my dear,' his darling Dolly had said to him more than once, 'Robin owes such a lot to you.' Townshend certainly remembered. But he was no longer sure his brother-in-law did.

Spencer House should have been a place of hushed mourning. Instead, it was a tumult of scurrying servants and bustling Treasury clerks. Several of the latter were loading tea-chests crammed with papers into a closed cart under the sheepish supervision of the Duke of Kingston, who cast Townshend a doleful look and shrugged his massive shoulders.

'He's been busy in Sunderland's study since dawn,' Kingston said, neither troubling nor needing to specify whom he meant. 'I found it locked, you know. I had to force the door open. Every drawer as well.' It was unlikely that Kingston had personally forced anything, but his point was made. 'Damned unseemly, I call it.'

'But necessary, no doubt,' said Townshend.

'Who's to say? All this' – he gestured at the tea-chests – 'is bound for Chelsea.' Walpole's London residence, then, not the Treasury. It was an eloquent distinction.

'How's the Countess?'

'In a torrent of tears, as you'd expect. And horror-struck to find a pack of inky-fingered clerks clumping about her home, as you'd also expect. She may have miscarried by now, for all I know.'

'Where's the, er . . .'

'Corpse? Taken away, thank God.' Kingston lowered his voice. 'They're talking of a post mortem.'

'Why?'

'Why do you think? The fellow was in rude good health when I last saw him.'

'You're surely not suggesting—'

'I'm suggesting nothing. But others won't be so circum-spect, will they?'

'I dare say not.'

'Well, don't let me keep you. He's in no mood to greet late arrivals.'

'I'm not late.'

'No?' Kingston's voice sank to a whisper. 'If you ask me, we're all late when it comes to keeping up with him.'

There was unquestionably an air of pre-emptive industry in Sunderland's plundered study. Walpole sat at his dead foe's desk, a late breakfast mug of cider at his elbow and a drift of papers before him, his face flushed and beaming, like that of a farmer in their native Norfolk at the conclusion of a tiring but ample harvest.

'Ah, there you are, Charles. Welcome, welcome. How's the day?'

'Well enough,' Townshend conceded, though in truth he had only the faintest awareness of the weather.

'Better than well, I reckon. This is a day I didn't think we'd see.'

'What have Sunderland's papers revealed?'

'Much. You might almost say all. But—' He broke off and glared across at a pair of clerks filling boxes on the other side of the room. 'You two! Get out!'

'Yes, sir,' they chorused. 'At once, sir.' And out they got.

'Close the door behind you!' It clicked respectfully shut. 'I've had them under my feet all morning, damn their eyes.'

'It looks as if you've needed them.'

'For porterage, yes. It's about all they're good for. But sit down, Charles. Make yourself comfortable. You may as well.'

'Comfortable? In a dead man's study? I don't know about that.' Nevertheless, Townshend drew up a chair. As he did so, his eye was taken by a portrait above the fireplace of a good-looking young man in military costume of the Civil War era. 'An ancestor?'

'The first Earl. Killed at the battle of Newbury, a few months after he was given the title.'

'Sunderland's grandfather?'

'Yes. Note that. The grandfather, not the father. The second Earl was the same brand of scheming trimmer as his son. Maybe Sunderland wanted someone more inspiring to look at over his mantelpiece.'

'Have you found anything inspiring to look at?' Townshend nodded at the slew of papers on the desk.

'You could say so. Sunderland seems to have been mighty selective about passing on what the Secret Service brought him.'

'Has he held back anything important?'

'It's only the important stuff he *has* held back. You and Carteret can pick out the bones when it's all been collated. Carteret tells me, by the way, that he may have found someone who can give us more reliable information on the doings of the Pretender than the kilted drunkards we normally employ.'

'Baron von Stosch.'

'That's his name. The genuine article, you reckon?'

'About as genuine as a diamond necklace on a Haymarket whore. But he could be useful.'

'He'll need to be if I read these runes aright.'

'What is it, Robin?' Townshend sat forward, his curiosity aroused. 'Jacobite rumblings?'

'There are always rumblings. This is something more. What do you make of these?' Walpole plucked a batch of papers from the pile before him and tossed it across the desk.

It was a list of names, running to several pages, arranged under county headings. The names were familiar to Townshend. Many of them were known Jacobites. Many more were not. 'These surely don't all belong in the same basket,' he said. 'You're not suggesting . . .'

'Look at Norfolk.'

Townshend leafed forward to their own county and read the names, with rising incredulity. 'Bacon, l'Estrange, Heron, North, Wodehouse.' He stopped. 'Some of these are our bought men.'

'But some men sell themselves twice over. Ever hear of a lawyer called Christopher Layer?'

'I don't think so. Hold on, though. Not Layer of Aylsham?'

'You have him. Not a credit to his profession, as you know. That list seems to be his handiwork. And Secret Service reports say Layer visited Rome last summer.'

'He's gone over to the Pretender?'

'To the extent of boasting he'll be Lord Chancellor under King James, apparently.'

'Then . . . how did Sunderland . . . come by his list?'

'There's the question, Charles. How indeed? Perhaps he was simply sent it. Perhaps he asked for it to be drawn up. Sudden death leaves no time for the disposal of incriminating documents. That's the best of it. On the one hand the Secret Service is busy telling Sunderland that Layer's an active Jacobite plotter known to be in regular communication with one James Johnson, an alias, they believe, of none other than George Kelly.'

'Secretary to the Bishop of Rochester.'

'Exactly. Our least loyal prelate. That, as I say, is on the one hand. On the other, Sunderland has Layer's list in his possession, bearing every appearance of a muster-roll of traitors and their camp-followers, including twenty-three peers and eighty-three Members of Parliament.' Walpole grinned. 'I counted.'

'How long has he had the list?'

'Who knows? Long enough to alert the King's ministers to its contents, I'd have thought. But he didn't, did he? And this may be the reason.' Walpole slid a single sheet of paper across the desk to join the pages of Layer's list.

Townshend picked up the sheet of paper. It was a letter, addressed to Sunderland. As he read it, his mouth fell open in surprise. Then he read it again, this time aloud. ' "I am greatly obliged to your lordship for the service you have rendered my cause and wish to assure your lordship that such service will be well rewarded. Your privileged foreknowledge of the Electoral itinerary will be our sure and certain guide in determining when it would be most propitious to set our enterprise afoot. It will be an enterprise of honour and of right and to find that you have as keen a sense as did your grandfather of where honour and right abide is to me a distinct and pronounced pleasure." '

'You didn't know the Pretender had such a florid style of expression, did you, Charles?'

' "Jacobus Rex." ' Townshend read the signature in no more than a murmur. Then he looked at the date. 'This was written less than a month ago.'

'So it appears. In perfect confidence, so it also appears. But I could hardly ask Galfridus to rifle through Sunderland's post-bag, could I? There are limits.' Walpole sighed. 'This is what comes of abiding by them.'

'I can hardly believe it, Robin. Sunderland . . . and the Pretender.'

'He'd have thrown in his lot with the Devil himself to get the better of me.'

The use of the singular pronoun registered somewhere in Townshend's confused thoughts. *Me*, not *us*. It was telling, in its way. But not as telling as the letter in his hand. 'What's meant by the . . . "Electoral itinerary", do you suppose?'

'The date of the King's departure for Hanover, I'd surmise. He's set on going this year. As to precisely when, who'd know sooner than his Groom of the Stole?'

'They plan to strike when the King's out of the country?'

'Or worse – to assassinate him on the road to Hanover.'

'Surely Sunderland wouldn't have put his name to that.'

'He put his name to something. Of course, if he'd succeeded in packing the House with his creatures and ousting us from office, he could have exposed the plot and claimed the credit for saving the kingdom. No doubt he only meant to go through with it if the elections went against him. As our managers seem to reckon they generally have. A desperate man, our Sunderland. And now a dead one.'

'What are we to do?'

'Nothing, for the moment. I want the ringleaders, Charles. And I mean to have them.' Walpole sat back in his chair. 'So, let them think they're safe for a little longer yet. Let them plot away their days while we gather the evidence to damn them.'

'Where's such evidence to be found? This letter condemns Sunderland, not his co-conspirators.'

'We must draw them out.' Walpole smiled. 'And I think I may have found a way to do just that. Sir Theodore Janssen came to see me a few days ago.'

'Is he still complaining about his treatment?'

'With decreasing energy. No, no. He came to see me because of an undertaking I secured from him while he was in the Tower – an undertaking to keep me advised of any developments in the matter of the Green Book.'

'How can there be any developments now?'

'I expected none, certainly. But what Janssen said gives me—' There was a sudden commotion outside. Kingston's voice could be heard above that of another man. 'Ah! That'll be Lord Godolphin.'

'Godolphin? What will he say when he finds us taking our ease in his brother-in-law's study?'

'Very little, when we show him that letter. I suggested he call, as a matter of fact.'

'Why?'

'So that one of Sunderland's relatives could witness our destruction of the letter.'

'You mean to destroy it?'

'Certainly. As an act of compassion, to spare the noble Earl's reputation and his family's feelings. That should take the wind out of Madam Marlborough's sails, don't you reckon?' Walpole winked. 'It's not the dead we need to snare, Charles. It's the living.'

Chapter Thirty

The Wanderer Returns

'Hello, Ma.'

Spandrel's greeting was hardly equal to the momentousness of the occasion. His mother gaped at him in astonishment for fully half a minute, seemingly – and understandably – unable to believe that he was standing before her, alive and well, alive and *uncommonly* well, to judge by his healthy complexion and newish clothes. Fifteen months of unexplained absence, during which she had often been reduced to believing him dead, had ended on an April morning of fitful sunshine, with her opening the door in answer to a strangely familiar knock and finding her son standing before her, smiling a smile she knew so well.

'Aren't you going to give me a kiss?'

She did kiss him, of course, and hugged him too. Tears started to her eyes. She hugged him again, then stood back and frowned at him. 'I thought you were dead, boy. You know that?'

'Not dead, Ma. As you can see.'

'Come inside and close the door before we have half the neighbourhood goggling at you.'

'I bumped into Annie Welsh in the yard.'

'What did she say to you?'

'Something about a bad penny.'

'She probably remembers what I said to her when you first went missing.'

'What was that?'

'That I hoped for your sake you had a good excuse for leaving me in the lurch.'

'I don't know about in the lurch.' Spandrel looked around the room. The piles of washing and the rack-load drying before the fire indicated that his mother was still plying her trade as a washerwoman. 'You probably found living was cheaper without me.'

'Cheaper, maybe. But not easier.' She grabbed his left ear lobe, as she often had when he misbehaved as a child. 'What have you been up to?'

'Ow!' Spandrel's exaggerated cry persuaded her to let him go. 'Some breakfast would be nice.'

'I'm surprised you don't expect a fatted calf.'

'Have a heart, Ma.'

'Lucky for you I've a bigger heart than's good for me. I'll make breakfast. While *you* explain yourself.'

Explaining himself was something Spandrel had already given much thought to. The Green Book – and the secrets it contained – was a subject he had no intention of broaching to his mother. He doubted she would be able to comprehend what he himself now found difficult to believe. The year that had passed since his departure from Rome had cast the events that had led him there in the first place into a semi-fabulous compartment of his memory. And he was content for them to remain there. Accordingly, while admitting that Sir Theodore Janssen had sent him on a secret errand to Amsterdam, he claimed that he had no idea what the package he had been charged to carry might have contained. He had been robbed of it in a tavern in Amsterdam, so he related, and, ashamed of such foolishness, had remained abroad rather than return home empty-handed to face Sir Theodore's wrath.

His account grafted itself at this point onto the truth. For the past year, he had worked as a surveyor's assistant in the French city of Rennes. He had met the surveyor, a kindly but ailing fellow much in need of assistance, by the name of Jean-Luc Taillard, during a coach journey (from Brest, a detail he omitted). Taillard, having no family of his own, had appointed Spandrel his heir. And Taillard's recent death had left Spandrel in possession of his life savings, amounting to 15,000 livres – about £1,000. This was a fraction of what Spandrel had dreamt the Green Book might bring him. But it was also far more than he had ever had to his name. And it meant he could return to England without fear of being imprisoned for debt.

'All the debts are paid, Ma,' he said, as he finished his breakfast. 'And there's plenty left over.'

'To spend on what, may I ask?'

'Somewhere better for you to live, to start with. You'll be sending washing out, not taking it in. And I'll be finishing the map.'

'That old dream of your father's?'

'This is one dream that's going to come true.'

'You mean that?'

'I certainly do.'

'All our troubles are over?'

'Yes. Thanks to Monsieur Taillard.' He plucked a flagon of gin from his bag and pulled out the cork. 'Let's drink to happier times.'

'You'll be the ruin of me, boy,' said his mother, unable to stifle a grin.

Viscount Townshend hurried into the Treasury that morning with an altogether lighter tread than he had felt capable of when entering Spencer House the previous day. This time, he had news for Walpole, not the other way about, and it was a rare enough experience for him to relish.

Walpole was standing by the window of his office, munching an apple and gazing out at a leash of deer in St James's Park. He looked exactly what Townshend knew him not to be – a man without a care in the world. But Townshend also knew that the cares of state were what lent him such a genial aspect. They were what made him happy.

'What do you have for me, Charles? Something, I'll be bound. I've seen that twinkle in your eye too often to be wrong.'

'A despatch from Sir Luke Schaub.' (Schaub was the British Ambassador in Paris, second only to Rome as a centre of Jacobite plotting.) 'Sent two days ago.' (Sent, then, on the day of Sunderland's death.)

'What does Sir Luke have to say?'

'Cardinal Dubois has alerted him to a request from the Pretender for the use of three thousand French troops.'

'When?'

'Within weeks.'

'How fortunate we are that the French Foreign Minister is such a devious man.' Walpole raised the window and tossed his half-eaten apple out through the gap, then turned to Townshend with a broad smile. 'It seems we'd have known something was afoot even without the run of Sunderland's study. But no doubt Sunderland would have persuaded the King there was nothing to worry about.'

'We should inform His Majesty.'

'I agree. We'll see him this afternoon. You'd better bring Carteret with you. It'll give the impression we're all of one mind.' Walpole chuckled. 'But then we are, of course.'

Shopping for anything but the barest necessities was for Margaret Spandrel a half-forgotten indulgence. Shopping for a new home was something she had not expected to do this side of Heaven. But that afternoon, equipped with a copy of the *London Journal* and the addresses of several reputable house agents, she accompanied her son on a tour of properties which were considerably larger and more elegant than many of those where she had latterly called to collect washing and which – miracle of miracles – William assured her they could afford.

Yet she was not to be lured into extravagance. Such money as they had should be used wisely. There were only two of them. They deserved no more than they needed: a modest level of comfort. This they found to her satisfaction – though not entirely to William's – on the second floor of a house on the southern side of Leicester Fields.

'Four rooms and a palace in view whenever you look out of the window for fourteen shillings a week,' observed the agent. 'You'll not do better.'

The palace in question was actually Leicester House, whither the Prince of Wales had fled after falling out with his father a few years previously and being expelled from St James's. It was not a palace and it did not look like one. But the square was quiet and its residents respectable. It would do. It would do very well indeed. They took the lease.

In the King's closet at St James's, which really was a palace even though some had been rude enough to suggest that it looked no more like one than Leicester House, what would do and what would not do were also matters of moment.

The King was not in one of his more pliable moods. Sunderland's death had shocked him to whatever lay at the core of his Germanic being and his reaction veered between the lachrymose and the suspicious. The triumvirate of ministers facing him – First Lord of the Treasury

Walpole and Secretaries of State Townshend and Carteret – wished, it seemed, to vex him with problems beyond his fathoming while failing to answer the questions that most troubled him.

'What made Lord Sunderland to die?' he demanded, not for the first time that afternoon.

'Pleurisy,' said Walpole. 'According to the doctors.'

'Pleurisy? So sudden?'

'It is a puzzle,' remarked Lord Carteret, despite a sharp look from Walpole. The youngest and best bred of the three, Carteret impressed the King by his fine manners and independence of mind. Would that he could have more such courtiers about him, instead of coarse-tongued, beetle-browed Norfolkmen. 'But of puzzles we have no lack.'

'Nor of plots, Your Majesty,' said Townshend. 'There seems no doubt that the Pretender is set upon another attempt.'

'They tell us his son may die also.'

The ministers needed to exchange several glances before realizing that the King was referring not to the Pretender's son but to the Honourable William Spencer, youngest son of the late Earl of Sunderland. 'The boy has smallpox, sir,' said Walpole. 'It's not connected with—'

'Where is the Duke of Newcastle?' barked the King. 'We are needful.'

'I'm sure the Lord Chamberlain will wait upon you directly, sir,' said Townshend. 'He has as yet, however, no knowledge of the threat to your person.'

'Person? Threat?'

'We fear it does amount to that,' said Carteret.

'Who? When? How?'

'The Jacobites,' said Walpole darkly. 'When you travel to Hanover. An assassin on the road. Simultaneous with—'

He broke off, then began again, expressing himself more simply. 'At the same time as a rising here in London.'

'In the circumstances . . .' Townshend began.

'It would be best to postpone your visit to Hanover,' Walpole continued. 'We must have regard for Your Majesty's safety.'

'I will go to Hanover.'

'Perhaps not this year.'

'*I will go.*'

'There is still much resentment among your subjects on account of the *Angelegenheit South Sea*,' said Carteret, smiling faintly at his own Germanism. 'That is what the Jacobites hope to exploit. We should give them no opportunity.'

'It is easy enough to frustrate their plans now we know of them,' said Townshend. 'We can station troops in Hyde Park and expel all papists and non-jurors from the city. That, together with Cardinal Dubois' refusal of assistance for the Pretender and his withdrawal of Irish regiments from the Channel ports—'

'And the postponement of your visit to Hanover,' put in Walpole.

'Should render us safe,' Townshend concluded.

'*Ja, ja.*' The King chewed at his knuckles. 'I stay here,' he conceded glumly.

'But for the moment,' said Walpole, 'we should do nothing.'

'Nothing?' The King glared at him. '*Nichts?*'

'Nothing to alert them to our knowledge of their plans. Once they know the game is up, they will go to ground. We will not catch them then.'

'So how will we – how will *you*, Mr Walpole – catch them?'

'By luring them into betraying themselves.'

'We believe the Bishop of Rochester to be at the bottom of it,' put in Townshend.

'No doubt he dreams of becoming Archbishop of Canterbury,' Carteret remarked.

'*Verräter*,' growled the King. 'Why do we let Atterbury to give sermons in Westminster Abbey when he plots behind us?' Francis Atterbury was Dean of Westminster Abbey as well as Bishop of Rochester. His sermons in the former capacity, uttered a mere stone's throw from the Palace, had often been thinly veiled dalliances with treason. Small wonder that the King did not understand why he had to tolerate him. But there *were* reasons. And they were good ones.

'He is undeniably popular,' said Townshend.

'A veritable darling of the mob,' said Carteret, smiling weakly. 'Against whom there is a singular lack of evidence.'

'Evidence that would secure his conviction in court, that is,' added Townshend.

'But give me a few weeks,' said Walpole, 'and I think I can gather such evidence.'

The King frowned at him. 'How?'

'You'll remember, sir, the . . . Green Book?'

'*Das Grüne Buch?*' The inflexion of horror in the King's voice suggested he was hardly likely to have forgotten it.

'Indeed, sir.' Walpole smiled at him reassuringly. 'I believe we can use it to bait a trap . . . that will snap shut round Bishop Atterbury's overweening neck.'

Margaret Spandrel returned to Cat and Dog Yard that afternoon to commence the less than daunting task of packing her belongings in readiness for the move to Leicester Fields. William did not accompany her. On the pretext of visiting the engraver who was holding the completed sheets of the map (and who he would later say had not been at home), he left her to make her way back there alone. He headed north to Bloomsbury, an area of the city favoured by those who had sufficient money to buy themselves a charming view of the meadow-patched hills of Hampstead and Highgate. George Chesney, a director of the New River Company, which piped Hertfordshire spring water to a goodly portion of Londoners from its reservoir at Islington, was one such person. His home in Great Ormond Street backed onto this vista of rural meadowland, while presenting an imposing Palladian face to the city.

The Chesney residence was not Spandrel's destination, much as he would have liked it to be. The year he had spent working for Monsieur Taillard had rid him of many delusions, most notably the idea that anything could be had for nothing, be it beauty *or* wealth. Life could only be bettered by honest endeavour. He was financially independent because of such endeavour, whereas fortune-hunting across half of Europe had yielded only fear and a fugitive's despair. All that was behind him. He missed old Taillard, he really did. He wished the poor fellow could have lived longer. But his death had handed Spandrel an opportunity to improve his station in society. For that he needed a wife, not a dangerously alluring dream-lover. And as a wife Maria Chesney would be ideal. But was she still available? He could hardly knock on her father's door and ask. He could, however, enquire of the Chesneys' loquacious footman, Sam Burrows, who was unlikely to let a Saturday afternoon pass into evening without calling at his favourite local tavern, the Goat.

'Mr Spandrel, as I live and breathe.' Sam was already pink-gilled and grinning when Spandrel found him. He had enjoyed a profitable afternoon at the cock-fights, so he explained, and was celebrating. But an excess of ale did not quite swamp his surprise. 'I had you down as dead – or in the clink.'

'You were nearly right on both counts.'

'Instead of which, here you are, looking the real gent.'

'That's because I am one.'

'If you say so, Mr Spandrel.'

'I do.'

'What brings you out this way?'

'Can't you guess?'

'Oh, that's it, is it?' Sam put down his mug and wiped his mouth. 'You're still set on Miss Maria.'

'I might be.'

'I'm sorry, Mr Spandrel.' To his credit, Sam actually looked as if he was. 'You're too late.'

'She's married?'

'All but. She'll be Mrs Surtees come July.'

Spandrel sighed. 'I suppose I should have—' Then he stopped and looked at Sam intently. 'Did you say Surtees?'

'I did.'

'Not . . . Dick Surtees?'

'Well, he calls himself Richard, but . . .' Sam frowned. 'Do you know him, then?'

Chapter Thirty-One

A Friend in Need

As apprentices, William Spandrel and his then very good friend Dick Surtees had often marked the close of the working day by adjourning to the Hood Inn near Smithfield. Spandrel had nominated it as a rendezvous in the note he had persuaded Sam to deliver for the highly practical reasons that he could be sure it would be open on a Sunday and that Dick knew where it was. Waiting there the following afternoon, however, the choice of venue began to prey on his mind, weighed down as it was by memories of the things he had lost in the years since they had been regular customers there, Dick's friendship not least among the losses.

Spandrel had been prepared to hear that Maria was married, or engaged to be so. He had almost expected it. But that her betrothed should be none other than Dick Surtees, failed mapmaker and aspiring man of the world, was a shock he had still not recovered from. He could have no fundamental complaint. Dick owed him nothing. Except an explanation. Yes, on that point Spandrel was clear. He *was* owed an explanation.

It seemed that Surtees agreed with him, for it was only a few minutes past the time Spandrel had specified in the note when a familiar figure threaded through the smoke-wreathed ruck to join him. The slim, slope-shouldered physique was the same, as were the dark, evasive eyes. But

301

Surtees' appearance had nonetheless been transformed. There were braided buttonholes and deep, embroidered cuffs on his coat, and the cream cravat and grey-black wig beneath the fancily brimmed hat singled him out not just as a gentleman but as a well-heeled student of fashion.

'Billy, I can't tell you how good it is to see you,' he said, clapping Spandrel on the shoulder and sitting down beside him. 'How long has it been?'

'Seven years.'

'Seven years that have treated you well, by the look of you. New suit?'

'Not as new as yours.'

'This?' Surtees flexed his cuffs. 'Well, you have to put on a show, don't you?'

'Not for old friends.'

'No. I suppose not.' For a moment, Surtees looked almost sheepish. 'I had your note.'

'I was surprised when Sam told me of your engagement.'

'Ah, that. Yes. Well, you would be.'

'How did it happen?'

'I sometimes wonder myself.' Surtees grabbed the sleeve of a waiter as he wandered by and ordered some brandy. 'Yes, I sometimes do.'

'My father died.'

'I know. I was sorry to hear of it.'

'How *did* you hear of it?'

'When I came back to London last autumn, I thought I'd look you up. For old times' sake. Reports had it your father had got into debt and then into the Fleet Prison and then . . .' Surtees shrugged. 'Sorry.'

'Did these . . . reports . . . mention me?'

'Oh yes. They said you'd fled abroad.'

'I didn't flee.'

'You don't have to explain yourself to me, Billy.'

302

'I'd be happy to. If you explained *yourself* to *me*.'

'Me? I made good. Simple as that.'

'Abroad?'

'Yes. Paris. You've heard of the, er . . .' Surtees lowered his voice. 'Mississippi Company?'

'I thought it crashed, like the South Sea.'

'Oh, it did. But I sold just at the right time. *Acheter la fumée; vendre la fumée.* It's a game. You have to know the rules.'

'A game of buying and selling smoke.'

'You, er, *parlez le français*, Billy?' Surtees looked quite taken aback.

'I spent some time there myself.'

'In Paris?'

'No. Rennes. Where I made good as well, out of something more substantial than smoke. And I came home, hoping I might still be able to . . .'

'Capture Maria's heart.'

'Yes, Dick. Exactly.'

Surtees' brandy arrived. He poured them a glass each. 'Sorry,' he said, by way of apologetic toast.

'But I find *you've* captured her heart.'

'Yes. Well, she's a lovely girl. You know that.'

'Yes. I do.'

'I'll, er, make her happy. You have my word.'

'How did you meet her?'

'That was . . . thanks to you, actually.'

'*Me?*'

'I remembered you'd said what a treasure she was. Even when she was no more than fifteen. So, when I heard you'd left London, I, er, decided to try my luck.'

'You seem to have had a lot of that – luck.'

'More than my fair share, probably. The father *and* the daughter have taken to me.'

'The mother too, I expect.'

'Since you mention it . . .' Surtees grinned nervously. 'Yes.'

'And you're to be married in the summer.'

'The thirtieth of June.'

'Perhaps I should congratulate you.'

'No need to be sarcastical. It couldn't be helped.'

'Couldn't it?'

'No-one had seen hide or hair of you in months and no-one expected to. I thought you'd forgotten all about her. So did she.'

'Encouraged by you, no doubt.'

'Be reasonable, Billy. How was I to know you'd turn up like this?'

Spandrel looked at his former friend long and hard before admitting, 'You weren't, I suppose.'

'It's damned unfortunate, but . . .' Surtees grimaced. 'There it is.'

'Be sure you *do* make her happy.'

'I will. You can rely on it. You could even, er, help me to.'

'What's that supposed to mean?'

'You've left her life, Billy. No sense trying to come back into it.'

'Are you warning me off?'

'Good God, of course I'm not. I'm just . . .'

'Asking me to give you a clear run.'

'Well, I, er, wouldn't put it quite like that, but . . .' Surtees shaped a smile that somehow suggested he was both grateful for not having to express the sentiment himself and a little ashamed of letting Spandrel do it for him. 'Yes. That's what I'm asking you to do. Leave well alone. For Maria's sake.'

Spandrel made his way back to Cat and Dog Yard as the sunny afternoon gave way to a pigeon-grey evening. Dick

Surtees was right, of course. Spandrel would achieve nothing by trying to come between Maria and her intended, unless it was to make a fool of himself. He had had his chance and it had slipped through his fingers. Now, the only sensible course was to seize the other chances that had come his way. As Maria had forgotten him, so he would have to forget her.

'William Spandrel?'

The voice echoed like a muffled bell in the cramped passage as Spandrel entered from the yard. A tall, broadly built man in dark clothes loomed in front of him and the shadow of another man fell across him from behind. He was suddenly surrounded.

'William Spandrel?' came the question once more.

'Yes. I . . .'

'Come with us, please.'

Powerful hands closed around Spandrel's elbows and shoulders. He was marched back out into the yard almost without being aware of it. 'What . . . Who are you?' An absurd thought came into his mind. 'I've paid my debts.' Then he remembered: it was Sunday. 'You can't be bailiffs.'

'We don't collect debts, Spandrel. We collect people.'

'What?'

'You're wanted.'

'Who by?'

'You'll find out soon enough. There's a carriage waiting. Do you want to go quietly?' The cold head of a cudgel pressed against Spandrel's cheekbone. 'Or very quietly?'

The carriage was shuttered and Spandrel was held fast by his captors, who remained as reticent as they were threatening. He could see no more than twilit shards of street corners through the gap between the shutters. But he

305

had not mapped every alley and highway of London for nothing. He tracked their route in his mind, judging every turn and every sound. Fleet Street and the Strand to Charing Cross; down Whitehall to Westminster Abbey, where the bells were summoning the faithful to evensong; round the southern side of St James's Park to Buckingham House, then out along the King's Road, through the darkening fields to Chelsea.

Why Chelsea? He could think of only one reason. And he did not want to believe it. But when they reached the Royal Hospital and drew to a halt in a courtyard to the rear of Orford House, residence, as all Londoners knew, of Robert Walpole, First Lord of the Treasury and Chancellor of the Exchequer . . . he had to believe it.

Chapter Thirty-Two

Reopening the Book

The room was high-ceilinged and ill-lit, the windows over-looking some inner courtyard engulfed in shadow. Shadow, indeed, seemed to fill the room, despite, or perhaps because of, a roaring fire, whose flames cast flick-ering ghosts of themselves across the walls and the gold-worked tapestries that covered them.

For a moment, Spandrel thought he was alone. Then he saw a figure stir on the vast day-bed that covered half the length of the far wall – a big, swag-bellied, red-faced man of middle years, in plain waistcoat and breeches, scratching under his wig as he hauled himself upright. He hawked thickly as he crossed the room, spat into the fire, then turned to face Spandrel, who had, with as much reluctance as incredulity, come by now to realize that this was the master of Orford House – Robert Walpole.

'Colic does not put me or any man in the best of tempers,' Walpole said in a gravelly voice. 'Try me, sir, and you'll regret it.'

'I have no wish to try anyone, sir,' said Spandrel.

'Nor to be tried, I dare say.' Walpole moved closer. 'Though the Dutch authorities would like to try you, I'm told, for the murder last year of one of their more eminent citizens.'

'I didn't—'

'Save your denials for your Maker, sir. I'll not hear them. You are William Spandrel?'

'Yes, sir.'

'The same William Spandrel who escaped from custody in Amsterdam in February of last year and still stands accused in that city of murder?'

'Well, I . . .' Something in Walpole's gaze told him prevarication was worse than futile. 'Yes, sir.'

'The United Provinces are a friendly nation. Surrendering a fugitive to them would be a common courtesy.'

'I am innocent, sir.'

'That's for them to say. However—' Walpole flapped his hand. 'I didn't have you brought here for the pleasure, if it would be one, of loading you aboard a ship bound for Amsterdam.'

'No, sir?'

'But I want you to understand that it can be done. It *will* be done.' Walpole snapped his fingers so sharply and suddenly that Spandrel jumped. 'Unless . . .'

The pause grew into a silence that Spandrel felt obliged to break. 'Is there something . . . I can do for you, sir?'

'There is.' Walpole moved to a circular table in the middle of the room and lit the lamp that stood on it. Then he unlocked one of the shallow drawers beneath the table, opened it and pulled out a book, which he let fall with a crash next to the lamp.

Spandrel flinched at his first sight of the book. It was a plain, green-covered ledger, with leather spine and marbled page edges.

'I see you recognize it.'

'I'm not sure. I—'

'I know everything, Spandrel. The whole squalid tale of scheming and double-dealing. Including your part in it. You do recognize this book, don't you?'

'Yes, sir.'

'And you're familiar with the contents?'

'I . . .' Spandrel strained to decide what it was best to say. Walpole's own name was to be found listed within those green covers. If Spandrel admitted he knew how big a bribe Walpole had taken, he was surely a dead man. But if Walpole already knew he knew . . . 'The contents made no sense to me, sir. I have no head for figures.'

'No head for figures? A bold try, sir. Yes, I compliment you on that. What about Dutch widows? Do you have a head for their figures?'

'I . . . don't understand, sir.'

'When I said I knew everything, that is exactly what I meant. *Everything.*'

Spandrel gulped. 'I . . .'

'Do you still not understand?'

'I do understand, sir. Yes.'

'Good. The book was delivered to me a year ago by an acquaintance of yours, Mr Cloisterman, of whose safe return from Rome you'll doubtless be glad to learn. Mr Cloisterman, incidentally, is now His Majesty's Ambassador to the Sublime Porte.' Catching Spandrel's blank look, he smiled and added, 'The Ottoman Empire.'

'Mr Cloisterman's an ambassador?'

'Thus is assiduous service rewarded. Yes indeed. Cloisterman is sampling the pleasures of Constantinople, which are many and varied, so I'm told. I've never been abroad myself. You know that? You, sir, are a better travelled man than me. But *not* a better informed one. Before he left, Cloisterman made known to me every detail of the Green Book's journey from London to Rome and back again. So, whatever lies you are tempted to tell, save your breath. I don't care how you managed your own exit from Rome. It matters not to me. Here you are, though, home again. Like the Green Book.' Walpole patted its cover, almost affectionately. 'And ready to do my bidding, I rather think.'

'How did you know . . . I'd come home?'

'Sir Theodore Janssen alerted me to the repayment of your debt to him, which could only mean you planned to return, wrongly supposing you were no longer of interest to the likes of me.'

'I did suppose that, sir, yes.'

'An expensive mistake, as it turns out. You passed Westminster Abbey on your way here?'

'I . . . think so, sir, yes.'

'*You think so.* You know so. Don't play the fool with me.'

'We did pass the Abbey, sir. Yes.'

'Are you acquainted with the Dean of Westminster?'

'No, sir.'

'The Right Reverend Francis Atterbury, Bishop of Rochester.'

'I, er . . . have heard of him.'

'As what?'

'As, er . . .'

'As a stiff-necked, silver-tongued Tory who was all for proclaiming the Pretender King when Queen Anne died. The Right Reverend Atterbury is a right renegade Jacobite.'

'Yes, sir.'

'And a plotting one to boot.'

'I know nothing of such things.'

'High time you learned, then. Certain papers have come into my possession following the recent death of the Earl of Sunderland. You knew his lordship had breathed his last? It's been the talk of the town, doubtless even your neck of it.'

The copy of the *London Journal* Spandrel had bought the previous day had been much given over to Sunderland's sudden death. Spandrel had not bothered to read the reports, wrongly supposing that the deaths along with the doings of such men were none of his concern. 'I heard, sir, yes.'

'Those papers leave no room for doubting Lord Sunderland's complicity in Atterbury's plotting.'

'Lord Sunderland?'

'Yes. *Lord Sunderland.* Don't look so surprised, man. Your perusal of the Green Book can hardly have left you with a glowing impression of your political masters' capacity for loyalty.'

'You're very frank, sir.' Walpole was being, in truth, disturbingly frank. Spandrel had felt safer being hectored than confided in.

'I'm frank when I need to be. Your value to me lies in your attested knowledge of the Green Book. Tomorrow is St George's Day. We can rely on Dean Atterbury presiding at evensong in the Abbey in order to lavish some patriotic prayers on the congregation. That'll be his brand of patriotism, of course, not mine. You will attend the service and afterwards bring yourself to the Bishop's attention. How you manage that is up to you, but manage it you must. Tell him you have something of inestimable value to the cause which you wish to discuss with him, something entrusted to you by the Earl of Sunderland.'

'But—'

'But nothing. He will rise to the bait. Sunderland's death has him all a-quiver, fearful about what it means and what it portends. He will agree to see you in private. You will ensure he does. At that meeting, you will tell him about the Green Book.'

'But—'

'Save your buts for a hogshead of ale!' roared Walpole, suddenly reddening. 'What do you mean by them, sir?'

'It's just that . . .'

'*What?*'

'If the Bishop is in secret communication with the Pretender . . .'

'As he is.'

'Then he'll know of my attempt to sell the book in Rome – and how it ended.'

'So?'

'I, er, got myself off the hook by telling the Pretender I'd made up the story. I said the Green Book was seized and sent to London when Mr Knight was arrested. I said I was a South Sea Company clerk trying to swindle him.'

'He believed you?'

'He seemed to.'

'Well, it's reassuring to know he's as big a fool as we'd always hoped. I suggest you make Atterbury believe that you were lying. Not difficult, since you were. Say Cloisterman made off with the book, leaving you to talk your way out of it as best you could. When you returned to London this spring, you were picked up by the Secret Service and taken before Sunderland. Sunderland had charge of the Secret Service, damn his memory, until the day he died, so that'll seem likely enough. Here's the wrinkle. Cloisterman was acting for Sunderland, not me. It was to Sunderland that he delivered the book and through Sunderland's influence, not mine, that he secured the Turkish posting. Well, Atterbury can hardly write to Cloisterman and ask him, can he? He'll swallow it. You'll say Sunderland seemed nervous, frightened almost, and threatened to have you sent to Amsterdam in irons unless you agreed to deliver the Green Book into Atterbury's hands. The nervousness is a nice touch. It'll play on the crazy suspicion that seems to have got about that I had Sunderland poisoned. His little son died last night, which only seems to have added to the rumours. You'll explain that you weren't supposed to reveal the source of the book, but, now Sutherland's dead, there seems little point in keeping his name out of it. You'll also explain that, now he *is* dead, you're free to impose your own terms. How much did you ask the Pretender for? A hundred thousand, wasn't it?'

'How did—' Spandrel bit his lip. 'Yes. It was.'

'You've learned from your mistake. Your price now is twenty thousand.'

'You want me to . . . try to sell it?'

'I want you to persuade Atterbury that it can be bought. The price is neither here nor there. I want him to believe this . . . bookful of gunpowder . . . is within his grasp. Then . . .' Walpole smiled. 'A letter to Rome, asking for instructions, or boasting of what the book will do for the Pretender's standing here – its publication as a prelude to a rising. It doesn't matter. But something, anything, to incriminate him. That's what I want. And that's what I mean to have.'

'I . . .' Spandrel's heart sank. There was no way out. He would have to do this. And that was not all. He was a pawn. And pawns tended to be sacrificed in quest of a bishop, especially pawns who knew too much. Perhaps Atterbury's involvement in his murder was just the kind of incrimination Walpole had in mind. 'I'm not sure I . . .'

'Do you want to be hanged as a murderer?'

'No, sir. Of course not.'

'Well then?'

'I, er . . .' Spandrel tried to look as if he meant what he was about to say. 'I'll do my best.'

'So you will.' Walpole slipped the Green Book back into the drawer, locked it and dropped the key into his waist-coat pocket. 'And you'd better pray your best is good enough.'

'Yes, sir.'

'No-one else knows where the book really is, of course, apart from Cloisterman, far away in Constantinople.

No-one but you and me. We make a strange pair to share such a secret, don't we? Of course . . .' He fixed Spandrel with his gaze. 'Should anyone else find out, I'll know who must have told them, won't I? That's the beauty of it.'

'I won't tell a soul, sir.'

'Be sure you don't.'

'And, er, when I've, er . . . accomplished the task?'

'How can you be sure I won't hand you over to the Dutch authorities anyway? Is that what's worrying you?'

'Well, no. I mean, not exactly.'

'I rather think it is. And, if it isn't, it should be. But the answer's very simple. You have my word. As a gentleman and a statesman.' Walpole treated Spandrel to a broad but fleeting grin. 'I can't say handsomer than that, now can I?'

Spandrel was left to make his own way back to London. Night had fallen and, as the lights of the Royal Hospital fell away behind him, darkness closed in on every side. Only his own footfalls and the mournful hoots of an owl somewhere to the north kept him company. He could not recall feeling so miserably desperate since his escape from Amsterdam. He should have left his debts unpaid and his mother unaware that he was still alive. Perhaps that was still the answer: to flee while he had the chance. But he could not abandon his mother so soon after re-entering her life and promising to transform it. There had to be another way out of this. There had to be. For if not . . .

He pulled up his collar against the deepening chill of the night and pressed on towards the city; and towards the task that awaited him there.

Chapter Thirty-Three

A Worm on the Line

The move from Cat and Dog Yard to Leicester Fields was accomplished with fewer difficulties than Spandrel's mother seemed to have anticipated. Her meticulous oversight of the removal man's work suggested that she half-expected some disaster to intervene before she could lay claim to being mistress of a respectable household at a reputable address. But, as the removal man muttered at one point, 'Nobody's going to make off with any of this,' nodding towards a cartload of their possessions. 'I've seen better stuff dumped in the Fleet Ditch.'

If Mrs Spandrel had overheard such insolence, she might have boxed the fellow's ears. Spandrel, for his part, would probably have told him to button his lip, had he been less preoccupied with a disaster whose proportions threatened to eclipse his mother's worst fears. 'Don't look so miserable,' she rebuked him as they stood together in their new and sparsely furnished drawing-room. 'I'll soon have this fit for the Princess of Wales to take tea in.'

'I'm sure you will, Ma,' Spandrel managed to say. And sure he was. But that did not make him any less miserable. 'Happy St George's Day.'

'Well, it's a happier one than I thought I'd ever see again, I'll say that.'

'Me too.'

'Then put a smile on your face, boy. And help me unpack.'

'I can't. I have to go out.'

'I might have known. Why?'

'Let's just say . . .' He put together some kind of a smile. 'I have to see a man about a dragon.'

Whether the congregation for evensong at Westminster Abbey that afternoon was larger because it was St George's Day Spandrel had no way to tell, since he had only ever been a reluctant churchgoer at best and then only on Sunday mornings. Evensong, especially in the august surroundings of Westminster Abbey, was for him a strange experience. His atheistical tendencies would not have made it an agreeable one in any circumstances. The circumstances that had led to his attendance, however, were such as to override religious scruples. What would have been merely disagreeable became instead an ordeal.

The nave was well filled with worshippers and Dean Atterbury made his entrance only after the choir had filed in. Spandrel caught a glimpse of an erect, sombre-faced figure in flowing robes soon lost to him behind a pillar. Even a glimpse was subsequently denied him by the Dean's position in the choir-stalls in relation to Spandrel's own beyond the screen.

But the Dean's voice was denied no-one. It tolled sonorously, like a bell, echoing in the vaulted roof. 'When the wicked man turneth away from his wickedness that he hath committed, and doeth that which is lawful and right, he shall save his soul alive.' What did Atterbury consider lawful and right? Spandrel wondered. Who *was* the wicked man? 'Dearly beloved brethren, the Scripture moveth us in sundry places to acknowledge and confess our manifold sins and weaknesses.' Sins and weaknesses. Yes. They were what had brought Spandrel to this pass. And very possibly the Dean too. 'Almighty God, the Father of our Lord Jesus Christ, who desireth not the death of a sinner, but rather that he may turn from his wickedness, and live; and hath given power and commandment to his Ministers, to declare and pronounce to his people, being penitent, the absolution and remission of their sins . . .'

'The grace of our Lord Jesus Christ, and the love of God, and the fellowship of the Holy Ghost, be with us all ever-more. Amen.'

'Amen.' Evensong was at an end, after nearly an hour of psalms and lessons and prayers. Most of the congregation was still kneeling, but the Dean was already leading the choir out. Spandrel's long-awaited chance had come, a chance he had no choice but to take. He had deliberately sat at the end of a pew and now rose and walked rapidly and unnoticed across the south aisle to the door that led out into the cloister next to the Deanery.

There was a pearly early evening light in the close. The choir was progressing round the cloisters towards the school. But the Dean, attended by a flock of chaplains, was bearing down on Spandrel, or rather on the side-entrance to the Deanery, next to which Spandrel had emerged from the Abbey.

'My lord,' he said, standing his ground. 'I must speak to you.'

Atterbury stopped so abruptly that several of the chaplains carried on past him, only to have to scuttle back when they realized what had happened. One of them advanced menacingly on Spandrel, as if intending to remove him from the Dean's path. But Atterbury held up a restraining hand. 'One moment, Kelly.' He examined Spandrel through cool blue eyes. 'Well?'

'It is a matter of the utmost importance, my lord. Affecting . . . a subject close to your heart.'

'What subject?'

'I cannot . . . speak of it openly.'

'Can you not?' Atterbury thought for a moment, then said, 'Deal with this, Kelly,' before sweeping past Spandrel and into the Deanery.

'But my—'

Kelly's broad black-robed back was suddenly between Spandrel and his quarry. The Deanery door slammed shut. The Dean and his retinue were gone. Save only Kelly, who slowly turned and gazed down at Spandrel from a considerable height, before cocking one bushy eyebrow and baring a fine set of teeth in what might as easily have been a snarl as a smile. 'Your name?'

'William Spandrel.'

'Your business with the Dean?'

'Is, begging your pardon, sir, with the Dean alone.'

'I'm the Dean's ears and eyes.'

'Even so—'

'I'll not bandy words with you, sir.' Spandrel was suddenly seized by the collar and hauled onto tiptoe in an unclerically muscular grasp. 'I am the Reverend George Kelly, confidential secretary to my lord the Dean and Bishop. What you tell me you tell him. And tell me you will.'

'Very well. I . . .' Slowly, Spandrel was lowered back to the ground. His collar was released. 'I'm sorry. I . . . didn't . . .'

'Out with it.'

'It concerns . . .' Spandrel took a deep breath. He was about to plunge into waters of unknown depth. 'The cause.'

'What cause might that be?'

'There is surely only one.'

'Hah! And so there is.' Kelly gave Spandrel a cuff to the shoulder that nearly felled him. 'Well, we have the cloister to ourselves. I'll allow you one circuit to tell your tale. One only, mind. I have no time to waste.'

'Nor have I, sir.' They started walking. And Spandrel started talking. But his thoughts travelled faster than his words. Walpole had told him to speak to Atterbury. Intermediaries, however confidential, however trusted, would not suffice. Yet Kelly would know half a story for the fraction it was. He would not be fobbed off, nor easily taken in. He had to be given enough – but not too much. 'I'm placed in a difficult position. I'm instructed to deliver an article to the Dean in person.'

'Instructed by whom?'

'The late Earl of Sunderland.'

'And what were you to the Earl?'

'Nothing. I . . . came to his attention.'

'By reason of the article you're charged to deliver?'

'You could say so, yes.'

'What is the article?'

'Something that will make the people of this country cry out for the restoration of King James.'

'And what is that?'

'The secret account-book of the chief cashier of the South Sea Company.'

'Hah!' Kelly pulled up and pushed Spandrel back against a pillar. 'You expect me to believe that?'

'It's true. I can give the Dean the Green Book.'

'And what will that avail him?'

'It lists all the people the company bribed. Up to and including . . . the Elector of Hanover.'

' "The Elector of Hanover." You choose your words like a man picking lice, Spandrel. What's the meaning of them?'

'The meaning's clear.' Spandrel looked Kelly in the eye.

'I have the Green Book. And with Sunderland dead, no-one knows I have it. Except you.'

'Why should Sunderland have entrusted such a thing to you?'

'Of all people, you mean?'

'Yes. *Of all people.*'

'I'll explain that to the Dean. I can answer all his questions. And I can give him what the King needs more than any number of loyal priests.'

'What does he need?'

'Ammunition. To fire a cannonade that will blast the Elector back to Hanover, where he belongs, and clear the way' – Spandrel nodded towards the Abbey – 'for a coronation.'

Kelly stared at Spandrel long and hard. Then a priest appeared in the far corner of the cloister and moved along the walk parallel to the one they were standing in. Kelly followed him with his eyes. A door opened and closed. He was gone.

'I must see the Dean.'

'But must the Dean see you? It's for him to say.'

'And for you to advise.'

'As I will.' Kelly nodded thoughtfully. 'Be at the Spread Eagle in Tothill Street this time tomorrow. I'll bring you your answer there.'

'But—'

'Be there.' Kelly stabbed Spandrel in the chest with a powerful thrust of his forefinger. 'That's all I have to say.'

Spandrel returned to Leicester Fields that evening by way of several inns other than the Spread Eagle. He fell to wishing that the matter could have been settled, one way or the other, rather than deferred for another twenty-four hours. Even then, there was no saying that his meeting with Atterbury, if he was granted one, would not be on yet a subsequent occasion. He did not seriously doubt that such a meeting would take place eventually. The lure was too strong for a true Jacobite to resist. But when would it be? And what would it yield? The uncertainty gnawed at him like hunger. And, as with hunger, time only made it gnaw the worse.

He was almost grateful to be able to spend most of the next day arguing with Crabbe, the engraver, over how much interest should be added to the long outstanding payment due for the completed sheets of the map. Crabbe drove a hard bargain, but had taken good care of the sheets and wished Spandrel well, though with a typically gloomy qualification. 'This is no time to be venturing into the market, young man. You'll get no subscribers till things look up. And it'd be best to wait until they do.' He was probably right. But Spandrel could not presently see more than a matter of days into the future. And he did not care for what those days promised to contain. He thanked Crabbe for the advice and went on his way.

Spandrel's mother was busy interviewing candidates for the post of maid-of-all-work in her new household when Spandrel arrived home. He took the sheets into his room and sat with them in the thinning late afternoon light, casting his eye over the intricately drawn and precisely scaled patterns of parks and streets and squares and alleys – and his memory across the weeks and months of labour needed to produce them. A map, his father had once said, is a picture of a city without its inhabitants. And how beautiful it looked without them, how clean and elegant. The people who had made the city were also those who had marred it. And even a mapmaker had to live among them. He could not walk the empty ways he had drawn. No-one could.

*　*　*

The Spread Eagle was one of several coaching inns serving the route from Westminster west out of the city. Its proximity to the Abbey made it a logical enough choice, even though Spandrel was surprised that a priest should nominate an inn as a rendezvous. But the Reverend Kelly was about as unpriestly as could be imagined, so the surprise was muted. Waiting in the tap-room that evening, Spandrel found himself wondering whether Atterbury employed Kelly more for the power of his arm than the depth of his piety. Perhaps, if he really was as busy a plotter as he was a preacher, he had need of such men about him.

Sure enough, when Kelly ambled in, he looked more like a half-pay army officer than a bishop's secretary. There was nothing remotely clerical in his dress and the set of his powerful shoulders, taken together with his swaggering gait, confirmed that humility was not a prominent feature of his character. He ignored Spandrel at first, preferring to buy a drink and exchange several guffawing words with the tapster before moving to speak to some lounging fellow in a corner. Then both men walked across to Spandrel's table.

'Good evening, Spandrel,' said Kelly, in a genial growl. 'This is a friend of mine, Mr Layton.'

Mr Layton was a smaller, less imposing figure than Kelly, with quick, darting eyes and a louche smile. He had been flirting with the pot-girl earlier. Spandrel had paid him no heed. But clearly Layton had paid him considerable heed.

'Mr Layton tells me you came alone and at the agreed time,' Kelly continued. 'That's reassuring.'

'No-one else is involved in this,' said Spandrel. 'I told you that.'

'Indeed you did. You also told me you had an article to deliver to my employer.'

'Yet you came empty-handed,' said Layton, with a feral twitch to his smile.

'You came without your employer.'

'You'd hardly expect a bishop to set foot in a tap-room,' countered Kelly.

'Is he willing to see me?'

'He wants to see what you have for him, certainly.'

'So he can, when we've agreed terms.'

'Terms, is it?' Layton snorted. 'I warned you, George. The fellow's out for what he can get.'

'Sunderland's dead.' Spandrel smiled gamely. 'I'm no longer bound by his instructions.'

'How much do you want?' asked Kelly, mildly enough, as if merely curious.

'I'll name my price, when I meet your paymaster.'

Kelly chuckled. 'You're the cool one and no mistake.'

'Perhaps we should warm him up a touch,' said Layton. 'See if he punches as well as he pleads.'

'No, no,' said Kelly. 'Let it go.'

'If you're sure.' Layton looked positively disappointed at being overruled on the point. 'Shall we send him up?'

'Yes,' Kelly replied. 'It's time.'

'Time for what?' asked Spandrel.

'Climb the steps to the galleried room across the yard,' said Kelly. 'Third door you come to. He's waiting for you.'

'The Dean?'

'*He's waiting.*'

Spandrel could see an ostler busying himself in the stable at the rear of the yard, but there was no-one else about. It was cool and quiet, away from the bustle of the tap-room. He glanced up at the windows of the galleried rooms above him, but there was no sign of movement.

He took the steps two at a time and marched smartly along to the third door. Through the window, he could see a fire burning, but the chair beside it was empty. He knocked at the door.

There was no answer. He knocked again. Still there was nothing. He turned the handle and pushed at the door. It yielded.

As he entered, a figure moved in the corner of the room, detaching itself from the shadow of the chimneybreast.

'So there you are, Spandrel.' The voice was not Atterbury's. Nor was the bearing. Nor yet the face. 'About time.'

Spandrel could neither move nor speak. He stared at the figure advancing upon him in a paralysis of disbelief.

'What's wrong with you, man?' said McIlwraith. 'You look as if you've seen a ghost.'

Chapter Thirty-Four

Back From the Dead

'Why don't you sit down, Spandrel?' said McIlwraith, gesturing to one of the two chairs flanking the fireplace. 'Before you fall down.'

'Captain . . .' Spandrel sat unsteadily down and gaped at the gaunt but otherwise unaltered figure of James McIlwraith. 'You're not dead?'

'Not unless you are too and Lucifer's decided to entertain himself by making us think we're alive.'

'I don't understand. Cloisterman said he left you for dead.'

'Left for dead and being dead aren't quite the same thing.'

'But you said . . . yourself . . . that you were dying.'

'I thought I was.'

'I wouldn't have left you if . . .' Spandrel shrugged helplessly. 'If I'd thought you'd live.'

'I'll do you the honour of believing that.' McIlwraith smiled. 'Have some brandy.' He poured a glass from the bottle standing on the mantelpiece and handed it to Spandrel, who gulped some gratefully down. 'Let me tell you it tastes even better when you've thought you might never taste it again.'

'How did you survive?'

'I don't know. I just did. It surprised that Bernese doctor even more than me. Must be the pure Swiss air. Or my long years of clean living. It was touch and go. Very nearly go. In the end, though, I came back. Maybe my immortal soul didn't care to leave so much business unfinished. That ball Wagemaker put in me hasn't gone, by the by.' He slapped the left side of his chest and winced. 'Still in there somewhere, they tell me. And still capable of killing me, if it lodges in something vital. So, if I drop dead in mid-sentence, you'll know the cause. But if I were you . . .' He moved to the back of Spandrel's chair and closed a crushing grip on his shoulder. 'I wouldn't count on it.'

'Count on it?' Spandrel looked up into McIlwraith's hooded eyes. 'I can't tell you how glad I am to see you alive, Captain. You surely don't think . . .'

'That you'd rather I'd stayed dead?' McIlwraith chuckled. 'Well, if you don't now, you soon will.'

'What do you mean?'

McIlwraith walked slowly across to the other chair and sat down. 'I've thrown in my lot with the Jacobites, Spandrel. With Atterbury and those two fellows down-stairs: Kelly and Layer.'

'Layer? Kelly introduced him as Layton.'

'A clumsy alias. His name's Christopher Layer. He's a lawyer. And a plotter. Not that there's a lot of difference.'

'But the Jacobites? You? Why?'

'Ah well, that's the question, isn't it? You see, it took me months to recover. By the time I was fit to leave Berne, there was no point going on to Rome. I knew the chase had ended long ago by then, one way or the other. So, I started back for England, by slow boat down the Rhine. I wasn't up to riding. And I was in no hurry. If I had been, I might have reached Cologne sooner. Which would have been a pity, because then I'd have missed Cloisterman.'

'You met Cloisterman?'

'I did. He was on his way south.'

'To Constantinople?'

'Aye. Constantinople. An embassy, no less. His reward . . . for services rendered.'

'What did he tell you?'

'Everything, Spandrel. Everything you and he did in Rome.'

'I see.'

'Do you now?'

'I can repay . . . the money you gave me.'

'It wasn't my money. It was the committee's. And they've disbanded. So, don't worry your head about the money. We'll let that pass. Breach of faith, now. That's a different matter.'

'I . . .'

'Why don't you tell me you never meant to sell the book? Why don't you say Buckthorn and Silverwood intervened just before you were planning to spring some sort of a trap on Mrs de Vries?'

'Because . . .' It had been bad enough to break his word to a dead man. Spandrel had often consoled himself with the thought that he would never have to account to McIlwraith for what he had done at Estelle's bidding. She had been worth it, after all. But she was lost to him now. And he *did* have to account to McIlwraith. 'Because it wouldn't be true.'

'No. It wouldn't be true. Nor would whatever you were intending to say to Atterbury, would it? Cloisterman delivered the book to Walpole, not Sunderland. He told me so. He was pleased to tell me. And he wasn't lying, was he?'

'No. Walpole has the Green Book.'

'And he has you, in his pocket.'

'Yes.'

'He set you on Atterbury.'

'Yes.'

'In the hope that the Green Book could be used to tempt the Bishop into betraying himself.'

'Yes.'

'And you had little choice but to do his bidding because otherwise he'd have handed you over to the Dutch authorities.'

'Yes.'

'Who don't know that de Vries was murdered not by you but by his secretary, with the connivance of his wife.'

Spandrel sighed. 'I should never have come back to England.'

'No more you should.' Then McIlwraith also sighed. 'And neither should I. They'd all given up by then, you see. Brodrick, Ross and the other members of the committee. They'd thrown in their cards. They'd abandoned the struggle. Walpole was cock of the dunghill. The Green Book was a dead letter. As for me, well, General Ross made it obvious I was an embarrassment to them now the game was up. They had to look to the future and make . . . accommodations . . . with their new master. I was politely encouraged to vanish. And so I did. As far as they were concerned. But when you've come as close to death as I have, when the Grim Reaper's brushed the hem of his cloak across your face and you can still catch the cold, grave-damp smell of it in your nostrils, you don't see things as other men do. You're not interested in accommodations. You can't be sent away. You won't be stopped.'

'Jacobitism is treason, Captain.'

'High treason, Spandrel. As high as Tyburn gallows.'

'You're really one of them?'

'Sworn and enlisted.'

'But why? You're no Jacobite. You were trying to stop the Green Book reaching Rome.'

'The case is altered. I won't let them win.'

'Won't let who win?'

'Walpole and his cronies. I'll have them yet.' There was a look in McIlwraith's eyes Spandrel had never seen before. His brush with death truly had altered him. Determination had become obsession. 'By hook or by crook, I'll have them.'

'It'll mean blood in the streets.'

'Then let it flow. I swore to make the truth known. No matter that those I swore to have sheathed their swords and slunk away. I still mean to make it known.'

'You won't succeed. Walpole knows everything. He has Sunderland's papers.'

'But he's biding his time. Because he thinks he has plenty of it. He doesn't know about me. If he did, he'd never have sent you to Atterbury. That's his mistake. And he'll pay for it, I promise you.'

'You can't win.'

'Oh, but I can. Not by listening to fools like Layer or waiting for instructions from Rome. They have some crazy plan to assassinate the King – the Elector, as they call him – on his way to Hanover. And they still mean to go through with it, despite Sunderland's death. But there's no need. There's another way to snare our fat Norfolk Robin. A surer way, by far. The Green Book, Spandrel. You saw it?'

'Yes.'

'My fellow plotters have persuaded themselves that Walpole destroyed it. But I never fell for that notion. He didn't get where he is by destroying the secrets that come his way.'

'You're not thinking of . . .'

'Stealing it back from him?' McIlwraith caught Spandrel's eye. 'No. It's a tempting thought, but a fatal one. Orford House is well guarded. And where would we look? He's not likely to keep it wherever you saw it. He'd like us to try, no doubt. A few of us shot down as common housebreakers would suit his purpose very well. It'd look bad for you, of course. Who but you could have told us he had it there? So, you'll be glad to know I have no intention of blundering into that trap.'

'What do you mean to do?'

'Nothing that you need worry your head about.' McIlwraith rose from his chair with more of an effort than he would once have needed to exert and leaned against the mantelpiece. 'You have more than enough to think about already. Such as what you're going to report to Walpole.'

'What can I report? I've failed.'

'No need to tell him that. *I* won't tell. Say Atterbury's agreed to meet you, down in Bromley, at his palace, next week.'

'Why next week?'

'Because by then Walpole will have more important things to worry about. I'll see to that.' McIlwraith grinned. 'I'm doing you a favour, Spandrel, though God knows why I should. I'm letting you off the hook.'

Off the hook? Spandrel did not feel as if he was. Quite the reverse. If he lied to Walpole and Walpole found out, he was finished. But if he told him the truth . . . he was also finished.

'Aren't I more trustworthy than Walpole, man? Aren't I just about the only one you *can* trust in all this?'

'It's hopeless, Captain. Don't you understand? He's too powerful. You can't defeat him.'

'Wait and see.' McIlwraith's smile grew wistful. 'Every man has his breaking point.'

'Not Walpole.'

'Oh, he has his weaknesses, never doubt it. One of them's the same as yours, as a matter of fact. *Exactly* the same as yours.'

'What do you mean?'

'Estelle de Vries.' McIlwraith refilled Spandrel's brandy glass. 'He keeps her as a mistress.'

'That's not true. It—' Spandrel stopped and stared into the fire. Estelle, with Walpole? It was not possible. It was not to be believed. 'It can't be.'

'But it can. It is. How is not for me to say. What did you think she meant to do when you left Rome?'

'We left . . . separately.'

'She had no more use for you once the Green Book was gone, then. Well, you can't have been surprised.'

'She went after Cloisterman.'

'Ever the huntress. You can't fault her for spirit. But Cloisterman went by sea from Leghorn. That put him out of her reach. And the Green Book likewise. Perhaps this . . . connection . . . with Walpole is her way of profiting from it nonetheless.'

'I don't believe it.'

'As you please. I hardly did myself. But I've seen her with my own eyes, man, riding with him in a coach. It's common knowledge. Walpole doesn't hide his vices any more than his virtues. He's installed her in a house in Jermyn Street. Phoenix House, near the corner of Duke Street, should you wish to see for yourself. An easy toddle from the house he keeps in Arlington Street. A wife in Chelsea and a mistress in St James's. That no doubt appeals to his sense of . . . husbandry. Oh, she calls herself Davenant now, by the by. *Mrs* Davenant, of course. I haven't told my . . . accomplices . . . who she really is.'

'I still don't believe it.'

'Yes you do. You just don't want to. Walpole didn't mention it to you, of course. He was hardly likely to. He needs your compliance, not your envy.'

'God rot him.' Surprised by his own vehemence, Spandrel pressed a fist to his forehead and closed his eyes. If only he could truly have said that it made no sense. But it did. It was, in some perverse way, just what he might have expected. He had thought he had succeeded, not in forgetting Estelle – for how could he forget such a woman? – but in setting aside his attraction to her. The months in Rennes, the women he had had there, the level-headed aspiration to Maria Chesney's hand . . . amounted to scarcely anything compared with the meagre portion of his life he had spent with her. And scarcely anything was virtually nothing.

'Do you hate him now, Spandrel?' McIlwraith's voice came as a whisper, close to his ear. 'Because, if you do, I have good tidings for you.'

Spandrel opened his eyes and looked up at McIlwraith. What was the captain planning? What could he do against someone like Walpole? What could he really do?

'I have the breaking of him.' McIlwraith's smile was broad and contented. He looked like a man at peace with himself – and at war with another. 'It's him or me.'

Chapter Thirty-Five

The Devil and the Deep Blue Sea

St James's was better lit than most parts of London, but there were still plenty of shadows large and deep enough to shroud Spandrel from view. He stood in the entrance to a service alley on the northern side of Jermyn Street, watching for signs of life at Phoenix House, handsome residence of one Mrs Davenant, a little way down the opposite side of the street. So far, there had been none.

Spandrel had several times asked himself what he was expecting to see at this hour of the evening. Estelle, if she truly did live there, was not likely to show herself to suit his convenience. The afternoon was a better time by far to watch for her. But he could not risk loitering in the area in daylight, any more than he could knock at the door and demand to see Mrs Davenant.

It made little sense, in all honesty, for him to be there at all. But the alternatives were hardly better. He could go home and listen to his mother describing the girls who might – or indeed the girl who had – become the maid their new station in life enabled them to employ. Or he could slink into a tavern and drink as much as he needed – which would be a lot – to forget the dilemma that McIlwraith had placed him in.

Should he tell Walpole that McIlwraith was alive and well and intent on meting out his own brand of justice? If he did, he would have to admit in the process that his attempt to gull Atterbury had failed miserably. Nor did he know what he would be warning Walpole against. It would certainly be easier to tell him the lie McIlwraith had suggested. But Walpole was a dangerous man to lie to. Only if McIlwraith really could destroy him, as he had pledged to, was such a risk worth taking.

Tomorrow, though, he would have to decide. Walpole required a report by then on what progress he had made, to be submitted by hand to the Postmaster-General – none other than Walpole's brother. Spandrel had to say something. And whatever he chose to say might easily rebound on him.

The need to see Estelle and to assure himself that what McIlwraith had told him about her was true was thus a distraction, in some ways, from a problem he had no hope of solving. More and more, he felt like a man trapped in a quagmire, whose every attempt at extrication only sucked him in deeper. Even his pleasure at McIlwraith's return from the dead was soured by the knowledge of the peril it exposed him to. And now—

There was a movement at one of the illuminated upper windows of Phoenix House. Spandrel caught his breath as a curtain was twitched back. A figure, outlined against the glow of a lamp, glanced down into the street. From where he stood, Spandrel could see that it was a woman. Her long dark hair flowed over bare shoulders above a low-cut gown. He could not make out a single detail of her face. And yet he knew, by the way she stood, head thrown back slightly, arm raised, that it was Estelle. He stared up at her, knowing full well that she could not see him, yet half-hoping, half-fearing, that she would somehow sense his presence. Then she released the curtain. Her shadow dwindled away behind it. She was gone.

Spandrel stood there for several more minutes, wondering what he had gained from this paltry glimpse.

McIlwraith had told him she lived there and he had not seriously doubted it. Yet he had felt driven to see her for himself. And now he had. It told him little. It proved nothing. Strictly speaking, he could not even be sure it was her he had seen. But it was enough.

With sudden decisiveness, Spandrel emerged from the alley-mouth and started walking east along Jermyn Street, head bowed, moving fast. He regretted now that he had ever allowed himself to be drawn to the area. Estelle rediscovered as Walpole's mistress was Estelle lost to him more conclusively than if she had been removed to the other side of the world.

He paid the few passers-by little attention as he pressed on. Seeing a man come round the corner of Eagle Street ahead of him, he did no more than move slightly to the left to accommodate him. But the man moved into his path, as if deliberately. He was a big, bulky fellow in a broad-collared greatcoat, full-bottomed wig and low-brimmed hat, flourishing a stick. And, far too late to avoid the encounter, Spandrel recognized him.

'Mr Walpole,' he said nervously, coming to a halt.

'*Mr* Spandrel.' Walpole prodded him in the chest with the point of his stick. 'What are you doing here?'

'I—' Spandrel broke off, but only momentarily. One of the few advantages conferred on him by his misadventures of the year before was speed of thought. Walpole was going to pay a late call on his mistress. He was not likely to believe that coincidence had led Spandrel to the very street where she lived. And Spandrel could not allow him to catch him out in a lie. But there were lies . . . and then there were lies. 'I saw . . . Estelle de Vries . . . in Pall Mall and followed her here . . . to Phoenix House.'

'Estelle de Vries? Here?'

'It seems so, sir.'

'You're sure?'

'I saw her with my own eyes.'

'Well, well.' Walpole lowered the stick and stepped towards the area railings of the house beside them, lowering his voice as he did so and beckoning Spandrel closer. 'Phoenix House, you say?'

'Yes, sir. Near the corner of Duke Street.'

'Very well. You may leave me to have this matter looked into. You'll do nothing about it. You'll make no attempt to approach her. You'll give her no means of knowing that you've returned to London. Is that understood?'

'Yes, sir.'

'Good. Now, then.' The stick tapped at Spandrel's shoulder. 'What of other matters? Since we have this chance of a private word, you needn't trouble to call at the G.P.O. tomorrow.'

Such relief as Spandrel felt at outwitting Walpole over Estelle was instantly banished by the realization that he could equivocate no longer about what he should report concerning Atterbury and McIlwraith. He paused only long enough to draw a deep breath, then chose his course. 'I have . . . secured an appointment . . . to call at the Bishop's Palace.'

'When?'

'A week today.'

'A week? Why so long?'

'He's a busy man, sir.'

'But busy with what? That's what we want to know.'

'It was the best I could do, sir.'

'Who gave you this appointment?'

'His secretary, sir. The Reverend Kelly.'

'See Kelly again. Tell him you can't – won't – wait so long.'

'But—'

'See him again.' The stick moved to Spandrel's chin and pushed it up, forcing his head back. 'Report to my brother

336

the day after tomorrow. I want prompter progress. You understand?'

'Very clearly, sir,' Spandrel said, as distinctly as the extension of his neck would allow.

'So I should hope.' Walpole whipped the stick away. 'Now, be off, damn you.' And with that the First Lord of the Treasury and Chancellor of the Exchequer strode past Spandrel and on along the street.

Even Robert Walpole could not always have what he wanted. Spandrel's problem was how to fend off the evil hour when he would have to explain that to him, hoping McIlwraith would spare him the necessity. It condemned him to an agony of uncertainty throughout the next day, during which his mother believed him to be scouring London for mapmaking equipment, while he was in truth wandering its streets in a state of aimless anxiety.

Thursday found him no better placed. Quite the contrary, since before it was out he would have to submit his report to Walpole's brother. He composed this work of fiction in a Covent Garden coffee-house, after searching the newspapers for some portent of McIlwraith's intentions – and finding none. *I have been unable to secure an earlier appointment*, he wrote. *I would have done my cause more harm than good had I persisted in the plea.* A nice touch that, he thought. *I am confident, however, of achieving much of what you require of me when I visit Bromley next week.* He was, of course, confident of absolutely nothing, except that he would not be going to Bromley next week.

He left delivery of the report as late in the afternoon as he dared, trudging out along the Strand and Fleet Street, then up Ludgate Hill to St Paul's and round by narrow ways he still remembered from his waywising days to the General Post Office on Lombard Street.

He was expected. The doorman directed him up to see

337

the Postmaster-General's secretary, a taciturn fellow who conveyed all he needed to by way of acknowledgement in one lingering look and a dismissive nod. The report was received.

Spandrel's apprehensiveness amounted now to a fluttering of the heart and a tremor of the limbs. He walked round to Threadneedle Street and looked into the courtyard of South Sea House, where only an air of neglect about the stuccoing and paintwork revealed the savage decline of its fortunes. He had never set foot across its threshold, yet, thanks to the Green Book, he knew the darkest secrets of its bankrupt workings – and wished to God he did not.

From South Sea House he wandered along Lothbury towards the cluster of inns between Lad Lane and Love Lane, eager to drown his identity as well as his sorrows in one of their cavernous tap-rooms. The route took him within sight of Guild Hall. A glance in its direction was enough to remind him of a visit with his father to one of the regular prize draws held there when the War of the Spanish Succession was still on and the Government took to organizing lotteries to raise money for Marlborough's army.

Two giant drums had been set up in the banqueting hall, one containing numbered tickets, the other tickets representing either blanks or prizes. Tickets drawn from the first drum won whatever was drawn next from the second drum. 'Look at these men's faces, William,' his father – an avowed non-gambler – had said. 'Can you tell which of them will be lucky?'

'No, Pa,' William had replied.

'No more you can, son. And no more you'll ever be able to. Just remember: the more desperately you need to win, the more certain it is that you won't.'

Good advice, then and now. Good advice, but bleak counsel. Spandrel's need of a prize to match his ticket was so acute that desperation was hardly the word for it. And the draw could not much longer be delayed.

Spandrel arrived home late enough to find his mother already abed, for which he was grateful, having no wish for her to see how drunk he was and hardly feeling equal to the task of pretending for her benefit that all was well. He took to his own bed at once and plunged instantly into a dark well of slumber.

From which he was roused by a commotion of raised voices and pounding feet in what the light seeping through the window suggested was early morning. He heard his mother protesting at something, with alarm bubbling in her throat. Then the door of his room burst open and several large, burly men, one holding a lantern, strode in.

'Take him,' came a shout.

'Who are you?' Spandrel wailed, as he was hauled from the bed. 'What do you want?'

'We want you, Spandrel. Put some clothes on. Mr Walpole won't want to see you in your nightshirt.'

'Mr Walpole?' The name hit Spandrel like a bucketful of cold water. Suddenly, he knew. It had happened. Whatever McIlwraith had planned to do . . . he had done.

Chapter Thirty-Six

The Biter Bit

Whitewash and a drizzle of sunlight through one of the barred windows set high in the wall did little to brighten the cellar of the Cockpit building in Whitehall to which Spandrel had been delivered. It was cold and damp, moisture clinging to the iron rings fitted to the floor, the vapour of his breath dissipating but slowly in the stale, frozen air.

The only other occupant of the room strode back and forth between the far wall and a trestle-table separating him from Spandrel. Robert Walpole was flushed about the face despite the prevailing chill and breathing heavily, his jaw working rhythmically, as if chewing on some irreducible lump of gristle. An intimidating presence at the best of times, he seemed now, in his evident anger, purely frightening, like a bull pawing the ground and choosing its moment to charge.

'You live with your mother, I'm told,' he growled, the remark striking Spandrel as just about the last thing he might have expected Walpole to say.

'Yes, sir.'

'She loves you?'

'Yes, sir.'

'Even if nobody else does. Because she *is* your mother.'

'Er . . . yes, sir.'

'And your father loved you too?'

'He . . . did, sir, yes. But I—'

'I have three sons and two daughters, Spandrel. My eldest daughter, Kate, is racked with illness. The doctors can do nothing for her. Such fits and fevers and purges as would grieve even you to see. She's not yet nineteen, but there's no hope for her. Not a one.'

'I am . . . sorry to hear it, sir.'

'You're sorry? Do you think that lightens my heart?'

'Well . . .'

'*No, sir.*' Walpole slammed his fist down on the table. 'It does not. She's dying slowly, at Bath, in an agony of mind and body. And I can't ease her suffering. Only my other children console me for that. Robert, Mary, Edward and little Horace. They're all well, thank God.'

'I'm glad to—'

'Or so I thought they all were. Until last night. When the news came from Eton.'

'What news, sir?'

'You don't know, of course. You don't know a damned thing about it.' Walpole rounded the table and clapped his hand to Spandrel's throat. His hand was large, his grip vicelike. 'Isn't that so?'

Spandrel tried to speak, but only a hoarse splutter emerged. He looked into Walpole's glaring eyes and could not tell whether the man meant to strangle him or not. He was about to try to push him away, indeed, when Walpole released him and stepped back.

'Yesterday afternoon, my son Edward was set upon by two masked men while returning to Eton College from some sport by the river. The boys who were with him say he was forced into a carriage at the point of a sword and driven away in the direction of Datchet. Those boys were given a letter and told to deliver it to the Provost, Dr Bland, a friend of mine from my own days at Eton.' Walpole whipped a folded sheet of paper from his pocket and handed it to Spandrel. 'Read it.'

Spandrel looked down at the letter. It was short, jaggedly scribed if elegantly worded, unsigned and very much to the point.

26th April 1722
Sir,
Be so good as to inform your friend, Mr Walpole, that his son will be released unharmed provided only that the full contents of the Green Book are published in the May Day edition of the *London Gazette*. Failure so to publish will result in his son's execution. Be warned. We are in earnest.

Walpole plucked the letter from Spandrel's trembling fingers and replaced it in his pocket. 'In earnest,' he said. 'Yes, I rather think they are.'

'I don't . . .' Spandrel's words dribbled out with his thoughts. 'I can't . . .'

'Account for it?'

'No, sir. I can't.'

'It's no more than a coincidence that this should happen so shortly after your approach to Atterbury?'

'What else . . . can it be?'

'It can be cause and effect, Spandrel. Damnable cause and bloody effect. Poke your stick into a beehive and you can expect to be stung. Prod a bishop and . . . what?'

'I'm sure there's no connection, sir.'

'Well, I'm not. Why else should Atterbury delay seeing you until next Tuesday?'

'You mean . . .' Spandrel uttered a silent prayer of thanks to whatever deity had decreed this one true coincidence. 'Because by then he believes he won't have to buy what I'm offering to sell him.'

'So it would seem.'

'I never had any inkling of such a response on his part,

sir. As God is my witness.' This much was true. What Spandrel did not add, of course, was that he also had not the slightest suspicion that Atterbury was responsible for the abduction of Walpole's son. McIlwraith had taken him. McIlwraith might even have written the letter. But McIlwraith was supposed to be dead. 'This is . . . dreadful.'

'Did you recognize the writing?'

'No, sir.'

'The boys say one of the men spoke with a Scotch accent. Kelly's Irish. They could have mistaken that for Scotch. Or it could be some bloodthirsty Highlander Kelly's recruited. Either way, Jacobites have done this. Oh yes. There's no doubt of that. Who else would stoop to punishing the child for their hatred of the father?'

'They say . . . he'll come to no harm, sir, if . . .'

'If I gazette the Green Book. Do you think I'm likely to do that, Spandrel?'

'I . . . don't know, sir.'

'You know what it contains. There's your answer.'

'But—'

'Which poses another question. How do the kidnappers know I *can* publish it?'

'I don't understand, sir.'

'You were to tell Atterbury that the book came from Sunderland, not me. Why then are the people he obviously put up to this so sure that I have it?'

'I didn't tell them, sir.' But he had told them. He had told McIlwraith, as McIlwraith had obliged him to, little thinking that the admission would rebound on him in such a fashion as this. 'I swear I didn't tell them.'

'Who did, then?'

Spandrel swallowed hard. 'There is . . . Mr Cloisterman.'

'So there is.' Walpole stepped closer. 'But Cloisterman is far away and greatly beholden to me. What would you say if I told you I was certain it wasn't Cloisterman?'

'What could I say, sir? It wasn't me. That's all I know.'

'And you truly have no idea who it might have been?'

'I truly have none, sir. None at all.'

'It really is a coincidence?'

'It must be.'

'Indeed.' Walpole took a slow walk to the wall beneath the windows and gazed up at the rectangles of milky sunlight that revealed the brickwork beneath the white-wash like the ribs beneath a starving man's skin. Then he turned. 'It's just a pity for you I don't believe in coincidences. Anyone who lays a hand on my son – or any child of mine – strikes at me as if he were thrusting a sword into my heart. And I strike back, as best I can. It may be that they saw through your offer of the Green Book. Or it may be that you know more than you're telling. I can't be sure which. And I haven't the time to spend deliberating on the point. I'll save my son if I can. What's certain is that I'll have the men who are holding him and I'll see them hanged, drawn and quartered for what they've already done, let alone what they've threatened to do. If I find that you bear so much as a shred of responsibility for their actions, I'll have you sent to Amsterdam to be hanged as a murderer . . . and I'll have your mother hanged as a thief.'

'My mother?'

'An honest woman, I'm sure. But no-one will believe that with her son swinging from a Dutch gallows and one of my wife's necklaces found about her person.'

'You wouldn't . . .'

'I would. And I will.' Walpole moved back to where Spandrel was standing and looked him in the eye. 'Is there nothing you want to tell me?'

There was much. But to confess the truth now was to confess to not having warned Walpole that McIlwraith was moving against him. 'There's nothing I *can* tell you, sir.'

344

'Then get out. And be sure you can be found when I want you. If you run, it's your mother who'll answer for it.'

'Should I still go to Bromley . . . on Tuesday?'

'Of course not. Do you think any of that will matter a damn by—' Walpole stopped and took a deep, soulful breath. Fear simmered beneath his fury: a fear of what would happen to his son. But it would not deflect him. It would not defeat him. 'Just get out of my sight, Spandrel. Now.'

Chapter Thirty-Seven

Allies in Adversity

'It was nothing, Ma. A misunderstanding. They were bailiffs who didn't know I'd settled my debts. And they were full of apologies once they realized their records were out of date.'

'Bailiffs?' Margaret Spandrel eyed her son doubtfully. 'They seemed more like, well, like Revenue men to me. And they didn't breathe a word about debts.'

'A hasty crew and no mistake. But that's all it was. A mistake.'

'We can't have this sort of thing going on now we've moved to a respectable neighbourhood, William. I have Jane starting on Monday.' Jane? Spandrel was momentarily at a loss. Then he remembered. The maid. Of course. 'How am I to keep staff if we have such carry-ons as this?'

'We won't, Ma. I promise. I've put a stop to it.'

'I surely hope you have, boy. Now, when are you going to get down to some work? Maps don't draw themselves.'

'This very minute. I have to see Marabout.'

'Marabout? Your father could never abide the man. What do you want with him?'

'A matter of business, Ma. He has something I need. Whether I can abide him or not, I still have to see him.'

Gideon Marabout kept a shop in Portsmouth Street, near Lincoln's Inn Fields, where he peddled more or less anything that came his way, from broken-down automata to wobbly clerks' stools . . . and 'maps for the discerning traveller', as he usually put it.

'Cheaper than hiring a guide and safer than leaving it to chance,' was another phrase of Marabout's that had lodged in Spandrel's mind as he hurried along Long Acre. If anyone could supply him with a more or less reliable map of any area he cared to name, it was Marabout. And this was more than a matter of business. It was a matter of life and death. So to Marabout he was bound to turn.

A few extra layers of dust on the stuffed bear still standing just inside the door were about the only changes Spandrel noticed as he entered the dilapidated premises. Marabout himself, a stooped and shuffling figure with strange flecked blue eyes the colour of lapis lazuli, abandoned sifting through a jumble of bent and chipped spectacles, gave Spandrel a coal-toothed grin and welcomed him as if he had been in only last week, rather than some time in the previous decade.

'Still not finished that map of your father's, then? You'll have to start all over again if you leave it much longer. Things do change that fast.'

'But not you, Mr Marabout.'

'No indeed. There has to be a still point to every spinning top.'

'It's maps I've come about.'

'Oh yes? Going a-travelling?'

'You could say so. How are you for Windsor Forest?'

'Well supplied. Not the call there was in the old Queen's days, see. This German King we have is no hunting man. Nor are you, though. It'll not be stag you're after.'

'I have business that way.'

'Then be on your guard. They say Maidenhead Thicket's thicker with highwaymen than trees.'

'What do you have, Mr Marabout?'

'Come through and see.'

Marabout twitched aside a curtain that looked more like a plague victim's winding-sheet and led Spandrel into a windowless, low-ceilinged back room, where a broad, shallow-drawered cabinet housed his collection of maps. They came in all sorts and sizes, ranging from fanciful impressions of the Americas to allegedly accurate street-plans of provincial towns. The light was too dim for Spandrel to tell one from another, but Marabout's eyesight was evidently equal to the task. He sifted through a well-filled drawer, then plucked out a large canvas-backed sheet and carried it out into the shop, where he laid it on the counter and weighed down the corners with four scratched and dented pocket-watches that came magically to hand.

'There you are. Reading to Egham one way, Cookham to Sandhurst the other. Every road and lane and most of the houses besides. Less than twenty years old, what's more, which is as good as yesterday in those parts.'

'I see no date.'

'No need. Datchet Bridge, look.' Marabout pointed to a span across the Thames east of Windsor. 'The old Queen had that built, in the year nought-six.'

Datchet Bridge. Spandrel's eye lingered on it. That was the direction Edward Walpole's kidnappers had taken. And there was the reason. They could not cross the Thames at Windsor for fear of being delayed by the toll long enough to be overtaken by any pursuit there might be. The Datchet route was obviously a safer way back into the Forest, whose bosky expanse the mapmaker had represented with dozens upon dozens of tiny tree-symbols. And the Forest was a place where they could hold the boy, safely out of sight, for the few days needed to force his father's hand – if forced it could be.

'What do you think?' asked Marabout.

'Not bad. Not bad at all.'

'To you, a guinea.'

'A guinea? That's steep.'

'You'd charge more if you'd drawn it yourself.'

'*Every* house, did you say?'

'I did not. But every house that matters, that's for sure. See for yourself.'

'You see more keenly than me, Mr Marabout. Can you find Bordon Grove?'

'Whereabout would it be?'

'Near the edge of the Forest.'

'Which edge?'

'I don't know.'

Marabout grunted and shook his head, but rose to the challenge nonetheless, as Spandrel had known he would. He traced a wavering circle round the ragged perimeter of the Forest with his forefinger, muttering, 'Bordon Grove,' repeatedly under his breath as he went. He was about three quarters of the way round when he stopped and tapped at the place. 'There it is.'

And there it was. Bordon Grove, family home of the Wagemakers. It lay about halfway between Bagshot and Bracknell, in the south-east quadrant of the Forest, no more than ten miles from Eton College. The boundary of its parkland was clearly shown and, within the boundary, additional to the inked square of the house itself, a smaller, narrower mark that could only be Blind Man's Tower.

'Do you want to buy the map – or commit it to memory?' Marabout was losing patience. 'I can go to nineteen and six.'

'Then you've gone far enough.'

'So I should think. It's tantamount to—'

The jingle of the door-bell caused Marabout to break off. Another customer had entered the shop, one more elegantly attired than most of his patrons: a woman, wearing an embroidered burgundy dress beneath a masculine-style jacket and fitted waistcoat. Her dark hair fell in ringlets to her shoulders. There was a white silk cravat, held by a brooch, at her throat. In her gloved hands she carried a feather-trimmed tricorn hat. She looked at Spandrel quite expressionlessly as she moved towards them, slowly removing the glove from her right hand.

'What can I do for you, madam?'

She made no immediate reply to Marabout's question, but gazed down at the map laid out on the counter. Then she said, more as a statement than an answer, 'A map of Windsor Forest.'

'This one's sold.'

'It will do.'

'But, as I say, it's sold.'

'No matter.' She smiled sweetly enough to charm even Marabout. 'I'm sure William can tell me what's to be found on it.'

Marabout looked round incredulously at Spandrel. 'You know this lady?'

'Oh yes.' Spandrel nodded. 'I know her.'

'This is appalling,' said Townshend, pacing to and fro across his office at the Cockpit. 'Kidnapped?'

'There's no doubt of it,' said Walpole, who might have seemed to an observer – had there been one – less distressed on his son's behalf than the boy's uncle-in-law. 'Nor any of their terms for his release.'

'How has Catherine taken it?' Townshend had little regard for Walpole's wife, but this calamity compelled him to spare her a thought.

'She hasn't.'

'What?'

'She doesn't know, Charles. And I don't want you to tell Dolly either.'

'His mother? His aunt? They aren't to know?'

'They'll be upset. Distraught in all likelihood. I can't have their feminine weaknesses brought to bear on the matter. I have to set aside my feelings – and theirs. I have to forget that he's my son.'

'But how can you?'

'I don't know. But I must. There can be no question of yielding to their demands. Can you imagine the consequences of publication? I can. Revolution, Charles. It would come to that, never doubt it. Blood and butchery. The city aflame. The King deposed. And you and I? The Tower, if the mob didn't get to us first. What would Edward's life be worth then? Not a groat. Even supposing his kidnappers released him, which I doubt.'

'What are we to do, then?'

'Find him. And rescue him. Before Tuesday.'

'But how?'

'I'm sending Horace to Windsor to organize a search. You and he and Galfridus are the only ones outside Eton College who know.' Walpole's two brothers, then, and his brother-in-law: so was the trusted circle defined. 'And I want it to go no further.'

'The King?'

'Must not be told.'

'He won't be best pleased when he finds out.'

'With luck, he won't find out at all. With luck, we'll have Edward free and safe by Sunday and those blackguards—' Walpole closed a fist on his invisible prey.

'He may be far from Windsor by now.'

'Yes. He may. Which is why I want you to conduct operations here in London. I want all the Jacobite bolting-holes and hiding-places watched. Discreetly, Charles. Very discreetly. If there's any suspicion that you've found where he's being held, I'm to be told before anything's done.'

351

'I'll see to it at once.' Townshend made to leave, then turned back and squeezed Walpole's slumped shoulder. 'He's a brave and resolute boy, Robin. He'll probably escape without any help from us.'

'A nice thought, Charles.' Walpole looked up into his old friend's face. 'But I can't afford to count on it.'

'I never thought we'd meet again,' said Estelle, as she and Spandrel walked slowly along one of the gravelled paths that quartered the rectangle of rank greenery known as Lincoln's Inn Fields. A group of ragamuffin boys were playing chuck-farthing ahead of them. Behind lay the narrow mouth of Portsmouth Street, from which they had recently emerged. Under his arm, Spandrel was carrying a canvas-backed roll, tied with string. 'Did you?'

'No,' Spandrel bleakly replied.

'You think very badly of me, don't you?'

'I think nothing.'

'Your mother told me where you were. *I* told *her* that we were acquaintances from your days in Rennes.'

'And who told you about my days in Rennes?'

'I think you know. My benefactor. The lessee of Phoenix House.'

'Walpole.'

'He's not the monster you think.'

'He threatened to have my mother hanged as a thief this morning. I'd call that monstrous. Wouldn't you?'

'He fears for his son's life. And he'll do anything to save him. Except what the kidnappers demand.'

'Then it's hopeless.'

'I don't think so. You have an idea, don't you? You think you know where the boy's being held – and who by.'

'Do I?'

'Yes. You do. I can read you as well as you can read that map.'

'Maps? They're my province, Estelle. You're right there.' He looked at her. 'But the human heart? I don't know my way around that.'

'A rebuke, William? Because I settled for the best I could hope for when I realized the Green Book was out of my reach? Well, rebuke me, then. I have nothing to apologize for.'

'How did you bring yourself to his attention?'

'I was taken in for questioning when Cloisterman reported my presence in London. I'd hoped he might not have surrendered the Green Book by then, that he and I could . . .' She sighed. 'I was too late, of course. He was on the point of setting off for Constantinople and keen to oblige his master in every way that he could. As for the master, he was curious about me. Cloisterman's reports had . . . whetted his appetite.'

'An appetite you were happy to satisfy.'

'I don't deny it. Why should I? A house in Jermyn Street. Liveried servants. My own carriage. Fine clothes. Expensive jewellery. What I give in return is little enough.'

'An ideal arrangement, then.'

'An acceptable one, certainly. But now endangered.'

'By what?'

'The Green Book. He's sure one of us has betrayed him. Possibly both, thanks to your encounter with him not far from my door. I deny it, of course. So do you. We may both be telling the truth. But that won't help us. Not if Edward Walpole dies. Then his father will seek vengeance. And he'll wreak it upon us. Even upon your mother. The boy's not yet sixteen. And Robin has such high hopes for him.'

'Robin?'

'He won't give in to the kidnappers, William. He'd rather let his son be killed than do that. And if he is killed . . . we're as good as dead.'

'There's nothing I can do.'

'You're going to Windsor Forest, aren't you?'

'Am I?'

'I'm coming with you.'

'No.'

'We'll make better time together in my chaise than you will alone on a hired nag.'

'You're not coming with me.'

'I'll go anyway and be waiting for you when you arrive. Why waste time when we have so little of it? We can be in Windsor by nightfall. It's my neck as well as yours. You can't refuse me.' She stopped and looked at him. 'Can you?'

Chapter Thirty-Eight

The Sylvan Chase

Acting against his better judgement was scarcely a novel experience for Spandrel. Nor had it always been a disastrous one. There was the rub. Estelle's arguments for combining their efforts were sound enough. About one thing he was sure she did not deceive him. Walpole would destroy both of them if his son did not escape alive. And he would almost certainly carry out his threat to destroy Spandrel's mother. With time pressing and their interests aligned, it made good sense for them to act in concert.

But past treacheries and present doubts travelled with them in Mrs Davenant's fine black and yellow chaise out along the Exeter road that afternoon, through the villages strung along the route, dappled and dozing in the warm spring sunshine. Spandrel still remembered Estelle as she had been at the river-port in Rome, proud and stubborn and untameable. That was her true nature and it would never change. Strangely, though, she was relying on him now, confident that he could yet avert the catastrophe that threatened to overtake them. He had refused to say precisely where they were going or why, but even this had failed to discourage her.

They knew each other too well, in their strengths and their weaknesses. That was the problem. There was too much understanding – too much bitter experience – for any form of trust. They were together because they needed to be. And in the silence that Spandrel strove to maintain lay his best hope of remembering that there could be no other reason. But silence held no appeal for Estelle.

'You keep to the Exeter road, I see,' she said as they failed to fork right beyond Hounslow. 'So, we aren't going to Windsor. Our destination must lie somewhere in the southern reaches of the Forest.'

'We'll put up at Staines tonight.'

'And in the morning?'

'We'll see whether this is a fool's errand or not.'

'You're not a fool, William.' (Of that Spandrel was presently far from sure.) 'You may have been once. But no longer.'

'Wrap your cloak about you.'

'I'm not cold.'

'It's not your comfort I'm concerned about. Hounslow Heath has more than its share of footpads. I don't want your fine clothes attracting unwelcome attention.'

'Then drive the horse faster. We can leave any footpad choking in our dust.'

'We'll need him fresh for tomorrow.'

'Why? Are we going much further?'

Spandrel smiled grimly. 'Do you never give up?'

'Why don't you just tell me where we're going?'

'I'll tell you tomorrow.'

'Why not tell me now?'

Why not, indeed? Because, as Spandrel could hardly admit, he feared that, if he did, he might wake in the morning to find her and the chaise gone. And this time he had no intention of being left behind.

Tired though he was, Spandrel did not sleep well at the inn in Staines. The landlord had a single room only for Estelle, condemning Spandrel to share a bed with a drugget merchant from Devizes who snored like a walrus and rolled much like one as well. Not that Spandrel could have hoped for carefree slumber in any circumstances. It was hardly more than a guess that McIlwraith was holding Edward Walpole in the vicinity of Bordon Grove, even if the guess had come to Spandrel with an eerie weight of conviction. If he *was* right, they still had to find the place and persuade McIlwraith to release the boy, an outcome which did not seem remotely likely, however Spandrel argued it out in his head. All he knew for certain was that he had to try. And then, of course, there was Estelle . . .

'Wagemaker?' The surprise in Estelle's voice was matched by the frown of disbelief on her face. It was the following morning, they were ready to start . . . and the time had come to reveal their destination. 'Surely that was the name of the Government agent who died in the duel with Captain McIlwraith.'

'Yes. It's his brother's house we're looking for. Bordon Grove. A few miles into the Forest, beyond Egham.'

'But why? What does Wagemaker's brother have to do with this?'

'I'll tell you when we find it.'

'How do you know where he lives?'

'I'll tell you that as well.'

Spandrel had never related McIlwraith's story of his feud with the Wagemakers to Estelle. Keeping it to himself had been his small act of homage to McIlwraith's memory. But McIlwraith was not dead. And soon, very soon, Estelle would have to find that out.

The horse began to show signs of lameness as soon as they set off. They were obliged to turn back and spend the better part of an hour waiting on a blacksmith to have him re-shod. It was late morning when they reached Egham and well gone noon by the time they came within sight of

Bagshot. The weather was clear and fine, a gentle breeze coursing like a murmur through the deep stands of the Forest that flanked their route. Spandrel should have felt fortunate to be riding in a handsome carriage with a beautiful woman on a perfect spring day. But what he actually felt was a growing sense of dread.

They stopped at the Roebuck Inn in Bagshot to water the horse. Spandrel suggested they take a meal there and overrode Estelle's objection that this was a waste of valuable time by pointing out that he wanted to ply the tap-room gossips for information concerning the master of Bordon Grove.

'What information do you need?'

'Any I can obtain.'

'To what end?'

It was the same, insistent question in disguise. Why had they come here? The answer was close now, whether Spandrel supplied it or not. He could delay the moment of revelation only a very little longer.

The wiseacres of the tap-room exchanged knowing looks when Spandrel mentioned the Wagemakers. A fresh flagon of ale between them sufficed to loosen their tongues. Bordon Grove had been a well-run and prosperous estate in the days of old Henry Wagemaker. But misfortune and mismanagement had been its undoing. The sudden death of young Dorothea Wagemaker (whether by accident or suicide opinion differed) so soon after her father's demise had sucked the vitals from the family and Tiberius, her brother, had subsequently proved himself to be the sottish wastrel all present had predicted from early in his feckless existence. Another brother, Augustus, had enjoyed a successful military career and his remittances were presumed till lately to have sustained Tiberius, their invalid mother and a soft-headed aunt who, together with no more than a couple of servants, comprised the household. Certain it was that the estate yielded nothing but thistles and vermin, being utterly neglected and overgrown. Augustus was reported to have been killed in a duel, somewhere abroad, a year or so before, so the family's fortunes could now be assumed to have reached their nadir. This doubtless explained why Tiberius had taken to filling his larder with royal game, earning himself a heavy and quite probably unpaid fine from the Swanimote Court at the rumoured bidding of chief woodward Longrigg, whose long ago courtship of Dorothea was sure to have a bearing on the case.

The name McIlwraith, dropped by Spandrel into the murky waters of so much rumour and reportage, sank at first without a ripple. Then, slowly, certain memories were dredged to the surface. McIlwraith. Yes, he was the last tenant of Blind Man's Tower, a folly on the estate, before it was abandoned, its windows bricked up, its outer stair-case left to crumble. It had been used for a while as a store-house for coppicing gear, but coppicing was but a distant memory at Bordon Grove. You could hardly see the tower now above the straggling trees. Owls had long been its only residents. As for McIlwraith, he had vanished shortly after Dorothea Wagemaker's death. And that, the stranger could rest assured, was no coincidence.

When Spandrel returned to the dining-room, he found, as he might have foreseen, that Estelle had already gleaned much of the same information from the landlady. Estelle had had no reason to mention McIlwraith, of course, so Spandrel could at least be sure that that element of the story was still unknown to her. It was, as it happened, the vital element. Blind Man's Tower was an overgrown ruin. No-one lived there any more; no-one went there. But might not its very abandonment make it ideal for

McIlwraith's purpose? Where better to hold a prisoner in secret for a few days? Where else, conveniently close to Eton College, could he be held?

Marabout's map showed a lane leading through the Forest to Bracknell, passing Bordon Grove about halfway along its winding route. They made slow going in the chaise through the many puddles and deep wheel-ruts. The boundary pale of Bagshot Park – residence, according to Spandrel's tap-room informants, of the Earl of Arran – curved slowly away from them into the Forest. After that, only dense, unfenced woodland met their gaze to either side. They glimpsed a group of barkers working in a small clearing at one point. Otherwise, the Forest was an empty domain of greenery and birdsong and filtered sunlight.

A low stone wall, moss-covered, fern-shrouded and much broken down, became visible away to their right. Spandrel stopped to study the map before confirming that they were now at the edge of the Bordon Grove estate, if estate it could any longer be called, rather than an indistinguishable part of the surrounding forest. 'The entrance should be about a quarter of a mile ahead.'

'And what do you propose to do when we reach it?' asked Estelle sharply. 'Drive up to the house and politely ask Mr Wagemaker to release Master Edward Walpole?'

'No.' Spandrel sighed. The time had come. 'It isn't Wagemaker we're looking for.'

'Who, then?'

'Captain McIlwraith.'

Estelle should have been dumbstruck by such an apparently perverse answer. Instead, she looked calmly at Spandrel and said, 'He didn't die in Berne, did he?'

'No.'

'I began to suspect something of the kind when you first mentioned the Wagemakers. I'm not sure why.'

'He's determined to see the contents of the Green Book made public.'

'Does he know what the contents are?'

'Oh yes. I told him.'

'Poor foolish William. You told him?'

'Yes. Strange, isn't it? Yesterday you said with such confidence that I wasn't a fool.'

'You aren't. You don't have to be one in order to do foolish things.'

'Good. Because I'm about to do another.'

'Which is?'

'I think I know where he's hiding the boy. And I think I can persuade him to let him go.'

'How?'

'By convincing him that Walpole won't yield to his demands under any circumstances. The captain isn't a cruel man. He won't want to harm the boy. If we can persuade him—'

'We?'

'He knows what you are to Walpole. He'll believe you understand him better than I do.'

'I'm not sure he'll believe a word I say.'

'He must.'

'Yes. If all's to end well.'

'It still can.'

'Perhaps. Perhaps not. You seem to have forgotten that young Edward was seized by two men. Captain McIlwraith has at least one accomplice, who won't necessarily share this kindly nature you credit him with.'

'Convince Captain McIlwraith and we convince however many others there are. He'll carry them with him.'

'You're sure of that, are you?'

'I'm sure of nothing.'

'Except that walking unarmed into a nest of kidnappers is a risk worth taking?'

'You don't have to come with me.'

'If I don't, you're even less likely to succeed than if I do.'

'But the choice is yours.'

'Yes.' Estelle looked away into the world of green shadows beyond the tumbled wall. 'And I made it when we left London.'

The entrance to Bordon Grove comprised two lichen-patched stone pillars between which gates no longer hung. The drive they stood guard over was a mud-clogged track, thick with weeds, but still passable. The house itself was nowhere to be seen through the tangle of trees. Not that the house was their destination. The map marked the tower away to the north-west of it, on rising ground. And Spandrel proposed to make straight for it.

They left the chaise in a glade a little way into the forest on the other side of the lane, the horse tethered and grazing. Such pathways as presented themselves in the woodland of Bordon Grove were no better than badger-runs. Estelle's dress soon became soiled with mud and frayed by thorns. But she made no complaint and kept pace with Spandrel as he steered a course by map and compass up the heavily wooded slope. She, indeed, was first to sight the tower ahead of them.

It looked like the turret of some strange castle that had otherwise vanished into the surrounding trees: a squat, three-storey-high structure of stone and flint, with arrow-loops for windows on the upper floors and a battlemented parapet round the roof. That these were mere architectural conceits was confirmed by the open, external staircase that zigzagged up one face of the building, serving doors on each level, not to mention the large, domestic windows on the ground floor. These had been bricked up, however, leaving the tower blind in fact as well as name.

'There doesn't seem to be any sign of life,' whispered Estelle, as they surveyed it from the shelter of the trees.

'They won't want to attract any attention.'

'Then how do you think they'll react to receiving some?'

'I'll approach slowly, but openly. Let anyone who's there see that I mean no harm. Wait here.'

He set off, breathing fast but walking as slowly as he had said he would. The undergrowth thinned as he reached a track leading to the tower entrance – a broad, stout-hinged door at the foot of the staircase. Looking back along the track, which soon curved out of sight, Spandrel guessed that it led to the house. Glancing down, he saw recent boot-prints in the mud, proving that Blind Man's Tower was not as neglected as some supposed. He turned and started towards the entrance. Still nothing stirred. A woodpecker began to hammer at a trunk somewhere close by. A rook flapped lazily from one tree to another above him, cawing as it went.

He reached the door. There was no knocker and rapping at it with his knuckles made little impression through the thick panels. He pounded at it with his fist and raised a muffled echo within, but no kind of answer. Then he tried the handle. The door was locked, as he had assumed it would be. He stepped away and stared up at the arrow-loops above him – then stumbled back in astonishment at the sight of a face staring down at him from the roof.

'Who the blazes are you, sir?' came the imperious demand.

'I—'

'Stand where you are. I'm coming down.'

He was a thick-set, red-faced fellow in a threadbare coat and stained waistcoat, a narrow-brimmed hat worn low and crookedly on his wigless head. He was carrying a fowling-piece under one arm that threatened to trip him at every stage of his unsteady descent. If not actually drunk, he was clearly far from sober. Spandrel had never met him before, but there was something familiar about him. And very soon the reason for that familiarity was revealed.

'I own this tower. And the land around it. You're trespassing, sir, and you'll explain yourself, if you please.'

'You're Mr Tiberius Wagemaker?'

'I am.'

'My name's Spandrel. William Spandrel.'

'Never heard of you. You don't look like a Forester to me.'

'I'm from London.'

'Then you can take yourself off back there.'

'I've come a—'

'Mr Wagemaker?' Estelle's voice carried up to them from the trees. Spandrel turned and saw her walking purposefully towards them. When he turned back, Wagemaker was smiling.

'Is this lady with you, Spandrel?'

'Yes, sir.'

'Then perhaps I should go to London more often. Your servant, ma'am.' Wagemaker plucked off his hat and essayed a stiff-backed bow, presenting a patchily shaved head for their inspection. 'You have the advantage of me.'

'I am Mrs Davenant, Mr Wagemaker. Mr Spandrel and I are here on a mission of mercy.'

'Mercy, you say?' Wagemaker creaked upright and replaced his hat. 'I shouldn't have thought you'd have any difficulty extracting that from the hardest of hearts, madam. And mine must rank as one of the softest for many a mile. How can I help you?'

'Mr Spandrel is my brother. I am a widow, as is my sister, who has a son at Eton.'

'A credit to the family, I'm sure.'

'He's been—' Estelle turned aside, apparently needing to compose herself. 'He's been kidnapped.'

'Kidnapped? Good God.'

'We think he's being held somewhere in the Forest,' said Spandrel.

'Have you informed Colonel Negus?'

'We're not acquainted with the gentleman, sir.'

'Deputy Lieutenant of Windsor Castle. If the Forest's to be searched—'

'The kidnappers have sworn to kill the boy if we approach the authorities,' said Estelle. 'We've had to let the college believe he's simply run away. Whereas, in truth . . .' She paused to take the calming breath that she so evidently seemed to need. 'The ransom is beyond our family's means, Mr Wagemaker. Our sister is beside herself. She fears she will never see her son again. Nor will she, unless we can find the place where they've confined him before the ransom falls due.'

'When does—'

'May Day,' put in Spandrel.

'And today is the twenty-eighth,' said Estelle dolefully.

'We're doing our best in the short time available to us,' Spandrel continued. 'Searching every disused or out-of-the-way building in the hope of finding him. Blind Man's Tower was mentioned to us at the Roebuck in Bagshot as meeting both of those requirements.'

'So it does,' said Wagemaker. 'Built by my grandfather, to celebrate the Restoration. I've, er, had no use for it in recent years. The strange thing is, though . . .'

'Yes, sir?' Spandrel prompted.

'Well, my housekeeper – an idle baggage, it's true, but sharp-eyed when she wants to be – reckons she's seen strange men in these woods over the past couple of days. I came up here this afternoon to take a look. No sign of anyone. Until you turned up.'

'There are fresh boot-prints yonder,' said Spandrel, pointing down the track.

'Probably mine.'

'I'd say they were the prints of more than one pair of boots.'

'Even so, you can see for yourselves the tower's empty. I keep it locked. And I'd swear no-one's so much as tried to force the door.'

'Do you have the key about you, Mr Wagemaker?' asked Estelle.

'Yes, but—'

'I'd esteem it a great favour if you'd let us look inside.'

'You would? Well, in that case . . .' Wagemaker fumbled in his waistcoat and produced the key – large, old and rusty. 'Anything to oblige a lady.' He propped his fowling-piece against the staircase, stepped past Spandrel to the door and slid the key into the lock. At first it would not turn, but after pulling the door tight against the frame – and deepening the colour of his face alarmingly in the process – Wagemaker succeeded. He turned the handle and pushed the door open. 'I'm sorry to say the only living creatures you're likely to find in here are mice and spiders, but you're welcome to see for yourselves.'

The door gave directly onto a dusty, cobwebbed chamber as wide and about half as deep as the tower itself. The floorboards were bare and large, jagged gaps in the plaster on the walls revealing the brickwork beneath. There were doors in each corner of the room, standing open to smaller rooms at the rear. The fireplace was a bare hole from which a fallen bird's-nest and other debris had spilt across the floor.

Spandrel stepped inside, disappointment already leaching away his hopes. Then he heard it: a scuffling, shuffling noise, followed by something midway between a moan and a whimper. 'Is there someone here?' he called.

And for answer a figure half-fell, half-rolled into view in the doorway of the back room to his left: a youthful figure in plain shirt and breeches, his hands and feet tied, his mouth gagged.

'God's blood,' said Wagemaker. 'It's the boy.'

And so it surely was, though not the boy Estelle had said they were looking for. Spandrel hurried towards him, aware of Estelle's footfalls on the boards behind him.

'Have they harmed him?' she said breathlessly.

'I don't think so.' Spandrel stooped over the boy, resisting the urge to recoil from the stench of urine. 'Never fear, young sir. We're here to help.' He prised at the knot securing the gag as the youth's wide, frightened eyes stared up at him from beneath a fringe of sweat-streaked hair. After a moment, Spandrel gave up trying to untie the knot, took out his pocket-knife and cut through the cloth. 'You are Edward Walpole?' he asked, pulling away the gag.

'You didn't say your sister had married a Walpole,' called Wagemaker from the front door. 'And it's strange you don't seem to recognize your own nephew.'

'We can explain, Mr Wagemaker,' said Estelle, turning back towards him.

'No need, madam.' Wagemaker smiled. 'I already know.' Then he pulled the door shut with an echoing crash. And darkness engulfed them even before they heard the key turn in the lock.

Chapter Thirty-Nine

Blind Treachery

The only light on the ground floor of Blind Man's Tower was a glimmer between the front door and its frame and a still fainter glimmer down the chimney. Spandrel moved across the room to the door and put his eye to the keyhole, but Wagemaker had made sure the escutcheon was back in place. There was nothing to be seen. And seemingly nothing to be done. Their attempt to rescue Edward Walpole had ended in them joining him in his imprisonment.

'Didn't you know that fellow was one of them?' snapped the boy, some of his father's arrogance revealing itself despite the dire straits he was in. 'There's a Scotchman in it too. And some other slinking rascal.'

'We did not know,' said Estelle softly.

'Did my father send you?'

'No.'

'I thought not. He'll have chosen people who know what they're about.'

'Perhaps,' said Spandrel. 'But we found you. And I doubt anyone else can.'

'What help are you to me?'

'Not much. Nor to ourselves, it seems.'

'Mr Wagemaker plays his part very convincingly,' said Estelle.

'Why have they done this to me?' There was a petulant

note to young Walpole's voice that Spandrel sensed he would soon find irksome, understandable though it was.

'They're trying to force your father to do something he's determined not to do,' said Estelle.

'Papa can't be forced.'

'They think otherwise.'

'What have they said they'll do to me?'

'They've said they'll kill you,' put in Spandrel.

Silence fell, long and heavy. Spandrel made his tentative way back across the room and began trying to untie the knotted ropes at the boy's wrists and ankles. But the knots were tight and in the darkness he could make little of them.

'You have a knife.' Edward Walpole had not been cowed for long. 'Cut them.'

'I was about to.' Spandrel took out his knife and went to work. 'But I'll have to be careful I don't cut through you as well as the ropes.'

'Hurry up, can't you?'

'You'll gain nothing by railing at us,' said Estelle.

'Will I not?' There was a thud as the boy kicked the wall with his pinioned feet, followed by a rustle of falling plaster. 'My father is the King's first minister. I can't be treated like this.'

'Perhaps you should have explained that to your kidnappers,' said Spandrel, sure though he was that young Walpole had done so just as often as he had been given the chance. 'Now, hold still.' Reluctantly, the boy did hold still. 'There. You're free.' Spandrel pulled the ropes away.

'Free of these ropes, but not this prison. What's to be done, damn it?'

'How often do they visit you?' asked Spandrel levelly.

'That fellow – Wagemaker – brings me bread and water. I can't tell at what intervals. I can't tell anything' – the boy's voice cracked – 'in this confounded darkness.'

369

'Calm yourself, Edward,' said Estelle gently.

'I'm Master Walpole to you, madam.'

'As you please.' There was an icy edge to Estelle's voice as she continued. 'Well then, *Master Walpole*, be so good as to keep to yourself any further reproaches of us that may come to your mind. We will all have to wait as patiently and as calmly as we can.'

Silence fell once more. But Spandrel reckoned it would not last for long. 'There might be something worth trying,' he said, rising to his feet and feeling his way round the wall to one of the bricked-up windows. There he stopped, took out his pocket-knife and gouged at the mortar between two of the bricks with the point of the blade.

'What are you doing?' called Estelle.

'Trying to scrape out enough mortar to dislodge a brick.'

'Do you think you can?'

'Eventually.' Mortar began to patter at Spandrel's feet. 'I doubt Wagemaker employed master craftsmen when he had this place sealed.'

'How long will it take?'

'I don't know.' Spandrel looked over his shoulder, sensing Estelle's presence close behind him, but seeing nothing. 'I may as well find out, though. Unless you have any better ideas.'

'I don't have any better ideas.' There was a touch of her hand at his elbow. 'But I'm sure there's a way out of every-thing – if you look hard enough.'

'One day there won't be. You know that, don't you?'

'One day. But not this day.'

'If you think you can do it, why don't you get on with it?' came a familiar whine from behind them.

'Out of the very mouth of babes and sucklings,' murmured Estelle.

'And spoilt brats,' added Spandrel, turning back to the wall.

Spandrel had loosened one brick, but was still a long way from dislodging it, an uncountable portion of time later, when Estelle called from the front door for him to stop.

'I think I can hear someone outside,' she explained. 'Footsteps. Voices. I'm not sure.'

But by the time Spandrel had joined her at the door, she *was* sure. And so was he. There was a burble of conversation. Who was speaking or what they were saying was not distinguishable. Then a boot scraped against the doorstep and the key was thrust into the keyhole. They moved back as the door opened.

The flood of daylight was at first dazzling. A figure loomed in the doorway, haloed by the glare. 'I'd bid you good afternoon,' came the voice of Captain James McIlwraith. 'But I fear it's not likely to be good for any of us.' He was holding a pistol in his right hand, which he proceeded to cock and point, not at Spandrel, but at Estelle. 'Particularly you, madam.'

'What became of your gallantry, Captain?' said Estelle, smiling defiantly at him. 'Imprisoning boys and threatening women is sorry work indeed.'

'As you say. Sorry work. But in a glad cause.'

'You'll pay for this,' said young Walpole, who for all his defiance hung back in the doorway of the rear room. 'You whoreson villain.'

'Another word from you, sir,' said McIlwraith, 'and I'll have my friend here tie and gag you again.' Tiberius Wagemaker loomed at his shoulder. 'Just one word, mind, is all the provocation I need.'

Edward Walpole stared dumbly at his captors, tempted to answer back, it was clear – but knowing better than to do so.

371

'What are we to do with you two, then?' McIlwraith pondered the point. 'The rat and the vixen we find in our trap. Have you succumbed to her charms again, Spandrel?'

'We have to talk to you, Captain,' said Spandrel. 'That's why we're here.'

'You *are* talking to me.'

'Alone.'

'Oh, alone, is it? So that Mrs de Vries can pour another sweet lie into my gullible old ear? I don't think so.'

'We risked our lives by coming here.'

'So you did.'

'Won't you grant us one small favour in return?' Spandrel looked McIlwraith in the eye. 'A private word, Captain. It's not much to ask.'

'Don't trust them,' said Wagemaker.

'I don't trust *you*.' McIlwraith sounded more than slightly testy. His strange alliance with an old enemy had clearly not been ordained in Heaven. 'But still I speak to you. Very well, Spandrel. You and Mrs de Vries go up to the roof. I'll join you there for your "private word". Lock the door behind them, Wagemaker. And stand by. Plunket!' A lean, narrow-faced fellow dressed like a scarecrow and closely matching young Walpole's description of a 'slinking rascal' appeared from round the corner of the building as Spandrel and Estelle stepped outside. 'Get back to the road and keep watch. And make it a keener watch than you managed earlier.'

'Yes, sir.' Plunket took off at a lope along the track.

'After you, madam.' McIlwraith uncocked the pistol and waved Estelle towards the stairs. 'And watch your step. Wagemaker is behindhand with his repairs.'

Spandrel followed Estelle up the stairs. There was a muttered exchange between McIlwraith and Wagemaker that he could not catch. Then the captain started after them.

*   *   *

The roof was a shallow pyramid of lead, centred on the chimney, with a walkway round all four sides behind the castellated parapet. Windsor Forest defined the horizon in every direction, green and deep and hazy in the mellowing sunlight. The sun was drifting through a cloud-rack away to the west and from its position Spandrel judged that the afternoon was turning towards evening. There was a chill to the air, though whether enough to account for the shiver he saw run through Estelle he rather doubted.

'Cold, madam?' McIlwraith, standing at the top of the stairs, had evidently seen the same thing. 'Or nervous?'

'Neither, Captain. A touch of vertigo, I rather think. I'm prone to it.'

'Then you shouldn't climb so high, should you?'

'I like to conquer my weaknesses, not be governed by them.'

'So I've seen. Now, this private word of yours, Spandrel. We'll make it quick, if you please. Mrs de Vries may not be nervous, but I have the impression Wagemaker is.'

'Does he know you killed his brother?' asked Spandrel.

'Oh yes. I told him myself. Little love lost there of late, apparently. The brothers had fallen out. Over this, as a matter of fact. The Forest. Walpole's been installing his favourites here just as he's been installing his whores in St James's. And those favourites have ridden roughshod over local rights and traditions. Tiberius blames the likes of Lord Cadogan, who's building a palace to rival Blenheim over at Caversham, for all his misfortunes. And the Jacobites have enabled him to dignify his resentment as a noble cause. There's no shortage of Jacobites around here, thanks to old King William's periodic expulsions of Catholics from London. The Earl of Arran lives nearby. And Lord Arran, as I'm sure Walpole knows from his perusal of Sunderland's papers, is thick with the Pretender.'

373

'This rising they plan cannot possibly succeed,' said Estelle.

'Not as things stand. But after Tuesday's edition of the *London Gazette* reaches the coffee-houses and taverns of England, it may not be so certain.'

'He won't do it, Captain,' said Spandrel. 'That's what we're here to tell you. Walpole won't give in. Tuesday's *Gazette* will make no mention of the Green Book.'

'We'll see as to that.'

'All you'll see,' said Estelle, 'is his son's blood on your hands.'

'I've no wish to harm the boy, in need of a thrashing though he clearly is.'

'What you wish is beside the point. What will you *do*, when Walpole defies you?'

'He won't.'

'He will. Trust me, Captain. I know him. As you so charmingly put it, I am his whore. His nature is clearer to me than it can ever be to you. He is immovable. He loves Edward. But he loves power more. And he will not give it up.'

'Then he'll have to—'

'You see?' Estelle stared intently at McIlwraith. 'You'll kill the boy, won't you? Or Wagemaker will. Or Plunket. Or the Earl of Arran's gamekeeper. It doesn't matter who. Someone will do it, rather than admit defeat and let him go free.'

'I cannot foretell the future.'

'We can. Tell him about your mother, William.'

'He says he'll have her hanged as a thief, Captain,' said Spandrel. 'After I've been hanged as a murderer.'

'And he means it,' said Estelle. 'He's only stayed his hand for fear of forcing yours.'

'And what does he say he'll do to you, madam?'

'He does not say. But he knows one of us must have told you what the Green Book contains.'

'How big a bribe he was paid, you mean? How much room he had to make in his pocket? I wouldn't worry your beautiful head too much about answering for that. If it comes to the point, I'm sure Spandrel here will manfully bear the responsibility, being the noble fool that he is.'

'It *is* my responsibility,' said Spandrel bleakly.

'There you are. It's back to the bedroom in safety for you, madam. Back where you belong.'

'Walpole takes nothing on trust,' said Estelle. 'He won't give me the benefit of the doubt.'

'You'll pardon me if I lose no sleep over that.'

'I hardly think you'll have much sleep to lose, with the forces Walpole can command on your trail. But that's beside the point. I'm not asking for your pity.'

'That's as well, since you'll get none from me.'

'I only want you to understand that we're here on our account, not Walpole's. We're here to save his son – and to save ourselves.'

'And you too, Captain,' said Spandrel. 'He doesn't know of your involvement. And he needn't. If it ends here.'

'In meek surrender? Is that your proposal?'

'You don't want murder on your conscience. That's what it'll be. Plain murder. And of a boy. An innocent boy, what's more, however guilty his father may be.'

'I told you, Spandrel. It's him or me.'

'Then it's him. I don't believe you're ruthless enough to go through with this. But he is. *I* told *you*. You can't win.'

'Only choose the manner of my defeat? That's no course for a soldier.'

'Release the boy,' said Estelle. 'We'll say we don't know who you are or where you've gone. I promise.'

'I know how reliable your promises are, madam.'

'You can rely on this one.'

'I think not. The brat knows too much already for you to protect my anonymity. Besides, what could have brought you here – other than that story of lost love I told Spandrel in Berne?'

'You could be out of the country long before anything was sworn against you.'

'Exile and hiding. What riches you do promise me.'

'Not riches, perhaps. But the best we can contrive.'

'And your reward? A long lease on Phoenix House, perhaps.'

'Perhaps.'

'But Spandrel's mother allowed to live out her days in peace. And Spandrel spared a miscarriage of Dutch justice. That's the sum of it, is it?'

'Yes.'

'The sum of all things.' McIlwraith sighed and looked past them across the rolling canopy of the Forest. 'Walpole's a keen huntsman, so they tell me. And it seems he no more wants for foxes than for hounds. He breeds the one as he breeds the other. What a grasp of economy the man does have. You're right, of course, Spandrel. My quarrel's with the father, not the son.'

'You'll let the boy go?' asked Spandrel, hope blooming suddenly within him.

'It seems it's either that or kill him. And I'd sooner hang for murdering the First Lord of the Treasury than his son. You may take it I—'

'McIlwraith!' It was Wagemaker's voice, raised in a shout of alarm. 'We're discovered.'

McIlwraith swung round even as did Spandrel and Estelle. There, below them, hurrying up the track, came a troop of infantry, their musket barrels glinting in the sun. Discovered they had clearly been. Or betrayed.

'Well, well,' said McIlwraith. 'It seems my mind's been made up for me.'

Chapter Forty

Under Siege

'Stand where you are!' came a shout.

For a second, Spandrel thought the order was directed at all of them. Then he realized that Tiberius Wagemaker was the real target. He had started up the stairs, a pistol clutched in his right hand, glaring upwards as he climbed. 'They've done for us, McIlwraith,' he bellowed. 'Spandrel and that she-devil.'

'*Halt or we fire!*'

But Wagemaker did not halt. It seemed to Spandrel that he did not even hear. Nor did he see, as they could from the roof, the musketeers taking aim below him.

'*Halt, I say!*'

Wagemaker raised his pistol, cocking it as he did so, and pointed it at Spandrel. In the same instant, there was a barked order and an explosion of musket shots.

Several of the shots took Wagemaker in the back. He arched backwards and fired into the air, the roar of the shot swallowing a last, grimacing cry. Then he fell, striking his head against the stairs behind him before plunging to the ground with a heavy thud like that of a laden sack being tossed from a barn-loft.

'Don't move,' said McIlwraith quietly, lowering his pistol out of sight behind the parapet. 'And say nothing unless I tell you to. I reckon Wagemaker's shown us what's likely to come of acting hastily.'

377

'You three on the roof!' The musket-smoke cleared to reveal the stout figure of a heavily braided senior officer. 'I'm Colonel Negus, Deputy Lieutenant of Windsor Castle. I have reason to believe an oppidan of Eton College, Master Edward Walpole, is being held here against his will. I require and demand his immediate release.'

'You'll find the boy in the room below,' McIlwraith shouted back. 'And you'll find the key to the door in the pocket of the fellow your men have just shot.'

'What's the boy's condition?'

'He's alive and well enough, though none too happy.'

'It'll be your neck if he's come to any harm.'

'I dare say it'll be my neck either way, Colonel.'

To this Negus did not respond. He sent two men scurrying over to Wagemaker's body. As they began searching his pockets, McIlwraith said to Estelle in an undertone, without turning to look at her, 'Have we you to thank for this, Mrs de Vries?'

'Yes,' she softly replied. 'The landlady of the Roebuck named you as the last person to live here and a rumoured lover of Dorothea Wagemaker. I'd already guessed you were still alive and that's when I realized William suspected you were holding the boy here. William was in the tap-room at the time, unaware of what I was doing. I paid the stable-boy to ride to Windsor Castle with a message for Walpole's brother, Horatio, whom he sent there yesterday to organize a search.' She paused, then added, 'I'd thought they might arrive sooner.'

'All this . . . negotiating . . . was just a delaying tactic, then?'

'Partly. But I bear you no ill will, Captain. I'd have been happy to—'

A sudden commotion below marked the discovery of the key. Negus sent his adjutant forward to open the door. He disappeared from their view, but they could hear the rattle of the key in the lock, followed by a creak of the door on its hinges.

'We were supposed to be in this together,' said Spandrel, slowly recognizing the deception to which Estelle was calmly admitting. 'We were supposed to trust one another.'

'But you didn't trust me, did you? If you'd told me where we were going and why, it mightn't have come to this.'

'That won't do,' objected McIlwraith. 'How did you know Walpole had despatched his brother to Windsor? He told you, didn't he? And he also told you to send a message to him there if and when you succeeded in gleaning the boy's whereabouts from Spandrel. So, if Spandrel had told you from the outset what was in his mind, you'd only have betrayed him the sooner.'

'What a hard woman you think me, Captain.'

'What a hard woman you are.'

'We could have ended this as I'd hoped,' said Spandrel, seeming to see in his mind a dream slipping away from him. 'We could all have escaped, with no harm done. There was no need for . . .'

'A military resolution,' said McIlwraith. 'Need or not, though, that's what we're to have. And in short order, I imagine, now they have the brat.'

At that moment, Edward Walpole appeared below, limping slightly as he walked towards the soldiers, supported by the adjutant. He cast a glance across at Wagemaker's body, then up at them on the roof, as he went. It was not a glance in which either mercy or gratitude was to be readily detected.

Colonel Negus led the boy away, patting his shoulder as he talked to him. Their discussion lasted several minutes, during which not a word was spoken on the roof. Spandrel stared at Estelle, daring her to look him in the eye. But she trained her gaze firmly on the scene below. Then Negus strode back to his position, leaving young Walpole in the care of someone who looked to be a doctor.

'Captain McIlwraith!' Negus called.

'Aye, Colonel?'

'Where's your other accomplice?'

'Taken to his heels, I assume.'

'Your companions there are Mrs Davenant and Mr Spandrel?'

'So they are.'

'Send them down. Mrs Davenant first.'

'As you please.' McIlwraith moved clear of the head of the stairs, waving Estelle forward.

The walkway was so narrow that she could not avoid brushing against Spandrel as she passed him. But still she kept her gaze averted. He watched her walk slowly to the gap in the parapet and turn to start her descent.

At that moment, McIlwraith moved smartly forward, raised the pistol and clapped it to her temple. 'That's quite far enough, madam,' he said, cocking the trigger. 'You surely don't suppose I'm going to let you go.'

'Don't do it, Captain,' Spandrel cried. 'She's not worth it.'

'There I must disagree, Spandrel. It seems to me she's eminently worth it, especially considering that killing her's unlikely to increase the severity of my punishment.'

'Lower the pistol,' shouted Negus. 'At once.'

'I can't oblige you there, Colonel,' McIlwraith replied. 'And if your men open fire, I should say they're as likely to blow Mrs Davenant's head off as mine. I advise you to stay your hand.'

'Let me go, Captain,' said Estelle, too calmly to sound as if she was pleading.

'Why should I?'

'Because, if you let me live, I can save William from the gallows. Kill me and you condemn him to hang alongside you.'

'And will you save him?'

'If you give me the chance to, yes.'

'No doubt I can have your word on that.'

'Would my word mean anything to you?'

'Not even if this tower was built of bibles.'

'I swear it, even so.'

'You're right anyway, damn it, whether you swear or no. A ball through your head is a noose round Spandrel's neck. And I'm as sure as you probably are that Negus will have been instructed to take me at any cost – even your life.' McIlwraith lowered the pistol. 'Go down and join your friends, madam. And remember your promise.'

'I shall.'

Spandrel watched her as she slowly descended the stairs, disdaining to put a hand to the wall to steady herself, an eddying breeze stirring her hair beneath the hat and tugging at her dress. As she reached the first landing and turned, she glanced up at him, but her eyes were in shadow and what her gaze might have conveyed he could not tell. Then she went on down, without a second upward glance.

'Spandrel may follow,' called Negus.

'Do as the man says,' said McIlwraith. 'You're better off down there than up here.'

'Will you surrender, Captain?' Spandrel asked as he moved to the head of the stairs.

'Do you think I should?'

'Walpole told me he'd have his son's kidnappers hanged, drawn and quartered.'

'Aye. And their heads left to rot on spikes at Temple Bar, no doubt. If that should happen to me, Spandrel, will you climb up there one dark night, take mine down and give it a decent burial, for the sake of the miles we rode together?'

'Yes, Captain. I will.'

McIlwraith smiled. 'Good man. I'll do my best to spare

you the need. Now, look lively on the stairs. We don't want Colonel Negus to suspect you of collusion with the enemy.'

Spandrel started down. He looked up twice during his descent, but McIlwraith was not watching him. He seemed to be scanning the horizon, his eyes narrowed against the sun.

It was no more than thirty yards from the foot of the stairs to where Colonel Negus was standing. In the few moments it took Spandrel to cover the distance, he became aware of a difference in the manner of his reception compared with that of Estelle. She was some way off down the track, with young Walpole, the doctor and a junior officer. Around the group they made hovered an atmosphere of solicitude and deference. But for Spandrel there was only Negus's stern gaze and gravelly voice.

'Place this man under arrest, Captain Rogers,' he said to his adjutant. 'We're unsure as to his allegiance.'

A pair of burly soldiers seized Spandrel by the arms and led him aside. He did not resist. He did not even protest. It was only what he had half-expected. As to what it portended, he could not find the energy to imagine.

'Captain McIlwraith!' he heard Negus call. 'Discharge your pistol into the air, lay down your sword and descend the stairs with your arms held aloft.'

'I'm a soldier like yourself, Colonel. I don't surrender lightly.'

'Your position is hopeless.'

'Aye. So it is. Whether I surrender or no.'

'Give it up, man. You've not harmed the boy. That'll count in your favour.'

'With God, perhaps. But not with Walpole. I advise you to withdraw your men.'

'Surrender, Captain, or prepare to be stormed.'

382

'You'll never take me, Colonel. And you'll lose most of your men in the attempt.'

'I'll bandy words with you no longer.' Negus turned to his adjutant. 'Captain Rogers—'

'Wait, sir,' said Rogers. 'What's he doing?'

The two soldiers holding Spandrel looked round at this, enabling Spandrel to do the same. He did so in time to see McIlwraith scrambling up the roof to the chimney and round to the far side of the stack.

'The man's mad,' declared Negus, his patience exhausted. 'Deploy your best marksmen and end this, Rogers.'

'I'll decree the ending of this, not you, Colonel,' shouted McIlwraith. He threw his gun down the roof to the walkway, then pulled something from inside the chimney-pot and fumbled in his pocket.

'Finish the man, Rogers. Now!'

'Yes, sir. But—'

There was a flash of some kind from where McIlwraith was standing, then a duller, trailing flame.

'He's lit a fuse, sir. Do you think—'

'My God, he must have mined the chimney. Fall the men back. Quickly!'

The realization of what McIlwraith was about communicated itself to the troops before Rogers could even issue an order. Once he did, they began a withdrawal down the track that soon became a pell-mell retreat. Spandrel's guards, intent upon saving themselves, left him where he was, staring up at the gaunt figure on the roof.

McIlwraith's coat flapped behind him in the breeze, his bare, grey-maned head lit by the sun. Though he could not be certain amidst the confused shouts and pounding foot-falls, it seemed to Spandrel that McIlwraith was laughing with genuine amusement at the scene below him. Then he stopped laughing. And slowly, with seeming relish, drew his sword. The sunlight glinted on the blade. McIlwraith held it out before him, as if to meet the charge of some other, invisible swordsman.

Then, with a flash and a roar, the mine exploded. The whole upper half of the tower vanished in a gout of flame and smoke and flying stone. And Spandrel's last thought, before something struck him near his right ear and darkness swallowed him, was that McIlwraith could not be hanged, drawn and quartered now. Nor would his head need rescuing from Temple Bar. He was out of Walpole's reach. For good and all.

Chapter Forty-one

Full Circle

Spandrel had a dim awareness of a wound above his ear being washed and dressed and of a bandage being wrapped round his head, but it was some unmeasurable time after that when he regained consciousness to find himself lying in bed in a bare, twilit chamber. The granular light from the window suggested either dusk or dawn, but he had no clear idea which and felt a strange lack of curiosity on the point. He fell asleep.

When he woke, the light was stronger and his mind once more in command of logical thought. The bed was soft and generously blanketed and there were no bars at the window, but nevertheless there was something cell-like about the chamber. He rose, slowed by a dull, pounding headache, and fingered the bandage round his head, faintly surprised to discover that he still had a head to be bandaged. Then he walked unsteadily to the window and looked out.

A high wall and a steep escarpment below it combined into a sheer and vertiginous drop beyond the mullioned panes. The river at the foot of the escarpment was surely the Thames and the town huddled on the other side Eton, to judge by the ecclesiastical building seeming to float above it that could only be the college chapel. He was in Windsor Castle. And not, the bareness of the room suggested, as an honoured guest. He crossed to the door and tried the latch. But the door was locked, as he had expected. So, he was a prisoner, as he had also expected.

He banged on the door loudly and for long enough to rouse any guard who might be near. But there was no response. Perhaps they had not supposed he would wake so soon. He went back to the window and pushed it open.

Church bells were ringing. It was Sunday morning. The events of the day before lay in the past. But they were fresh in his memory. In his mind's eye, clearer by far than the vista below of river and field and chapel, Spandrel saw McIlwraith standing on Blind Man's Tower, sword in hand, the instant before he and it were blasted into oblivion. 'You'll never take me,' he had said. And he had been as good as his word.

He was gone now, that strange, curmudgeonly warrior. He had used up the last of his lives. Spandrel wandered back to the bed and lay down, tears stinging his eyes as a grief he had never thought he would feel swept over him. It was a grief, he realized, sharpened by fear. McIlwraith had rescued him once before, when no-one else could. What would happen to him now? Who – if anyone – would rescue him this time?

The church bells had fallen silent, and the angle of the sun across the rooftops of Eton had altered with the advance of the day, when the door of Spandrel's room was at last opened, to an overture of jangling keys. A grim-faced guard, built like a bear but clearly not given to dancing, looked in at Spandrel, then made way for a kitchen-boy, who brought in a meal that smelt surprisingly good, deposited it at Spandrel's feet and scuttled out.

'What am I—' But Spandrel's admittedly tardy question was cut off by the slamming of the door. And a further jangling of keys.

*   *   *

Half an hour later, the door opened once more. Expecting the kitchen-boy, Spandrel picked up the licked-clean plate and held it out for collection. Only to find himself confronted by the corpulent, scowling, Sunday-suited figure of Robert Walpole.

'Put the plate down, sir. Do you take me for a turnspit?' Walpole looked round at the guard. 'Close the door behind you. And stay within call.'

'Yes, sir.' The door closed.

'Well now, Spandrel, how do I find you? Barely scratched, according to the doctor.' Walpole ambled across to the window and gazed out. 'And handsomely accommodated, I see.'

'Am I a prisoner, Mr Walpole?'

'Certainly you are, sir. But a well fed and softly bedded one, thanks to Mrs Davenant. She assures me you did your best to rescue my son. And he *was* rescued. But since you bear a large measure of responsibility for the peril he was placed in—'

'I had nothing to do with it.'

'*Don't interrupt me.*' Walpole turned and glared at him. 'You knew McIlwraith was still alive, yet you said nothing. I suspect you also knew what he intended to do, but still you said nothing, calculating that his plan, if it succeeded, would bring me down. Only when you realized that I would not yield to his demands and that you would therefore be complicit in my son's murder did you attempt to retrieve the situation. In which attempt you were only partially successful.'

'Your son *is* alive.'

'Indeed he is. But Colonel Negus's adjutant and two other members of his detachment of troops are not, having been killed by flying lumps of stone of the kind that merely grazed you. Nor are my son's kidnappers available for questioning. Two are dead and one is in hiding.

How am I to prove Atterbury's involvement in this plot without the evidence only they could have supplied?'

'But your son is alive,' Spandrel hopelessly repeated.

'Yes. And if I believed you'd tried to save him out of Christian charity rather than a concern for your own skin, I'd thank you fulsomely enough. But I don't believe it. And I doubt you have the gall to try to persuade me otherwise.'

'I did my best, sir.'

'To serve two masters and outwit each of them in turn. That's what you did your best to accomplish, Spandrel, and you failed, as you were bound to. Well, there's a price for failure. And you'll have to pay it. Mrs Davenant tells me she gave McIlwraith some sort of undertaking to save your neck, but I have to tell you she was in no position to give such an undertaking. Your neck is at my disposal, not hers. And her whims are not my will. That is something both of you need to understand. She seems to think I should set you free. But then Kelly would squeeze the truth out of you and Atterbury would know better than to carry on with his treasonable designs. As it is, he still doesn't know the extent to which I've seen through them and I mean to keep him in ignorance as long as possible. I also mean to teach you – and Mrs Davenant – that disobeying me is a grievous offence.'

'What are you going to do with me?'

'Send you to Amsterdam.'

'To hang?'

'That'll be a matter for the Dutch court to decide.'

'But you know what they'll decide.'

'Not at all.' For a moment, Walpole seemed about to smile. Then his face hardened. 'You must address yourself to your own salvation, Spandrel. I'm done with you. Tomorrow, you'll be moved to the Tower of London and held there while a message is sent to the Sheriff of Amsterdam and a reply awaited. You'll be allowed no visitors, I'm afraid. I can't have your situation becoming the talk of the city. As for letters, you may send one to your mother if you wish. I'll read it before it's delivered, of course, courtesy of the Postmaster-General, so you'll need to watch what you say in it. A flight to foreign parts might be a merciful lie to tell in the circumstances. Your mother needn't know anything of events in Amsterdam. I shan't inflict them upon her. Nor, if you conduct yourself with suitable reticence at your trial, will my wife's jewellery ever be found about her. You have my word on that.'

'Your word . . . as a statesman?'

'That blow clearly hasn't addled your memory. Yes. My word as a statesman.' Walpole walked slowly across the room towards the door, then stopped and looked round at Spandrel. 'We shan't meet again. Nor will you and . . . Mrs Davenant. If you have a message for her . . .'

'There's no message.'

'Good.' Walpole permitted himself a grin. 'I wouldn't have passed it on if there had been.'

Spandrel was surprised by the mildness of his own re-action. This was, after all, the plight he had been struggling to evade, one way or another, for more than a year. Perhaps that was the reason for the fatalistic lethargy that held him in its grasp. He could do nothing. There was no escape. He was done for. Days would pass, journeys be undertaken, procedures followed. But the end was fixed and known. In that certainty lay a strange kind of comfort. He did not have to think any more. He did not need to struggle. Everything would be done for him. Except dying, of course. He would have to do that for himself.

Looking through the window, he thought how easy it would be to scramble out onto the chamfered sill and decree his own end, falling through the Windsor air to the ground far below. It would spare him a deal of suffering later. But he had not the courage for that. And his store of hope, he realized, was not quite exhausted, though why not he failed to understand. 'While there's life,' his father had often said, 'there's hardship.' And so it seemed there was.

Spandrel pulled his bed across to the window and sat by it to write the one letter Walpole had said he could write and for which a single sheet of paper had been provided. He would tell the lie Walpole had suggested. He would let his mother go on believing that she might yet see him again. At least she did not have to do so as a washer-woman living within the rules of the Fleet Prison. As a well set up widow, she might find a new husband and forget her wayward son. She might, indeed, be better off without him. She could hardly be worse off.

The letter written, he lay down on the bed and stared out at the sky, watching the afternoon wear towards evening. How odd it was, he thought, that a man who has never done anything wrong, nor borne anyone the least ill will, should nevertheless be required to pay with his life for the crimes and conspiracies of others. It was not fair. It was not right. But it was how the world turned. From light to dark. And back again. For some.

Robert Walpole's arrival that evening at the Townshends' London residence was a surprise, though a pleasant one, for the Viscountess. The Viscount pretended for his wife's benefit that he shared her surprise. The truth was, however, that Walpole had said he would call upon his return from Windsor, to speak of matters which his sister knew nothing about.

After an exchange of family gossip which the Viscountess found disappointingly short and shallow, Walpole and his brother-in-law retired to the Viscount's study, where, behind closed doors, fortified by port and tobacco, they turned at once to urgent debate.

'Edward is well?' Townshend asked, knowing already that his nephew-in-law was safe, but not yet certain that safe also meant sound.

'Oh yes,' said Walpole, smiling the broad smile of a relieved parent. 'He doesn't seem to have had to endure anything worse than I was put through at Eton in the normal course of a typical day. You oppidans never knew the brutalities we collegers were subjected to.'

'I did, Robin. You complained to me of them in unfailing detail at the time and have often reminded me since.'

'Lest you forget.' Walpole laughed. 'Edward will be able to entertain you with tales of his incarceration when you see him in the summer. He's likely to mention a dark-haired lady who'll sound confoundedly like Mrs Davenant.' He held up a hand. 'I know you've always wanted to know nothing about my mistresses, Charles. I blame your prudery on a happy marriage. And I thank God for it as well, of course. You and Dolly are luckier than you know. It was because of your . . . sensibilities . . . that I failed to tell you of the lady's involvement in this matter.'

'Say no more.' Townshend gave his brother-in-law a knowing look. 'I gather there was . . . some kind of explosion.'

'The tower where Edward was held turns out to have been mined. It was blown to blazes.' Walpole chuckled. 'My son seems to have enjoyed the fireworks.'

'Were many killed?'

'Negus's adjutant and two soldiers. Along with two of the kidnappers. A third made off. I needn't tell you I'd like to have had at least one of them to squeeze for evidence.

As it is, we're back where we started so far as Atterbury's concerned. The fugitive's called Plunket. He's known to the Secret Service as a Jacobite hanger-on. The smallest of fry, but worth landing if we can catch bigger fish in the same net.'

'This dishes your efforts to tempt Atterbury with the Green Book, I assume.'

'I fear it does, Charles. That, as you might say, is now a closed book.' Walpole smiled wryly. 'We must make the best of what we have.'

'Should we show our hand, then?'

'Not yet. I want our discredited emissary safely lodged in a Dutch gaol before we make the threat to the King public. Horace is ready to leave for The Hague tomorrow. How many troops do you think he can persuade Hoornbeeck to promise us?'

'Not as many as Heinsius would have done.' (The previous Grand Pensionary of Holland had indeed been an unswerving ally. His successor was a notably cooler one.)

'Hoornbeeck may feel more accommodating when Horace tells him that the Englishman who murdered one of Amsterdam's most eminent citizens last year and then escaped from custody can now at last, thanks to us, be made to answer for his crime. We've neatly, if inadvertently, attended to the destruction of the blackguard responsible for his escape as well. All in all, I reckon the burghers of Amsterdam are greatly indebted to us.'

'So, it's the noose for your redundant mapmaker?'

'Indeed. Which is nothing less than he deserves.' Walpole took a thoughtful puff at his pipe. 'Irksome as the fellow is, though, I've done my best for him. Horace will ask for an assurance that he won't be tortured into confessing.'

'Nor into disclosing anything not strictly relevant to the case, presumably.'

'True enough, Charles. But mercy was naturally my prime consideration.' Walpole blew a noose-shaped smoke-ring towards the ceiling. 'As ever.'

Chapter Forty-two

Dutch Reckoning

Spandrel spent a week of comfortable if scarcely contented solitude in the Tower of London. By coincidence, his quarters were next to those previously occupied by Sir Theodore Janssen. But though the view they commanded of the river and the wharves of Bermondsey was the same, there was an important difference ever to the fore of Spandrel's thoughts. Sir Theodore had been waiting for his case to be heard by Parliament, fearful about how much of his lovingly accumulated wealth – of land and houses, jewels and china, paintings and tapestries, horses and carriages, cochineal and pepper – he would be allowed to keep. But his life had never been threatened. He sat now at his house in Hanover Square, less wealthy but at several fortunes' remove from poverty, contemplating an old age of ease and security. For Spandrel, old age had joined a long list of experiences he knew he would never have.

Being led in chains through Traitors' Gate, loaded aboard a launch and conveyed downriver to a waiting Dutch frigate was, by contrast, an experience he had never expected to have and would have preferred to be spared. But his preferences counted for even less than they ever had. The *Kampioen* took delivery of its prisoner in Limehouse Reach on a dull May morning of spitting rain. And turning for a last glimpse before he was led below,

Spandrel took his leave of the city – and the country – of his birth.

The day after Spandrel's unheralded departure, Viscount Townshend wrote to the Lord Mayor of London, instructing him to expel all papists and non-jurors from the city by reason of the Government's recent discovery of a Jacobite plot to overthrow – indeed, assassinate – the King.

Even as the papists and non-jurors left in their paltry hundreds, the troops arrived in their armed thousands to set up camp in Hyde Park. The King, it was announced, would not now be going to Hanover. A threat to his life, as well as his crown, was said to have been revealed in an anonymous letter to the Duchess of Kendal. Arrests, trials and executions were promised. And the London mob settled to await an exciting summer.

For Spandrel summer was less of a prospect than a memory. Not that the seasons made themselves apparent in the cells beneath the Stadhuis in Amsterdam. There the shadows were always deep and long and the days very much the same. Spandrel's cell was not the one he had been incarcerated in fifteen months before, but might as well have been for all the differences there were. Big Janus was still the friendliest of the turnkeys, bearing no grudge, it seemed, over the affray at Ugels' shop. He seemed, indeed, positively sorry to see Spandrel back, though not as sorry as Spandrel was to be there.

How and when the authorities would deal with him Spandrel did not know. Soon and summarily was his expectation. This time, he felt certain, the British vice-consul – if one had been appointed in succession to Cloisterman – would not come calling.

In that he was correct, though only because the dandily attired visitor shown into his cell a few days after his arrival was not the vice-consul. Evelyn Dalrymple, as the plum-voiced fellow introduced himself, was at pains to emphasize that he held a senior post at the British Embassy in The Hague. He would not normally endure a *trekschuit* journey halfway across Holland for the dubious privilege of visiting the Stadhuis cells. That he had done so was a measure of the British Government's concern for the due and proper process of the law.

'I'm not sure you appreciate how much we've done for you, Spandrel.'

'Oh, I do appreciate it, Mr Dalrymple, believe me.'

'We've specially requested that you be spared torture.'

'That was good of someone.'

'Indeed it was. But it *was* only a request, you understand. Throw wild accusations around at your examination – muddy the water, so to speak – and the Sheriff may seek what he conceives to be the truth by rack and screw. The Dutch are a tenacious people, especially if you try to put them right. Are you familiar with the concept of Dutch reckoning, Spandrel?'

'I don't believe I am.'

'Query a bill at an inn in this country and the landlord's apt to send it back to you with further additions. In the same way, if you protest your innocence overmuch, you may find yourself punished more harshly. Hanging can be mercifully swift, if competently done. And the Dutch are a competent people. I should look more to their competence than their tenacity, if I were you.'

'Thank you for the warning.'

'Don't mention it.' Dalrymple glanced around at the four dank walls and up at the ceiling – though he scarcely needed to, given how close it was to the crown of his hat. 'It's not too bad here, is it?'

'No, no. A regular home from home. I can't think why I wanted to leave it.'

Dalrymple looked at him sharply. 'I shouldn't recommend sarcasm at your examination, Spandrel.'

'I'll remember that.'

'I have to ask you . . . if you'll require the services of a priest.'

'Won't that question arise only after I've been condemned?'

'I suppose so.' Dalrymple shrugged. 'But there's no harm in looking ahead.'

'In that case . . . no.' Spandrel forced out a smile. 'A priest might muddy the water.'

In London, muddied water was available by the bath-load. Hardly a day passed at the Cockpit without the questioning of one or more specimens of unpatriotic riff-raff. But where were the serious plotters, where the genuine conspirators? Ten days after the papists and non-jurors had been sent packing from London, an answer seemed to be supplied by the arrest at his lodgings in Little Ryder Street of George Kelly, secretary to the Bishop of Rochester.

It soon became common knowledge, however, that Kelly had been able to hold the arresting officers at bay for some time, thanks to his distinctly unsecretarial skills as a swordsman, while most of his presumably incriminating correspondence burned merrily on his sitting-room fire. Walpole, it was said, would make someone suffer for such bungling, not least because he was bound to suffer for it himself.

'We'll have to release him,' was Walpole's conclusion when he and Townshend met two days later to consider the Deciphering Department's report on those papers of

Kelly's not consumed by the flames. And it was a conclusion that clearly pained him. 'There's nothing here.'

'But if we can't touch Kelly . . .'

'We can't touch his master. I'm well aware of that, Charles. Damnably well aware.'

'What's this about . . . Harlequin?'

'Atterbury's dog, damn his paws. Half Europe seems to have been writing to Kelly enquiring after the cur's health, obviously as a cipher for the vitality of the plot. But we can't prove that's what it means.'

'How are we to proceed?'

'Stubbornly, Charles. That's how. Stubbornly and tirelessly. We can't dig this fox out of his hole. But he'll have to come out of his own accord eventually. And when he does . . . we'll be waiting.'

At the waiting game Walpole knew no peer. For Spandrel, however, waiting was a game he could only lose, though one he was nevertheless forced to play. While in London the First Lord of the Treasury and the Northern Secretary pored glumly over the Deciphering Department's report, in Amsterdam Spandrel was taken before Sheriff Lanckaert for examination.

Lanckaert himself said very little, and that in Dutch. His English-speaking deputy, Aertsen, conducted the brief but pointed interrogation. He and Spandrel had last met on the occasion of Spandrel's escape from custody, an event to which neither of them referred directly. In short order, however, the long dormant evidence of Spandrel's association with Zuyler that had emerged just prior to McIlwraith's dramatic intervention at Ugels' shop was cited as confirmation that Spandrel and Zuyler had conspired to rob Ysbrand de Vries and had ended by murdering him. The even hoarier accusation that Spandrel was a secret agent of the government of the

Austrian Netherlands was not revived, due, Spandrel assumed, to some subtle change in the balance of political expediency. Instead, Aertsen invited him to admit that he had killed de Vries when discovered by him in the act of breaking open the chest in his study in search of the money and valuables Zuyler had told him he would find there.

'No,' Spandrel hopelessly declared. 'That's not so. Zuyler tricked me into sneaking into the house so that I'd take the blame for his murder of de Vries. I told you the truth last year and it hasn't changed.' No more it had. But he knew more of the truth now. He knew it all. Yet there was nothing to be gained by telling it. 'You should be looking for Zuyler and Mrs de Vries.'

'We have looked for them. But we have found only you.' They had in truth not even done that. Spandrel had been served to them on a plate, lacking only a sprig of parsley by way of garnish. Zuyler was dead, but they did not seem to know it. And Estelle de Vries had transformed herself into Mrs Davenant, mistress of Phoenix House *and* Robert Walpole, for which information they would probably not be grateful. 'We have a sworn statement from an elderly servant of Mijnheer de Vries that you killed his master, Spandrel. Against that all your denials and allegations count for nothing.'

'I didn't do it.'

'Then why did you flee when you had the chance to prove your innocence?'

'Because I had no such chance. As this examination demonstrates.'

'That is enough.' Aertsen glared at him. 'That is quite enough.'

There was a lengthy conferral in Dutch, then a rambling pronouncement of some kind by the Sheriff, of which Aertsen supplied a brisk translation.

'Your guilt is established, Spandrel. Formal judgement and sentence will be passed tomorrow. Do not expect leniency.'

Aertsen's parting warning had hardly been necessary. Leniency did not feature in Spandrel's expectations. He tried, as far as he could, to harbour no expectations at all. A future governed by the forces pressing in upon him was unlikely to be either long or relishable. The authorities had to bend over backwards to avoid confronting the inconsistencies and contradictions in the case they had made against him. But it was clear that bend they would. And equally clear that Spandrel would be the one to break.

Back in his cell, he thought, as he often had of late, of McIlwraith, and wondered what that indomitable champion of lost causes would do in such a situation as this. Try to escape, perhaps. But the solid walls and thick bars of the Stadhuis would probably prevent him. Proclaim the truth as he knew it in open court, then – the whole truth, Green Book and great men's greed and all. But that would only win him hours of useless agony in the torture chamber. He would be as helpless as Spandrel to avoid the fate that lay in wait.

Between the bars of his tiny window, Spandrel noticed a spider spinning a web. He half-remembered some legend of McIlwraith's homeland, in which Robert the Bruce had been inspired by the indefatigable spinnings of a spider. But, more clearly, he remembered a superstitious saying of his mother. 'A spider in the morning brings no sorrow; a spider in the afternoon brings trouble on the morrow.'

Was it still morning, or had the afternoon already come? For a few moments, Spandrel struggled to decide. Then, irritated with himself for making the effort, he stopped. What difference did it make? Morning *or* afternoon, he knew what the morrow would bring.

Chapter Forty-three

The Wheels of Justice

In the Stadhuis of Amsterdam, two flights of stairs were all that separated the cells from the civil chambers. The short journey between them, which Spandrel had never previously undertaken, was a bewildering transition from gloom and squalor to opulence and grandeur. The Magistrates' Court was a vast and glittering chamber, the magistrates themselves a sombrely clad half-score of solemn-faced burghers arrayed beneath pious paintings and allegorical friezes. Sheriff Lanckaert directed proceedings, with occasional interventions from one of the magistrates who seemed to outrank the others. Aertsen perched mutely at a desk to one side. Spandrel, guarded by Big Janus, was required to do nothing but stand and listen, understanding none of the words spoken but having a shrewd idea what they would amount to.

It was not long before the chief magistrate was intoning a formal verdict, a translation of which was helpfully muttered into Spandrel's ear by Big Janus. 'Guilty, *mijn vriend.*' It was no surprise. But somehow, until that moment, Spandrel had half-believed it would not happen. It had been the purest self-deception, of course. It had been bound to happen. Telling himself otherwise was merely an indulgence in one of the few comforts not denied him. But even those few were being stripped from him now, one by one. And soon there would be none left – none at all.

Spandrel was marched back down into the bowels of the building, which he thought strange, since no sentence seemed to have been passed. An explanation of sorts was supplied by Aertsen, who led the way and glanced back over his shoulder once to say, 'The Chamber of Justice is on the other side.' Spandrel took him to mean the other side of the Stadhuis, an indirect route to which was presumably used to spare any wandering city fathers a distressing encounter with an unwashed prisoner. Any figurative significance to Aertsen's words Spandrel dismissed as improbable.

Re-emerging in a hall yet vaster than the court and glimpsing a gigantic statue of Atlas supporting a star-spangled globe at the far end, Spandrel was taken into a marble-lined chamber where the Sheriff and the magistrates, accompanied this time by a pastor, were waiting for him. He was tempted for a moment to object to the pastor's presence, having told Dalrymple he had no use for one, but he supposed Dutch law insisted a pastor be there and to the insistences of Dutch law he was clearly a slave. With little ado, the chief magistrate pronounced sentence on 'Willem Spandrel'. And there really was no need for Big Janus to tell him what it was.

As it happened, Aertsen took it upon himself to remove any doubt there might be about the import of the words used. 'It is death, Spandrel. You understand?'

'I understand.'

'The sentence must now be publicly pronounced. This way.'

They descended some stairs to another marbled chamber, this one boasting open windows at ground level

402

on one side, through which passing Amsterdammers could observe the scene. Spandrel noticed half a dozen or so of them watching, their figures outlined against the bright sunlight filling the square, before he was turned to face the magistrates once more, seated now on the marble steps that ran along the opposite wall. Above them were statues of weeping maidens and above the maidens a frieze filled with gaping skulls and writhing serpents. The Old Bailey it was not. And for that Spandrel was grateful. He had seen men condemned to die at the Bailey amidst cat-calls and laughter. Here a dread dignity prevailed.

The chief magistrate said his piece again, less perfunctorily than in the Chamber of Justice. A clerk scribbled something in a book. And it was done. Big Janus sighed soulfully, then led Spandrel away, as gently as a shepherd leading a lamb.

Aertsen accompanied the pair as far as the door of Spandrel's cell. There he looked Spandrel in the eye for several seconds before saying, 'You have been sentenced to die by hanging from the public gallows at Volewijk. Do you have any questions?'

'When will it be?'

'The next hanging day is eleven days from now.'

'What is today?'

'Do you not know?'

Spandrel shrugged. 'I lose count.'

'It is the second of June.'

'The second?'

'Yes. Does it matter?'

'It's my birthday on the seventh.'

'Not here, Spandrel. Here, that would be the eighteenth. And you will not see the eighteenth. Lucky for you, I think.'

'How is that lucky?'

'You do not have to grow any older.' There was a faint curl at one edge of Aertsen's mouth.

'Is that what they call Dutch reckoning?'

The curl vanished. Aertsen turned to Big Janus and snapped, '*Sluit hem op.*' Then he stalked away.

Viscount Townshend climbed the stairs of the Treasury in Whitehall with a lightness of tread only the carriage of good news can impart. The gloom that had hung over Walpole since the farcical mishandling of Kelly's arrest was about to lift, or at least to thin, thanks to the intelligence Townshend was bearing. And his brother-in-law's gratitude was always a wonderful tonic.

As he approached the door of Walpole's outer office, it opened and a familiar figure emerged – that of Walpole's brother and loyal man-of-all-work, Horatio. As a Treasury Secretary, whose financial duties were confined to buying elections and selling favours at the First Lord's direction, Horatio was commonly to be seen about the place. Townshend was nevertheless surprised to see him on this occasion. There had been a letter detailing his discussions with the Dutch Government concerning troop loans, but Townshend would have expected a personal report from Horatio upon his return. His tread grew fractionally heavier.

'I didn't know you were back, Horace.'

'What? Oh, Charles, it's you.' The younger Walpole looked distinctly flustered. 'Yes. I arrived last night.'

'When shall you call on me?'

'I can't. Confoundedly sorry, old fellow. There it is.'

'There *what* is?'

'Robin's sending me on my travels again.'

'Where to?'

'Can't say. Sorry. Sworn to secrecy. He'll tell you, I'm

sure, but I can't. He leads me a dog's life, you know. And, like a dog, I must run.' With which Horatio did precisely that.

Townshend was wise enough not to ask Walpole what manner of mission he had sent his brother on. Walpole would tell him or not, as he pleased. Of late, he had told him less and less, which grieved Townshend as much as it irked him. They had once trusted each other completely. Now . . . But perhaps, he reflected, his news would bring some of that trust bubbling to the surface.

'We have him, Robin.'

'Who do we have?' came the frowning response.

'Plunket.'

'We were bound to, sooner or later.'

'But Plunket's the weak link in the chain. He'll give us all the rest in time.'

'You think so?'

'Yes. Don't you?'

'I'm not sure. Perhaps.'

'Are you quite well, Robin?'

'Yes. Just a little . . . distracted.' Walpole rubbed his forehead and gave a crumpled smile. 'It's nothing you need to worry about.' Which really meant, Townshend well knew, that it was nothing he was going to be *allowed* to worry about. 'As for Plunket . . .' Walpole's shoulders sank. He pushed out his lower lip. 'We'll see.'

'Wake up, Spandrel. It's McIlwraith. I'm back. And I'm heezing you out of here before you have your neck stretched longer than an Edinburgh Sunday. Put your boots on, man. We're leaving.'

'Captain? That can't be you. You're—' Spandrel woke and McIlwraith vanished into the dream that had

405

summoned him. There was no-one there. Spandrel was alone in his cell, save for the spider that still kept him company, morning *and* afternoon.

He looked round at the patch of wall on which he had been keeping a tally of the passing days since his sentencing. The broken toothpick he had found wedged in a crevice, doubtless left by some previous prisoner, served well for the purpose. There were five scratches. He would make a sixth today. It was the halfway point of his journey from court to gallows and nausea swept over him at the very thought. He held his breath until it had abated, then stretched up for the toothpick.

'It'll be good to see you again, Captain,' he murmured to himself as he swung round and scratched at the grimy surface of the wall. 'And it won't be long now.'

'Mrs Spandrel?'

'Yes.' Margaret Spandrel looked doubtfully at her visitor. 'What can I do for you, sir?'

'Don't you remember me?'

'I don't . . .' She peered closer. 'My Lord, it's Dick Surtees. After all these years. Come to finish your apprenticeship, have you?'

'Not exactly.' Surtees smiled awkwardly.

'Not remotely, dressed like a dog's dinner as you are.'

'I was, er, sorry to hear about . . . Mr Spandrel.'

'Were you now?'

'Billy told me . . . just recently.'

'You've seen William?' Some mixture of hope and anxiety lit her features. 'When?'

'Oh, a month or so ago.'

'Oh.' Mrs Spandrel's shoulders sagged. Her expression shrank back into disappointment. 'I thought . . . Well, he didn't mention it to me.'

'Is he here?'

'Who?'

'Billy, of course.'

'No.' Mrs Spandrel sighed heavily. 'Gone abroad to better himself, apparently.'

'Abroad? Where?'

'He didn't say. The truth is . . .' She wiped away a tear with the back of her hand. 'I haven't the faintest notion where he is or what he's doing.'

'Oh.' Surtees too looked disappointed. 'I see.'

'What do you want with him?'

'Nothing, really. It doesn't matter.'

'It must do, to make you come here.'

'No. It *really* doesn't matter. It can't—' He stood looking at her for a moment, rocking back and forth on his heels. Then he blurted out, 'I have to go,' and turned for the door.

Such money as Spandrel had had about him when taken into custody was still his, at any rate notionally. For a genuinely modest commission, Big Janus had agreed to put it to good use: supplying Spandrel with a daily flagon of *jenever* that drowned the sour taste of fear and reduced his expiring allotment of life to a painless haze. There were eight scratches on the wall now and the coiner in the next cell, destined to hang the same day as Spandrel but denied the soothing effects of *jenever*, could often be heard wailing in sheer terror at the prospect before them.

There was no good or noble way to approach death, Spandrel decided in one of his long stretches of inebriated lucidity. It was the same for everyone. The variously pattering and shuffling footsteps he could hear in the street outside were leading their owners to death as certainly as Spandrel's sojourn in his cell was leading him.

The only difference was that he knew when his journey would end. And that end was close now, so close he could almost smell it. He reached for the flagon of *jenever* and raised it to his lips. And death shrank back into the shadows. But only a little way. Only a very little.

Alone in his study at Orford House, Robert Walpole threw another log onto the fire and watched it blaze up the chimney. It was not a cold evening, but he had need of flame and heat. He walked across to his desk, picked up the green-covered ledger lying there and leafed randomly through its pages. So many names. So much money. So many glorious secrets. It went against the grain to part with them. It offended his every political instinct. But this latest turn of events had shown him how dangerous the Green Book was, to him as much as anyone. Even if Horatio could manage the present crisis, there was no saying another would not flare up. The entire Spandrel affair had been partly Walpole's own fault, after all. The Green Book was simply too tempting. Ultimately, there was only one way to solve the problem it posed. With a regretful sigh, Walpole walked back to the fire and sat down in the low chair beside it. Then he began tearing the pages out of the book and feeding them, one by one, into the flames.

There were nine scratches on the wall now. The light was failing in the world beyond the window of Spandrel's cell. Tomorrow would be the last complete day he spent in it, the last complete day, indeed, that he spent anywhere, unless there really was a place beyond the end of life.

His reverie was interrupted by the unlocking of the door, which came as a surprise to him, so regular and predictable had the guards' ways become. He looked round to see Big Janus framed shaggily in the doorway.

'*Opstaan, mijn vriend. Opstaan.*'
'What's wrong?'
'Mijnheer Aertsen. He wants you.'
'What for?'
Big Janus shrugged. '*Ik weet het niet.* You come. Now.'

Chapter Forty-four

The Quiddities of Fate

Aertsen was waiting for Spandrel in the examination chamber. But he was not waiting alone. Seated next to him at the long table beneath the chandelier was Dalrymple, whose purse-lipped expression suggested that a second journey from The Hague had pleased him no more than the first. On Aertsen's other side sat a narrow-shouldered, black-wigged fellow with a face the colour and texture of an old saddle. At the far end of the table, lounging back in his chair with one hand thrust inside his waistcoat, the better it appeared to attend to an itch somewhere near his armpit, was a fourth man, less smartly dressed than the others but somehow giving the impression of being in charge of them. Sheriff Lanckaert was nowhere to be seen.

Aertsen fired some instructions in Dutch at Big Janus, who led Spandrel to a chair in front of the table and sat him down, then left, without troubling to shackle his leg to the block. Spandrel thought that almost as strange as the absence of pen and paper from the table. There was something strange about this gathering altogether. That much was clear before a word was addressed to him.

'Mr Dalrymple you know,' said Aertsen, after eying Spandrel for a moment with his strange squinting indirectness. 'This gentleman is Mijnheer Gerrit de Vries.' He nodded to the grim-faced figure on his right. 'Son of the late Ysbrand de Vries.'

'And I'm Horatio Walpole,' said the fourth man. 'Brother of Robert.' There was indeed, Spandrel realized as he looked at him, a distinct resemblance. Horatio was fat, though not quite as fat as Robert, with a round and ruddy face, though neither quite so round nor quite so ruddy as his brother's. And there was a softness to his gaze Spandrel did not recognize. Horatio was the poor man's Walpole, but no doubt impressive enough to those who had not encountered the real thing.

'What can I . . . do for you, sirs?' Spandrel ventured.

'It's more a case of what *we* can do for *you*,' said Walpole.

'I'm a condemned man, sir. There's nothing anyone can do for me.'

'What if you were no longer condemned?'

'I . . . don't understand.'

'Tell him, Dalrymple. This isn't a Commons debate. We gain nothing by dragging it out.'

'Very well.' Dalrymple cleared his throat and glanced at Aertsen. 'By your leave, mijnheer?'

'*My* leave?' Aertsen tossed his head irritably. '*Mijn God.* Tell him, yes. Why not?'

'Your . . . situation, Spandrel,' Dalrymple began, 'has altered.'

'Altered?'

'Yes.' Dalrymple seemed to wince. 'Shortly after sentence was passed on you . . . someone else confessed to the crime for which you were convicted. Since you have all along maintained your inn—'

'Someone else?' Spandrel stared at Dalrymple, half-stupefied. 'Someone else has confessed?'

'Yes.'

'Who?' But there was, of course, only one person it could be. 'Not . . . Estelle?'

'Mrs de Vries,' said Dalrymple flatly. 'That is correct.'

'She can't have done.'

411

'But she has.'

'She . . . admits it?'

'Fully and completely. Thus exonerating you . . . fully and completely.'

'I don't believe it.'

'It is hard to believe, certainly. But it is true. The confession was made in person to Sheriff Lanckaert. Mijnheer Aertsen was also present.'

'It is true,' said Aertsen through gritted teeth.

'Why? Why would she do such a thing?'

'To save an innocent man from hanging was the reason she herself gave. Was it not, Aertsen?'

'Ja.'

'I'm not going to hang?'

Dalrymple shook his head. 'You are not.'

'But Estelle?'

'Worried about her, Spandrel?' asked Walpole.

Yes. He was. Almost in spite of himself, he was suddenly very worried indeed. '*She* will hang? Instead of me?'

'As in our country,' Dalrymple replied, 'a wife who murders her husband is not hanged, but, er, burned at the stake.'

'Oh my God.'

'Fortunately,' said Walpole, 'it needn't come to that.'

Spandrel turned to look at him. 'What do you mean, sir?'

'We have a proposition for you, Spandrel. Get on with it, Dalrymple, for pity's sake.'

'The circumstances are complicated as well as delicate,' said Dalrymple, choosing his words with palpable care. 'Mrs de Vries's confession establishes the primary guilt of her husband's secretary, Zuyler, who, according to Mrs de Vries, has since—'

'He's dead,' said Spandrel.

'Quite so.' Dalrymple smiled tolerantly at him. 'To

412

proceed. Mrs de Vries could not be tried without your conviction first being quashed. Such a public admission of judicial error would be . . .'

'Damned embarrassing,' said Walpole.

'The embarrassment is not all ours,' snapped Aertsen.

'He's referring to Mrs de Vries's confessed reason for the murder.' Walpole looked at Spandrel and shrugged. 'A certain green-covered book.'

'The contents of which we would prefer, especially at this sensitive juncture of national affairs, not be bruited abroad,' said Dalrymple. 'You follow?'

'I . . .' Spandrel glanced at each of the four men in turn and was no clearer about their intentions. 'I'm not sure I do.'

'Our proposition,' Dalrymple continued, 'is simply this. If your conviction were allowed to stand, but you somehow . . . escaped from custody . . . again . . .' He paused, marshalling his thoughts, it seemed, setting aside his scruples. 'Mr Walpole and I have persuaded the Dutch authorities to release you, Spandrel. Formally, you will have escaped. Informally, you will be allowed to return to England on the clear understanding that no attempt will ever be made to re-arrest you, provided that you never visit Holland again.'

'You'll let me go?'

'You have it, Spandrel,' said Walpole. 'It must almost be worth the fright of being condemned to hang for the relief of learning you don't have to after all.'

Spandrel was tempted for a moment to tell Walpole how very far from being worth it the experience had been. But there was a puzzle here he did not understand. He was naturally eager to snatch this unexpected chance of life from the jaws of death. Yet he had the strange impression that the two Englishmen and the two Dutchmen were almost equally eager that he should snatch it. And one of them was de Vries's own son. 'What about . . . Mrs de Vries?'

'The V.O.C. will look after her,' said Dalrymple.

'How will they "look after her"?'

'*Mijn stiefmoeder,*' said Gerrit de Vries suddenly, '*doet wat ik zeg.*'

'Mijnheer de Vries has succeeded to his father's position within the V.O.C,' said Dalrymple, smiling awkwardly. 'He has interceded with them on his stepmother's behalf.'

'I don't understand,' Spandrel protested. 'What has the V.O.C.—'

'Your understanding is not required,' Aertsen cut in, so loudly that his voice echoed in the shadowy recesses of the chamber. 'Do you accept the proposition?'

'I . . .'

'She'll come to no harm,' said Walpole, with a reassuring grin. 'My brother wouldn't hear of it.'

'Do you accept?' Aertsen repeated.

'Yes. I do.' A sudden fear that his salvation was about to be rescinded gripped Spandrel. 'I'm sorry. I didn't mean— I'm grateful, sirs, more grateful than I can say. I accept . . . unreservedly.'

'Of course you do,' said Walpole, a grin still fixed to his face. 'Who wouldn't?'

'*Mijn stiefmoeder,*' growled Gerrit de Vries, '*is mijn zaak.*'

'What—'

'Enough,' declared Aertsen, frowning at de Vries. 'We have said enough.' He rose abruptly from his chair, took a key from his pocket and tossed it onto the table. 'Can we leave you to end this as agreed, Dalrymple?'

'Most certainly, Aertsen.'

'Thank you. Mijnheer?' Reluctantly, it seemed, and with a scowl at Spandrel, de Vries also stood up. '*Laten we gaan.*' Aertsen glanced round the table. 'Good evening, gentlemen.'

The two men strode off into the shadows that shrouded the door, which was heard to open, then slam shut behind them. Silence settled over the unlikely gathering. Walpole scratched under his wig. Dalrymple adjusted his cravat.

'What is to happen, sirs?' asked Spandrel.

'What is to happen is that you are to pick up that key,' said Dalrymple. 'It opens the back door of this chamber, beyond which steps will lead you to a store-room, where someone has negligently left a window unfastened. You will climb out of the window, cross Dam Square and make your way up the near side of Damrak to the harbour. A boatman will be waiting for you near the toll-house. You will identify yourself as William Powell.'

'Powell?'

'That is correct. The boatman will row you out to a pinnace sailing tonight for the Texel roadstead, where she is to deliver mail to an East Indiaman, the *Tovenaer*, shortly to embark for Java. The master of the *Tovenaer* has instructions to deliver you by launch to any convenient port along the south coast of England and to furnish you with money for your onward journey. At that point, you will become a free man, in fact if not in name.'

'And Mrs de Vries?'

'Is already aboard the *Tovenaer*. But she will not be leaving the ship . . . until it reaches Java.'

'Is that what you meant by the V.O.C. looking after her?'

'Reading between de Vries's pouts and grimaces,' said Walpole, 'I reckon his stepmother knows more about the V.O.C.'s inner dealings than's good for their peace of mind. Hence her banishment to Java. Which is good for *our* peace of mind as well, in view of all she knows about the South Sea Company. You're a nonentity, Spandrel. But the fair Estelle? *Her* trial? *Her* execution? Too much attention. Far too much. For everyone. So, we've compromised. You go free. She goes . . . a long way away. And we breathe more easily. You're a lucky man.'

'Thanks to Estelle.'

'Yes. That's the damnably unaccountable part of it. You and I both know what she's given up. *How much* she's given up. And it might have cost her her life. Her life, for yours. Not a bargain that my brother gives me to believe a woman of her character would dream of entertaining. But she has. Why? She doesn't love you, does she?'

'No. She doesn't love me.'

'And there's nothing you can do for her.'

'Not a single thing.'

'So, why did she do it?'

'I don't know.'

'I should ask her, if I were you.'

'Yes.' Spandrel reached unsteadily for the key. 'I will.'

Chapter Forty-Five

Homeward Bound

The *Tovenaer* made way slowly as she headed out into the North Sea. The weather was clear and settled, sunlight dancing and sparkling on the gentle swell. The following wind was scarcely more than a breeze. It was a fine early summer's afternoon, the last afternoon, as it had threatened to be, of Spandrel's life, but instead the first of the rest of a life restored.

Spandrel and Estelle de Vries stood on the quarter-deck, watching the Dutch coast drift away behind them. It was the first time they had been allowed to leave their cabins since Spandrel's dawn arrival from Amsterdam, the master of the vessel, Captain Malssen, following the instructions in this regard of a senior V.O.C. merchant, identified by Estelle as Gustaaf Dekker, who was also aboard. Dekker apparently no longer feared the two might jump ship or play some other trick on him and was content to leave them to their own devices. This was thus also Spandrel's first opportunity to thank Estelle for what he still found it hard to believe she had done.

'You saved my life,' was the lame but simple truth he finally put into words. 'I shall always be in your debt.'

'And you will always be in my heart,' said Estelle, smiling at him. 'Even though you don't believe I have one.'

'I believe it now.'

'But it's a surprise, isn't it?'

'I admit it is.'

'For me too. After all I've done. If you'd asked me, I'd have said there wasn't any burden my conscience couldn't bear in exchange for a life of ease and pleasure. That's what Walpole gave me. And that's what I could have gone on enjoying.' She breathed deeply as the mizzen-sails filled and flapped above them. 'All I had to do was forget my promise to Captain McIlwraith. Oh, and I had to forget you as well, William, which I couldn't seem to do. I begged Walpole not to send you to Amsterdam. I pleaded with him as I'd never pleaded before and never would have again. But he refused me. He told me it was a matter of . . . political expediency. But there he lied. The truth was that he was jealous of the place you hold in my affections. And angry, of course, because he believed you'd endangered his son. He sent you to Amsterdam out of spite. And he thought there was nothing I could do to save you. Well, he was wrong, wasn't he?'

'Did you know what you were risking? Worse than the noose – the stake.'

'Risk agrees with me. Besides, I felt sure it wouldn't come to that. Don't over-estimate the sacrifice I've made. I left Walpole a note, telling him I still had a copy I'd made of the contents of the Green Book, which, while not as damaging as the original, would still cause him a great deal of embarrassment if it fell into the wrong hands.'

'*Do* you have a copy?'

'Leave me with some of my secrets, William, please. The possibility that I had a copy was enough for Walpole to send his brother racing after me. Poor Horace has but recently negotiated a troop loan with the Dutch Government. He wouldn't have wanted them to think better of it, as they well might have if they'd felt the British Government had placed them in an intolerable position.

The Dutch are no friends of King George. As Elector of Hanover, he has trading ambitions in the Baltic which they keenly resent. A copy of the Green Book could be a potent addition to their armoury. Trade is, after all, their lifeblood. I was married to one of them. I know how their minds work. When you were first arrested last year, you were accused of working for the Marquis de Prié, weren't you?'

'Yes. But—'

'Ysbrand was in secret communication with de Prié on behalf of the V.O.C.'

'What?'

'How much do you know about the Barrier Treaty of 1709?'

'Nothing. I've never even heard of it.'

'Be grateful I have. It granted the Dutch control of a series of fortresses along the border between France and the Spanish Netherlands – now the Austrian Netherlands – as a barrier against future invasion. The Dutch are supposed to be paid an annual subsidy towards the maintenance of the fortresses by the Flemish provinces they're sited in. Those subsidies are in arrears, amounting to many millions of guilders. The V.O.C. was worried – still is – lest de Prié persuade the Emperor to establish a Flemish East India Company to compete with them. Ysbrand was Flemish by birth and thus the obvious choice for a secret mission to negotiate a compromise with de Prié. The V.O.C. would use its considerable influence in the States General to have the arrears written off if de Prié would use *his* influence to have the idea of a Flemish East India Company quietly forgotten.'

'How do you know all this?'

'I've been the wife of an eminent Dutch merchant. And the mistress of a *pre*-eminent British politician. I know more than either of them thought I had the chance of

419

learning. Secrets aren't for telling. They're for storing against the day you may need to *threaten* that you'll tell them. That's why I told Sheriff Lanckaert last year that you'd admitted to travelling to Amsterdam by way of Brussels. Partly to incriminate you, of course. But partly also to let the V.O.C. know that I could, if I chose, reveal their secret dealings with de Prié, causing a rupture within the States General.'

'What a deep game you play.'

'Oh yes. Deep and dark. A man may have me as his mistress, if he is rich and powerful enough. But I am ever my own gamestress. I judged how it would be. Neither Walpole nor the V.O.C. could afford to let me answer for the crime to which I confessed, for fear of what I might make *them* answer for. So, I do not burn and you do not hang. I am sent away and you are allowed to escape.'

'But you've given up so much, Estelle. Ease and pleasure. You said so yourself.'

'All for you, William. I wasn't certain I could when I left England, you know. But when I stood outside the Stadhuis and watched you being condemned to—'

'You were there?'

Estelle nodded. 'I was. And when I saw the weary, hope-less despair on your face as the death sentence was passed, I knew I had to do my best for you. You didn't abandon me in Rome, did you, small thanks though you had for it? Well, *I* couldn't abandon *you*. It was a bewildering discovery to make about myself. That there really was someone in the world I cared about, even though he's neither rich nor powerful, nor ever likely to be.'

'Didn't you care about Zuyler?'

'If you're asking me whether I'd have done the same for him, the answer's no. You're a different kind of man, William, I'm glad to say. You should be glad too. But don't let the difference go to your head. I think I was looking for an excuse to leave Walpole anyway. It was a beholden life. And I prefer to be beholden to no-one. Besides, ease and pleasure cloy after a while, don't you find?'

Spandrel laughed at the absurdity of the notion that he would have any way of knowing and shook his head at her sheer incorrigibility. 'What in Heaven's name will you do in Java?'

'I can't imagine. Fortunately, I don't have to. I'm not going to Java.'

'You're not?'

'Certainly I'm not. You've met my stepson. If he's an example of the effects of the East Indian climate, not to mention East Indian society – and I'm assured he is – I'd be mad to go. Gerrit has me marked down as good marrying material for the wife-hungry merchants of Batavia. He – and they – are to be disappointed, however.'

'But Dekker and Captain Malssen have orders to take you there.'

'Indeed.' Estelle lowered her voice to a whisper. 'I intend to come to a private arrangement with one or both of those gentlemen. I have it from the boatswain that we're to call at Madeira on the way. I shall disembark there.'

'They won't allow you to.'

'Do you doubt my powers of persuasion?'

'No. But—'

'Then leave me to employ them. On which subject . . .'

'Yes?'

'Don't look round. Dekker has just commenced observing us from the shelter of the companion-way. It would be helpful to my managing of him on this voyage if you and I appeared to be at odds. You'll forgive the pretence, I know, disagreeable as it will be for both of us. All will be well for you from now on, William. You have nothing to fear from Walpole. He knows certain bargains must be honoured, especially those struck by his brother in his name. He will leave you completely alone. And you will prosper. Of that I feel strangely certain. Finish your map. Maps *are* the coming thing, you know. People have need of them. At any rate, they think they do, which is even better.'

'Not you, though?'

'No. I prefer an unmapped future. Now, I hope we will be able to contrive a more fitting leavetaking closer to the time, but for the moment—' Suddenly, she tossed her head and raised her voice. 'It is all very well for you, Mr Spandrel. What do I have to show for it?'

'Enough, I think, madam,' he snapped back, rising to the occasion so well that there was the sparkle of a smile in her eyes that she did not allow to reach her lips. 'Go to the Devil.'

'I very likely shall.' She turned on her heel and strode towards the companion-way, where Spandrel glimpsed Dekker's black-clad form shrinking back out of sight. There was no way to tell Estelle's simulated anger and frustration from the real thing. That was the wonder of her. And for Spandrel it always would be.

Early the following evening, the *Tovenaer* hove to off Hastings and set down a launch, with Spandrel aboard. He could see Estelle watching from the quarter-deck, her pink dress turned blood-red by the wash of golden sunlight. She did not raise a hand and nor did he. The rules of the game she was playing had still to be observed. Each knew what the other's gaze conveyed and that was enough.

Spandrel wondered if he would ever see her again. If not, this last, fading sight of her was the end. He did not want to believe that, likely though it was. She was still alive and so was he. There was no telling what the future might hold. Except that, throughout as much of it as lay before him, he would think better and more fondly of her than he would once have supposed to be possible.

'Fare you well, Estelle,' he murmured under his breath as the launch drew further and further from the ship. 'Fare you ever well.'

Chapter Forty-Six

Looking to the Future

After a night at the Smack and Mackerel Inn in Hastings – named, he decided, because a stomach-turning tang of stale fish pervaded everything, including the bedding – Spandrel was eager to be on his way. But it was Sunday and no coaches were running. The skipper of a coaster sailing for London that afternoon was willing to take on passengers, however, so Spandrel left Hastings as he had arrived, by sea.

The coaster had many calls to make on its way, the number and duration of which far exceeded Spandrel's expectations. Tuesday morning found the vessel no further on than Deal. There Spandrel lost patience. After a salty exchange with the skipper, who declined to refund any portion of his fare, he went ashore and continued his journey by road.

He spent that night at Faversham, whence the mail-coach bore him on to London the following day. He could have reached Leicester Fields by early evening, but a whimsical notion had occurred to his mind. He put up for the night at the Talbot Inn in Borough High Street.

After a meal and several reviving mugs of ale in the tap-room, he walked up to London Bridge and stood by the railings in a gap between the houses, watching the light fade over the city he had never thought he would see again. It was good to be back. And better still to know that, this time, he could stay.

The following morning, Margaret Spandrel breakfasted in low spirits. Her attempts to shake off the sadness William had caused her by his second abrupt and unexplained departure had been undermined by the realization that today was his twenty-seventh birthday. Sighing heavily and deciding to set off for Covent Garden in the hope that haggling over vegetables might improve her state of mind, she rose from the table and walked across to the window to judge the weather.

But what the weather was like she suddenly did not care. For there, standing at the edge of the lawn in the square below, was a familiar figure. And he was waving at her.

She flung up the sash and leaned out. 'William?' she called. 'Is that really you?'

'Yes, Ma,' he called back, smiling broadly. 'It really is.'

Later that day, another traveller returned to London from the Low Countries. Horatio Walpole, devoutly hoping he would not be sent straight back again this time, reported promptly to his brother at the Treasury.

Resilience was one of Robert Walpole's abiding traits. He had long since rid himself of the despondency that had gripped him on the occasion of their last meeting. It seemed to Horatio, indeed, that he had already forgotten the charms of Estelle de Vries, alias Davenant, thanks either to the alternative charms of some newly discovered mistress or to a happy turn in his pursuit of Atterbury. As it transpired, both emollients to Robert's mood had been applied.

'You've done well, Horace,' the great man and grateful brother announced over a bumper of champagne. 'The

East Indies is as far from harm's way as anyone could ask for. As for Spandrel, I suppose the fellow's never really *meant* any harm. And now he can do none. We have Atterbury by the tail.'

'Has he been arrested?'

'Not yet. But Plunket is beginning to see the attractions of turning King's Evidence. When he does . . . we'll have them all.'

'I can rest my weary limbs at home for a while, then?'

'Indeed you can. Take a well-deserved rest.'

'And what will you do with Phoenix House?'

'Oh, I have someone in mind for that.' Robert winked at his brother. 'When a mare throws you, mount a sweeter-tempered one, I say.' At which they both laughed immoderately and recharged their glasses.

Two days later, at the Goat Tavern in Bloomsbury, Sam Burrows' customary Saturday evening soak was enlivened by the not entirely unexpected arrival of William Spandrel.

'You've heard, then, Mr Spandrel?'

'Heard what?'

'Come on. It's why you're here.'

'I've been away, Sam. Apparently, Dick Surtees came looking for me. But, when I called at his lodgings, his landlady told me he'd moved – without leaving a forwarding address.'

'Shouldn't wonder at that.'

'What's it all about?'

'Bigamy, Mr Spandrel. Well, it would've been bigamy, if the marriage had gone off. Seems old Mr Chesney reck-oned your friend was too good to be true, so made some inquiries. And what pops up but a wife, in Paris, legally churched and well and truly living. Didn't see Mr Surtees for dust, did we? Handsome of him to try and let you know the coast was clear, though.'

'How's Maria taken it?'

'Oh, much as you'd expect. Whey-faced and weeping at first. A little better lately. But she still keeps to her room a lot. In need of consoling, I'd say.'

'Would you?'

'I would, now I've met the man to do it. Not got a wife tucked away somewhere, have you, Mr Spandrel?'

'Definitely not.'

'Nor any skeletons in the closet likely to rattle their bones?'

'Not a one.'

'There you are, then. You're just the man she needs. And an altogether finer one than Mr Surtees, if you don't mind me venturing the opinion.'

'No, Sam. I don't mind at all.'

Spandrel took his place early for matins at the Church of St George the Martyr in Queen's Square the following morning, then settled back to watch as the pews filled around him with the pious pick of local society. About ten minutes before the service was due to begin, Mr and Mrs Chesney, accompanied by their daughter, Maria, entered the church and moved to their private pew near the front. They did not notice Spandrel. But Spandrel noticed them, Maria in particular. She was looking pale, as Sam had led him to expect, and thinner than he remembered.

A tender feeling of pity for Maria stole over Spandrel, a feeling he knew, in favourable circumstances – beginning with a brief but telling encounter at the conclusion of the service – might lead to a revival of the affection they had once proclaimed for each other. It would be a delicate business, at least at first. But he was confident that he could manage it. He could not in fact recall feeling so confident about anything before in his life.

Many of the congregation were kneeling in prayer. So as not to appear out of place, Spandrel dropped to his knees, folded his hands and closed his eyes. As he did so, a strange and exhilarating thought came to him. Queen's Square stood at the very limit of London. Beyond the gardens at its northern end lay open fields to north and east and west. This was the edge of the map. It would not always be so. The city would grow, around and beyond it. The map Spandrel had not yet even finished – the map he had helped his father draw – would be redundant. What then? Why then, of course, as the future unfolded, he would draw another. And quite possibly another after that, helped, perhaps, by *his* son. In its way, the thought was a kind of prayer. And Spandrel uttered it solemnly.

Postlude

July 1722–March 2000

Chapter forty-seven

Tragedy, Comedy and History

History is the geology of human experience, a study, as it were, of tragedy and comedy laid down in the strata of past lives. In death there are no winners or losers, merely people who once lived but can never live again. What they thought, what they believed, what they hoped, is largely lost. That which remains is history.

The *Verenigde Oostindische Compagnie* vessel *Tovenaer* called at Madeira early in July 1722. It is not known if any passenger disembarked. Certain it is, however, that none of its passengers can have reached Java. The *Tovenaer* was lost with all aboard in a storm off the coast of New Holland (later to be renamed Australia) in the middle of October 1722. She has lately become the object of the eager attentions of aqualunged treasure-seekers, by virtue of her cargo of gold and silver bullion, intended to be traded for tea, textiles and porcelain, but which has served instead as a waterlogged memorial to Dutch commercial enterprise.

This disaster is unlikely to have been reported at the time in England. It almost certainly therefore did not intrude upon the early married life of William and Maria Spandrel, whose wedding had been solemnized at St George the Martyr's Church, Queen's Square, Bloomsbury, on Michaelmas Day of that year.

*   *   *

By the time of the Spandrels' wedding, the evidence given by John Plunket had led to the arrest on charges of treasonable conspiracy of Christopher Layer, George Kelly, Lord Grey and North, the Earl of Orrery and, of course, Bishop Francis Atterbury. As soon as Parliament met in October, the Duke of Norfolk joined them in the Tower. Walpole then pushed through the suspension of Habeas Corpus for a year and the imposition of a special tax of five shillings in the pound on Roman Catholics and non-jurors to meet the alleged cost of putting down the conspiracy.

Layer was tried and convicted of high treason and sentenced to be hanged, drawn and quartered. In the hope of extracting information from him to use against the others, his execution was many times delayed, but in vain. Eventually, Walpole had to acknowledge a lack of clinching evidence. He therefore proceeded against Atterbury and Kelly by a Bill of Pains and Penalties, calling only for presumptive evidence. The delinquent peers were released on indefinite bail. Kelly was sentenced to life imprisonment (as was the wretched Plunket), Atterbury to permanent exile. Layer was at last put out of his misery in May 1723. A month afterwards, Atterbury was loaded aboard a man-of-war and despatched to France, whence he was never to return. Of the multitude of Jacobites Walpole feared and/or hoped might come to see the Bishop off, only the Duke of Wharton put in an appearance.

Layer's head was duly displayed at Temple Bar, only to be blown down in a gale some years later, almost literally into the hands of Dr Richard Rawlinson, the Oxford theologian and non-juring bishop, who was so taken with this relic of Jacobite fervour that he asked to be buried with it in his right hand. It is not clear whether the request

432

was carried out. Kelly languished in the Tower for fourteen years, then staged a dramatic escape and re-entered the Pretender's service. He was one of the 'Seven Men of Moidart' who sailed with Prince Charles Edward, the Young Pretender, from Nantes for Eriskay in June 1745. He later served as the Prince's private secretary. He died in Rome in 1762. Plunket, meanwhile, had died in the Tower two years after Kelly's escape.

Power breeds jealousy, especially in him who wields it. Robert Walpole, *Sir* Robert as he soon became, can hardly have expected to remain at the head of the nation's affairs for the next twenty years, but remain he did, growing more lonely and more ruthless in the process. He had his private griefs to bear, no question. His invalid daughter Kate died in the midst of his campaign against the Jacobites. His other daughter, Mary, was also to die young. His sister Dolly, Viscountess Townshend, and his brother Galfridus died within a few months of each other in 1726. And with Dolly died also his forty-year friendship with Charles Townshend.

Walpole had already engineered the disgrace and dismissal of Lord Carteret, whom he saw as a potential rival. Now, without Dolly to unite them, he began to weigh Townshend's loyalty in the balance and find it wanting. King George I expired unexpectedly of a stroke en route to his beloved Hanover in June 1727 and many thought the new King would give Walpole short shrift. But Walpole had been assiduously cultivating the Princess of Wales with just this contingency in mind and Queen Caroline's favour enabled him to manage George II much as he had managed George I. Townshend's ministerial days were thereafter numbered. Offended by Walpole's ever more frequent interferences in foreign policy, he resigned and retired to Norfolk to pursue his theories on crop rotation, which were to win him a form of immortality as 'Turnip Townshend' of the Agricultural Revolution. He died in 1738.

By then Walpole was a stubborn and bloated old man, twice a widower, tortured by the stone, baited by the press and plagued by a rising generation of ambitious young office-seekers. He was forced into a war against Spain he had no wish to fight, thanks partly – irony of ironies – to a long-running dispute between the Spanish Government and the South Sea Company. The war went badly, the general election of 1741 hardly better, and at length, early in February 1742, he resigned, retiring to the Lords as Earl of Orford.

The newly ennobled Lord Orford was an immensely wealthy man. No satisfactory explanation of his extraordinary accumulation of riches has ever been advanced. He put much of it to use in assembling, at vast and heedless cost, a collection of the very finest paintings and sculptures. Raphaels, Rubenses, Rembrandts, Titians, Vandykes, Poussins, Murillos and Domenichinos found their way to Houghton Hall, his Norfolk residence, by the priceless crate-load. A less likely connoisseur is hard to imagine. But posterity has proclaimed his taste, if not his morals, impeccable.

Walpole died at his London home, of a remedy for the stone that turned out to be worse than the disease, in March 1745, aged sixty-eight. The doctor who attended him in his final illness, James Jurin, is now believed to have been a crypto-Jacobite. The earldom – and with it the bulk of Walpole's fortune – passed to his eldest son, Robert junior, while his surviving brother, Horatio, lingered on in the Commons until belatedly granted a peerage a few months before his death in 1757. By then Robert junior had been succeeded as Earl of Orford by his son, George, who devoted the prime years of his manhood to the seemingly impossible task of squandering his inheritance. In this he was so successful that in 1779 he was forced to sell the entire Houghton collection to Empress Catherine of Russia for a meagre £36,000. Most of the pictures now adorn the Hermitage Museum in St Petersburg.

Walpole's youngest son, Horace, the famous dilettante and epistolizer, lamented the sale. 'It is the most signal mortification to my idolatry for my father's memory that I could receive,' he wailed. 'It is stripping the temple of his glory and of his affection. A madman excited by rascals has burnt his Ephesus.' What Horace's elder brother, Edward, thought about this is not known. His many years as the inactive and almost completely silent Member for Great Yarmouth had been succeeded by an increasingly reclusive existence, from which even his nephew's gross sacrilege failed to rouse him. He died in 1784. His brother Horace inherited the earldom from the profligate George in 1791. With Horace's passing, in 1797, the title became extinct.

The end of the Robinocracy brought an end also to the long exile of Robert Knight. Upon payment of £10,000 for a royal pardon and another £10,000 to appease the South Sea Company, he was permitted by the new Administration to return to his homeland. It appears that financial consultancy had not been unprofitable. He was able at once to buy back his estate in Essex that had been sold in his absence. And there he died in 1744. His son later sat in Parliament as the Member for Castle Rising, a Norfolk pocket borough in the gift of the Walpole family, made over to him for reasons that can only be guessed at.

Whether Knight senior ever visited Sir Theodore Janssen at his house in Hanover Square following his overdue homecoming is unknown. Certainly the wily old Flemish financier was still to be found there by those who sought him out, though not for a great deal longer. This founding director of both the Bank of England and the South Sea Company died in September 1748, aged ninety-four.

The South Sea Company itself lost its only tangible commercial asset – the *Asiento* for the supply of slaves to Spain's American colonies – in an opaque and tardy sub-treaty of the none too transparent Treaty of Aix-la-Chapelle in 1750, for a flat payment of £100,000. The company lingered on pitifully for another hundred years until Gladstone arrived at the Exchequer in 1852, noticed that it was still in being and promptly administered it out of existence.

By contrast, the last gasp of the Jacobite cause was in many ways its most glorious. What would have happened had the Young Pretender's army marched on south from Derby in December 1745 will never be known. The fact that a yacht loaded with King George II's valuables was kept ready at Tower Quay while news from the Midlands was anxiously awaited suggests that the conclusion was far from foregone. In the event, the rebel army marched back to Scotland – and destruction at Culloden four months later. Among the unanswered questions they left behind is whether Walpole would ever have allowed them to get so far in the first place. But Dr Jurin's ministrations had ensured that Walpole's counsel was not available to the Government of the day.

James Edward, the Old Pretender, died in Rome in 1766. By the time of his son's death, in 1788, even pretending had ceased to seem worthwhile.

While the King was packing his valuables, politicians were pondering their allegiance and depositors were clamouring for their money at the Bank of England during those tense December days of 1745, calmer heads were mapping the present for the benefit of the future. *An Exact and Definitive Map of the City and Environs of London in the Reign of His Britannic Majesty King George the Second*, the work of William and James Spandrel, father and son, was published in sixteen separate sheets at monthly intervals between November 1748 and February 1750. It can be assumed to have taken anything up to ten years to produce.

The surviving subscription list shows the commercial bias one might expect. But commercial considerations are unlikely to account for the presence on the list of Sir Nicholas Cloisterman, retired Ambassador. There are, of course, many reasons for wanting to buy a map. Some of those reasons have less to do with planning journeys than remembering them.

Every map has its history, largely lost though it may be. That which remains may become, if it survives long enough, the stuff of saleroom speculation. Two hundred and fifty years after its last sheet was published, an original bound copy of the Spandrels' map was sold at auction in New York for $148,000 – not far short of £100,000. Back in 1721, such a sum would have made a man rich beyond the dreams of avarice. It would have been, quite literally, a King's ransom.

Appendices

Appendix A

Directory

A complete list of named characters featured in the course of the story in alphabetical order of title or surname (or forename where only this is known), with a note of their circumstances in 1721/22. Those listed in italics will not be found in any history book.

Aertsen, Henrik. Deputy to Sheriff Lanckaert of Amsterdam.
Aislabie, John. Chancellor of the Exchequer until forced to resign over South Sea scandal.
Albemarle, Arnold van Keppel, Earl of. Allied Commander at Battle of Denain, 1712.
Anne, Queen. Last reigning British monarch of the Stuart line. Died 1714. Succeeded by George I.
Arran, Charles Butler, Earl of. Jacobite landowner in Windsor Forest.
Atterbury, Francis. Bishop of Rochester, Dean of Westminster. Jacobite plotter.
Barlaeus. Supposed name of Zuyler's landlord in Amsterdam (see Ugels).
Blain, Percy. British Consul in Florence.
Blain, Elizabeth, 'Lizzie'. Wife of Percy Blain.
Bland, Dr Henry. Provost of Eton College.
Blunt, Sir John. Director of South Sea Company.
Bortolazzi, Cardinal. Pro-Governor of the City of Rome.

Bouvin, Host of card-playing and musical evenings in Geneva.

Brodrick, Thomas. Chairman of House of Commons Secret Committee of Inquiry into South Sea Company.

Buckthorn, Giles. One of two supposed Grand Tourists whom Spandrel meets with Estelle de Vries in Switzerland (see Silverwood).

Burrows, Sam. Footman to the Chesney household in London.

Cadogan, William, Earl. Army general, sometime British Ambassador to The Hague and Windsor Forest landowner.

Calderini. Banker used by Spandrel and Estelle de Vries in Rome.

Caroline, Princess of Wales.

Carteret, John, Lord. Secretary of State for Southern Department from March 1721.

Caswall, George. Banker to and former director of South Sea Company. Also Member of Parliament.

Chandos, James Brydges, Duke of. Former Paymaster-General.

Charles Edward, Prince. The Young Pretender. Son of James Edward, the Old Pretender and heir to the Stuart line. Born December 1720.

Chesney, George. Businessman. Director of New River Company.

Chesney, Louisa. Wife of George Chesney and mother of Maria.

Chesney, Maria. Daughter of George and Louisa Chesney.

Clement XI. Pope until March 1721.

Clementina, Princess. Wife of James Edward, the (Old) Pretender.

Cloisterman, Nicholas. British vice-consul in Amsterdam.

Crabbe. Engraver of the Spandrels' map.

Craggs, James the elder. Postmaster-General until March 1721.

Craggs, James the younger. Son of James the elder. Secretary of State for Southern Department until February 1721.

Dalrymple, Evelyn. Chargé d'affaires at British Embassy in The Hague.

Davenant, Mrs. Name used by Estelle de Vries in London.

Dekker, Gustaaf. V.O.C. merchant aboard the *Tovenaer.*

van Dillen, Jacob. Deceased mutual friend of Sir Theodore Janssen and Ysbrand de Vries.

Dirk. Pickpocket with whom Spandrel shares a cell in Amsterdam Stadhuis.

Drummond, Lachlan, Colonel. British Government spy at Pretender's court in Rome.

Dubois, Cardinal. Foreign Minister of France.

Edgar, James. Secretary to James Edward, the (Old) Pretender.

Geertruid. Maid at de Vries house in Amsterdam.

George I, King of England and Elector of Hanover. Governor of South Sea Company.

George, Prince of Wales. Son and heir of George I. Governor of South Sea Company.

Godolphin, Francis, Earl of. Brother-in-law of Earl of Sunderland, both having married daughters of the Duke of Marlborough.

Gordon, Sir William. Commissioner of Army Accounts. Also Member of Parliament.

Grey and North, William, Lord. Jacobite plotter.

Harlequin. Francis Atterbury's pet dog.

Harris. Clerk at British Embassy in The Hague.

Hatton, John, Captain. Soldier. Fiancé of Dorothea Wagemaker. Died of wounds during War of Spanish Succession, 1712.

Heinsius, Anthonie. Former Grand Pensionary of Holland. Died 1720. Succeeded by Isaac van Hoornbeeck.

Henrik. One of three ruffians who try to kill Spandrel in Amsterdam (see Jan and Roelant).

Hondslager, Cornelis. Name given by Zuyler to Spandrel as that of leader of the ruffians who try to kill him in Amsterdam (see Jan).

van Hoornbeeck, Isaac. Grand Pensionary of Holland.

Innocent xiii. Bishop of Osimo, elected as Pope in succession to Clement XI, May 1721.

Jacquinot, Madame. Proprietress of Auberge du Lac, Vevey.

James Edward, Prince. The (Old) Pretender. Son of King James II of England and claimant to the British throne.

Jan. Leader of the ruffians who try to kill Spandrel in Amsterdam.

Jane. Maid-of-all-work taken on by Mrs Spandrel after her move to Leicester Fields.

Janssen, Sir Theodore. Director of South Sea Company and Member of Parliament.

Janus, 'Big'. Turnkey at Amsterdam Stadhuis.

Johnson, James. Alias of George Kelly.

Joye, Charles. Director and Deputy Governor of South Sea Company.

Jupe, Nicodemus. Valet to Sir Theodore Janssen.

Jurin, James, Dr. Physician. Secretary of Royal Society.

Kelly, George. Secretary to Francis Atterbury. Jacobite plotter.

Kemp, Mr and Mrs. Travelling aliases of Estelle de Vries and Pieter Zuyler.

Kempis. Alias used by Pieter Zuyler in The Hague.

Kendal, Ehrengard Melusina von der Schulenburg, Duchess of. Mistress to King George I.

Kingston, Evelyn Pierrepoint, Duke of. Lord Privy Seal.

Knight, Robert. Chief cashier of South Sea Company.

Lanckaert. Sheriff of Amsterdam – the city's chief law and order officer.

Layer, Christopher. Lawyer. Jacobite plotter.

Layton. Alias of Christopher Layer.

Longrigg, Esmund. Chief woodward of Windsor Forest. Local landowner.

Lorenzini. Chancellor to Grand Duke of Tuscany.

McIlwraith, James, Captain. Soldier of fortune. Secret agent for Brodrick's Committee of Inquiry.

Malssen. Captain of V.O.C. vessel *Tovenaer.*

Mar, John Erskine, Earl of. Commander of Jacobite army in Scotland during the Fifteen.

Marabout, Gideon. Shopkeeper who sells Spandrel a map of Windsor Forest.

Marlborough, John Churchill, Duke of. Captain-General of the Army during War of Spanish Succession.

Marlborough, Sarah Churchill, Duchess of. Wife of Duke of Marlborough and mother-in-law of Earl of Sunderland.

Master, Harcourt. Director of South Sea Company.

Maybrick. A tile merchant Spandrel meets on his way to Amsterdam.

de Medici, Cosimo, Grand Duke of Tuscany.

Mehemet. Turkish Groom of the Chamber to King George I.

Monteith, Father. Secretary to Cardinal Bortolazzi.

Negus, Francis, Colonel. Deputy Lieutenant of Windsor Castle.

Newcastle, Thomas Pelham-Holles, Duke of. Lord Great Chamberlain.

Norfolk, Thomas Howard, Duke of. Jacobite plotter.

Orrery, Charles Boyle, Earl of. Jacobite plotter.

Pels. Sir Theodore Janssen's banker in Amsterdam.

Phelps. British Consul in Milan.

Platen, Clara Elizabeth von Meyerburg Züschen, Countess of. Secondary mistress to King George I.

Plenderleath, Josiah. Deceased father of Estelle de Vries (according to her).

Plunket, John. Jacobite plotter.

Powell, William. Alias used by Spandrel when leaving Amsterdam for the last time.

de Prié, Ercole di Turinetti, Marquis de. Minister Plenipotentiary to Governor-General of Austrian Netherlands.

Rawlinson, Richard, Dr. Theologian at Oxford University.

Roelant. One of three ruffians who try to kill Spandrel in Amsterdam (see Henrik and Jan).

Rogers, Captain. Adjutant to Colonel Negus.

Ross, Charles, General. Member of Brodrick's Committee of Inquiry; former commanding officer of Captain McIlwraith.

Schaub, Sir Luke. British Ambassador to Paris.

Siegwart, Frau. Proprietress of Pension Siegwart, Berne.

Silverwood, Naseby. One of two supposed Grand Tourists whom Spandrel meets with Estelle de Vries in Switzerland (see Buckthorn).

Sloper, William. Member of Brodrick's Committee of Inquiry.

Spandrel, Margaret. Mother of William Spandrel.

Spandrel, William. Mapmaker. Son of William and Margaret Spandrel.

Spandrel, William senior. Bankrupt mapmaker. Died 1720.

Spencer, Hon. William. Infant son of Earl of Sunderland.

Stanhope, Charles. Treasury Secretary until forced to resign over South Sea scandal. Cousin of Earl Stanhope.

Stanhope, James, Earl. Secretary of State for Northern Department until February 1721.

Stosch, Philip von, Baron. German bibliophile recruited by Carteret to spy on the Pretender in Rome.

Sunderland, Charles Spencer, Earl of. First Lord of the Treasury until forced to resign over South Sea scandal.

Sunderland, Judith Spencer, Countess of. Wife of Earl of Sunderland.

Surtees, Richard, 'Dick'. Former apprentice of William Spandrel senior.

Taillard, Jean-Luc. Surveyor for whom Spandrel works in Rennes.

Townshend, Charles, Viscount. Secretary of State for Northern Department from February 1721; old friend and brother-in-law of Robert Walpole.

Townshend, Dorothy, 'Dolly', Viscountess. Wife of Viscount Townshend and sister of Robert Walpole.

Turrettini. Banker used by Estelle de Vries in Geneva.

Ugels, Balthasar. Amsterdam shopkeeper who rents his basement to Zuyler.

Ugels, Rebekka. Daughter of Balthasar Ugels.

de Vries, Estelle. English-born wife of Ysbrand de Vries.

de Vries, Gerrit. Son of Ysbrand de Vries by first marriage.

de Vries, Ysbrand. V.O.C. merchant and old friend of Sir Theodore Janssen.

Wagemaker, Augustus, Colonel. Secret agent of Robert Walpole.

Wagemaker, Dorothea. Sister of Augustus and Tiberius Wagemaker. Fiancée of Captain Hatton. Died in a fall, 1713.

Wagemaker, Henry. Father of Augustus, Tiberius and Dorothea Wagemaker. Died 1712.

Wagemaker, Tiberius. Brother of Augustus and Dorothea Wagemaker.

Walpole, Catherine. Wife of Robert Walpole.

Walpole, Catherine, 'Kate'. Eldest daughter of Robert Walpole. An invalid.

Walpole, Edward. Second son of Robert Walpole. Oppidan at Eton.

Walpole, Galfridus. Youngest brother of Robert Walpole. Postmaster-General from March 1721.

447

Walpole, Horatio, 'Old Horace'. Younger brother of Robert Walpole. Treasury Secretary from April 1721.

Walpole, Horatio, 'Young Horace'. Youngest son of Robert Walpole.

Walpole, Mary. Younger daughter of Robert Walpole.

Walpole, Robert junior. Eldest son of Robert Walpole.

Walpole, Robert, 'Robin'. Paymaster-General until April 1721. Thereafter First Lord of the Treasury and Chancellor of the Exchequer.

Welsh, Ann, 'Annie'. A neighbour of the Spandrels in Cat and Dog Yard.

Wharton, Philip, Duke of. Eccentric hell-raising Jacobite.

Zuyler, Pieter. Secretary to Ysbrand de Vries.

Appendix B

Glossary

Recommended reading only for those with a taste for historical detail: an explanation of some eighteenth-century terms which may not be familiar to the contemporary reader, with notes on their significance in 1721/22.

The Austrian Empire and the Austrian Netherlands
The Holy Roman Empire, a medieval attempt to unite central Europe under a single Christian Emperor, had long since become moribund. The Habsburg Emperors ruled effectively only in their Austro-Hungarian heartland, most of which actually lay outside the notional boundaries of the Empire thanks to recent conquests from the Turks – hence the growing trend to refer to this hotchpotch of territories as Austria. For finishing on the winning side in the War of the Spanish Succession (q.v.) Austria was rewarded with most of Spain's subject territory in Italy plus the Spanish Netherlands – the southern half of the formerly Spanish-ruled Low Countries, more or less equivalent to today's Belgium and Luxembourg. The Austrian Netherlands (as they were thereafter known) offered the Emperor a definite but far from straightforward opportunity to compete with the British, French and Dutch in maritime trade.

Coffee-Houses
These establishments, which had begun to spring up in the middle of the previous century, provided rather more than coffee. They were male-only eating, drinking, debating, gambling and newspaper-reading dens, distinguishable from taverns by virtue of (slightly) higher standards of décor and behaviour.

Debtors' Prisons
Imprisonment for debt was a Sword of Damocles hanging over the head of anyone who accepted any form of credit. It was also a Catch-22, since, once imprisoned, how could a debtor pay his creditors? Even in debt, however, there was class distinction. In London, the King's Bench Prison was reserved for gentleman debtors, the Marshalsea and the Fleet for the lower reaches of society. There were also gradations of imprisonment, since not all debtors were penniless. Some could pay to live outside the prison itself but within its rules, in designated lodging-houses, from which base they might hope to earn some money and claw their way back to solvency. Alternatively, a debtor could flee to a different county (which in London meant crossing the river), where there was no writ for their arrest, or take refuge in one of the recognized debtors' sanctuaries, such as Whitefriars in London and Abbey Strand in Edinburgh (the sites of ancient and legally protected monastic foundations). Debt also enjoyed a sabbath. No debtor could be arrested on a Sunday.

The Fifteen and the Forty-Five
The two famous Jacobite (q.v.) risings of the eighteenth century, the first a recent memory, the second yet to happen. The Fifteen was intended to exploit popular resentment of the shipping over of a German prince to succeed Queen Anne in the summer of 1714. The leader of

the rebel army, the Earl of Mar, proved a disastrous military strategist and the rising was already a lost cause when James Edward, the Pretender, landed at Peterhead in December 1715. He retreated to France, along with Mar, in February 1716, leaving the remnants of their army to be hunted down by Lord Cadogan's forces. Thirty years later, the Forty-Five was to prove an altogether more serious rising under the personal leadership of Charles Edward, the Pretender's son.

Hanover
The Electorate of Brunswick-Lüneburg, commonly known as Hanover, qualified as an electorate because its ruler was one of the German princes traditionally entitled to vote on the choice of Holy Roman Emperor. It became attached to the British crown at the death of Queen Anne in August 1714. The Act of Settlement of 1701 had settled the presumptive succession on Princess Sophia of Hanover, granddaughter of King James I and Anne's closest Protestant relative. Sophia died in May 1714 and it was thus her son George, who had ruled Hanover since 1698, who succeeded to the British throne. Hanover, however, remained officially a foreign country, with a completely separate (benignly despotic) form of government, coincidentally reigned over by the same man.

Jacobites
Any person who maintained (as many did) that King James II remained the rightful King after and despite the Glorious Revolution of 1689 was, by definition, a Jacobite (the name being derived from the Latin version of James, *Jacobus*), but slowly the expression became limited in application to those who wanted to do something about it and engaged in treasonable conspiracy to that end. Following James II's death in exile in 1701, Jacobites

recognized his son as King James III. The succession of George I in 1714 outraged them even more, since Anne had at least been a daughter of the royal blood, but it also raised their hopes of a restoration of the true line – hopes destined ever to be dashed.

The Mississippi Company
When King Louis XIV of France died in September 1715, he was succeeded by his five-year-old great-grandson, Louis XV. Power was vested in a Regent, Louis XIV's nephew, Philippe, Duke of Orléans, an insecure and impressionable individual who was rapidly seduced by the economic theories of the Scottish financier, John Law, a far-seeing advocate of paper money, who founded the Banque Générale in April 1716 and soon turned it into a quasi-national bank. In August 1717, Law took over the ramshackle Mississippi Company, which held the monopoly on trade with France's North American colonies, renamed it the Company of the West (though the old name somehow refused to go away) and transformed it into a vigorous commercial enterprise with, it soon came to be believed, such limitless wealth-making possibilities that only a fool would refuse to invest in it. The company's stock soared in value and soared again as it gradually acquired every other overseas trading monopoly at the Regent's disposal. It was accordingly renamed the Company of the Indies (although everybody still called it the Mississippi). In August 1719, Law played his trump card: the conversion of the entire National Debt of France (standing at more than £100 million) into Mississippi shares. The calculation on which the scheme was based – that the shares would continue to rise in value – proved a self-fulfilling prophecy, fuelled by generous instalment arrangments for payment and a flood of paper money from Law's bank (by then the official Banque

Royale). What Law had failed to foresee, however, was the resulting hyper-inflation, which soon began to dislocate society. In his newly appointed role of Finance Minister, Law resorted to ever more draconian measures to control the beast he had let loose, culminating in May 1720 with an edict halving the face value of banknotes and Mississippi shares. Three days of rioting in Paris persuaded the Regent to overrule him. The shares sank like a stone and the bank was besieged by mobs demanding coin for their notes. Want and ruin had suddenly taken the place of glut and prosperity. Not long afterwards, plague arrived in Marseilles to add to France's woes. By November 1720 paper money was dead and the Banque Royale broken. Law fled the country and a full-scale inquiry was launched into the disaster, the laggardly conclusion of which, in October 1722, was that all documents relating to the affair should be destroyed, by public burning in specially designed cages. The Mississippi Company lived on, but its secrets were not permitted to. The Duke of Orléans also lived on, but only until the following year. He is commemorated by the city of New Orleans, Louisana, named in his honour. Law died in Venice in 1729 and is commemorated by every colourful chapter in the subsequent history of financial speculation.

New Style, Old Style
The Julian Calendar (credited to Julius Caesar) counted every fourth year as a Leap Year, an insufficiently precise adjustment which led to a gradual separation of the calendar and tropical years. The Gregorian Calendar (promulgated by Pope Gregory XIII in 1582) solved this problem by omitting the Leap Year at the turn of three out of every four centuries. It was rapidly adopted by most European countries, but not by Great Britain until 1752. The result was that in 1721/22 the British calendar lagged

eleven days behind most of the rest of Europe. This was further complicated by the British practice of beginning the year for legal and civil purposes on 25th March (Lady Day – the Feast of the Annunciation of the Virgin Mary) rather than 1st January. Businessmen dealing with the continent took this in their stride, moving easily between the two systems and often employing double dating. Hence Sir Theodore Janssen would probably have dated the letter he sent to Ysbrand de Vries after his meeting with Robert Knight at the outset of this story 19th/30th January 1720/21. Dates in the continental calendar were referred to as New Style, those in the British as Old Style. (When Great Britain finally adopted the Gregorian Calendar, it also moved the beginning of the year to 1st January. Money-lenders did not care to lose eleven days' interest, far less the better part of three months', hence the financial year has begun ever since on 6th April, being 25th March plus the missing eleven days.)

Non-Jurors
To regularize the clearly irregular arrangement of 1689 whereby the deposed King James II was succeeded jointly by his elder daughter Mary and her Dutch husband, Prince William of Orange, all office holders under the Crown were required to swear allegiance to the new dual monarchs. The four hundred or so clergy (including five bishops) who felt unable to do so because they had already sworn allegiance for life to James were expelled from their livings and described as Non-Jurors (i.e. persons who had not taken an oath). Death and recantation made steady inroads into this number. Those who continued to hold firm even after James's death in 1701 were suspected (at least by the Government) of latent if not actual Jacobitism. The most Jacobite prelate of all,

however – Francis Atterbury – had no difficulty in swearing the oath, only in keeping it.

Northern Department, Southern Department

The seemingly obvious and natural arrangement whereby one Secretary of State deals with Foreign Affairs and another with Home Affairs was not adopted by the British Government until 1782. Back in 1721/22, two Secretaries of State shared responsibility for Home Affairs (according to which of them was on hand at the time) but divided between them responsibility for relations with the so-called Northern Powers (Scandinavia, Poland, Russia, Germany and the Netherlands) and the so-called Southern Powers (France, Spain, Portugal, Italy and Turkey), hence the names of the two departments. Seniority was vested in whichever of the Secretaries had been in post the longer. At the start of 1721, this was Earl Stanhope, by its end Viscount Townshend.

The Ottoman Empire

The Turkish Empire was named after its ruling Ottoman dynasty and was also known as the Sublime Porte, a French translation of the formal title of the central office of the Ottoman Government in Constantinople (now Istanbul). It had recently lost control of Hungary to the Austrian Empire, but still held sway throughout the Balkans, as well as in the Holy Land and North Africa as far west as Algeria. An ambassadorial posting to Turkey was not without its complications. Edward Wortley Montagu was despatched to Constantinople in August 1716. He and his wife (the celebrated poet and letter-writer, Mary Wortley Montagu) arrived the following spring after an arduous overland journey, only to be recalled within months because of a ministerial upheaval back home (the resignations of Walpole and Townshend). They ended up spending sixteen months in Turkey (most of them waiting for the new ambassador to arrive) and ten months on their way there or back. Wortley Montagu's successor, Abraham Stanyan, reached Constantinople in April 1718. He may well have anticipated his own recall when he learned of another ministerial upheaval back home three years later (the return to office of Walpole and Townshend).

The Papal States
A large area of central Italy (corresponding more or less to the present-day regions of Latium, Umbria, the Marches and Emilia-Romagna) was reserved for the Pope in his capacity as a temporal sovereign. As such, the Papacy was not revealed in a flattering light, the region, beyond the city of Rome itself, being a byword for poverty and maladministration.

Pocket Boroughs
Whilst the county constituencies of the British Parliament represented local landowning opinion with a fair degree of accuracy, many of the borough constituencies had such limited electoral rolls and arcane electoral procedures that they were, to all intents and purposes, in the pocket of a local magnate. The most notorious example of this was Old Sarum, a deserted Iron Age hill-fort near Salisbury, whose two Members of Parliament were returned by an electorate of three, tenants of Thomas Pitt, whom, not surprisingly, they unfailingly elected. Many such boroughs were transparently for sale. Hence Robert Walpole's brothers, Horatio and Galfridus, as well as his son, Edward, all sat at one time or another for the Cornish borough of Lostwithiel, controlled by a venal local landowner named Johns, who charged £20 per vote and a

modest £300 for his travelling expenses on election day. (A very rare example of a pocket borough somehow slipping out of the pocket came in the 1722 general election, when Carr, Lord Hervey, son and heir of the Earl of Bristol – and father, persistent rumour had it, of Robert Walpole's youngest son, Horatio – failed to be re-elected for Bury St Edmunds, which his father had donated to him, apparently by reason of drink-sodden negligence. Hervey died the following year and it is not clear whether he was ever sober enough in the interim to appreciate his loss.)

The South Sea Company
The South Sea Company originated in the ambitions of a group of businessmen headed by John Blunt to turn the Sword Blade Company (which had originally manufactured and sold sword blades but was, by the beginning of the eighteenth century, serving sharper purposes) into a bank rivalling the Bank of England, whose directors had been profiting handsomely from underwriting the currency since its foundation in 1694. Their hopes of doing so relied on the favour of Robert Harley, who became Chancellor of the Exchequer in the summer of 1710 and was immediately faced with the problem of how to manage unsecured war debts of £9 million. Blunt was ready with a solution, which Harley eagerly adopted: the unfunded loans were to be converted into shares in a new South Sea Company, which would hold the monopoly on trade with Spain's American colonies. The company came formally into existence in September 1711, with Harley (by then Lord High Treasurer and Earl of Oxford) as Governor, the Sword Blade group prominent among the directors and one Robert Knight appointed to the post of chief cashier. Under the Treaty of Utrecht, which finally brought the War of the Spanish Succession (q.v.) to a close in March 1713, the company was granted a thirty-year

contract for the supply of slaves to the Spanish colonies (the *Asiento*). They never actually managed to turn a profit on this business, but at political manoeuvring they knew no master. Oxford's fall from power and King George I's accession were smoothly accommodated, with the King and the Prince of Wales replacing Oxford as joint Governors. By 1719, Blunt and Knight had the entire National Debt of £31 million – and the consequent eclipse of the Bank of England – in their sights. This seemed to be rendered certain by the passage of the South Sea Bill in April 1720, the rapid conversion of most of the Debt into South Sea shares and the vertiginous rise in the value of those shares. But what went quickly up came even more quickly down. It came to be understood that even political corruption – the true basis of the entire scheme – had its limits. And there really was nothing quite as safe as the Bank of England.

The War of the Spanish Succession
As the seventeenth century drew towards its close, the dominant preoccupation of the European powers was how to carve up the Spanish Empire on the death of the ailing and heirless Spanish King, Carlos II. In October 1700, Carlos nominated his distant cousin Philippe of Anjou, grandson of King Louis XIV of France, as his successor. A month later, Carlos died. Great Britain, the United Provinces and the Austrian Empire were pledged never to allow the union of the French and Spanish crowns and formed a Grand Alliance in September 1701 to secure Spain's possessions in the Netherlands and Italy for Austria. War raged in Spain, Italy, Germany and the Low Countries for the next twelve years. When the war ended, in 1713, it did so very much on the Grand Alliance's original terms, with a guarantee that Philippe and his successors would never claim the French throne.

An historically very significant feature of the peace treaty was that the British seizure of Gibraltar in 1704 was rendered permanent.

The Stone

Why so many men and women of the eighteenth century – Robert Walpole among them – should have succumbed to stones and gravel in the kidneys and bladder is something of a mystery. Diet seems the likeliest answer. Most people were probably chronically dehydrated, the drinking of water being a hazardous undertaking at the best of times. Dehydration is now thought to be the primary cause of stone formation. The fashion for coffee consumption can have been no help in this regard. And the widespread use of chalk to whiten flour must also have played its part. The only effective treatment was lithotomy – surgical removal of the stone, without the benefit of anaesthetic. The odds against survival were long. As Walpole discovered, however, the odds against surviving such supposed cures as lithontriptic lixivium – the potion Dr Jurin poured down his throat in March 1745 – were even longer.

Swanimote Courts

Forest law was a thicket of ancient offences and penalties governing land use and peat, timber and game rights in the Royal Forests. It was exercised, inconsistently and irregularly, by local Swanimote Courts (the name Swanimote meaning literally a meeting of swains). Their judgments could only be enforced if confirmed at a trial before the Chief Justice in Eyre (*in Eyre* being a judicial term similar to *Errant*, indicating an itinerant circuit court function). No Chief Justice in Eyre had actually sat in Windsor Forest since 1632. This did not render the Swanimote impotent, however. It could detain offenders, confiscate their guns, dogs and traps, and bail them to appear before the next Justice Seat in Eyre (whenever that might be) on ruinous recognizances. Paying its fines tended to be a better course to follow. And fines there were aplenty in Windsor Forest during 1721/22, discontent at the acquisition of Forest land by Whig grandees being at its height. The Windsor Swanimote was allowed to lapse in 1728 when it began exercising its power of acquittal rather too freely for Walpole's liking.

The United Provinces
Those provinces of the Netherlands which successfully rebelled against Spanish rule in the sixteenth century (known today simply as the Netherlands) formed an independent federation, governed by representatives of the provinces meeting at The Hague as the States General. In practice, Holland, the largest and richest province, determined national policy, articulated by its Grand Pensionary, selected from the pensionaries of the States of Holland. They had deliberately left the office of Stadholder vacant at the death of William III in 1702, preferring a collective leadership. In the course of the seventeenth century, the United Provinces won a reputation as Europe's most orderly, prosperous and civilized nation. (In 1670, Amsterdam became the first city in the world to introduce a truly effective system of street lighting.) Crime was minimal, poverty hard to find. But nothing lasts for ever. By 1721/22, the country's power and wealth had begun to decline – even though most of its inhabitants probably did not know it.

The V.O.C.
Spanish embargoes on trade with the Mediterranean drove the Dutch to develop the East Indies market far faster than either England or Portugal, their principal competitors in

the region. To regulate this market, the States General established in 1602 a United East India Company – the *Verenigde Oostindische Compagnie*. The company was federally constructed, with directorships allocated to the provinces in proportion to their capital contributions, and was delegated the power to maintain troops, garrisons and warships, govern the inhabitants of the East Indian colonies (comprising most of what is now Indonesia) and treat with local potentates as it saw fit. The V.O.C. became, in a sense, a state within a state, albeit one exercising its power on the other side of the world. It reaped huge rewards as the years passed, supplying Europe with tea, coffee, spices, porcelain and textiles. But it also incurred serious losses, with one or two shipwrecks every year. Those wrecked vessels, lying still in the Atlantic and Indian Oceans, are ironically all that remains today of the V.O.C.'s once vast and mighty fleet. The company itself was dissolved in 1795 and not a single example of the many hundreds of its vessels that did not sink has survived.

Appendix C

Map

The map overleaf illustrates the political structure of western Europe in 1721/22, marking places and states featured in the story. (It should be noted that the mosaic of German states is a *simplified* version of the bewilderingly complex and virtually unmappable reality!)

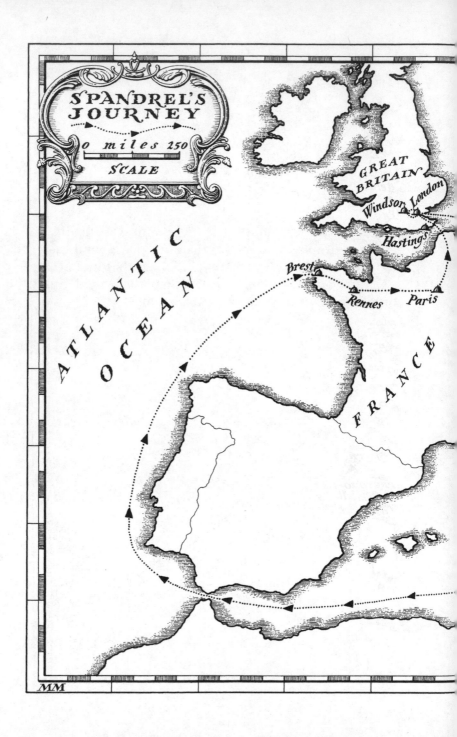

SPANDREL'S JOURNEY

0 miles 250

SCALE

ATLANTIC OCEAN

GREAT BRITAIN

Windsor London

Hastings

Brest

Rennes   Paris

FRANCE

MM

UNITED
PROVINCES

The Hague
Amsterdam
Antwerp
HANOVER
AUSTRIAN
NETHERLANDS
Brussels
Cologne
PALATINATE
Heidelburg
BREISGAU
Freiburg
Vienna
Berne
Basle
SWITZERLAND
Geneva
SAVOY
Milan
Turin
Genoa
AUSTRIA
Florence
TUSCANY
Marseilles
Leghorn
PRESIDIO
Orbitello
Civita Vecchia
PAPAL STATES
Rome
OTTOMAN
EMPIRE
Naples

Gower